SOMEONE TO WATCH OVER ME

A Novelized Memoir

Judi McMahon

Meet the Author

A long while ago, some very savvy people suggested I write a book about my life. I wasn't ready then. I am now. And I've so much more to add. I've finally found my focus, written on matters close to my heart, and also developed a holistic skin care company. Most important, I adopted my daughter Valentina from an orphanage when she was a child and I was alone and divorced. Valentina, the light of my life, is now 17. This is my first book of fiction after a varied career as a newspaper reporter, entertainment editor, columnist, and as an author of how-to books. I hope you'll find within these pages both entertainment and some wisdom from the lessons I've learned, and that you also have a special someone to watch over you.

Someone to Watch Over Me is a novelized memoir that captures the shifting spirit of the past six decades. Because it's based on true events and real people, many of whom are well known, I've fictionalized my story to protect the identities of the main characters and the people who passed through their lives.

The three women who share center stage come of age in New York City during the 1960s. Annie Ryan becomes a writer, Maureen McDermott a well-known singer, and Sabrina Aldrich a television newscaster. At times all three meet and share their hopes, their challenges and tribulations - in short, their humanity.

This novel takes a searching look at dysfunctional families, childhood rape, interracial romance, divorce, addictions, redemption, and love. It is serious in sections, humorous in others, and deeply human throughout.

The story ends just after 9/11, a date that changed the world. Do all three survive? Sabrina is at the TV station when the first plane hits the World Trade Towers, Maureen has an apartment nearby, and Annie has been married to a New York City fireman who is on duty that fateful day. The drama is moving and real and the ending thought-provoking.

PRAISE FOR
Someone To Watch Over Me

Your book has so much of my own life in it I can't believe it. Damn those men! And hail the good ones! This is really a book that tells a woman's story like it really is. Thank you so much for being so honest and genuine and not being afraid to let it all be told!
Martina Marin, California

We just returned from a wonderful trip! Costa Rica is beautiful! I really enjoyed reading your book on the beach. I especially enjoyed how each one of the character's lives developed and intertwined with one another. It is always interesting to me how we react in life to our family upbringing.
Melissa Bishop, Pennsylvania

I started reading your wonderful book ...I'm loving it and I think you're an amazing writer. I especially love the Maureen character. I've known so many Maureens in my life but none as colorful as she is!
Peggy Byrne, New York City

What a wonderful treasure your book is! Thank you for devoting so much time to inspire all of us. I laughed, I cried and shall be reading it again and again!
Anne Gentry, Baltimore

Thoroughly enjoying your book!!!! You are an excellent writer, and characters are wonderful! The chapters on taking care of the aging father were so very touching too.
Brandi O'Ryan, Colorado

I just finished your book and I really enjoyed reading it! What other books have you written? I would love to go to my local library and read more of your works.
Christie Schubert, Idaho

SOMEONE TO WATCH OVER ME

JUDI MCMAHON

To order additional copies of this book, contact:
Fulfillment Services, Inc.
526 E. 16th Street
Tucson, AZ 85701
(800) 311-7817 Tel
(520) 798-1514 Fax

To contact the author directly, go to RebornAngel.com
(or call 1-520-323-0833)

Preface

— ❦ —

What a trip it's been! In my 60 plus years on this earth, I've been witness to truth and deception, to many lives well and badly lived. As
for me - I'm a survivor. An eternal Sondheim lover, I'm still here. But
where are they now, the people who have crossed my path? What's
happened to their hopes and dreams? So many souls have disappeared
- some precipitously while still in their 30s, others in their 70s. Lately
their spirits come to me in sleep and linger in wakeful moments.

I've survived the era of self-help books and laugh tracks, theme parks
and wrinkle cures. And I've dared to love again and again. Yet like
many women enduring in mid-life and cloistered in creature com-
forts, I'm facing the last years alone. This is my recollection of a life
endowed with highs and lows, with some exceptional characters and
circumstances. I've chronicled the lives of three women whose paths
crisscrossed again and again in situations that spanned fifty years.
Some portrayals bring laughter; a few tears. All of it is based on true
events and real people. Where necessary, names and circumstances
have been changed to protect the living and the dead.

Dedication and Acknowledgements

— ❦ —

This book is dedicated first to my darling Valentina who I love with all my heart. You came into my life when I was 58 and made me young again. I also want to thank so many others who have played vital roles in my life and were the impetus for writing this book — most especially, for Bill W. and his friends, I'm grateful to be a member of the greatest alliance in the world; for Lincoln Chase — a most generous talent and gentleman — thanks for the memories, and, for Father Victor Yanitelli — the beloved and brilliant Jesuit — bless you for always believing in me. For Joe McMahon, the great passion of my life, and, for my darling brother Donny, whose days were cut too short, I'll always remember the good things. And last but not least — to my incredible grandmother Tillie, who was always my mainstay and support — thank you for being an always-present part of my life. And odd as it might seem - for their immense inspiration in illuminating my life through their talents — I want to single out George Gershwin, Stephen Sondheim, Fred Astaire, Gene Kelly and the muses that inspired them to heavenly things.

You realize of course that we all start out the same, growing little by little inside our mother's womb. Then we come on out and for some of us the circumstances aren't as good as they are for others. Take Annie. She wasn't born into a famine somewhere in deepest Africa, or one of just too many unwanted girls in China, and didn't begin life with a debilitating disease, or some kind of deformity — yet there was something missing right from the start, something that made her feel constantly uneasy, unsafe — something that made her yearn to feel wanted, protected, loved. She searched all over for It, for Him, for Them, for Meaning, for Love. If only she could find...someone to watch over her.

— ❦ —

Chapter 1

Annie...

On October 9, 1935, in the borough of Brooklyn in the city of New York, a baby girl weighing 9 ½ pounds — double wrists — chubby thighs — came into this world. Her name was Annie. Her older sister Joanie was born a year and a half before, while two years after Annie's birth a baby brother was delivered. That was it. Genug! — Enough already! Sara Rosenberg told her husband Sam that another child was the *last* thing she wanted.

Sara's enduring talent wasn't mothering. It was suffering. And she never tired of talking about her troubles - real or imagined. Worse, for some unexplained reason, Sara saw Annie as the primary source of her misery. Each time Sara heard about a baby being born to a neighbor or family member and Annie was in earshot, she never missed an opportunity to remind her daughter: "Such a fat little baby you were. Over 9 ½ pounds! It was torture, such torture. The doctor, he had to cut a little *down there* to get you out - you had such a big head. Wait 'til you have a baby. It's *agony!*"

On the whole, the Rosenbergs seemed to be genial folks, enjoying life in the tranquil middle-class area of Brooklyn to which they'd recently moved. It was 1940, a safe time. You could walk outside at any hour and most people never locked their doors. Big old sycamore trees shaded lush green lawns fronting comfortable detached brick homes. Bicycles on most of the front porches, chalk-marked sidewalks, the sounds of children playing, depicted a family-oriented neighborhood.

It all seemed so simple, so right with the world. Each spring and summer one could hear the jingle of the bell announcing the Good Humor Man. Magically, front doors opened, excited kids ran out to the curb and lined up to buy their favorite ice cream. There was a soothing regularity to life — the milkman delivered daily, the knife-sharpener truck came once a week and the Fuller Brush man made monthly visits. It was the picture of normalcy, a trouble-free way of living in a time long gone by.

Such a nice neighborhood. Such a pleasant family.

Don't trust appearances.

— ❧ —

The Rosenbergs had moved from their tiny apartment to their dream house in Flatbush when Annie was four. The spacious colonial-style brick house cost $8,000, a hefty amount in 1939 since the Depression was just ending. Her father had worked long hours of overtime at his plumbing job to accumulate the $2,000 down payment that bought into the American dream. He was so proud of his achievement that it's doubtful he ever realized how discontented his family was. Nor of the horror that happened to his little daughter Annie before they even moved in.

"Let's play hide and seek," Anthony Jr. whispered in Annie's ear. They were playing in the empty rooms where the cedary scent of new wood and fresh paint permeated the air. His smile made the little girl uncomfortable. It was kind of weird. The new house was so big. So much to fix up, her daddy had said. Where was her daddy? Inside somewhere? Checking on

something outside? She could hear the sound of a hammer somewhere in the distance. Annie's mom was on the porch reading a book — so far away. Every time she told Anthony she wanted to find her mother, he grabbed her arm and wouldn't let go. "C'mon Annie. We're not done playing yet." She was only four years old. And there weren't any grown-ups close enough to see or hear her.

Junior was Mr. Bianco's 13-year-old son. Mr. Bianco was her Daddy's friend. He was helping him renovate their new house. She really didn't like being alone with Junior. He was creepy. But her daddy had told them to go and play and let the grownups get their work done. She had to do what she was told.

Then he grabbed her hand and pulled Annie after him, upstairs, into an empty bedroom. "We're going to play in that closet, Annie." That smile again. "I don't wanna! I wanna find my daddy!" she yelled. He didn't even answer this time, just pulled her into the closet, closing the door behind them, leaving just a crack open for air. It was very very dark. He was breathing hard, like he was running. It didn't feel like a game. Little Annie was afraid.

Her heart was pounding in her chest. She was scared to death. She could hear the sound of hammers echoing somewhere in the house. But they were far away. Should she scream for help? Junior's hands were sweaty. He held her very close to him. His body smelled. Then he pulled her panties down. He took his big thing out and shoved it between her legs. Her brother's was so tiny. Why was his so big? And sticking out? "Stay still and listen to me," he had said. He turned around and tried to shove it into her rear end. It felt like she was tearing inside. She felt pain and terror. Annie began to SCREAM . He clamped his hand over her mouth and told her in a mean voice she better be quiet or she'd get into real bad trouble. He kept pushing his thing into her. It hurt it hurt it hurt. Tears were pouring down her cheeks. She felt sick. And hot. And terrified. When would he ever let her go?

Finally he did. Finally it was over. And no one anywhere in that house noticed anything. He told her to shut up. Not to tell or she'd be in real trouble. So she kept this terrible happening inside of her. Secret. For years and years. There really was no one to tell.

Chapter 2: The Families

The Rosenbergs

Immigrants from Eastern Europe began flooding our shores toward the end of the 19th century. Fleeing violent prejudice and abject poverty they continued the exodus into the 20th century; it really wasn't difficult to forsake their motherland for America, the land of opportunity. Gittel and Aaron Rosenberg had scrupulously saved their zlotys for years to escape the terrible conditions Jews lived under in Poland, and now with their youngest son Sam, the Rosenbergs joined this tidal wave in 1925.

Like everyone before them, they had made the crossing in steerage crammed into a crowd of refugees speaking Yiddish, as well as a number of strange-sounding languages. Each one clutched just the bare necessities from the home they'd left behind. Gittel was apprehensive. "*Chap nit!*[1] — What's to worry about, Gittel? When we get there, we'll do well," Aaron assured her. After all, he was the man of the family and had to sound strong, but he really didn't know what would come to pass.

1. Take it easy

"Oy, Got tsu danken[2]!" Gittel Rosenberg couldn't contain herself any longer. As their ship slowly made its way to Ellis Island, she stood on deck, gazing in wonderment as Lady Liberty loomed above the sea of heads swaying in front of her. "Finally, maybe we'll have a little *mazel*[3] in our lives! Look Aaron, look—we're in America!" Then Gittel hugged 14-year-old Sam, their youngest son, holding him as tight as she could, tears rolling down her cheeks as she thought of their two older boys left behind. There was only enough money for the three of them. She had no idea that her other sons would die in the Warsaw Ghetto uprising; that she would never see them again.

The Rosenbergs found a small apartment in Williamsburg, Brooklyn, a poor section where Jewish immigrants could find cheap housing. Sam, Gittel's pride and joy, was a solidly built, good-looking kid with a strong jaw, nice nose and winning smile. He resembled the dancer Gene Kelly, (though he was never that good on his feet). But oh boy, was he good at knowing what he wanted to do with his life. "I've gotta learn a good trade," young Sam announced to his parents. "I want to make a decent living, make something of myself here in America." His mother gazed at him with pride. Meanwhile his father talked to Mr. Stern, their downstairs neighbor, whose son Yankel was a successful plumber out in Queens.

"Sammileh," Mr. Stern said the next time they ran into each other, "my son Yankel, the plumber, he could use a good assistant. I hear you vant to learn a trade. Vat you tink?"

"Oh thanks, thanks very much Mr. Stern," Sam answered with excitement. "If I can train — learn how to be a plumber...."

The very next Sunday Sam was introduced to Yankel when he and his young wife came for dinner. They discussed an apprenticeship. "Sure I'll take you on. My poppa tells me you gotta good head on your shoulders. But I warn you— it's gonna be long hours and you gotta take the trolley over the bridge and then the

2.*Thanks to God*   3. *luck*

train. But if you stick with me and pay attention—you'll do okay," Yankel said in his heavy Brooklyn accent.

Sam Rosenberg toiled hard for four years, working long hours, taking night school classes and always helping out at home. He learned his trade well, and first time out, passed the exam. He'd forever be proud of his plumber's license and the money it enabled him to earn so he framed and hung it on the wall. Wherever Sam went, the license went with him, renewal after renewal.

— ✿ —

The Freemans

Max Freeman—Sara's father, had emigrated from Russia with his family in 1920. He met Tillie, who would become his beloved bride, in the crowded Bronx tenement where she lived with her family. The first day they talked, they discovered they'd grown up in nearby villages. "So we had to travel half way around the world to meet each other!" Max laughed, a twinkle in his eye. Tillie was one of four sisters, orphaned young, when their mother died. Their eldest sister had married and settled in England while the other three girls came to America with their father, who eked out a small living as a butcher. Tillie was young and lovely, fiery and strong, always the optimist. "What a beauty," Max decided; he'd found himself the perfect wife. It didn't take long before they were married. "*Tillie, tsum glick, tsum schlimazel,*[4] you are my treasured wife," Max would whisper at night as he held her in his arms. And Tillie would snuggle even closer.

Max Freeman was the immigrant's fairy tale come true. Within ten years he'd earned a fortune. Working 14 hour days, he developed a small grocery store in the Bronx into a much larger one, while Tillie made a comfortable home and cared for the two little girls who had come along the way. Soon, with Tillie's encouragement, he built a supermarket in the up-and-coming borough of Queens. Then came the day when he arrived home for dinner and proudly announced:

4. *Through good times and bad times*

"Tillie, we're getting out of this crowded place. The market is going beautifully out in Queens. I want you and the girls out there too."

"Wonderful!" Tillie said. They were moving up in the world, which pleased her no end. She loved the prospect of decorating a new home. And oh what a house Max had picked and in such a fine neighborhood! And so the Freemans moved from their row house in the Bronx to a five-bedroom home in Forest Hills where they were now living in splendor. *Only the best is good enough for my family* could have been the motto on their front door.

Max especially adored his younger daughter, Sara. He wanted nothing but *naches*[5] for her, and after she and Sam married, the grandchildren Sara gave him made him *kvel*[6] like nothing else.

— ℃ℛ —

While the Freemans prospered, Sam's family did not. The Rosenbergs could afford no more than their railroad flat in Williamsburg. But it was neat and spacious, certainly better than where they came from. Besides, they had their favorite son with them and Gittel catered to his every need. Once Sam learned the plumbing trade and began bringing home significantly more than his hard-working tailor father, she valued him even more.

Yes, life in America was very very good, that is until Sam, the light of Gittel's life met Sara Freeman.

In the summer of 1933, Sam had landed a sizeable assignment. He was to upgrade the plumbing system in the Freeman's supermarket. Sam was a hard-working 23 and Sara a sheltered 18. As fate would have it, that July Sara had come to help her father with the bookkeeping; she'd always had a good head for figures. The first time Sam walked in to the office, she was working at her desk—a tiny delicate pale blonde with little ringlets encircling her hairstyle almost like a halo. Sara looked up when he walked in, taking his measure with big saucer-like blue-green eyes. She liked what she saw. So did he. Later that day Sam heard her infectious giggle. What

5. *joy*   6. *glow with pride*

a fine-looking little lady, he thought, I've never seen anyone so pretty! He fell head over heels. As for Sara, she loved the attention and his handsome good looks. Why, the very first time he smiled at her, she was sure he was the man of her dreams!

Sam's work took much of the summer so that he and Sara had many opportunities to make conversation and soon, with her father's permission, they went out to lunch. The more time they spent together, the more irresistible was the attraction. For once in her life Sara was the center of attention and wasn't playing second fiddle to Anna, her older sister, who always had beaux coming to call. By summer's end Sara was very much in love and had high expectations for a grand future. Sam made it clear he wanted to marry her. Surreptitiously she was tickled to death that she might be able to beat her sister Anna to the altar—and finally get *all* the attention.

Years later, when she'd be in one of her rare sentimental moments, Sara would tell her children how wonderful it had been when their dad was courting her—*before* the changes, before she learned about his temper. Back then, he was all sweetness and promise.

When Sam told his mother about Sara, Gittel was beside herself. "What is wrong with you, Sammy? Are you *meshugginah*? What are you doing with this girl?" she demanded. Sam tried to reassure her. "Mom, you have to get to know her. Just you wait and see. She's such a nice girl and from such a good family. And she's very pretty."

"What do you need Queens for? There's *pretty* right here. Besides —she's too young. And she's spoiled," Gittel insisted. She couldn't imagine much worse than having to give up her precious son, and the *income* he brought home every week. Sam's mild-mannered father, Aaron, as usual, went along with his wife's decisions.

"Please give her a chance," Sam pleaded. "If you get to know her you'll see what a nice girl she is!"

But he knew it was hopeless. He also knew it had little to do with Sara.

Six months—almost to the day—after Sara and Sam first said hello in Max's store, the Freemans finally gave the young couple their consent. They had been objecting that Sara was too young and didn't know Sam well enough, but one day Tillie convinced her husband that it didn't matter. Sam might be Sara's best chance—and they had better not lose it. "Max, Sarah is so happy. He's a hard worker, is earning a decent living. And besides, they're not exactly lining up for her. Not like they do for our Anna," Tillie sighed. "Such a shame. Even though Sara is pretty, let's face it — Anna has the better personality. But we're lucky this Sam came along and actually wants her." And so the Freemans gave their younger daughter their blessings.

The Rosenbergs—Gittel, that is—never did.

When Sara Freeman became Sara Rosenberg on a snowy day in January 1934, Sam's parents sat silently in their drab living room in Williamsburg. They had told Sam it was the snow. But Sara knew better. It cut her to the quick. After that, when Sam made his weekly Sunday morning visits to his parents' apartment, he went alone.

Sara Rosenberg sat at home and nursed her unhappiness. But it wasn't long before her in-laws were not the only cause.

Sam's arrival at the end of his workday had long ceased to be a time of joy. In fact, Sara had come to dread the sound of his key in the front door. He'd take off his hat and jacket and carefully hang them up. Affectionate by nature, he'd go over to give Sara a kiss. Most of the time she'd turn her head ever so slightly so that the kiss landed on her cheek. "I'm busy Sam," she'd say, as she peeled a potato or stirred something in a pot. Then Sam went to shower, a ritual he performed at least twice a day, morning and night.

After cleaning up Sam would walk apprehensively into the kitchen and look into the pots on the stove. Sara tensed—and waited. Sometimes he grunted and went into the living room to listen to the radio. Other times he scowled, and shot her a look of annoyance. But most often he exploded. The pot roast looked dried out, the string beans overcooked. "Damn it!" Sam would shout. "What have you been doing all day? I don't want this crap for supper!" One awful time she'd never forgot, after he bit into stale bread on the table – (oh how he hated day old bread) — he took note of a new leopard print vest she was wearing. "And where did you get that *schmatte*?[7] You call that fashion? Wasting my money on that *drek*?[8]" Sara didn't move fast enough, so he'd grabbed at her new vest—and tore half of it off.

It hadn't taken Sara long to realize she'd married a man with a brutal temper. My God, what was wrong with him? The explosions began within their first year of marriage. They grew increasingly frequent until they had become the rule, not the exception. And almost always, it was over the way she kept house—or rather, the way she didn't.

For Sara — one was a lonely number. Being married was every woman's goal; in her world divorce was unheard of. But she grew more and more discouraged. As much as she avoided the cruel reality, deep down inside of her she feared she'd made a terrible mistake. Sara was ashamed to confide in her parents because it would be admitting that they'd been right—she hadn't known Sam Rosenberg long and well enough. She couldn't unburden her heart to Anna, who was so damned condescending – that would only make her sister feel more superior than ever.

And then the kids came along. Sara was only 19 the first time she was pregnant. Two more kids followed within the first five years. So much to endure, too much, too much. Sara kept her bitterness carefully hidden. And hurt like hell inside. Then she made a discovery. Food made her feel better—even if it was just for a little while. Not any food. *Sweets and starches.* Any kind of chocolate candy or cakes. And nuts, especially Indian nuts, which she kept in a paper bag in her nightstand and would crunch on late at night when everyone else was asleep. Soon Sara began to stuff her mouth with junk food day and night—whenever her nerves demanded numbing.

7. Rag   8. crap

She also escaped from her disgrace and anger with an endless
succession of pulp fiction and romance novels.

— ❦ —

Few of Sara's relatives had any idea at all of what was going on.
Although her father sensed there was some discord, she revealed
next to nothing. But Max, who visited as often as he could, suspected
his daughter wasn't that happy.

At least twice a month — usually on a Sunday morning — Max
would drive to Brooklyn from Forest Hills with presents for Sara —
usually a stack of the *True Detective* magazines she loved to read. And
once the kids were old enough he'd bring them a variety of candy bars.
And of course there was always one of Tillie's Jewish specialties — a
lukshen kugel one time, a *tzimmes* another, maybe some *latkes* to reheat.
Annie would never forget her grandmother's crusty potato kugel.
Spicy, spongy, delicious. No other *kugel* ever measured up to it!

Annie's mother revered her father. Sara's permanent look of
suffering vanished from the moment Max walked in the front door
till he left back for Queens. These visits were the high point of her
otherwise depressing week.

"Where are the *kinder*[9], Sara?" he'd ask, after hugging his
favorite daughter. Then he'd call out in his big booming voice:
Children, come here and give your *zaideh*[10] a kiss!" It didn't take long
for them to come running. After Annie's grandfather distributed the
presents — (there were always presents) — the two adults sat down
at the kitchen table, talking while they sipped freshly brewed coffee.
The one good thing you could say about Sara Rosenberg's kitchen is
that she sure knew how to make a pot of first-class coffee — the one
thing her touch didn't ruin. Annie's mom and grandfather talked in
hushed tones, but she heard a lot more than they ever realized. And
their conversation always ended with the same refrain.

"What is *wrong* with him?" her grandfather would finally say. "I
want to help my daughter, my flesh and blood. Please, let me give

9. *children*   10. *grandfather*

you the money to pay off the mortgage. I'll never even know it's gone. And you and Sam can use the extra cash to buy some good furniture for this place. Like what you had at home. This is a crime by him?"

"Papa, Sam would have a fit if he knew you even suggested it," Annie would hear her mother whisper. "He refused the down payment from you. And it's gonna be just the same with this. You should know him by now."

"So — tell him it's a loan, for God's sake!" "I can't do that. Sam has to be a *gantseh macher*,[11] poppa. You know that by now. He earns enough to manage the mortgage payments. He'd think you don't respect his ability to provide for us. Just be glad he didn't refuse the beautiful bedroom set you bought for the girls."

"I know him, but I don't understand him, Sara. Sometimes I think he's completely *meshugine*.[12]"

"That's how he is, daddy. Sam's very proud. He needs to be the provider. No help from *nobody*. Here, have another cup of coffee." Annie's mother also cut a hefty slice of coffee cake for her father, and there the conversation ended.

Annie's grandfather took a few sips, wiped his mouth with his napkin, and called the children over for good-bye hugs. With a "*zei gezundt, bubbelah*,"[13] he embraced each child with genuine affection and slipped two shiny nickels into each one's hand. "Take care of yourself, my darling Sara. Come out and see us more often."

They all walked out with him, watched him get into his fine-looking new Oldsmobile and drive off. They waved like crazy — until the car became a tiny speck and finally disappeared.

— ❧ —

Sam Rosenberg was an intelligent man, but without a single drop of introspection. As far as he was concerned, his mother had been right. Sara was spoiled. But she was also very young, and at

11. big shot   12. crazy   13. Bye bye sweethearts

first he calmed himself with the thought that time was all she needed to learn to become a decent cook and housewife. But of course, she never did. Sam grew increasingly frustrated with the years. Anger became his full-time occupation at home, and it dominated the family with darkness and despair.

As the years went by, he never had a clue at how frightened — and angry — his family was, or why his wife was so aloof — why she stayed up reading half the night and was still asleep when he'd leave for work. Sam's shame at having a wife who kept a home that embarrassed him had rapidly turned into an uncontrollable rage at his misfortune. It evolved into epithets and bullying and an awful way to live.

Sam began to spend more time at work. He thrived on the hard work that earned him respect and prosperity as a master plumber. He put in a great deal of overtime. He was making more money and besides — it avoided tensions at home. But once he was home, his displeasure didn't take long to boil over. Sara just never grew to care about things that mattered a lot to Sam — things like proficiency at cooking and laundry and cleaning. "Why do you always end up ruining the food? What the hell is wrong with you, anyway?" he screamed at her. "You can eat off my mother's floors, for crying out loud. But look at this pigsty! Why dirty dishes in the sink all day? All you're good at is sleeping late and reading your garbage and ruining the food you buy with my good money!" The litany went on and on, over and over. Sara would finally burst into tears and run out of the room.

As the years went by and Sara felt more paralyzed with fear, she wasn't capable of shielding the children from her husband's anger either. Nor did she try to soothe their upset. Instead she did an instant about face and bullied the kids in her own complaining, manipulative style.

"Don't slam the door!" "Stay out of the refrigerator!" "Get those dirty shoes off before you come in and get *schmutz* on the carpet!" "Lower your radio!" "No cookies — it'll ruin your appetite!" "Stay off the good furniture!" Those rare times the kids actually sat in the living room, it was on the floor, not the plastic-covered furniture that always looked new. And no showers after 6 in the evening because the sound of the running water might wake their dad, who napped and snored on the living room sofa as soon as dinner was over. The breadwinner could break all the rules, including using the living room couch.

The *no-showers-after-6pm* rule wasn't for Sam's benefit. It was for Sara's. She wanted her angry husband to be out of her way as much as possible. That meant either out of the house — or asleep. Since the shower would wake him, then no showering. And so Sara tried to put some order into her own life by keeping her children in her own prison of "don'ts."

The three kids grew up in a house of rigid and far-ranging rules and regulations. And because they were at the mercy of their parents' roller coaster moods, it meant someone would be in tears before the day was over.

Suppertime was the only meal the family shared together. And it was dreaded. Every night, Annie and her brother and sister approached the dinner table with their stomachs in knots while they waited for their father's face to start turning red. Then — *crack!*

"Shoe leather, that's what you give me" Sam might shout. "You buy this expensive T-bone steak — and you *know* after all these years that I *hate* steak that isn't rare — and you *still* can't manage to get the meat off the broiler in time? And look at these goddamned carrots. When will you cook the vegetables *long* enough so they're *not* raw? You're wasting my hard-earned money with this *crap*, this *drek!*" he yelled, glaring at them with murder in his eyes. The veins in his neck were bulging ominously. Then he'd lift his plate of food in his strong laborer's hand and hurl it across the dinette. *SMASH!!* As the shattered dish hit the floor, the food would slide down the wall. Sam's glare would be met by frightened silence. Sara, biting her lip, would be struggling to hold back her tears. And by then Annie's stomach was churning. Sid was trying to disappear in his chair. "You act like a goddamned sissy!" Sam would turn and attack him. Joanie was digging her nails into her palms, scared and angry and desperately hoping the fighting would stop. They'd all leave the table with a stomachache.

— ∝ —

When Annie was younger, she hated her father for his frightening anger. And she felt sad for her mother, who seemed so vulnerable, so pathetic. But as she grew older, and understood more of the interplay between her parents, Annie came to resent her mother as well. She realized Sara could have avoided most of these scenes by watching the damned clock and getting the meat off the broiler and leaving the vegetables to cook long enough or not too long. Damn it! Why the hell didn't she do it? Why did she insist on making all of them suffer!

Sure, Annie realized that some kids had it even harder – they had drunken parents, or parents who beat them, or no parents at all. But that couldn't stop her tears.

So home sweet home just wasn't that at the Rosenberg's. Annie spent as much time outside with her friends as she could. Soon after the family had moved to Flatbush, Annie made friends with the girls who lived on her block. She'd run out and meet them-to skip rope, play potsie, organize a game of ring-a-leevio or tag. She couldn't invite friends over—no place to sit or relax, no snacks – after all, snacks would make crumbs on the floor. And her mother would have a fit at the noise. No noise! So *outside* was Annie's dominion, the only place for sure she could giggle like a girl.

Annie's two best friends were Adrienne Yehegian, whose family
were Armenian immigrants, and Margie Coleman, the only girl in
a family of four boys — though not for long. Once the US entered
World War II and the fighting in Europe had escalated, young men
were being drafted. Poor Margie lost two of her older brothers within
three months of each other. The two gold stars hanging proudly in
the Coleman's parlor window couldn't begin to make up for the
enormous pain of this loss. Margie fell apart whenever she heard
one of the patriotic songs on the radio, like "Praise the Lord and Pass
the Ammunition", or if there was a war movie in the double bill at
the movies on Saturday mornings, (and in those years, there always
was,) Margie would sit in the dark and cry. Annie cried along too.

— ❧ —

For Annie, one of the best things about living in Flatbush was
the Brooklyn Dodgers, the first integrated baseball team in history.
She was a dedicated Dodgers fan. She began listening to their games
on the radio in 1945. Once her father had bought their first television
set, a 10-inch black-and-white Philco, she and Sid — the family sports
fans — would be riveted to the screen for the weekend and night
games. Annie remembered nostalgically when Jackie Robinson
joined the team that included Gil Hodges, Pee Wee Reese, Carl
Furillo and Duke Snyder. And wow, they even got to see them play
once at Ebbet's Field. When they won the World Series in 1955 — the
only time they ever won it as the Brooklyn Dodgers – Annie was
ecstatic. When they moved to Los Angeles, neither Brooklyn nor the
Dodgers would ever be the same.

— ❧ —

Being a Rosenberg meant walking on eggshells. Above all
else: children were to be seen and not heard — regardless of what
was going on. Talking about anything that bothered them was
unacceptable. So feelings of pretty much any kind — especially fear
and anger — were not acknowledged. Each child had to find an outlet-

to help cope with the inner turbulence and the pervasive gloom that-was their normal environment at home. Soon enough Joanie became a *femme fatale*, vamping her way through adolescence. "Hey Annie, look at this super scarlet lipstick. Terrific, huh?" And she'd smooth on the third coat of what was always too vivid a color for her fair skin and slather on her Max Factor pancake makeup and the rest of her war paint like she was going into battle. And maybe she was. Joanie dressed and walked like she made up her face — overdone, obvious, and totally inappropriate for her age. She wanted to be voluptuous and desirable like Rita Hayworth or Betty Grable – or any of the stars in the *Movie Screen* fan magazines she devoured every day.

Poor Sid. He was the most frequent target of their dad's rage. It destroyed any positive feelings that might have had a chance to develop. He was really short for his age, and horribly shy — and the only one in the family to suffer from acne. He squeezed the pimples, convinced it would help, and walked around with a mess on his face that left permanent scars. It only added to his sense of hopeless inadequacy. Sid also chewed his nails to the quick. For years his father would yell at him, call him a sissy or a *shmendrek*.[14] He hated it. And he hated his father.

Sid was a lost soul. In high school he joined a neighborhood gang, but even there he never found the respect he desperately wanted. He started at Brooklyn College but lasted barely a year. Then nerdy little Sid suddenly shocked everyone. He ran off and joined the Marines. For Sid it turned out to be the right move. What a change when he returned home two years later. Even Sam appreciated the difference, and actually bragged about his son the *marine*. Sid set his sights on success. So he went back to college — and this time he graduated.

As for Annie, her path to finding approval was at school. She was smart, and she loved to read, and she got really good grades at P.S. 138. But it never seemed to get her anywhere at home. When Annie was about 6 she'd actually tried to write a song. She'd seen

14. *An inept bungler*

the ads in the back of comic books — "You too can become a famous songwriter. Just send us your lyrics…." So she decided to make up her own version of a popular song. She was so proud, and ran to show it off to her mother.

"This is so *stupid*, Annie! I'd be ashamed to show it to anyone!" her mother laughed. And when her dad came home Sara couldn't wait to tell him all about it, laughing derisively as she said, "Sam, look at this — your daughter thinks she can write songs!" Annie's heart was in tatters, she was so embarrassed. She went up to her room and cried until she fell asleep. Yet, as Annie grew up, she still assumed that being a star pupil would make her parents admire and love her. She just didn't get it.

Inevitably Annie would daydream about a life that was like the movies she loved — where the girl was always pretty and lovable and the story always had a happy ending. Maybe Judy Garland in an Andy Hardy movie. Most of all, she could hardly wait till she was old enough to leave this house that was like a prison — the anger, the fighting, the verbal abuse. "Quiet? You want quiet, go live in a cemetery," her father yelled at her one day when he noticed that she'd stuck her fingers in her ears to shut out his cursing about Sara letting him run out of clean underwear once again.

After P.S. 138, Annie attended Erasmus High. (Later on she loved telling people that Barbra Streisand and Neil Diamond had gone to *her* high school.) It was at Erasmus that Annie began to write. She joined the school newspaper where she reported on class happenings as the gossip columnist. She was also allowed to contribute her own poetry. From the abundance of what she used to call the "pity poems" she had written in her journal — "*And the Lord Said, Love is Near, and I answered, What should I wear?*" was one of her briefer ones — she chose a few less personal ones. Having them published in the school paper gained Annie much needed admiration from her peers.

Annie's favorite subject was English, and her favorite English teacher was Phillip Bodgan — tall, 40-ish, and married. Mr. Bogdan was passionate about teaching and an inspiration to his students — and he was a big fan of anything Annie wrote. Annie practically worshipped him, with a huge crush in the bargain. A light went out for her when spring semester ended and her junior year came to a close. No more Mr. Bogdan.

For Annie's last year of high school, things had gotten even worse at home — criticism from her mother was constant now. Joanie was out of the house so she became the main target of her mother's frustration. And there was even more quarreling between her parents. They fought over absolutely *everything*. Annie began writing with a new seriousness, expressing her deep feelings in poetry and prose. It began as a life-saving outlet. And once she decided to show some of her pieces to Mr. Bogdan, it became her means for recognition and praise, and prolonging her relationship with her idol for another year.

Whenever Annie had written something new, she'd wait for Mr. Bogdan in the hallway when she knew he was finishing his last class. She knew he'd always have a few minutes for her. He'd read the pages she held out to him and suggest ways to improve what she'd written, never forgetting to add his praise: "I like it, Annie. Just flesh out a little more about how these two met and you'll be right on track. It's really quite well done." And then he'd smile. Annie's feet barely touched the ground on her way home.

She was so grateful that Mr. Bogdan saw promise in her writing — and let her know it. He seemed to realize that Annie's wisecracking disposition hid deep unhappiness. And he knew from veiled comments she'd made — plus the fact that her parents had never attended a single play she had been in — that Annie received little support of any kind at home. He seemed only too delighted to be her mentor.

When she graduated from Erasmus in pre-Women's Lib 1953, Mr. Bogdan wrote in her autograph book: *"To that rara avis, a female with a mind."* Coming from a man whose opinion she respected above all others — Annie treasured it beyond reason.

Now that she'd graduated from high school, Annie was determined to search out her own path. Brooklyn College was out. That's what everyone else did.

Go on, run away, try to hide. But where are you going, little girl, what do you think you can do all on your own? It's the 50s you know, and nice girls get married.

— ℭℜ —

Chapter 3

Park and Lexington Avenues in the East 60s region of Manhattan is one of the most exclusive areas of the city, with luxury high-rise buildings and a dense concentration of expensive shops on nearby Madison Avenue. Occupying a full city block-between the two avenues and stretching from 68th to 69th Streets, stands the modern-looking white stone and marble building that houses the once prestigious (and in the 50s, strictly a girls' school) Hunter College of the City of New York.

For Annie Rosenberg of Brooklyn, attending Hunter College fulfilled a secret ambition; one she had fantasized for many years. "Your cousin, Beatrice Brown and her friend — Bess Myerson — they attended in the 1940s," her maternal grandmother, Tillie, used to remind her. "Beatrice, she arranges now for Leopold Stokowski, and such a fine viola player she is, and Bess, well you know she was the first Jewish Miss America," her grandma would announce with pride. "You'll have only *nachas* my darling Annie, if you go there," she added. *Nachas* — or good luck — that sounded good to Annie.

She had the necessary 85+ average to apply. Tuition would be dirt cheap, so her parents couldn't object — just $8, *including* books.

Annie was grateful her grandmother was continually supportive, the one person in her life she could always count on. She wasn't sure yet what she'd major in; sometimes she thought she wanted to become a social worker and help other people, at other times she still wanted to be a writer. All she knew was that her road to independence would begin at Hunter.

She applied, crossed her fingers and toes, wrote hopeful messages in her diary and prayed daily that she'd make it. It took two months before she received the marvelous news — that she had been accepted, was really, truly, actually going to be a Hunter College freshman! Annie could barely believe her luck. Finally things were looking up. Some how or other, in spite of any obstacles and backbiting she felt from the family, she'd make it into the city each day, begin discovering what life was all about. And do it *her* way. Whatever that meant.

Manhattan Island was only five miles away. You could see it from some parts of Brooklyn. To little Annie Rosenberg the distance always seemed more like a thousand, but now she was finally going to cross that chasm and as much as she wished she could find an alternate route — she'd have to rely on the New York City transit system. And so in early September 1953, she began her daily commute, which amounted to an hour and a half traveling each way.

Through good weather and bad, Annie trudged the nine long blocks to the bus stop and waited with the rest of the crowd for the B-45. There were no backpacks then so she schlepped all her books as best she could. Day in, day out, rain and snow sometimes, shivering as she waited in the worst of weather. Why did her mom make it even harder? Complaining constantly about everything and holding back her meager $5 weekly allowance, her mother made many a day a miserable one.

Annie took a bus to the train station and then began a 45-minute ride into the city, changing subway lines twice in Manhattan to reach the 68th Street stop on Lexington Avenue. During morning rush hour, it was very crowded. Finding a seat was difficult. Too many times trains stalled, too often there was standing room only, and worse, some of the passengers *smelled* – why, Annie never understood, but they didn't deign to use underarm deodorant.

By her sophomore term, Annie was crestfallen. The arguments at home were escalating; she didn't know if she could take it much longer; she was becoming a nervous wreck. It was too hard to study with all the yelling, too damn many distractions. Maybe, she thought, it would be better to get a job — a *full-time* job — and carry fewer credits — finish school at night if necessary? Then she could move out. Something had to change.

At home, she'd flee the inevitable arguing by closing herself in her room and quietly listening to her favorite Elvis songs. She also daydreamed a lot — hoped she'd meet someone as handsome, as sexy as Presley. Twenty in 1956, and still a virgin, Annie reacted like the millions of other Elvis fans who were swooning over the swivel-hipped sex symbol. Yes, Annie sought independence, but she also wanted romance and fantasized that her *Prince Charming* would come along and rescue her from all the unhappiness and uncertainty.

Annie's habitual daydreaming began in the 1940s when the silver screen was the major egress for escape and entertainment. A partaker in the early ritual of movie going – she'd watch the romantic portrayals of larger-than-life stars like Humphrey Bogart and Ingrid Bergman, of Bette Davis and Paul Henreid whose soul-stirring performances left such an indelible mark that for a very long stage of her life (or was it forever?) Annie waited for her own great love, that *knight-in-shining-armor* who'd save her from all the bad things. She fantasized often of this special hero, the one who'd love and watch over her 'till death they did part.

Actually, Annie's wishes were rather ordinary. Every girl wanted a boyfriend, a special man, wanted to be a bride one day.

In the 1950s and the 1960s women were expected to marry, to make the best alliance they could. For a young Jewish woman, a doctor, a lawyer, or a C.P.A., that was the epitome of success. To gain such a husband meant you would have "*a good provider.*"

But Annie hadn't met anyone yet. What was wrong with her? Maybe she wasn't attractive or worthy enough. She was forever comparing — her features were ordinary; actually there was a tiny bump on her nose that she saw as huge and an impediment. And she was kind of short and could never measure up to the tall, svelte, beautiful models in the women's magazines. The few dates she'd had didn't work out; schleps, losers, damn it, she wouldn't go out with any of those jerks! She wanted someone like her movie heroes, handsome, courageous — real men. But was she attractive enough? Deserving enough? She felt ugly, useless and helpless.

— ℭ℞ —

Annie searched through the Sunday newspaper want ads, determined to find a decent job. She'd worked part time through her freshman year at an orthopedic surgeon's office, putting in as many as 20 hours a week, keeping his books, so she looked under office positions with bookkeeping experience. She figured she could wing it.

And that was how at the tender age of 20 she found herself with a job as office receptionist, bookkeeper, and *chief bottle-washer* at Triumph Records, a new record label, begun by a former dentist, Arthur Ginsberg, who had in fact been one of the founders of Atlantic Records.

Ginsberg was bought out of Atlantic with a few hundred thousand dollars when his marriage to his wife Myriam, who held stock in the company, ended. He named the new company after his favorite sports car. He would create a new, no, a better record label than Atlantic Records, they'd see.

The only problem with his ambitious plans was that Ginsberg was newly married to a young, long-legged ex-adult film star

and spent his days screwing to his heart's content at their new
sumptuous apartment on Central Park West. He would spend his
evenings at recording sessions, working with a stable of new singers
like Tony Middleton, but he rarely appeared at the new offices he'd
opened on West 74th Street. He left the details to his *gofer*, Marty
Torino, and of course, to Annie Rosenberg — the young girl he
hired to answer the phones and handle the artists and writers, the
wannabes who came in all day long.

Suddenly Annie found herself with more responsibility and
freedom than she'd ever imagined. Marty Torino, (who was
supposed to be helping Art find promising new artists and sign them
to contracts,) was in reality busy with his latest blonde bombshell,
Anita Diva, a porn queen for whom he had a mad passion. Torino
knew he could get away with murder. Ginsburg was too busy with
his own pussy to care what Marty was doing. Besides, Arty was the
actual diviner of talent, he'd listen to 'em at night, take home some
of the demo recordings, and ultimately select the new talent for his
record label.

And so it was left to Annie to chat with the Cashbox and
Billboard salesmen and to meet artists, managers, writers — some
well-known and some has-beens, all of whom would wait all day
in the hopes of seeing the big man, Arty. It was fantastic. She could
hardly believe that she was in this position of trust. She was learning
a lot. It was a very good experience though at the time Annie really
wasn't aware of how much she was absorbing. Those first few
months she had no idea when Ginsburg would show up; he'd call
hourly and say he was on his way, but rarely got there before 4 p.m.

It took her months to get it — that he'd never set foot in his
office before 4 — and then he'd work until 10 or later. But all day,
the desperate, the hungry, the impatient, would call, drop by, keep
waiting, hoping to see the big man with the cash to back them, to
make their songs into hits, to shape the singers among them into
stars.

Women's roles in the post war world began to show signs of change when Katharine Hepburn played a lawyer opposite Spencer Tracy in *State of the Union*. But it was slow, the changes that would eventually come with the woman's movement. In 1950 Elizabeth Taylor was still playing a traditional role in *Father of the Bride*, and in 1953 Marilyn Monroe sang about diamonds being a girl's best friend in *How to Marry A Millionaire*.

Working full time was good for Annie. It was worth it to take a term off from school and to save enough money to move out. Next year, she'd take 12 credits, be able to manage it, get on with college, but best of all be practiced enough to move out of the house. She was gaining a little more confidence each day as she discovered she was able to handle the daily activities and run the office on her own. Why even that good looking young singer Gene Pitney, befriended her and later asked her if she wanted to manage him. Pitney hated the control of the overbearing and overweight Marty Flugelman, who had slyly signed him to an absurd 10-year contract, and was making most of the money by managing the young singing talent.

Annie was flattered, but knew that wasn't right for her. Besides, she hoped to return to Hunter in the evening and was looking for her own apartment or one to share. While she was out all day, she was still living at home. It was easy to avoid her mother at her worst moments, and there was less tension when she arrived home at 6 or later, but she also knew she'd have to get out once and for all. Now that she was making $200 a week, she could do it. Art Ginsburg paid very well for those days, and with average rents for studio apartments on the West Side going for $125, Annie could make it on her own.

— ◌℞ —

"I've left the schmuck, Annie," Joanie announced. "And I've found a decent walkup on West 76th Street. You can move in with me if you want, and we'll share the rent, hon." Annie wasn't surprised at all. Joanie's marriage to Philip Stern seemed wrong from the get-go; but then it was Joanie's way to get out of their unhappy home life. Annie was overjoyed; finally she had a reason, an anchor and a good excuse to leave home. And she certainly didn't need any further explanations from Joanie. It was obvious that she and Philip were living together more like brother and sister than husband and wife.

The 1950s, a decade of conformity, began to change. Gene Kelly and America were singing in the rain, and Eisenhower was president. And for once in her young life, Annie Rosenberg felt enormously happy. She'd share an apartment with her sister — get out of the house in the best way possible. How could anyone object? And now that she had a job, she felt a real independence.

In the autumn of 1956, Annie and Joanie moved into the furnished one-bedroom brownstone. Close to Triumph Records offices, it was so very convenient. Joanie found a job teaching on the upper West Side. They'd have each other. Annie finally breathed a sigh of relief.

It didn't last long. A few months later Joanie came home and excitedly proclaimed that she'd found the love of her life. He was the assistant principal at her school. Unfortunately, he was married, she confided, unhappily. "But don't say a word, Annie. Not a word! He loves me, he'll get a divorce, this is good for both of us," Joanie said with assurance.

Annie was concerned, but said nothing. After all, her sister was two years older, had been married; hopefully she knew what she was doing. And anyone was probably a better option than Phil Stern. Stern was an English professor and the Rosenbergs were very pleased with Joanie's choice. A *nice Jewish man*, of course. But the marriage only lasted three years. Philip was pathetic, a Wally Peepers look-alike with absolutely no sex appeal. Annie even wondered if Philip was gay. And she certainly could understand why Joanie was attracted to Andre when she finally met him. He was very handsome. He'd been the drama teacher at the school, and he was interesting too. "Andre was just appointed assistant principal. He'll be making a better salary and we'll make it," Joanie predicted.

Five days before Christmas Joanie called Annie at the office. She was on Cloud Nine! She and Andre had booked a 7-day vacation in the Bahamas; he had indeed separated from his wife, and was planning a divorce.

"Oh that sounds like a fabulous trip, Joanie. I'll miss you but am glad he's taking you away. You deserve it."

Happy for her sister, but alone and lonely, Annie desperately yearned to meet someone of her own. Little did she know how soon her wishes would be answered.

...No one ever said life was supposed to be fair. But some get better breaks than others. Roosevelt Jones played the best hand he was dealt, played it well and left a lasting legacy of music that would live on — long after he was gone.

— ❧ —

Chapter 4

July 1928 —

It was 1928, the end of the jazz age and Calvin Coolidge, 30th president of the United States, was still in office. It was also the year that 40-year-old Lillie-May Jones, a hard-working cotton-picker from Alabama suffered a massive stroke and died. It was a tragic end to a hard life — Lillie-May's death left behind five fatherless children, including her only daughter and the youngest, Rosella, 13. The burial was swift and simple. Now Rosella was alone. She gently folded up her mother's few nice belongings and her Sunday-go-to-church outfit to give to an aunt. The cabin was sweltering with the heat of the day. Sweat poured down her face. She walked outside. It was going on 9 p.m. but the air hung heavy with the summer's heat. "Oh Momma, what should I do," Rosella cried out.

The brilliant stars in the navy blue sky shimmered like the tears trickling down her cheeks. "How do ya live without a wonderful momma like we had?" Rosella implored the night air. There was no one else to ask. Two days after they buried Lillie-May, her brothers had gone off to seek work. Her stomach growled from hunger, but Rosella had no appetite. A sudden burst of wind, which meant the air was changing, swept along the dusty dry terrain. A piece of it caught in her eye. It stung, but not as bad as the hurt she was feeling. It was cruel to lose the person who cared the most about you.

"What am I gonna do now, without you? What can I do Momma?" she cried out again. But in the dark summer's night no one heard her. What will become of me?" she screamed even louder, feeling far younger than her thirteen years on earth. Suddenly the scriptures she'd been taught returned to remind her that she must honor her mother, not worry about her own fate. With all the strength left within her, Rosella Jones called upon her fading faith. "Oh momma, dear momma, I pray you're in the Lord's loving hands."

— ❧ —

1928 was also a year when the financial state of the world was teetering. Happy days were coming to an end. President Coolidge left office just before the stock market failure of 1929 devastated the economy. Within a year the crash destroyed lives and fortunes and led to the Great Depression. Millions of people were about to find themselves unemployed and in need of public assistance.

In the deep South, where Rosella was raised, blacks were already used to an impoverished existence. Life was harsh, real hard for the poor and uneducated. Rosella and her family's meager beginnings were out of Childersberg, Alabama, a dirt-poor farming area many miles from Birmingham. Her parents had been tenant farmers, toiling in the cotton and cornfields. Called "day-hands," many were the children of slaves. They worked from dawn until dusk. It was grim. It was dismal. But what else could "colored" folk do?

At the south edge of the farm, six simple cabins stood in a field of grass. Generations of whitewash were peeling from the mud-brick walls. All but one front porch had rotted away, and there were gaping holes where doors and windows used to be. One of these decaying cabins is what Rosella called home.

Alabama was always sizzling hot and dusty. Rosella was six when her father — miles of life written all over his face — died working the fields one sweltering August day. Then the final blow came when her mother suffered the stroke, and then passed on. Rosella was devastated. Two weeks later, relatives took her in but it was still an unforgiving life. Family or not, they didn't really need another body to house and feed. She hated it, being alone, so dependent upon the benevolence of others. "Thank you, Auntie Lucy, thank you Uncle Marcus, thank you, thank you, thank you," she repeated over and over and over again. She bit her tongue so often there was a real red mark there, all to keep her feelings inside.

"There's no two ways about it 'chile, we just don't have enough to go around," her aunt explained. Rosella was forced to drop out of school to help pay for her keep. Her four brothers had long ago gone off in different directions looking for work cross-country. She never did hear from them again.

"Oh Jesus, are you there? Can you help me, please?" she'd cry out silently, laying her head down on the old pillow, dirty, smelly, without a case, her only buffer against the hard mattress beneath. Finally she'd fall asleep.

It was the dark days just before the depression. A desiccated, difficult time for millions of Americans, black and white. For Rosella, life was sometimes unbearable. All she had left of her beloved mother was a modest bible and the positive philosophy she'd preached. It wasn't enough.

December 1931 —

Christmas was coming but so what. No money to buy gifts. When Rosella found herself pregnant at 16, she was humiliated.

It was so wrong, a flawed choice made early in life. Worse, it was the one time she'd committed a sin. She craved affection, a warm kind word from anyone. And now this. Rosella shed quiet tears for months. Mortified, she didn't dare tell anyone. They had their own burdens. But she knew she could only hide it just so long.

What'd become of her? "Dear Lord, please show me the way out of this," she'd pray.

She continued to work, in spite of the awful morning sickness that came upon her. She needed to keep the secret. "What on earth was she going to do?" Rosella asked herself, time and time again. Mercy, Jesus, Mercy! — how could she take care of a baby?

She saved every spare penny, worked seven days a week and as many hours as possible. "Oh lord, show me what to do," she wailed, muffling the sounds into the pillow as she cried herself to sleep. Her two cousins slept nearby, all in the same small windowless room. She didn't dare let anyone know.

Finally Rosella devised a plan. She'd go to Freddie Mae's, a cousin living in New York City, somewhere on 125th Street. She'd heard her relative, who'd left Childersberg in 1925, was doing real good. Everyone said she was a good kind person. Rosella couldn't hide her condition much longer. The baby was beginning to show. She copied Freddie Mae's address into her mother's tattered bible. She'd beg her cousin to take her in. She'd enough money to pay her keep 'til the baby was born.

Rosella took her savings, rolled it up tightly in a tiny rag and knotted it into her bra for safekeeping. Packing her meager belongings she slipped out at the crack of dawn to get to the main dirt road. There was always some traffic there.

She stood on the lonely road all day long, the hot sun beating down on her swollen belly. Her feet were hurting, her back was aching, and the sweat was dripping down her face. It wasn't easy getting someone to stop. Not too many Negroes had cars. Many passed by without slowing down. "Hey little lady, hop in" the old man said, stopping a few feet up the road. His old Ford pick-up truck was laden with bushels of potatoes. Finally she'd been able to hitch a ride with a good Samaritan.

"The name is Henry," he said, "Headed for Birmingham."

"Oh very good, sir, I need to get to the Greyhound station there," she answered.

The rest of the trip was easy. The truck driver was friendly and talkative, didn't ask many questions. He figured a girl of Rosella's age was running away. Wherever she was headed had to be better than where she was coming from. Hell, he didn't mind helping. Finally they arrived at the bus depot. "Thanks Mister, thanks a lot for the ride," Rosella said gratefully.

"Hey times are tough. You go where you can do better for yourself, girl," he said with a smile big enough to reveal a few of his front teeth missing. Life wasn't easy for him, either, but at least he had a job.

Rosella bought a ticket and waited all night on the wooden bench for the morning bus. Finally she boarded a Greyhound departing for New York. It was 1932. A new life lay ahead.

Into that world, a baby boy destined to become a force in the music business, would be born. His name was Roosevelt Jones. Smiled on by fate, this man who began life in poverty and grew up in a Harlem tenement, would ultimately achieve enormous success and rub shoulders with people from all walks of life. Among those he'd meet would be Annie, and he'd make a difference in her life.

Franklin D. Roosevelt had taken office on March 4, 1933. His "Forgotten Man" speech lifted Americans out of their deep malaise. It would become an inspiring era in American history. "The only thing we have to fear is fear itself" came over the air like a ray of sunlight. For Rosella, too, there was hope.

"Of course, child, we got room for you," Freddie Mae said, hugging her warmly. Rosella found the uptown apartment easily, but the rickety stairs up to the third floor was tiring. She was exhausted. She didn't have to explain much to Freddie Mae. Wise beyond her 26 years, Freddie Mae knew Rosella wouldn't have traveled three days on a bus if she didn't have a real strong reason to come there to stay. She could tell Rosella was pregnant, and didn't sit in judgment. That was the Lord's job.

While it was a modest railroad flat, to Rosella this refuge was more like a palace. Besides, she was thrilled to learn there was a bathroom down the hall. No more having to walk out the back way to the outhouse like she had to do back home. Things were looking up.

After a delicious hot meal of ham hocks and turnip greens, a plate Rosella downed so fast she burned the roof of her mouth, she was shown to the room she'd make her own. She quickly lay down on the neat single bed. She fell into a bottomless sleep and slumbered for hours and hours.

On August 16, 1932, her only child, Roosevelt Lincoln Jones, was born. Rosella had named him after the presidential candidate she admired, the one she believed could do the most for the poor — and for good measure, gave her newborn son the middle name of the first president who cared about her people.

Soon after Roosevelt's birth, Rosella took up housework to make ends meet. It was a hard life, but Freddie Mae looked after a few infants, and another one was just fine. And the work was better than down south, that they all agreed, anything was better than Alabama. Some days Rosella made as much as $5, including the ironing she took in.

Sensitive and soft-spoken, Rosella worked hard, saving every penny she could. Resolute, unwavering she'd make sure her boy had a much better life. She was determined he'd never have to struggle like she and her brothers. Rosella was indomitable in helping her child — Yes — anything was possible, if only you believed.

She taught her son that even though he would grow up never knowing a father, that he was a *Somebody* — to stand tall, to mind God and to believe in himself. She guided him gently, but made sure he developed an interest in learning. It would serve him well.

When Nathaniel Brown came courting, Rosella spurned his advances. Nothing was going to interfere with building a better life for her boy. She went without fancy clothing in order to buy Roosevelt a second-hand piano so he'd develop the talent that was so obvious when she saw him tinkling with the keys after Sunday church services. They squeezed it into the small living room. Hell, Freddie May liked gospel music and she loved the idea of a piano even if there was little room. Rosella believed music could open doors in Roosevelt's life. She always dressed him in the best clothes and taught him to care about his appearance. Yes, she made sure Roosevelt had the finest she could afford.

All she had to do was look around her to realize the alternatives. Rosella saw the wasted lives, the dreams that drink and drugs depleted. Possessing a wisdom well beyond her years, she had a keen instinct for what was good for her child. She never let a moment go by when she didn't inspire him towards the best he could do.

Over the years, Rosella would dispense advice to her son like a doctor giving pills. Hers were coated with sugar. She wanted him to be careful with his money. "The quickest way to double your money is to fold it in half and put it back in your pocket," she warned.

Roosevelt Jones remembered all his mother's advice. He followed her good words and example, earnestly studying, seeking every opportunity that came to him. Yet somewhere along the way, neither knew that fate would take it's own stance.

— ∞ —

The civil right protests that gripped the South in 1968 followed years of upheaval. It rippled north, where Negroes who were supposed to have equal rights damned well knew they didn't. But the courageousness of those who stood up and wouldn't take it any more made it better for everyone. Being called a "nigger" was the cruel rite of passage for black children the country over. "Nigger. Nigger. Nigger." They were sick and tired of it all.

In the end there wasn't much sense of victory among blacks, for barriers came down slowly and integration arrived only after years of battle. Progress, many blacks said, had gone only so far. Many remained in their separate world, profoundly wary of whites. In New York, in the tenements of Harlem, bitterness and suspicion were everywhere. Unless you were one of the lucky few who broke through the economic barriers you knew you were destined to live your life in poverty.

Not Roosevelt Jones. Nurtured and nourished with attention and love he grew up and up into a giant of a man. "Lord, I told you to drink your milk, but I never expected you to have to bow your head to get through the door, son!" Rosella said lightheartedly. Six feet 6 inches tall, you couldn't miss him.

Roosevelt's size 16 shoes turned in a trace giving his stance a military manner. While his gait was slower, his stride was longer than most men. His music was his mission in life and the work he was to accomplish would be measured in small, vital victories.

And my oh my, Roosevelt was handsome. He never possessed bodacious black male vanity, yet he was the quintessential black male — tall, lean, muscular with a wonderful energy about him and a warm, open smile that beguiled women and men alike. Walnut-skinned with chiseled features, his nose resembled a Roman warrior more than his African American heritage. His voice, deep and resonant, was good enough for him to demonstrate his own songs. (In fact, later on, he cut a few records of his own.)

But it was his mesmerizing laugh, rich and throaty, that everyone remembered most.

Roosevelt wasn't bothered being black, though blacks were often bothered. "Hell, mom, others have it so much harder," he said when he won the music scholarship that enabled him to study composition at the Julliard School of Music. He knew how his mother, against all odds, had labored six days a week to take care of him. This empowered him, gave him the energy to want to be all she knew he could be. What a damned good woman she was!

When later he faced barriers of bigotry, he forever held his head high, shoulders set back and straight — for he was a man with a healthy sense of himself. Bright, talented, a musical genius, he wrestled his way through injustices. The shadow that he would cast would be one of greatness.

Roosevelt ventured forth at a time when some progress was made, but not enough to give him his due. But he was a risk taker and the record business was the stage upon which he would gamble. The stakes were many, the rewards substantial.

In the late fifties and sixties, Rock'n'Roll and Rhythm and Blues were the rage. Groups like the Platters and artists like Bobby Darin dominated the record charts. Their music was being played over and over on the radio. Songwriting teams like Leiber and Stoller were turning out hits like "*Spanish Harlem*", while the duo of Pomus and Shuman were writing hit after hit, eventually getting some of their songs sung by mainstream singers like Dean Martin and Frank Sinatra.

Enterprising young men masterminded record companies like Atlantic. A dentist named Herb Abramson and his associates Jerry Wexler and Ahmet Ertegun built the recording label into a giant in the industry, producing hits by Bobbie Darin, Lloyd Price and by groups like the Drifters. Later on, down in Detroit, what became to be known as the Motown Sound fashioned the Temptations and the Chiffons into hit groups and of course, the Supremes.

Sports and music. Those were the best avenues to success for Black men in postwar America. The GI Bill of Rights allowed many to get a college education, but the jobs available to them were few in major corporations. Those who became professionals became doctors and lawyers who worked within their own communities. The color line was up all over, and when jazz stars like Lena Horne traveled, she still had to stay in sub-standard hotels, and use the back doors of the major hotels to enter, even when she was starring there.

But there were major breakthroughs in the entertainment and sports fields, giving hope to any Negro child who had a morsel of talent.

In sports Jackie Robinson had broken through the color line in baseball. Robinson had said, "I'm not concerned with your liking or disliking me. All I ask is you respect me as a human being." He got more than respect as he changed sports history forever. His courage in playing stoically while many southern ball players cursed at him was not wasted. And his brilliant playing rapidly helped break the segregation line in baseball.

The success stories were the exceptions. Especially in the record industry where sleazy manipulators stole whatever they could from the naïve. Dozens of black artists had one or two hits, and then faded away. Most had poor management — crooked con artists who sold them a false bill of goods. They would sign contracts giving 50 percent of their royalties to their agents. Others had drug habits that made them vulnerable. However talented the writer was, he'd sell a song for a quick fix. And the vultures, the greedy operators were out there, waiting to grab the golden ring out of the hands of the weaker ones. An entire subculture of slimy managers and agents worked behind the scene and scalped much of the profits from the innocent amateurs.

The fortunate few who had good guidance grew into major stardom, as Diana Ross did after she left the Supremes. Gordy Berry, the founder of Motown, one of the few Blacks to take a leading role in those days helped many get their start.

Roosevelt always had an ear for music. While he had a serious bent, and played the classics during his stay at Julliard, his passion was in the rhythm and blues that was the Black sound of the day. It was a way out, a way to make the big bucks he saw flashed around by the entertainers who had made it.

His mom helped; first with the old Spinet piano she bought so he could practice at home. Then she paid for formal lessons so he could learn to read the music. After a year of studying composition, Roosevelt was ready. Using his favorite pencil, an Eberhard Faber Blackwing 602 — soft enough to write the flats and notes he needed to tell his story — he began to develop melodies, fast and slow with clever lyrics too. He worked hard, and for the rest of his life kept a supply of freshly sharpened Blackwings near him at all times.

Soon Roosevelt was one of many black songwriters walking the streets of Tin Pan Alley, knocking on the glass door offices of small publishing firms at 1610 and 1650 Broadway, selling a song or leaving a demo disk here and there. His ability to carry a tune was good enough to rate his being backup on a number of demonstration discs, and later, he did arrangements for such names as Dinah Washington and LaVerne Baker. His talents as a writer and composer would exceed all his dreams. During his life he would write more than three dozen songs that made it to the top of the charts. He also was called upon to write special lyrics and music for leading singers as well as special musical scores used in Hollywood movies.

By 1958 he had made the first rungs of the ladder, having sold four songs that topped the Cashbox and Billboard lists, including the one about the name game, banana fananana.

The foremost element of his success was that Roosevelt was able to buy his mother a comfortable home in Jamaica, Queens. He made sure his mother was safe. She wouldn't have to work any longer. He'd see to that.

Rosella loved the little house but even more the large plot of land outside that she developed into a wonderful vegetable garden, planting everything imaginable that would grow in the east. Rosella was back to her roots — the land — and she made the most of it. Her greatest joy was having Roosevelt travel out in the summer to take in the bags of vine ripe tomatoes, the corn and the rest for his family. She was so glad to see him, to know he was doing well.

Roosevelt did have a family, having married in his early 20s a beautiful black schoolteacher, Mavis Johnson, whom he met in the 42nd Street library. His mother was disappointed that he had tied himself down so early, but she soon took to Mavis, who was a lovely young woman. The children came quickly, one after another. Mavis no longer could teach. More mouths to feed, more reason to walk the pavements of Broadway, to sell a song or two.

It was a part of his life he'd keep very private. In fact, many intimates didn't know he was married. While Roosevelt strayed from time to time, he always respected his family, remained a devoted father and for the first decade was a faithful and good husband. But he was young and the temptations were many. Eventually he succumbed — there were so many beautiful women trying to seduce him — hell, just a little on the side. He'd do his thing in show business, keep and sleep in a midtown hotel suite and travel uptown as many weekends as he could. That's where his family lived — in a grand brownstone home on the outskirts of Harlem. He had bought it with his first big record hit. Yes, he wandered, but he always made certain his family was well provided for.

"Mom, you always find something to smile about, don't you?" Roosevelt teased his mother, as he took the two shopping bags filled to the brim with her freshly picked tomatoes and green beans. She had also pickled watermelon rinds, made current jelly, gave him a dozen jars of each to take to Mavis and the kids.

"You don't stop smiling because you grow old, son. You grow

old because you stop smiling," she responded. "Now you take the goodies to Mavis and the boys," she reminded him. She always made sure that her grandsons got some of her prized homegrown produce.

He hugged his mother tenderly. She was growing frail with age, but that smile on her face could light up the grayest of days.

Roosevelt headed back to the city — to his ever-present crusade to get his songs sung, to get his music played. That was the name of the game. It was all a game.

By the early 60s, the record industry was in its heyday. Cousin Brucie and Dick Clark could make or break a record. The infamous payola disc jockey scandal erupted earlier, when it was learned that record company promoters were buying off the radio stations' top DJ's. Powerful radio personalities like Alan Freed were ruined by the exposés in the city dailies that revealed the truth on how hit songs were made.

And so, in a natural evolution, record company executives, who would bestow a gold record upon their latest hit group, were now improvising crooked deals. That gold record represented a million records that were sold, but what the company's creative bookkeeping never disclosed was the profits from the other 400,000 or more in sales that they pocketed. The artists never knew so much more money was due them.

By the late 50s Black songwriters also emerged, their names now credited on many hits. Some also did arranging, and a rare few became part of management. At a brand new record company called Scepter, the Shirelles broke through with "*Will You Love Me Tomorrow?*" The company, started on a shoestring by Frances Rosenfeld, an overweight, overbearing, married woman from New Jersey, with her clandestine black lover, Benny Anderson, soon had a stable of artists and hits on the charts. Ensconced at 1650 Broadway, in new offices, their record label was the talk of the town.

Anderson was one of the few Blacks to make it on the

management side, until Motown out in Detroit with Berry Gordy at the helm wrested some of the power away. There were also mob connections. All the clubs where the artists would appear were run and operated by the Italian and Jewish Mafia of the day.

Too many helpless songwriters, who scrambled for enough money to pay their rent, had to share their royalties and credit with the singer who made the song a hit, (many unethical publishers and greedy A&R people at the management level added their names to the composer's or lyricist's credits). A songwriter eager to make a record, sold his song for a quick $50, and spent it the next hour by going and getting a fix. Heroin was the drug of the day, and too many bright lights were quickly extinguished.

Roosevelt saw how the hard stuff had done in some talented brothers. The vacant look in the eyes, the dozing off in the middle of a conversation, it was hell to witness. He stayed away, but he loved *pot*, felt it made him write better. He conducted summits at the Dorsey hotel on 7th Avenue where he'd taken a suite of rooms after his third big hit. His work became even more prolific; soon he was writing a battery of hits. His talents were in demand by publishers, who often called to request a new song for one of their top recording artists.

He also arranged acts and rehearsed with singers like Dinah Washington, with whom he also had a brief affair. It was an especially flush time for Roosevelt; he was making good money and could support his mother, his wife and children, and be generous to others. He gladly helped the down and outers, giving fives and tens with an understanding smile and a pat on the back to those down on their luck.

Coley Wallace, a handsome young black actor who'd played the lead in the *"Joe Louis Story"*, showed up regularly – to share a joint – to borrow some bucks. There was a cadre of followers who knew Roosevelt was good for a sawbuck or two. Roosevelt helped; it was part of his nature. "Hell, if you loan someone $20 and never see him again, it was probably worth it," he smiled. But he never asked for repayment and was always willing to lend a hand.

Finally, he was *The Man*, successful, a black who had made it, who had held on to the main money his hit songs were making. He hadn't let anyone swindle him. He'd done it on his own.

Roosevelt was thinking higher, reaching further — did some important work on the West Coast, arranging and writing for the movies — began working on a musical, involved in raising sufficient funds to get it produced on Broadway. But his bread and butter was still the rhythm and blues and rock and roll of the 60s. And so he kept on keeping on, turning out #1 songs that topped the charts of Billboard.

He would not get to produce the Broadway musical nor live to hear the soundtrack of the new movie that opened in February of 2001, where one of his many hits was featured.

— ∞ —

There's a somebody I'm longing to see, I hope that he turns out to be...

— ❦ —

Chapter 5

Annie and Roosevelt

The recording industry changed rapidly in the 50s. Fly-by-night labels could go legitimate with one or two hit records. Neophytes rented modest office space — and if they couldn't afford that — some began working out of basements or the garage. The object: to cut a record, and then get the "A"-side well-known fast. Everyone in the business knew how critical it was to get as much *play* as possible. An audience who heard a new record getting lots of turns by the disc jockey would buy it. The problem: you needed to know someone at the radio station to get your record played. Publicizing songs became an all-important venture. And so the *song-plugger* was born. Men were paid to go 'round the country to promote new recordings at radio stations.

Some of the more voracious song-pluggers began greasing the palms of a few greedy disc jockeys willing to show favor. That's how the payola scandal came to pass. Too many people pushing too many songs, all in the name, the quest for fame. And *money*.

This was the uncompromising milieu in which Roosevelt Jones had to succeed — a cutthroat one where manipulators with no talent looked for a way to get rich quick. Parasites, they looked for the vulnerable, the dreamers desperate to make it. Making money fast was like a reflex action, a hiccup in the record business of the 50s. Whites owned major record labels, and while many were legitimate businessmen, too many were not and numerous black performers were exploited.

Wannabe artists knocked on Tin Pan Alley doors hoping to be heard. How to catch the golden ring? A singer, who achieved one smash hit on the charts, could build a career. It was the same for the songwriter. New fresh talent was always wanted.

No matter how gifted, few would make it. It was those performers who were disciplined who had the best chance, while the others, the disoriented and lost — were reduced to the addictions of the day. Selling their songs for a nickel bag of heroin, they were quickly left behind. But the strong prevailed. Always staying ahead of the pack, never losing their ability to communicate ideas, some rose to incredible heights. One of the best of them was Roosevelt Jones.

Roosevelt had known Art Ginsberg at Atlantic Records, cut a few records with him, already had a few hits under his belt. Learning about the new Triumph setup, he stopped by Art's new headquarters and left his card. Admiring Roosevelt's unique talents, Ginsberg soon called upon him.

"Hey man. Glad to hear from you. I'm cookin here with this new label," Ginsberg said. "I have some good strong artists on board. Major new talents. There's a new singer, Shirley King, good looker, with a voice as good as it gets. I'm going to make Shirley into a big star. And I'm gonna need some new material, and you are the Man, R.J."

Roosevelt chuckled. "Sure, whatever you say, Art."

"I'll get to the office by six. Why don't you go on up there and relax? There's a piano, coffee, whatever you need. Wait for me, man," Ginsberg urged.

Then the record exec phoned the office. Naturally he got Annie. "Annie, I need a favor. Can you stay late — keep the office open 'til I get there? I'll make it by six. I'll pay you time and a half. I've scheduled a meeting with 'R.J.'," he announced. 'R.J.' was the nickname he had long called Roosevelt.

"Sure I will," she quickly answered. She could use the extra money for staying overtime.

Annie wondered why Art Ginsburg ever hired her for 9-to-5 hours when he never ever got to his office before 4 p.m. Some days he didn't make it at all. He'd better make it tonight. She had to put in an appearance at the family dinner and that meant traveling to Brooklyn. Meanwhile, feeling excited about this extra assignment, she put on some fresh lipstick and checked herself in the mirror. She wanted to look good. After all, until Mr. Ginsburg arrived, she'd be spending some time with the great Roosevelt Jones. Not too bad of a work assignment, she thought, and what's more she'd get paid for staying late.

Annie became sensitive to Roosevelt's presence the first time he walked through the door. Tall, charismatic, he personified warmth and charm. He was good looking and sexy too — damned sexy, if you got right down to it. Always the center of attention, Roosevelt had a grace and a smile that could light up the darkest corners of a room. Women in particular were attracted to his self-assurance and his good manners. He knew how to talk to them, was kind and thoughtful. Just what Annie needed.

No matter that he was a Negro, (that's how black men were described in the 50s) — Annie wasn't prejudiced, she was beyond all that. Furthermore he was a "hunk" — sort of a better-looking version of Sidney Poitier or today's Denzel Washington. She was attracted, she knew it. Besides, this man was in *show business*. And successful. It appealed to her fantasies for she was forever smitten with the limelight.

Annie was familiar with two of Roosevelt's biggest song hits. Starry-eyed, she hummed them often. Especially *Such A Night*. She loved that song. And now today, lucky her had to keep him occupied until Mr. G. arrived. Her heart was beating overtime.

And so on that gray December afternoon Annie sat at the front desk and passed the time as best she could. It was cold outside and she was bored. Everyone had left early. Annie thumbed through the latest Vogue magazine, ever enthralled with fashion. She hoped the lacey blouse she was wearing and the velvet bell-bottom jeans looked good. The jeans were tight enough to get her good figure noticed. Ta Da! She sat and waited, checked her face again, added some rouge.

Maybe she'd better phone Joanie to say she'd be late and she'd also tell her about this fantastic songwriter whom she'd be talking to in a few minutes. No one answered. She's probably already on her way to Brooklyn.

At that moment she saw his tall silhouette approaching the office door. "Hey, Babes," Roosevelt greeted Annie, with a twinkle in his eye. "Art told me to wait for him here. Would you like some coffee? I can go downstairs and pick up some donuts to go along with it" he added.

Wow! No one in her life had ever called her Babes. She was flattered that this successful songwriter addressed her in this manner. It felt good. She felt like she belonged. She smiled back. "Sure, I'd love some." She spoke so low she could hardly be heard, damn it! She was nervous. This man was so gorgeous, so charming, so, so, so – Annie was smitten.

And that was how it began. Just coffee, sometimes donuts, always flattering words. And Annie, why, she was feeling so bedazzled, so very warm and content with this idyllic attraction. It was just what she needed.

From the beginning she was enamored of this man who towered over her, whose words were being sung on the radio, played on jukeboxes and enjoyed by millions. He was what she once wanted to be — a songwriter. And better still, he was successful at it. When he sat down at the piano in the next room, and played some of his hits, she couldn't believe she was really there. "Pinch me to see if I'm awake!" He was a wonderful pianist. Could play anything. Even the classics. Annie was agog with a sense that here she was, all the way from Brooklyn to Broadway and this very special man was actually playing music for her. Now who could resist?

"One more drink and I'll be under the host."
— *Dorothy Parker*

— ○? —

Chapter 6

A nnie gazed out the window. It was a cold December evening but snow had not been in the forecast. A light mantle was beginning to cover the street below. While it was pleasant being in the office with Roosevelt, the waiting was getting wearisome. As usual, Art Ginsberg was late. Within the hour the flurries became heavier and soon major drifts began enveloping the area.

"Oh my God, I don't even know if I can get home, never mind to Brooklyn if it continues coming down like this," Annie commented.

"I can call a private limo service I've used," Roosevelt offered, calling out from the next room, where he was at work at the piano. All of a sudden Roosevelt played a few bars of *Let it Snow, Let it Snow*.

She smiled. "Do you take request numbers?" Annie teased.

"Sure, I can play Chopin as well as Gershwin – or even Jones, if you like," he chuckled.

"How about *Melancholy Baby*," Annie joked. They both laughed.

Annie felt apprehensive, as if the weather outside, the mood within and the moment were all charged with anticipation.

Feathery snowflakes were outlining the windowpanes while the lights inside created an inviting atmosphere. The heat from the radiators kept the office warm and cozy and the low hissing of the steam was comforting. Roosevelt continued at the piano – back to working on a new composition he'd intended to play for Art. The melody was beautiful, haunting and romantic.

Annie could feel her heart thumping in her chest. Her lips felt awfully dry. She reapplied some lipstick and hoped the spritz of *Joy* cologne she'd applied earlier still had some oomph. *Joy* was her favorite – she'd saved up to get the small bottle at Saks. "*Should she stay in this room, or walk in and listen to him up closer?*" she wondered.

As luck would have it — on this very evening Annie had plans. It was Chanukah, the "Festival of Lights." Joanie and she had promised their parents they'd come for a holiday meal. As long as they didn't have to live there, they didn't mind going home. Latkes (potato pancakes) were a tasty part of the celebration. They loved them! (And while it was out of character, for some reason their mother made this dish rather well.) Now it was getting late and Annie was worried. Her family had their meals on the early side. It was already 6:30 and they'd wonder where she was. She nervously picked up the phone receiver.

"I'll be there by 8, Mom. I'm taking the train. The express still runs at that hour. Hopefully the snow will stop. I'm sorry but I have to wait until my boss shows up," she explained, looking up at Roosevelt, whom she suddenly noticed, was holding up a bottle of champagne.

"So be it. You know we eat early. Why you have to always do things your way, I'll never know. But we'll save some latkes for you. Here, say hello to your father," she said, anger in her voice.

"Annie, Annie, how could you do this? Your mother is upset.

She made the whole dinner. Your sister is here, so is Cousin Fred and Helen. And you? Shame on you. Hurry up, please." And he hung up.

Now Annie was sorry she called. She hated it when her father became annoyed with her. But he'd always defend her mother. Well, she'd try to get there soon. Mr. Ginsberg must have gotten stuck in traffic or something. And it was snowing out – didn't her parents realize it was snowing? Annie's mind was racing on and on. "*Shit! No! Stop it*," she thought – she wasn't going to be upset when she had this unique, this precious moment right here. An opportunity to talk to someone creative and bright and nice and she wouldn't let them spoil it for her.

When Roosevelt had arrived, he'd handed her a bottle of champagne, which she had put into the small office refrigerator. She went to the closet and took out two glasses, put the bottle on a tray and ambled into the next room. Roosevelt placed the bottle of champagne atop the piano. He had been playing some new composition and was now writing down the bars of music with his Eberhardt blackwing pencil.

"I'd love a drink," she requested, holding up the bottle so Roosevelt could pop the cork and pour some champagne. She didn't know if he'd brought it as a celebration gift for Ginsberg or what – but she really didn't care. It was pink and bubbly and would be nice, so nice to drink. Her hand was trembling a bit. She hoped he didn't notice.

— ଔ —

The first time Annie had tasted alcohol was when she was five. It was a hot summer's day, Annie's brother was crying. Sid cried so easily. But Annie took charge. She deployed Sid, only two years younger, to climb up on the stool to reach atop the refrigerator where a Manischevitz wine bottle stood unopened. "Come on, let's get some cookies. And the bottle on the Frigidaire," she commanded.

They were alone in the apartment. Joanie was at school. Their mother had gone down to the corner ice cream shop, telling them, "don't worry, I'll be right back." She wasn't. It was an awful feeling, being alone. Maybe she was only gone 20 minutes but to Annie and her brother, it seemed like forever.

They snuck the big bottle of wine into the bedroom, where, while her brother nibbled on cookies, Annie had more than a taste. In fact, the family frequently told the story later of how her mother and father discovered her asleep on their bed. Waving a rattle in front of her giggling face, they were saying, "baby is dwunk, baby is dwunk," laughing at their little girl who'd obviously imbibed a quarter of the bottle. And they thought it was cute.

She stayed away from the grapes from then on. Well, most of the time she did – except on those traditional holidays spent at her grandparents. Dinner was always accompanied by wine—rich, sugary, sweet, Jewish wine. She loved the taste. And she'd always get giddy, every single time. As a matter of fact, later on, when everyone was in the living room, she'd steal back to the dining room table to finish off any glasses she could find that had remains of wine in them. The signs were already there.

— CR —

The champagne Roosevelt had brought was delicious, bubbly, effervescent and mellowing Annie out more and more by the moment. Delicious to be intoxicated, to feel warm and wonderful and no worries at all. Aahh, the stage was set.

The office phone rang. Finally.

"Annie, it's icy and treacherous out here. I've been on the Henry Hudson. I couldn't call until I got to a rest stop. Tell R.J. to wait; I should be there by 8," Ginsberg said and hung up before she could explain she had to leave, that she had to travel to Brooklyn that same evening.

Annie peered out the office window six floors below. The snow was beginning to accumulate. A layer of white covered the otherwise grimy garbage cans stacked outside the smaller buildings. At the beginning it was charming—everything looked cleaner in the city with fresh snow.

"Oh well, let's celebrate some more," she bravely suggested, as Roosevelt poured another glass of the bubbly for each of them.

"Maybe you should eat something—this stuff can go to your head," he suggested.

"Nahh, I'm fine," she giggled. It made her feel at ease, drinking something alcoholic. Odd, how quickly she felt self-assured and confident after just a few drinks. Giddy too.

Feeling warm, very warm, (and definitely attracted to this forceful man before her,) Annie didn't hesitate a moment when he gently took her hand. "You're a very pretty young lady, you know that don't you?" he said softly. "You really light up this office, Annie." He leaned over, gently kissed her on the forehead. She rubbed his shoulder to show him she cared. He smiled and then kissed her on the lips.

The kiss was warm, tender, sweet, not grabbing, nor sexual. So her mother was wrong. She wasn't such an ugly duckling after all, look who thinks I'm attractive, look who cares! She felt terrific. Roosevelt Jones, the songwriter, the performer, the handsome young black man, he really liked her. A tingling sensation overtook her body. She had another drink.

The next time she looked up, the hands on the clock on the office wall stunned her. Could she be reading them right? It was 9 o'clock. She must have fallen asleep on the reception room sofa, while Roosevelt had gone back to the piano in the other room. It was very dark out. Where on earth was Art Ginsberg? What would her parents think? Oh my God she was in trouble!

"It's alright, Annie. Art called to switch our recording session to Friday. You were tired; I didn't want to wake you. Let me call you a cab," Roosevelt suggested, as she walked barefoot into the other room.

"I've gotta call my family," she said weakly, scared to death. Her heart was pounding so hard she thought it was going to come out of her body.

"Hey, there's already six inches of snow on the ground, baby. Your parents, they'll understand you couldn't really make it. The radio said we're due for a few more inches. This is not a night for traveling on trains. Relax. It will turn out all right. You'll see," he tried to reassure her.

Little did he know. Annie panicked. What could she say, what was her reason for not calling back, what excuse could she give to her mother and father — to Joanie? They were waiting for her in Flatbush. Dinner had to be long over. It was too late now! She was frightened and embarrassed. She picked up the phone to call. She'd come up with an alibi — "the IRT local train broke down in the tunnel," she told them shaking, trembling, scared out of her wits. And then without knowing how it happened — from the fear of it all, she passed out.

Yes, Annie had actually fainted from the reality that she was lying and maybe they knew it. She didn't want her family to find out she was deceitful and drunk; that she was with a married songwriter alone in the office; that something, no, a lot about this scene was wrong.

Roosevelt walked into the room slowly. He carefully rolled the slender cigarette. *Reefer* is what they called it back then. "Here, have a puff," he invited, handing her the hand-wrapped cigarette. The acrid yet pungently sweet smell of the marijuana filled the room; it was her first sampling of the stuff that would transport her to a different level, to feel light-hearted and silly and to say wild and funny things. She loved it.

The champagne, the marijuana, but most of all the longing she felt to be close to another human being, especially a male to whom she was wildly attracted, made Annie feel uninhibited enough, warm enough to allow him to touch her, to hold her and then to put his gentle hands between her legs. She loved how it felt. Her body throbbed all over. She became very excited. He taught her how to come.

That's how it started, one snowy winter night. The passion, the attraction between them was real. And so were the differences. From then on having this secret liaison was like subsisting in a netherworld — or playing a role in a movie. Most of the time she felt glamorous and important and best of all, always warm and *wanted*. How delicious a feeling. Right or wrong — Annie didn't want to ever let it go. She had a secret romance, one she couldn't even share with her sister. The mystery of it only enhanced the glamour in her psyche.

Then there was the music, which was always exciting and dominated the mood. It took her to another dimension — made her feel absolutely marvelous. She envisioned Fred and Ginger dancing and Judy Garland singing and everything was in gorgeous living Technicolor, lifting her to another level where all was warm and loving and glamorous. It was as if Roosevelt had seduced her into his world with evenings of song. But that wasn't quite true — Annie had volunteered for the role and went along willingly — for his planet was her pleasure. He'd sit at the piano, the place where he spent hours composing some of the most beautiful music Annie ever heard. Was there anything better in this world than being a participant in the creative process? *"Oh Lord, I'm so happy,"* she tearfully thought.

Roosevelt's long slender fingers performed with joie de vivre, even when he was only playing chords. And when he created a song in her presence, this was a magical, wonderful event. He wrote two for her, two with words meant for her alone. For the very first time in her life Annie felt someone really believed she was special. So unique that he told her he *loved her*. And like many men in the heat of passion, Roosevelt probably meant it when he said it.

Chapter 7

The social climate in the 60s did not make seeing one another easy. It surely wasn't acceptable for inter-racial couples to date. Annie felt particularly uncomfortable walking along the street with Roosevelt. Not because he was black and she was white. Of course, this turned heads. (Even blacks in those days resented a white woman with one of *their* men.)

Don't laugh, but more than the black/white disparity, it was the enormous height difference that embarrassed Annie. She was all of 5'2 and he was 6'6. Roosevelt would have to stoop down to hear her. They really resembled an odd couple strolling along the street. Oh, they looked all right when he was seated next to her, after all, he had exceptionally long legs, but standing, Roosevelt towered over Annie by a foot and a half. Of course she immediately purchased the highest heels she could find and stumbled around in them most of the time.

But to hell with height differences and the color barrier. They shared a loving connection. And for Annie, well the ardor, the tenderness she experienced — it felt so very good. She could barely believe that she was noticed, never mind needed by someone "important" — a well-known songwriter like Roosevelt Jones.

She learned swiftly how to hide the illicit relationship. From Art Ginsburg, from her family, from everyone. Sure, some had their suspicions; a few of the *brothers* knew Roosevelt liked young girls. When he'd come by the record company Annie couldn't always hide a blush that appeared on her face or she'd laugh a little too loud at his remarks. A small number wondered if there was something going on. Others, knowing his penchant for new pussy, was sure something was going on.

What they never knew was that this man took Annie seriously. Eventually Roosevelt moved out of his home, left his wife and three children, and the couple moved in together. It was the only time in his life that he did this. He respected his family. Kept that part of his life separate, going home most weekends, always keeping his obligations to his wife, children and to his adored mother. But somehow, Annie believed, she'd stirred something within him that he valued most of all. At least for a while he did.

At the beginning of their affair, Annie learned to take the elevator in the hotel to the 11th floor or 9th, and then go to the 10th; She never let on she was visiting the black songwriter who kept a suite of rooms up there on the 10th floor.

He taught her how to be discreet. No sense causing talk, now was there?

At first she followed blindly. He was almost like her Svengali. He taught her how to make love. He also inspired within Annie the energy and aspiration to want more from herself, to write, to return to school, to make something of her life. Those first few months, they shared an intense passion and love. It was wonderful, no, magnificent — to have a man care so much for her, and such a special man. Annie was divinely happy, deliriously dizzy with the attention paid to her.

It took time, but eventually she sensed the domination, in his taking special interest in her going down on him. "Saves the energy, baby, I gotta record date later, and you doing this is real good, so good, aahh," he'd close his eyes and sigh, finishing the last drag on the reefer. She was high, not only from the pot, but because on her own she began drinking vodka. It was clear, didn't smell much, she thought it wouldn't be detected on her breath. She purchased the smallest size bottle, a size she'd hide in her purse and then she'd pour some of it into her can of Fresca soda, which she drank at the office, thereby keeping herself feeling an all-day little buzz.

At night, especially when he was composing, Roosevelt would have a joint or two. There'd also be a bottle of scotch around or wine. Annie carefully siphoned enough off to keep herself on an even course. Or so she thought. There was no one there who knew her before to notice that most of the time now she was just slightly off the ground, out of it. But then again, she had the kind of personality that was a little ditsy anyway, and probably no one would have noticed the difference. At the beginning she was careful to measure her usage, to control it. It hadn't taken over yet, wasn't totally controlling her.

And so it went. For the first three torrid months they engaged in the most intense, exciting love affair, fueled by music and marijuana and a magic madness making the forbidden facet of it all the sweeter. It was *their* secret. Annie didn't dare tell Joanie. Besides, Joanie was busy, and barely there that she hardly noticed if her little sister was at the apartment or not.

Soon enough Roosevelt rented a small apartment for them to share on West 72nd Street, situated in a quiet residential-style hotel where no one noticed who came and went. Annie wanted to play house but it was hard in a hotel without a real kitchen and more important a playmate. Roosevelt was busy with a rigorous writing and recording schedule. His retinue of songs kept growing. More and more artists were recording them. Dinah Washington. Elvis Presley. She was thrilled. After all, didn't most people know and sing his hits, including the one about climbing the mountain, the one he really wrote with her in mind? "This one's for you, Baby," he said, finishing it off one night at the office. "Every time you hear it played, remember I wrote it for you." She'd remember this, always.

"This is a great book, first-rate writing, good story," Roosevelt said, bringing Annie home a new book to read. He loved reading, enjoyed sharing his love of literature. Besides, he thought the examples of writing would be helpful to Annie. He also was a giver, and liked giving her presents. Last month he had brought her Steinbeck's *The Grapes of Wrath*." This time it was a leather-bound copy of *Pride and Prejudice*. "It's a woman's story, told very well, Austen is a great writer — you'll like it kiddo," he promised. He was thoughtful and caring in so many ways.

Now six months had passed and Annie began noticing that Roosevelt was becoming distracted - a little distant. It began when he started working with the new singer, Shirley King. Really, it wasn't just jealousy on her part, but she thought he spent far too much time with Shirley. Annie grew increasingly resentful. It was lonely having to stay in the hotel apartment they shared while he was out so many nights. True he was working — that's show business, but she felt awful being all alone. She was restless, insecure. She didn't have enough to do, didn't know how to spend time alone. Being alone meant being with *herself*. She didn't know how to do this.

She read the books he brought her. She tried watching TV. Sometimes getting lost in a good movie helped. Some quiet, lonely nights she'd turn on the RCA. And watch the late movie on Channel 2. She saw Errol Flynn in "*Captain Blood*" and Tyrone Power shooting up the railroad as Jesse James, and of course, those romantic epics — her favorites being "*Casablanca*" and "*An Affair to Remember*." Annie always loved tearjerkers.

But it wasn't so much fun any longer. She was alone, feeling insecure, quickly growing lonely. There was still such a hole inside of her. So much to fill up and with what she didn't know. She wanted Roosevelt to be there with her, to share more time with her, to take her with him, to fill up the void. She just didn't understand why she couldn't be with him all the time. Oh how Annie needed *ALL* the time.

Soon she'd gone over the edge — was certain there was more to the rehearsals then just rehearsing. It was also obvious that this new singer was very important to him. Roosevelt kept writing songs for her, and they were planning to record an album together. Worried, Annie took to writing her heart out, trying to win him with words. She'd write mostly pity poems but some of them were credible. A few of them, she thought, were worth saving; persuasive traces of poetry that showed a spark of talent. She wrote her heart out because she didn't know what else to do.

Damn it. She'd call Joanie. But Joanie was never at home. She must have been sleeping at Andre's. Just as well. If Annie reached her at some late hour she'd end up telling her everything and besides, sometimes Joanie knew Annie's words were slurred from drinking. What a pair they were! "Hey Mom, your daughters are dallying around with married men. *Unavailable Men* — that's what they are! I wonder why," Annie laughed to herself.

Annie never did like being alone, nor was she patient in waiting for Roosevelt to finish rehearsing. She'd sleep for an hour or two, and then awaken. Always restless, she sipped some more wine. She couldn't stand it any longer. Nothing took away the emptiness inside.

"Is Roosevelt there?" she'd ask, calling the rehearsal hall. She knew he didn't want to be disturbed. But she couldn't help it. Yes, she recognized that she was checking up on him, that he might get annoyed with her but she had to know — was he really rehearsing or somewhere else? If they called him to the phone then she'd ask him some inane question; anything to get his attention.

He did come to the phone.

"Please, Annie, go back to sleep. We'll talk later…when I see you."

"And when will that be?" she asked, knowing he disliked her questioning him. "Now you know I don't know how much longer we have to work. Please, Babes, watch a movie — do some more reading — but don't keep calling me here."

She'd sleep fitfully. Sometimes she had odd dreams, about wanting to be what she wasn't. Like she had this recurring fantasy — that she died, went to heaven and when she got there she unzipped herself and got out of her body and turned into a 5'6" 120-pound beauty who ate all she wanted and never ever gained a pound! Wow, what a really nice dream!

Roosevelt was out until the wee hours. He was in the habit of waking her up when he returned, usually about 3 in the morning. "It's time to have a bite to eat with me," he'd suggest. He'd order in or they'd go down to the all-night coffee shop on Broadway. Annie eagerly showed him the poems she'd scribbled in a drunken haze, hoping he'd like at least one of them. And some of them, they weren't bad, she knew it. "This one's real good, Annie, real good. Keep it up, you're on the right track," he reassured her. God, that made her feel special.

When one day in June Roosevelt informed Annie he might have to go out on tour, she was devastated. She realized she might have to spend time at the apartment her sister and she shared on West 76th Street. It was better than being on her own at the hotel. No, she didn't like being alone. But alone she'd be, even on 76th Street.

For Joanie had moved into Andre's apartment. He lived on the east side of town. She stored some clothes on 76th St. and helped pay the rent — that way their parents wouldn't know she was living somewhere else. Ironic — both of the girls still cared what their parents thought.

"I know Andre is getting a divorce; it's just that his wife found out she was pregnant right after we came back from Jamaica," she announced one day. "It isn't right for him to desert her. So he goes back and forth, Annie." Somehow Annie didn't think even Joanie believed what she was saying.

"Maybe the biggest lie on the planet is when you get what you want then you'll be happy," Annie answered. "Look at you. You say you've gotten what you want but you're not satisfied at all — because you have legitimate doubts, Joanie."

"I know he doesn't care for her, like he does for me," Joanie said. Her response seemed hollow. A baby was a major development. Joanie suspected that their sizzling love affair, which had been cooling down lately, might not hold him. A baby was a good enough reason. Maybe Andre would go back to his wife after all. Yes, both of them were seeing married men. But Annie didn't dare reveal Roosevelt to Joanie, let her know she was involved with a *Black* man.

The next evening during dinner Roosevelt announced he'd be leaving on the road trip, worse, that it would last at least a month. Annie's gut level jealousy grew when she learned it was with Shirley, who was introducing his latest songs. In fact, within three months, Roosevelt had written three hits for this phenomenal new singing star, and had taken on managerial duties as well. Shirley was taking the town by storm and he knew he had a winner.

"Why can't I go with you?" she asked, desperately hoping he'd agree. Of course, she ignored the reality that she had a job, that she really couldn't just take off for a month anyway. Damned if this wasn't frustrating. She knew making demands on Roosevelt wasn't a good idea. He made up his own mind on everything. He'd learned to ignore most of her crying jags when she'd had too much to drink; she was young and he understood her loneliness, but other pressures she attempted to employ didn't sit well with him. He reacted irritably. "Cut it out, Annie. Shirley is too new, too raw to perform on the nightclub circuit without my going along as accompanist. That's all there is to it," he insisted. But she didn't believe him because she'd already heard rumors — that the two were having an affair.

A week before Roosevelt was to leave on the tour he walked in and found Annie crying bitterly. This time, feeling guilty about leaving her for the month — he was more sympathetic. "Why all the tears," he asked lifting up her chin gently. "How can I help you baby?"

"I hate how I look, I wish I could make my nose smaller. Look at the bump in it. It dominates my entire face!"

He laughed. "You're pretty, babes, real pretty. Don't you see this?" he answered, smiling. "Hell don't you notice how guys look at you when they come into the office?" All Annie could see was a nose. Too big. Maybe if she could fix it she could fix up her life.

It was easy. Dollars were flowing and Roosevelt soon assuaged her by writing a check for fifteen hundred dollars, the price Annie was quoted after a consultation with one of the best cosmetic surgeons in New York. It was trouble-free, one night in the hospital, and then she could rest at the apartment. Damned if she wouldn't do it!

— ∽ —

Chapter 8

Maureen

March 1967

The room swirled round and round. Oh Jesus, Joseph and Mary — did Maureen feel woozy. She tried to raise herself up but she just couldn't lift up her head which was throbbing away. It was almost like an iron weight was tied to it. She felt the room spinning once again and detected the smell of strong disinfectant.

Where was she?

A sea of nausea was clouding over her. She felt powerless and so very tired. She tried to open her eyes, but her lids felt heavy. Within a few moments she fell back asleep.

Hours later she awakened. This time she could see a sliver of light illuminating the room. It must have been nighttime. She tried to raise herself up but felt a weight on her arm. It was attached to a board. There was a bandage and a needle coming out of her hand. She could just about see it…she was getting some kind of IV treatment.

"Maureen, come on in for supper now, lass, it's late," she heard her mother shout. There was no mistaking her mother's Irish brogue. Now she saw herself playing hopscotch on the city street. But she was only 8 years old. That wasn't the present. Was she dreaming? The room spun around again. Her head still felt heavy.

She finally recognized the smell that was still lingering... the antiseptic odor of a hospital room.

"Help!" she cried out. No one answered. Where was her mother, her father? Anyone? Who could lend a hand? Was she crying out loud or to herself? Was this just a bad dream? She wanted to wake up and be okay. Help me, someone, help me. What am I doing in a hospital? Again she felt heavy-lidded. She passed out again. This time she would sleep through the night.

"Poor child, such a terrible fever with this peritonitis. It's been three days already," whispered the desk nurse to another, who was about to take the tray of medication into the rooms.

"I was here yesterday," another nurse commented. "She had only one visitor and with such a serious condition, not a soul that was family," another nurse commented.

"Right now we have to concern ourselves with helping the doctors with breaking the fever and getting rid of the infection, rather than who comes to visit her or not."

"Still, it's sad, isn't it? A young pretty woman like that — seems a shame she's all alone."

— ∞ —

...1963

It was June of 1963 and the Soviets had put the first woman into space. Valentina Tereshkova, age 26, orbited the earth in the spacecraft "Vostok 6", a stunning achievement for any woman.

It was also the era of the Beatles. You could define the '60s in their warm and witty songs; their first hit, *"Please Please Me,"* was now Number 1 on the charts. Everyone loved the Beatles — even Maureen McDermott, who usually preferred folk songs she could strum on her guitar.

Beautiful at 25, with sparkling blue eyes the color of sapphires and a few faint freckles that marked her Celtic heritage, Maureen's natural blonde tresses fell loose and long, a shank of golden hair persistently covering one eye. Her skin was so translucent that the veins visibly beat in the delicate pads of her temples. She had a fine-looking figure, a bit on the slim side, but a perfect 36B on top, her breasts solid and lush at the same time. Although she dressed down and didn't wear more than lipstick, she had an incandescence about her that quickly drew notice.

Maureen found comfort in the eclectic Village neighborhood in which she lived. If you didn't fit in to the rest of the world, you would likely fit in Greenwich Village. The Village name aptly described an area with winding streets, brownstones, little shops and cafes and, best of all, affordable rents that attracted struggling artists and writers from all over. Magically they melded into one community in downtown New York City.

While she devoted herself to painting in her Village studio, in her leisure hours Maureen took the most pleasure in playing the guitar. She would strum away softly except when she had a few too many. Then, pitching her voice a little higher and louder she would amuse her friends with flippant songs like *"If you don't like my peaches, why do you shake my tree?"*

Maureen was a product of her time. She had become an adult in the 1950s when the culture was turning inside out and made her and so many others over. Now in the turbulent 60s, she was still searching for that something elusive, a sense of self. While she appeared fragile, she was more the *Iron Butterfly*. Too much had happened to her not to have toughened up. No one was going to take advantage, not any more. The times had tested and challenged her. In the end it would become living plasma that would help her become her true self.

When she was feeling sad Miss McDermott would croon morbid Irish folk tunes, songs her father sang to his five children before he left them for good. And when the new Beatles hit, *"Yesterday,"* was released, it fit Miss McDermott's magnetism for the melancholy and so she quickly learned it; "Yesterday…All my troubles seemed so far away…." she warbled with a rich, silvery sound.

Her voice was lyrical and exposed nerve ends that drew applause. Maureen would put it to use at the parties she learned about in the bars — small groups of interesting people would gather together in walkups, private places where pot could be smoked and no one minded. There she would go, guitar at the ready gaining a little extra attention and sometimes applause. She needed the attention. The applause wasn't bad either.

Maureen had been painting for the better part of three years. Large abstracts, glistening in vibrant acrylic colors, were stacked up against the walls. Stacked up and unseen. But her work was stunning and evident and everywhere, dominating every square inch of her small apartment. She had to believe they were worth something, that some day, some time, they would earn praise. She didn't always believe.

"Oh Christ! This is a damned waste, she thought, flinging her paintbrush onto the floor and wiping her hands on the old shirt she was wearing. Maureen felt she would never get the acknowledgment she sought. Sure she should be painting for art's sake. But what about her sake? And if no one saw her visions, were they visions or empty dreams?

She heard that one of her fellow students from Hunter had a major exhibition and sold some of his work. Others had group shows. Yet it had been years and she was still painting, with little space left for the piles of work that eclipsed most of the apartment leaving only room for a bed, table and lamp.

While she stretched the canvasses herself, they were still costly. Art supplies were expensive when you painted day in and day out and no one bought your work. The best she had done so far was to rent a space at the Greenwich Village Outdoor Art Show.

"All I was able to sell were my 'artsy fartsy' necklaces — cheap glass beads I had strung together as a backup...and at a dollar a collar, that amounted to forty bucks in sales. Hardly enough to save the day," she reported back to her buddies at the neighborhood watering hole. "I feel like I'm having an out-of-money experience," she quipped.

"Hey Honey, I submitted my novel to 20 different publishers and got just as many rejection notices. That was after spending two years writing it. I'm finally getting an agent, who just might make a difference. No one ever said life was easy," Billy reminded her.

Maureen smiled. Billy was yet another dreamer, who spent most of his nights driving a taxi to earn a living so he could write during the day. He was good with words that she knew, from the poetry she heard him read over at the Bleecker Street Cafe where writers were given a stage where they could bare their souls.

"You do have a way with words, Billy. You'll make it some day," she said rubbing his shoulder tenderly.

"Some day. That's the trick, isn't it? It's always some day but not now," Billy scowled.

"I'll drink to that," Tait Hansen said. Tait was an out of work actor, although he had done an off-Broadway play the prior summer. It opened and closed the same week. "It isn't easy, my friends, but hell this beats some boring office job now, doesn't it!"

They all sniggered at that.

While the rent on the fifth floor walkup on Cornelia Street was only $75 a month, Maureen owed just about everyone. She couldn't wait tables to pay the bills any longer. Didn't make near enough money at it. She also owed a hefty tab at the White Horse Tavern. Murphy the bartender told her to pay up by the end of the month or else. Although she fancied herself an abstract artist the real world beckoned. She needed a real full time job.

She began studying the classifieds in the *New York Times*. A few didn't sound so bad. She had been an art major at Hunter, and did have a talent for drawing. What the hell — she'd sell out for a while, do what she could to make some money so she could get back on an even keel.

She had enjoyed her long indulgence, barely working at all these past three years, but *Prince Charming* hadn't come along to save her and no one had rung her bell to tell her she was a grand prize winner, so indeed, it was time to get a job.

After a few false starts, she applied for work as a fashion illustrator at B. Altman, an upscale department store on 34th Street. All she had in her meager portfolio were a dozen sketches. She had worn the one long skirt she owned with a brightly embroidered Mexican-style blouse. And beads, lots of beads. It wasn't much of a fashion statement.

The outfit hadn't mattered. To Maureen's surprise they hired her, and right away. Evidently the copy chief liked her work. She had always been good at drawing human figures. Maureen smiled. What the hell, she needed the money. It was ironic, sketching gorgeous women in pricey gowns for the Sunday papers. She had absolutely no interest in clothes.

That night she celebrated. On the juke box at the White Horse Tavern, *"Where Have All the Flowers Gone,"* was playing, sung by the movie star Marlene Dietrich trolling out her anti-war version, a hit of the day. It went well with the radical protesters who frequented the place.

"I'm feeling good...I've landed a real job. Why soon I'll be able to settle my bar bill," she told Murphy, a big smile on her face.

"Actually I'll have more than enough to pay *all* my bills and still buy paint supplies."

"Well, now, my lass, things are looking up," the big burly bartender responded.

"Pour me another drink, will you hon, I'm going to be a nine-to-fiver soon, and that's cause for celebration!" she said.

"Jesus, Joseph and Mary — will wonders never cease," howled O'Casey, overhearing Maureen's announcement. O'Casey, another regular, was grinning from ear to ear. "Hey, if you can get an honest to goodness real job, there's hope for a lot of us, now isn't there? Hey Murphy, the lass's drink is on me."

Chapter 9

March 1967

"Miss McDermott, don't try to talk. You've had a very close call," the doctor said, leaning over her hospital bed.

"I want this damned needle out of my arm," she said, in a raspy voice, trying to pull the IV out of her hand. Her hand was black and blue from all the places they'd inserted the needle.

"You've been in and out of a very grave fever for 5 days now. You're going to have to rest and let us help you," he said in a soft voice.

Maureen felt warm. Very warm. Too tired to fight. And she was frightened.

"Can you tell us any family member we can contact? " he asked.

A tear came to Maureen's eye. "You can call my brother, Danny, he'll tell my mom, but I don't know who could visit. They live way out on Long Island."

"Now you don't worry about that. Just give me the phone number and

I'll try to reach someone."

She gave him the number, but soon felt drowsy and fell back asleep.

...1963

Maureen had a penchant for being a rabble-rouser. At college, she was the first woman ever expelled for being found in a *'compromising'* position in the art department with a male student. So what, she thought, she had learned enough. She regularly cut the other courses, like math and economics. And gawd, how she hated science! She'd rather be painting.

And so, after only five semesters at Hunter, which had a notable Fine Arts department in the 50s, Maureen left and soon found a job waiting tables at a coffee shop on West 46th Street. It was in Hell's Kitchen — the neighborhood of old crowded tenements where she'd grown up.

It was a crisp and sunny afternoon in late October as Maureen began the afternoon shift at *Haymore's Coffee Shop.* She was feeling particularly cruddy, having received a notice that her telephone would be turned off if she didn't pay up. Besides that, she really would love to be out walking in the park on such a gorgeous autumn day.

She'd just taken out her order pad and prepared the carbon sheet when she chanced upon some old friends. Chanced upon them because Maureen had to serve them. They were seated in one of the red leatherette booths in her service route. They seemed surprised to see her. She wished she could have been swallowed up into the coffee shop's cheap linoleum flooring.

"Well Mo, fancy finding you here. I thought you were in the halls of ivy somewhere and wouldn't be in these parts no more," said Joan Dempsey. The Dempsey's had lived upstairs from the McDermott's, and Joan and Maureen used to swap Archie comic books and sometimes play jacks together. But Joan always had a more conservative agenda planned for herself. She'd taken a civil service exam, and was now a bona fide employment counselor with the New York State Department of Labor. She was safe, secure, smug — and now engaged.

Joan's gum-chewing friend, Eileen McMahon, had a beehive hairdo stiffened with so much hairspray that it could knock over a full-sized man. She whispered something to Joan. She appeared to be amused at Maureen being their waitress. Arrogant bitch! Maureen had to make light of it. She didn't have a choice.

"This is a transition time for me. I did two years at Hunter College and left and I'm now painting and on my own. I have a great little studio in the Village. This job helps. But I'm still finding myself hon, still looking. And you know, sometimes I feel like I'm diagonally parked in a parallel universe," she added with a wink and a smile.

Maureen was instantly sorry that she'd tried to "explain" where she was at. Who were these people anyway? They were no better than she was, damn it. She wouldn't let these *dese, dems* and *doze* jerks get to her. Dempsey was a dope anyway.

"You were always the joker, Maureen. Listen; next time you find yourself looking for a *real* job, you can call on me. Here's my card," Joan said, handing her one from her State Employment Service. As if that would help.

Maureen bit down on the inside of her lip. Waiting on tables wasn't where she wanted to be. But at that stage, what she wanted wasn't always what she could get. God, she wished she didn't feel so rotten if anyone gawked at her like those two idiots did, like she was a failure. *I mean, it takes time to find one's place in the cosmos,* and damned if she would settle until she felt it was where she was supposed to be. Hell, the work was honest, it gave her the free time she needed to paint, and she had nothing to apologize for.

She was relieved when the two of them finally left. Still, she wasn't feeling good about herself — or the fact that she was happy that they had left her a decent tip.

She had liked college and was easily accepted because she had an over 85 average; they didn't take just *anyone* into Hunter College. It was the best of the City College system. Her dilemma was that while she loved her elective courses, she just didn't want to do the other work, the math and science, the economics, the tedious stuff.

The art department was really nifty. She'd miss Robert Motherwell, the famed abstract expressionist who taught her favorite course at the school. Devoted specifically to Picasso's *Guernica* – the course analyzed the details of the master's great mural on the Spanish Civil War. Coupled with a philosophical discussion of Ortega Y Gasset's book, *The Revolt of the Masses*, it had captured her attention, as it had all the students attending this philosophical dissection of art. But art wasn't all. While the $8 tuition, which included books, was affordable, she really disliked the discipline of having to study for tests. She wanted the opportunity, for the first time in her life, to be totally free, and independent, to make her own decisions, good ones or bad.

Maureen also craved affection, somebody in her life. Maybe that was her downfall. While Hunter College was an all-girls school, men were admitted to the Fine Arts Department. My, now didn't it make everything a little more interesting! She had a big crush on Peter O'Connor, one of the students in her architecture class, so when they got into it that day, with the classroom empty, who knew they'd be discovered? So how come she was expelled and not him?

It was true. It was a man's world. Couldn't live with 'em and couldn't live without 'em. Men weren't to be trusted, of course, her mother had taught her that. Look how their father deserted them. He didn't give a damn. He had disappeared one November morning, never sent a Christmas or birthday card to any of them. It was awful how it hurt. As far as she was concerned he was dead. It was obvious he never cared about what happened to his kids.

Still as much as she put on the persona of someone strong and indifferent, Maureen frequently felt lost and lonely. Life wasn't that easy. There was a hole somewhere inside. She wasn't sure of how to fill up the emptiness. It occupied her being. And so she sought short-term liaisons, and nightlife in the bars. The talk there was intelligent, peppered with politics and social consciousness and a few good laughs. When that wasn't enough, she'd take someone home to fill the void.

Thank heaven her mother didn't know too much about her lifestyle. Maureen's mother, Mary Catherine, had been a good woman. Though not well schooled, Mary Catherine was a devout Roman Catholic and did the best she could for her kids. She was in the habit of holding her own life up to the candle of faith, in the hope it would make visible the designs of God. Not that she always trusted; her life had been hard, with her husband a drunk and abandoning her with all those little children to care for. But care for them she did and she would proudly boast of those who had done well.

Two of them actually graduated from college, while Billy and Danny, her two eldest sons, had respectfully joined the New York City police and fire departments, good civil service jobs in those days. The boys had been schooled by nuns and intent upon living up to their mother's high goals for them. They wanted to know nothing about the rude and the lewd types their sister hung out with in Greenwich Village. They never could understand her living down there.

Maureen was the only one who had gone her own way. No take-care-of-me marriage. No civil service job for her. No safety net. She had set her sights on the art world, somehow a dissolution of her past. She knew the smirks her brothers made and her mother's open criticisms were because she chose a different path. One that was vague, that didn't bring in a regular income. How ridiculous, they thought. No, they'd never understand.

But it was what Maureen needed at that time in her life. She

would weave a tapestry of illusion for herself in boldly painted
images, mostly cubistic abstracts of Mondrian-like arrangements. It
helped the harm she often felt. While she empathized with the flower
children of the 60s, Maureen would flaunt traditions in her own way.
Laugh, drink, be merry, and when all else failed, sing out a song.
She would never think again about the philandering man who had
abandoned himself to booze and his family at the same time. No
one ever know too much of her past. She would never talk about it.
In fact, when anyone got too close and asked she'd say her father
was dead, "six months ago," to explain the tears that came with one
drink too many. "Don't ask me anything more, okay, darlin?" she'd
respond. "Just pour me another, I don't like to talk serious."

Up in her studio, she'd often get lost in the painting. But there
were the other times when it was too lonely, listening to Jimmi
Hendrix's first album and painting alone. Going out for a while
— to the 9th Circle on Christopher Street or the Kettle of Fish on
Macdougal Street — brought her some solace. She wanted to talk
about the *present*, be it the latest stupid movie by the rat pack, or
even how odd the Maharishi Mahesh Yogi, the Beatles' spiritual
teacher seemed.

By the time she'd reached her quarter-century mark, Maureen
had experienced a profusion of one-night stands and a few brief
affairs. Weird, to feel old at 25. Most of the women she knew from
the old neighborhood and from school had married and settled
down. Women's Lib was only just starting, and few women could
handle making it on their own.

Sometimes it seemed like she was the only one to remain single.
Why not! She liked her freedom. Maureen sought out her buddies,
the mostly male faction of would-be authors and artists who drank
beside her in the Village bars. They understood her need to paint,
to express herself in visual images. And if she had a little too much
to drink, and didn't want to be alone, it was okay to sleep together,
legs entwined, to feel warm and satisfied. She'd be the one doing the

asking, without using words.

She remembered her early Catholic teachings but hadn't been to church in years. Sure there was a little guilt, but these were the 60s. Fueled by the warmth of vodka martinis, one-night stands were good enough for her. It was years before the AIDS virus, and long before even the knowledge of genital herpes made most people cautious as hell.

— CR —

The narrow, windy gray cement platform of cement for the Long Island Railroad trains was cold and lonely. An awful place to have to stand and wait. She hated climbing up the many stairs to reach the platform and loathed even more the wide spaces between platform and train entrance. Worse, she feared she'd fall through the space and die between the trains some day. She hated the train almost as much as where it would take her — to a long put-off visit to see her family.

Thanksgiving of 1964, Maureen decided to go out to Levittown, a small area on the South Shore of Long Island where her mother now lived with one of Maureen's brothers. The entire family was expected. She'd successfully avoided seeing them for so long, and wasn't quite sure why she was doing this. It was a lengthy trip on the Long Island Railroad. Besides, it freaked her out getting on the damned trains. She couldn't understand why anyone would want to commute an hour each way to come home to a patch of grass.

She carried gifts for her nephews and nieces. She was also carrying a pint of Smyrna in her shoulder bag. As long as she had a few drinks to while away the time on the train, she'd be okay.

The trip now involved getting a taxi at the station. More money, more wasted time. She finished the tiny bottle of vodka and sucked on some mints. No tell-tale breath.

— CR —

"Well, well, glory be, she's finally here," her mother said, opening the door. They hugged, she kissed her mother on the cheek, but it felt strange. Did she look all right? Would they like their presents?

The small house was filled with relatives. She tried to feel at ease. After all this was her family — or was that the problem? After a bountiful turkey and ham dinner she listened to talk about baby formulas, rising fuel costs, football games. "If you think nobody cares if you're alive, try missing a couple of car payments," a sister-in-law said. They all laughed. But Maureen was bored. She felt like a fish out of water. They didn't approve of her; it was obvious.

Her mother had a new hairdo. At least it was far different than the last time Maureen had seen her. Tight curls that looked good on her silver gray hair. Mary Catherine McDermott still had a pretty face, but it was lined with years of disappointments and the marionette lines that led from her mouth turned down in a negative manner.

"Life's precious moments don't have value unless they're shared," her mother began.

Maureen knew what was coming. *Speech number 783.* And as her mother started in all over again about why she didn't come out and "live like a decent person?" and then the chorus of assenters chimed in, she had more than enough.

"Hey, I don't mean to run, but I have to catch the 6:15 train and I'd better leave now," she announced. Not a minute too soon. They would never understand. And she was beginning to accept that they just couldn't. People had to live their own lives, and hers would not be one of quiet desperation.

— ❧ —

Later that same winter Maureen had an intense affair with Joe Garrison, the handsome super of her building. Joe was a writer, eking out a living doing the maintenance on three buildings. He was from North Dakota, a simple guy. And of course he was married, and needed to support himself and his family while hopefully writing the great American novel. Why were some of the better guys married, she wondered?

The super's wife, Annette, worked part time at St. Vincent's hospital, in between raising their two daughters, 3 and 5. Maureen didn't feel guilty. Well, just a bit. Annette was a nice person, sensitive, and had no idea that when Joe would come up to fix the sink, he was also fixing Maureen's loneliness. She finally broke it off. Too complicated, living in the same building. Besides, she didn't feel right about it, not at all.

Peter, Paul and Mary were one of the singing groups Maureen played regularly on her 45 discs. She also loved Pete Seeger, Joan Baez and Bob Dylan, the protestors who voiced her own concerns and sensitivities.

Music was a good escape. A few times, early on in high school, she would cut classes to get on line at E.J. Korvette on 34th Street, to buy the latest hit single. She'd saved quarters, taken from the wash money when she had to do piles of laundry to help out her mother. She didn't think there was anything wrong with that; after all, she spent three hours hauling baskets of dirty laundry four blocks away to the Laundromat. Later on, when she was working and had extra money, she'd attend Dylan's concerts at Carnegie Hall, even if the seat were so far back she could barely see the curly haired minstrel on the stage.

By 1967, Abbie Hoffman's bestseller, *Steal This Book* was making the rounds. The Viet Nam war was an unpopular one, and most of the idealists who lived in the West Village, like Maureen, would attend rallies and be prepared to march. The times, they were a changing, as Dylan forecast. Dr. King had already been jailed 14 times, stabbed once and in March of 1965 marched to Montgomery, Alabama, intensifying his peoples' hope for justice.

Then one night, sitting at a Bring-Your-Own party going on

down the street, Maureen and Annie ran into one another. They
were both pleasantly surprised! The girls had spent some quality
time trading jokes and experiences at the lunch table — what was
it? — seven years ago in the college cafeteria. Annie liked Maureen
— she was a unique and bright light with a good sense of humor.
Though they came from different backgrounds, they shared much in
common when it came to cobweb dreams and sensitivities.

"Well, will wonders never cease? Imagine running into you
here," Maureen exclaimed. They soon discovered they were both
living in the Village.

"You look great kiddo! I love your longer hair," Annie replied
with equal enthusiasm. Maureen looked absolutely beautiful. But
then she was always a knockout!

"And you look absolutely gorgeous," Maureen responded,
admiring Annie's psychedelic top — the one with just enough glitter
to play up her figure. Annie knew it. She did look good that night,
but then she always dressed to the nines.

They talked of life and living in the Village.
"Hell, it's great downtown, friendly, non-judgmental, good for
finding out about life and about how to live your own," Maureen
philosophized.

"You're so right! I love it here," Annie exclaimed. "There's more
thinking people, young ones too, and I'm crazy about all the little
shops and winding streets. Fancy that we've both been living in the
same neighborhood and only ran into each other now!"

They hugged, delighted to have found each other. And while
it was a long time ago, seemingly little had changed. Maureen was
still the sharp kid always filled with witty wise cracks. While it was
apparent she had her own dilemmas with which to deal, it was
easy to tell that her passion for life illuminated most of what she
did. Annie especially appreciated Maureen's colorful disposition.
Actually it was similar to her own. Hell, they were both bright lights!

— ෬ —

They'd first formed an alliance at Hunter because of what they would *not* do. They'd chosen not to bother with the snobbish bridge-playing sorority crowd that gathered at the next two cafeteria tables. Those superficial idiots, they thought they were superior. Annie and Maureen knew better. Most of these students' goals focused not on learning, but landing the right husband. They concentrated on dating only pre-med or dental students, deciding the best catch was someone with a doctor before his name.

"Doctor, my ass, I want someone who will be around for me," Annie said. "My dad makes just about as much money as the dentist down the block, but what good is it? My parents still never spend it, enjoy what they have," Annie commented. Back then she'd felt a bond with Maureen. After a while Annie shared her secrets — the arguments that constantly went on at home. She had to. There were far too many days when Annie would arrive late for class, her eyes red and puffy, telltale signs of tears shed earlier. There was a tension, a nervous tone in her home that made life harsh. Maureen was no dope. She caught on fast. She didn't exactly have it easy herself.

What Annie never bothered sharing was how much she adored her father, though she could never get too close to him. It was these two sides of herself and her on-again, off-again relationship with him which would haunt her most of her life. For, while her mother Sara had retreated into a self-protective cocoon, she was also jealous and possessive and reacted when anyone came too close to her Sam. She couldn't even share him with her own daughters. There was a careful line one didn't cross. While their dad wanted to be warm and affectionate towards his daughters, their mother would resent his giving them the slightest attention. And to keep the peace, he gave in.

Years later Annie was forced to examine her own emotional needs. Finally she realized that some of the lacks she suffered in her earlier life came from her mother's own difficulty relating to *her* mother. The legacy was a perverted one, for both her sister Joanie and herself found it difficult to relate to men when they grew up, always looking for the love and attention they hadn't received from their father, often seeking that attention from men who were emotionally unavailable.

"I guess I've been looking for my father in some of the men I chose. But, you know something, Maureen — they weren't there for me. But then, neither was my father."

Maureen shook her head in assent. She was also seeking to fill up a deep dark empty hole that had never been brimming with affirmations—that at times hurt like hell. She would seek her father in the men she brought home to love her, though in the end they never would. Now there they were at a Village party with men they barely knew, strangers, who in the end would remain so.

Maureen picked up her guitar, and sang one of Annie's favorite songs — *Someone To Watch Over Me.* She had always loved Gershwin. And was always looking for someone to come save her.

Poor kid, does she really think there's anyone real out there? Maureen was thinking to herself as she sang the lyrics for Annie. No, Maureen knew there was no one to watch over her, she truly doubted that there was such a thing as true love.

Now, after all this time, they'd met at this village gathering. Small world, wasn't it? The party was at a well-known painter's brownstone, just a dozen guests casually sitting around, some in pairs, some alone. A friend at work had invited Annie, said there'd be some interesting men. Candles gave a golden glow to the darkened room. The odd scent in the air was a combination of commercial air freshener and some candlewood incense that left a small dark billow of smoke — all in a vain attempt to hide the acrid odor of the marijuana being passed around.

Annie looked around to see if there were any interesting men.

She felt someone's eyes fixed upon her, noticed a tall slim man with a beard. He smiled at her. Soon they were talking. She moved over and sat down closer to where he was. She took a few puffs of the reefer handed to her and passed it on.

The Answer My Friend Is Blowing In The Wind, sang the small circle of party dwellers that remained after 2 that morning. Bob Dylan's lyrics fit the mood of the mellowed-out participants who ordinarily questioned everything. A joint was passed around and the giggling began. Annie was still there. But now that she had hooked up with this good-looking guy named Steve, who told her he was a painter, she was thinking of leaving.

Maureen looked up to see where her friend was. She noticed Annie, her head leaning on a bearded man's shoulder. It was Steve Smythe; Maureen recognized him from the bar scene. He was a total womanizer. Annie looked like she was falling asleep. Maureen picked up her guitar to strum another song. *Embraceable You* — another Gershwin number both women liked. The next time Maureen gazed their way, the couple were gone. Good thing Annie and she had exchanged phone numbers. She wanted to keep in touch.

— ෬ —

Chapter 10

...Maureen and Sabrina

Time. Where had it gone? Or did it stand still? Everything was a blur. Maureen had slept through most of it. Once she could put it all together, she learned she had been hospitalized for 15 days.

"You've been lucky, to be in a first-rate hospital, and get such good care," a composed but guarded Sabrina said. "It's been a long haul, but thank Heaven, you're going to be all right."

She'd visited often. Buddy and Annie had also come up near the end. But Maureen remembered only fragments. The heavy course of antibiotics and painkillers had diminished her sensibilities.

"When...when did they say I can get out of here?" Maureen asked excitedly.

"You'll be discharged tomorrow. Buddy and I will both be here to take you home. Don't worry about anything but getting well. I've already been to your apartment and had it cleaned. Your refrigerator is stocked with fresh juices and nourishing foods. You'll need to take it easy before you can *go back to work. They're waiting for you, Maureen. They hired a temp to do the drawings. But <u>you're</u> the one they want back."*

Maureen was grateful. She knew Sabrina had sacrificed time to do this for her. "Sabrina, I...."

"Please don't say another word. You were very ill...we were worried. And remember, I'd already given notice. So I could afford the time."

"By the way...you've been without a cigarette for more than two weeks. I'd say that's a good start on giving them up."

...."Please, Sabrina...I hate to disappoint you but I've been smoking in the lounge the last few days. I bummed a few."

"Well, who am I to preach. But eventually, I hope you'll stop."

"Easy for you to say, you never started. But I'm going to kick 'em eventually, I promise," Maureen said and she meant it.

The two women embraced. A bond had been formed that wouldn't be easily broken.

"By the way, you slept through St. Patrick's Day, didn't even know it had come and gone," Sabrina said with a smile.

"Well, now, I suppose I still have the luck of the Irish, to have survived this horror. I'll settle for that!"

— ଔ —

1966

SABRINA

Sabrina Aldrich knew she was beautiful. After all, hadn't she been told that since she was a little girl? It didn't hurt that Sabrina's mother had been one of the leading cover girls in the 40s. Sabrina had inherited her mother's high cheekbones, lithe, lean body, and great legs. She had the kind of body that suggested she was holding a winning ticket in the lucky genes lotto.

Sabrina shared a warm bond with her mother and was proud

of her many accomplishments. Jane Aldrich was not your run-of-the-mill society gal; nor was she the kind of vapid woman born to staggering wealth and towering position — the type who just travels — follows couture and generally makes herself useless.

No, Sabrina's mother had come from modest beginnings. She was raised in a succession of foster homes after losing her parents when she was five. An older child, she had never been adopted. It would always leave a core emptiness within her. She never forgot her experiences and wanted to protect other children from falling prey to the foster system, from moving from one family to another.

And so when Jane's modeling career ended and after she was well ensconced in her marriage to the very social Dr. Martin Aldrich, she decided she'd go back to school. Jane acquired her degree and pursued a career as a social worker, specifically in the placement of orphans. She was determined to provide a safe haven for children; there were so many poor and abused children all over the United States, never mind in the world.

She worked in this field for years, refusing far easier assignments so that she could make a difference and she did.

She also made a difference in her daughter's life and how Sabrina viewed the world.

Sabrina had the innate sensitivities of her mother and her father's intellectual curiosity. Martin Aldrich, a third-generation physician, was one of three men who helped develop a vaccine against a vicious strain of malaria. His endeavors took up a half-dozen paragraphs in *Who's Who*.

Though the Aldrich's were a secure, wealthy family residing in Greenwich, a toney upscale area of Connecticut, what was more significant to Sabrina were her mother's concern for others and her father's important research that earned him an historic place in medical annals. She'd been raised with a social conscience and a respect for others.

Most of all, Sabrina didn't want to be dismissed as just another pretty face. True, she was a cheerleader, a high school prom queen, and for the standards of her time, she'd been an achiever, a *star*. But Sabrina was very bright and definitely confident — and damned if she didn't want to make her own mark. "In the 50s, we weren't encouraged to do anything other than be good children, get a good education, make the right marriage and raise families," she explained. Ah, but she knew better.

As she finished high school, Sabrina knew she wasn't interested in a serious relationship. That could wait — what was more important to her was achieving a higher education and then to make something special of herself. As always, her parents were supportive.

After graduating Barnard College with honors in 1962, Sabrina took some time off, knowing after the summer she would pursue a career.

She decided to share a summerhouse on Fire Island — a popular area off Long Island — with three other young women, all from *good* families.

It was a summer of discovery singing hits like *I Want to Hold Your Hand*, from that brand new group, The Beatles. But after the fun, stumbling, drink in hand along the crooked boardwalk; from one party to another, Sabrina had had enough. Feeling restless, she was ready to do something with her life. Yes, she was sure of it — she wanted a good job — some way to test her own value.

While her parents would have liked her to come back home she convinced them she'd have to live in Manhattan, where the job market was extensive. She was determined to make it to the top and Sabrina didn't mind using family connections to get a foot in the right door. It wasn't difficult to persuade her mother to help. With her Grace Kelly looks, bouffant hairdo of the day and a strong academic record in tow, Sabrina would be one of the few women who'd shatter the *glass ceiling.*

At the beginning — even with the right school and background and connections — it wasn't that easy. She spent many months knocking on doors. Before long Sabrina could recite the standard rejections of the era: *"We like you, but if we hire a woman and she gets married and moves on, then the training we invested is gone. Also, women do get pregnant, and...."*

Teachers, social workers — these were suitable positions for women. If a woman wanted to enter the more masculine arena of competition, where CEO's of companies were always men, and directors — even of creative departments — were male; women had major barriers to surmount.

After four months of fruitless searching, Sabrina heard of an opening in the ad department of B. Altman's. The position: head of the copy department, really quite a plum spot for anyone, never mind a young woman with no experience at all. She asked her mother for help. Jane Aldrich knew the family that still had major control of the Fifth Avenue store. One call was all that was necessary to begin the course of action that would install Sabrina in this top position.

Having natural writing ability (she always did well on her term papers at Barnard) Sabrina hastily put together a portfolio of composite ads. Some of them were quite clever; others were obviously borrowed from successful ad campaigns. But it was enough to get an interview and consideration. Her makeshift portfolio and family connections got her the position that paid a phenomenal (for that time) $300 a week.

The portfolio went over well. They really liked her ideas. But she had no expertise with the scheduling of ads, supervising two other copywriters (with far more experience than she) or working with the art director and artists.

All Sabrina's life, things were made easy. Besides her good looks and family background, she never had to be concerned about money.

And so until she was ready to move out on her own, Sabrina knew she could live in her parent's pied-a-terre on 58th Street and Park Avenue.

Now, Sabrina had a challenge before her and loved the idea. She worked her tail off, spending the next six months learning every aspect of the work so she could prove she was more than up to the task. She read books on retail advertising. And she didn't care how many hours she'd have to work to prove herself. Sabrina single-mindedly dug her heels right in and stayed long hours. Every morning she turned up at the office at 8 a.m. before anyone but the cleaning crew had arrived. And she'd get right to work. She became skilled at every facet of running a retail-advertising department. She learned how to oversee the production of slick, well written ads on the fast-paced schedule that was the cadence of this up-scale department store.

Soon, she'd gained the respect of everyone in the department. She effectively supervised the writing and scheduling of ads on house wares, fashions, sports and gift pages that ran regularly in all the major New York newspapers. No matter that she was just 22. She knew she deserved their respect. She bought a sign for her office desk that confirmed her philosophy: 'SUCCESS STOPS WHEN YOU DO'.

— ⅋ —

"Maureen, this is a fabulous illustration," Sabrina exclaimed, admiring the beautiful sketches Maureen had made for her first Sunday double fold. She liked Maureen, always glib, funny, a cigarette constantly in her hands, or between her lips while she sketched away at the drawing board.

Soon the two young women — from such diverse backgrounds — became after-hour drinking partners. Maureen introduced Sabrina to the folk singing set down in the Village. They would regularly spend Friday nights laughing, drinking, and flirting with the men they met.

After midnight, when Maureen was showing signs of having a little too much to drink, and the cigarette smoke at the bar was getting to Sabrina's more sensitive lungs, Sabrina would take a taxi home. She knew Maureen wouldn't mind. Maureen bid her a quick adieu, and then retreated to a back booth with the crowd, trading jokes, discussing politics, and thoroughly enjoying herself. On the floor next to her in an old case, was her guitar. She never knew when she would feel a song coming on. She'd always loved singing.

While the Beat Generation had peaked in the 50s, Maureen and her set still looked up to Jack Kerouac and Allen Ginsberg as semi-deities. Some of her drinking companions had gone south in the 60s, to be part of the non-violent protest movement first begun by Rosa Park's refusal to sit in the back of a bus followed by a young Reverend Martin Luther King, a Ph. D at 26, taking up the gauntlet.

On November 13, 1956, the Supreme Court had ruled that segregation was against the law. Many courageous Negro college students would invade all-white lunch counters waiting to be served. They would wait for hours and hours. They would not be served.

The sit-ins began in Greensboro, North Carolina in 1960 and then spread throughout the South. *For deep in my heart, I do believe, we shall overcome someday;* a lyric attributed to Pete Seeger became the theme song of the 60s. After the alienation of the 50s, with icons like Marlon Brando on his motorcycle and James Dean, starring in the movie *Rebel Without A Cause*, a new generation wanted to achieve independence. Brando and Dean were forces of an age group searching for a different identity.

For those who could only talk about independence but were emotionally bogged down — too much baggage, old scars that didn't heal, there was the discovery of Milltown in the 60s, soon followed by the popular Valium, one of the many, "I Don't Give A Damn" drugs that would dangerously mix with booze and cause many tragedies in ricochets and overdoses that could not be reversed.

There at the Whitehorse Tavern, seated in a back booth, guitar in hand, Maureen strummed as her group of fellow inebriates sang the defiant songs of the age. By 2 a.m. she had enough. Ben Tolson, the handsome reporter from the Times had come by. She took him home that night, her latest trophy, she thought. What she didn't learn until months later was that she had also picked up a vicious strain of gonorrhea that would eventually impair her reproductive system.

An interest Maureen and Sabrina both shared was an affinity for modern art. In 1959, the most controversial creation of Frank Lloyd Wright had opened on Madison Avenue. It was a bold, circular structure called the Guggenheim Museum of Art. Maureen loved it, and went monthly.

A rare exhibit of Picasso's *Guernica* opened that spring and brought both young women there. "I wish I could do something 1/100th as good," Maureen sighed. "It's such a magnificent, bold work." It was amazing, how art could soothe her soul.

"Hey, what the hell, we've been here for an hour, let's go see if there's a line over at Cinema II; they're playing the new Beatles' movie, and I need a laugh or two," Maureen finally suggested. *It's Been A Hard Day's Night* was upbeat, light fare.

"Sure, a good idea," Sabrina agreed.

After the movie, the two friends walked along Third Avenue, stopped at a local pizza joint for a slice. Maureen wasn't feeling so good.

Maureen looked awfully red and flushed. "Are you all right?" Sabrina asked.

"I don't know, I have an awful stabbing pain in my right side." She winced. "It was bothering me all through the movie."

Within a few moments both knew Maureen was having some sort of excruciating attack. Appendicitis? "I can't eat this thing," Maureen said, and put her pizza down. She was sweating profusely.

"You need to see a doctor, immediately," Sabrina said, grabbing her handbag and Maureen's. "Let's get out of here."

Sabrina found them a taxi, helped Maureen, who was wincing in pain into the cab. "Take us to the emergency room at Lenox Hill Hospital," she told the driver. Maureen looked awful, like she might pass out from the pain. Sabrina waited patiently for hours while her friend was diagnosed and then admitted. "She's running a 104 degree fever and we don't think it's her appendix. We'll know more after tests," the young intern reported.

That weekend would be touch and go. Maureen had unknowingly developed peritonitis, the result of a fallopian tube that had finally ruptured, infected by the disease she had picked up from that handsome reporter two months earlier. Two weeks later she left the hospital weak, pale, run down. The spirit had been drained out of her. She still would need two more weeks of antibiotics.

When Maureen's mother, a God-fearing woman who still attended daily mass, learned that her willful daughter had been hospitalized, she chose not to visit. "Jesus, Joseph and Mary!" she cursed. "It *had* to lead to something like this, that damned fool would never listen!" She was convinced that her rebellious daughter had finally been punished for her erring ways.

"That's what that kind of life has brought her," she sobbed to the local priest at the parish house. Worse, she feared her daughter had had an abortion or something equally evil. She was ashamed, determined to keep it a secret. She'd confide only in Father O'Reilly, who promised to pray for her wayward daughter. No, she couldn't visit her; it would be too hurtful, and it might seem like she was condoning her daughter's shameful behavior.

"You go if you want," she said to her boys. "But I can't. The girl has to change her ways."

Most of the family, conservative, siding with their mother, stayed away. But Danny, Maureen's youngest brother, finally came in the day before she was discharged. He handed her a bouquet of flowers. "I'm sorry about this, kiddo. Here's fifty bucks from the gang to help out," he said, handing her a white envelope.

"Mom isn't up to coming in, I'm sorry...she means well, she really does, Maureen," he stuttered.

"Tell Mom I understand," she answered. But she didn't.

That was the last Maureen heard from her family. In their own ignorance they'd determined that she deserved whatever happened to her. They were always of the mind that she was too damned wild, living alone as she had, and then not even finishing college. Didn't they tell her to move out their way, return to school, become a nurse or a teacher — make something decent of herself? If not a secure career, then she should be marrying and raising a family. Mary Catherine would light a candle for Maureen daily, praying to St. Jude for her salvation. But she could not bring herself to see her willful daughter.

Marriage? A family? The concept to Maureen seemed remote at this point. The doctors had explained that the infection had badly damaged Maureen's tubes. If she should marry and ever hoped to have children she'd need surgery to try to reverse the impairment. Right now she was too damned sick to care.

When Buddy had learned that she was at Lenox Hill, he came to visit every day that final week, often bringing her Breyer's coffee ice cream, her favorite flavor. Just a few days before she was released, Annie Rosenberg, her old friend from Hunter College, who'd learned about her illness through the grapevine, had also come to see her. A new Annie, happy, smiling, glowing with news.

"I'm engaged — a wonderful guy, so handsome, so sexy," she shouted. "And we've known each other for only two months — talk about love at first!"

All Maureen could learn was that her friend had placed a

personals ad in the *East Village Other,* an alternative newspaper, in
the personals column. Met a damned fireman named Tom Ryan,
for God's sake, and was going to marry him. Would wonders never
cease?

She hugged Annie, wishing her the best of luck; really hoping
this man would be good to her. The only firemen she knew —
including her own brother — were male chauvinists. She'd dated
a couple, and while they were hunks, they were cheap bastards,
including her brother John. John had never called Maureen, asked
how she was doing after her hospitalization — and he was stationed
at a firehouse in the West Village, so he could have even come to
visit. It hurt but she didn't expect much from any of them. She knew
he was busy — worked two jobs and, had to travel all the way out
to Long Island where he lived with his wife and two sons. Maureen
had noticed those few times she had seen him at home, that he acted
dreadfully towards his wife.

As for dear Annie — who was she to pass judgment on this
happy soul? Maybe, finally, Annie would have good fortune — and
the answer to her dreams. She knew how much of a romantic her
friend was, and Maureen truly hoped she'd found her *Mr. Right.*

That July, men walked on the moon for the first time, Maureen
went back to work, and life started to feel better. But the nights were
something else. She grew restless and couldn't stay home any longer.
She just had to get out, go back to the Old Cedar Bar, and catch up
with her chums. She needed the companionship.

Dismayed at the doctor telling her that her system was all
messed up, Maureen decided, the hell with it all. Why would she
want to bring children into this mixed-up world anyway? And
marriage? She hadn't seen any award-winning ones, didn't think it
was worth the hurt. So though she'd been warned not to have any
alcohol in her system for the next six months, within three weeks of
being back at the bars she was sipping wine spritzers, smoking her

Marlboros and getting a buzz on. The age of Woodstock was still burning bright.

Ben Tolson. That mother fucker. Maureen had finally figured it out. She had slept only with Ben for the month and a half before she ended up in the hospital, so she knew. She was well aware of his reputation — he slipped his dick into any broad he wanted. After all, he wrote for the big deal Times. And dumb her, she was just another broad. So he'd been screwing around, infecting women all over town. But she'd do the right thing.

So Maureen sat down, wrote and mailed an anonymous letter telling Tolson he should check with a doctor before he destroyed any other lives. She never knew if the son-of-a-bitch did anything about it. Weird, but he never came around to the bars she frequented any more.

Years later — though Maureen wouldn't find out for a long time — Tolson, who had a passion for both sexes, was going to die of AIDS.

— ଔ —

Chapter 11

March 1967

Maureen had been in the hospital for a week. Lucky that she had medical coverage from the job at Altman's. She learned that Sabrina had been to visit, though she could only vaguely recall it. She began to remember the immense pain that had brought her to the emergency room.

"Can you call Buddy for me? He must be wondering where I am," she asked, the next time she saw Sabrina. "I bet he's leaving messages on my answering machine."

She knew the doctor had asked for a family contact. Ha! What a joke. What with the familial dysfunction of the McDermott's she didn't expect a response. Oh well. At least the IV had been removed from her sore arm. But now they were giving her gigantic needles in the butt. That was getting sore too. She was so uncomfortable; she didn't know which position to lie in. Being sick was no fun.

She was still in need of a heavy dose of antibiotics. "You're not out of *the woods yet, my dear," said the kindly head nurse. "Your fever, in spite of everything, goes up at night. You have to stay with us longer."*

"How much longer?" Maureen asked — eager to get out. She missed her apartment, her friends, and her work.

"Be patient. You've been a very sick young lady."

She was depressed. Lying like a prisoner in a bed so long. What could have happened to give her this infection that had contaminated her stomach and may have messed up her reproductive system? She was afraid to think.

Maureen turned away from the nurse and closed her eyes.

— ◌ৎ —

...1964

It was the morning after the party and Maureen, content in her bed, jiggled her toes and smiled. She felt toasty warm under the blanket. She was glad she ran into Annie after all these years. She'd call so they could get together. This time she was glad she'd come home alone.

She opened one eye to catch the time on the radio clock. It was almost noon, Sunday, a good day for sleeping late and then reading the papers. Her favorite activity was the Times crossword puzzle. She had a special dictionary that furnished esoteric puzzle definitions, like "corona," a six-letter word for "lunar phenomenon." With practice, she was getting good at it, now writing her answers assertively in ink.

The new job began the next day. She could barely believe it. She was going to become a nine-to-fiver! Maureen turned over, buried her head in the soft feather pillow and was about to go back to sleep when the phone rang. It was Buddy inviting her to brunch. Of course she'd go.

They met at the Bleecker Street Café. In the passionate voice of the 60s, when having coffee at an outdoor café could be an excuse to sit for hours, the two of them would have breakfast and argue the issues of the day. It was a volatile time. Police had now replaced the dogs snarling at the concerned civilians who were marching for civil rights and now irritating tear gas was used to break up overzealous protesters at peace rallies.

There were the doves and the hawks. Buddy was a hawk. As soon as they placed their breakfast order, he launched full swing into supporting the Viet Nam war. "They may have gone to the wrong war, but they went for the right reasons," was his manifesto over the orange juice.

"Sure, sure that's why they're coming home in body bags and no one is winning," she answered, puffing away on her third Marlboro.

"You're off the beam, Maureen. Our guys need support. And to a degree, well I think those protest rallies you attend, they're Commie-backed," he opined. Buddy enjoyed tweaking his friend.

"Well have it your way pal," she said, leaning her face very close to his to make her next point. "But we are born naked, wet and hungry. Then things get worse. Look how our dreary politicians have led us into bloodshed in a war no one can win," she continued, determined to convince him of her higher moral stance.

Buddy realized that on this subject there was no sense going up against Maureen. He scarfed down the rest of his omelet. There were two theories to arguing with women. Neither one worked. He had learned that lesson growing up with a mother who enjoyed arguing just to argue, but worse, who prevailed in every debate.

Still, engaging in ideas with Maureen was far more satisfying. "Hey, let's have another cup of coffee," he said, smiling at the waitress approaching their table. He leaned over to light Maureen's next cigarette.

"Now, if you smoked, you could do a Paul Henreid," Maureen

said laughing. She was alluding to the romantic scene in *Now Voyager* where Henreid lighted Bette Davis' cigarette and his own at the same time. She loved the movie.

"Hey, thanks but no thanks. You know smoking is not one of my favorite activities," he replied. "I'll light 'em for you, but I'm not joining you. I have enough bad habits," he added, pointing to his widening waist.

"I am in shape. Round is a shape," Buddy used to say.

"So work out, the gym is just down the street you know," Maureen reminded him. She was well aware he was not the athletic type.

— ❧ —

Buddy Berkowitz had met Maureen at the Café Wha, a Village basement nightclub where Bob Dylan had once sung his epic song, *Hard Rains Gonna Fall*. They both appreciated Dylan's compositions. It was 1963, the same year that Lee Harvey Oswald ended many American's dreams. The assassination of J.F.K. had troubled him, took away any illusions. Now with Johnson escalating the war, Buddy had tried to enlist. The military rejected him because of poor eyesight. The best he could do was pass out pamphlets supporting the troops at rallies where the opposition marched with banners screeching, GET OUT NOW!

Buddy was crazy about Maureen, though he never got to first base. At 5 foot 6, he was short. While his features were all right, the thick-lensed glasses he wore exaggerated his eyes. Actually he had nice eyes. Years later he would switch to contact lenses in an effort to help his appearance. But in those days, he was uncertain of himself. He knew he wasn't any woman's idea of a heartthrob and so Maureen's acceptance made him feel better about himself. After all, she moved in trendy circles, and often took him along.

Still, while he didn't want to complain — *Sex was like air* — it wasn't important unless you weren't getting any. Buddy wasn't.

The 1960s was a time of great turmoil. An ugly, divisive war was tearing America apart. It was also a time of idealism. While many watched the "I Have A Dream Speech" eloquently spoken on the Lincoln Mall, others enlisted in the Peace Corps. Buddy's parents, they talked him out of that one too.

So Buddy Berkowitz was a caseworker for the City of New York, a low paying but gratifying job. He had a good heart. While it wasn't the exotic Peace Corps, it made him feel he was doing something to help those in need.

Buddy had grown up in Queens, the only son of Anna and Willie Berkowitz, immigrants from Austria. The family lived in a modest garden apartment in an area called "Flushing" where many Orthodox Jews lived to be near the synagogue, the water, and each other. He never ever fit in.

His sense of humor sustained him and helped him gain a measure of popularity. Sometimes his jokes about his ethnic heritage were amusing enough that friends would tell him he had missed his calling — that he'd do better as a stand-up comic. When he wanted attention he'd tell a joke or do whatever he had to do to let people know Buddy Berkowitz was there. "Hey, it's like I dance around the room waving a chicken over my head. That way the others know I'm there. If it works, why not!"

Talking about celebrating the Passover holiday with his family, Buddy commented: "At our Seder, we had whole wheat and bran matzo, fortified with Metamucil. The brand name, of course, is *Let My People Go*." Another time Buddy amused his co-workers with *"What does the rabbi do during some sermons? The answer? Babylon!"*

Buddy, whose real name was David, never "got" the religion his parents wanted him to follow. After his bar mitzvah, he found excuses for avoiding synagogue services — though every Friday night he was part of the ritual lighting of candles and chicken soup meal that followed. He didn't mind the soup part. And there was camaraderie around the table, with good guidance shared, usually by his father, a decent and honorable man. More than once he would remind his son: "*If you tell the truth, you don't have to remember anything.*"Buddy followed that advice all of his life. It was years later that he learned his father had borrowed the axiom from Mark Twain.

Obtaining his B.A. at Queens College, Buddy studied for a masters in social work at New York University. It was what brought him to the downtown area of Manhattan that included Greenwich Village.

After N.Y.U. he accepted the first job offered, scoring high on a walk-in exam for case workers advertised in the Village Voice. He was assigned to work in the Bedford Stuyvesant area of Brooklyn, a neglected section where many southern Blacks had emigrated. Most were women living alone, with two or three or as many as five children, fathered by different men.

Buddy would get them the best doles he could; in those days, the city would give special grants for clothing and furniture. He bravely took one toothless woman shopping on Horatio Street in the West Village, where there was good, old, and sometimes antique, furniture for sale cheap.

He wasn't supposed to take his clients anywhere, but he felt for the lady, who had two beds for five kids, all less than 8 years of age, and lived in a cockroach-infested building with hot water problems. He didn't know if she appreciated the good oak table he had picked out for her, but it was a damned sight better than anything she had ever owned before.

Unlike his simple, hard-working family, Buddy enjoyed the nightlife and a beer or two in the local bars. He worked conscientiously all day. So why not? Besides, many of the taverns in the Village were really singles' meeting places. He wanted to find someone, which wasn't easy, meeting up with rejection after rejection until he found Maureen.

Buddy enjoyed Maureen's philosophy: "He or she who laughs — lasts."He laughed. She laughed. They traded witticisms. She was funny, nice and accepting. And she enjoyed his finely honed sense of humor.

He taught her some Jewish traditions delivering them in a satirical manner. Once he had her giggling at his definitions of Yiddish protocol: "What are other words for kishka, sukkah, and circumcision? A gut, a hut, and a cut!"

She practically adopted him, after all — he was such a sweetie and really so naive. Not really bad looking, though he had such low self-esteem. She figured his comedy routines were a cover-up, but so what. And he could be very clever. Maureen enjoyed jesting.

She thought he looked a lot like Dustin Hoffman, who was just emerging as a movie star. All Buddy needed was to get some confidence, and he'd do just fine. Of course, he was a nerd as a dresser so Maureen made him change his after-work attire. The short-sleeved white shirts and tie were ridiculous at night, she told him. "The white shirt *has* to go. Get a sweatshirt and denims," she told him, "learn to relax."

They became good friends, if not lovers. Greenwich Village was the perfect blending place, where the entire spectrum of human experience could be met. It was the eclectic neighborhood for those who had left their more conservative homes to explore their individualities and their common needs. The hippies occupied the East Village, the artists and writers congregated more in the West Village, and in between, on blocks like Christopher Street, gays met at bars like the Stonewall.

Buddy was like the brother Maureen never really had. Her real brothers were harsh and judgmental. Buddy was accepting, and thought everything she did was terrific, well everything but her views on politics.

"Buddy, darlin, I'm going to tell you an Irish saying. Write it down and learn it well. It's a lovely one," she said, introducing:

"May there always be work for your hands to do. May your purse always hold a coin or two. May the sun always shine on your windowpane. May a rainbow be certain to follow each rain."

There were some rainy days for Maureen. She was determined to be a free spirit, but often there was a price to be paid. While she kept it a secret how many men she brought home, she knew he was a real friend and would not judge her. Anytime that Maureen had a crying jag, if she didn't have anyone else, she knew she could reach Buddy, and he would come right over. He lived in the West Village too, right around the corner on Bleecker Street.

There's a saying old, says that love is blind
Still we're often told, seek and ye shall find
So I'm going to seek a certain lad I've had in mind...

— ❦ —

Chapter 12

Annie and Tom
November 1969

"Tom, wake up, wake up, please," Annie whispered.

He didn't budge. He'd been moaning, crying softly in his sleep.

"Wake up," she repeated, now shaking his shoulder gently.

He opened his eyes, looked bewildered for a moment. "It's nothing, absolutely nothing. Leave me alone, please – let me sleep."

Tom turned away from her, his body tensing up like steel. Annoyed at her waking him up, he was shutting her out again. It wasn't the first time this big, strong man, cried relentlessly during his sleep. What was wrong? Why couldn't he tell her? Annie moved towards him — put her toes next to his, inched closer, wrapped one leg around his, so that some part of their bodies were touching. But she knew there was a barricade between them. It didn't seem like he'd ever tell her what was bothering him. It was *his* secret.

The next morning, a beautiful crisp autumn day, Annie went downstairs to make breakfast. She'd charm him with a stack of pancakes. He loved pancakes and sausage and the way she made them. Tom was on a two-day shift off from work and later on they planned to take a drive to Sheepshead Bay, where they enjoyed dining at Lundy's, a famous Brooklyn seafood restaurant. Annie was looking forward to the fresh clams on the half shell, to the precious time alone with Tom. Then the phone rang. Of course it was his mom. She straight away asked to speak to her son. *Something was wrong with her kitchen sink, there was a flood on the floor, could he please come out and fix it?*

"I'm sick of it, Tom, sick of it up to here," Annie shouted, sliding her forefinger across her throat. Your mother's always making demands on you. And besides that, she ought to get off her high horse and be a little nicer. She's absolutely rude; didn't even acknowledge me. All she wants is *you*! She knows we're married and damn it, there's nothing she can do about it!"

He didn't answer. No, he'd never answer. He walked into the kitchen, ignored the pancakes she was making, drank some orange juice and went for the door. "I'm going down to the handball court. See you later."

The door slammed before she could say another word.

All because Ursula had brusquely asked to speak to Tom, with not even a cordial hello to Annie. And they had such nice plans for the day. What was he going to do when he came back? Get dressed and drive out to her house? Sure, he may have gone to play handball to let off some steam, but he'd come back and rush out there to take care of his mother's needs. Like she couldn't call a plumber.

Annie was furious, and hurt. Damn it! There went their great plans for the day. That Ursula…she always had some favor she'd ask of one of her boys. Like she was a weakling, a poor little old widow living all alone. Hah! That was so far from the truth. Somehow she called on Tom more than his brother, Joe. Anything to get Tom away, to spoil Annie's day. She hated Annie, of that Annie was sure. How could Tom not see it, how his mother was coming between them?

Maybe that's why they had so much turmoil in their marriage. It was a great part of the reason she would leave him and why she felt so sad.

— ❧ —

December —

Now that they had separated, Annie was reduced to a litany of regrets. She couldn't live with him and she couldn't live without him. Please, God, what should she do? Please, please answer. She heard nothing. Nothing at all.

Feeling the sharp teeth of the doomsday dragon tearing at her dreams Annie needed to write the heartache away. If there were guardian angels or otherworldly beings somewhere, anywhere out there — then please, she beseeched — "Dear angels — please send these words to Tom — let him know how much I want him back in my life."

She sipped some vodka. No, she guzzled it. Smelled like rubbing alcohol. Burned going down. But it dulled the ache, filled the bottomless hole. How dare she ask for him back? She knew it was no good!

Annie was out there alone in the cosmos. Seeking safe harbor, searching for a shimmering star that showed the way to a place, any place where she'd feel okay. And loved. She needed to be loved. Was that really asking too much? And so fearful all was lost, she wrote:

Dear You," her treatise began. *"I thought about you today. I was back to our living together, to our apartment in Queens, the swings in the park on a brisk autumn day. There I was pushing Colleen back and forth while singing, "You Are My Sunshine." And then I felt it all over again, the "what-ifs" and "why-can't-we-make-it" syndrome.*

Tom, why can't we get along? Why do we hurt each other? I love you with a passion words just can't convey. When we make love it's as if we are the only people on this earth. But then we argue. Over stupid stuff too. And so I'm here and you're somewhere else."

Annie poured another drink. Sure, she knew a successful marriage was about compromising. But it was always *she* who made the concessions — while Tom, he simply withdrew. It wasn't fair; it wasn't supposed to be that way. Or was it? She was getting the message: nowhere on one's birth certificate did it say life is fair, fun or easy. She hated, absolutely hated the idea.

But this marriage tested every aspect of her psyche. She was increasingly uncertain, yet terrified to admit that it was a mistake. How could she ever let go? It was so damned hard to let go.

Sometimes Annie felt possessed. What kind of spell had been cast over her? Was this real life or was this the movies? A bad movie at that. She had this absolutely insane hunger for Tom — he was so handsome, she took immense pleasure in just looking at his face. He met her movie-star image of what a husband should look like. But it wasn't all physical. Not at all. They could finish each other's thoughts and when there was no conflict, they were close and loving, the feelings beyond perfect.

She sipped some more, continued the letter to nowhere:

"I miss the security of hiding out in marriage, in a family setting. There is an implicit knowledge in a marital contract that says someone would notice if you weren't there for dinner, never mind if you were dead."

"Since I left, and am living on my own again, I wonder if anyone would wonder where I was if they called and reached my answering machine. Maybe a week or more would pass before anyone would show real concern. If I were sick or needed help, could I get it – would anyone know it? There are risks in living alone."

Of course Annie wouldn't admit that she was too frightened to stay on her own. Tom didn't know she'd been sleeping on the old sofa bed at Maureen's. She poured herself another drink, didn't bother with tonic, didn't care it was burning her throat. She was worn to shreds. At that moment she saw it clearly; knew where the real trouble was — it was with Ursula. The battle was really Tom's problem. How could he demonstrate loyalty to his mother yet exhibit allegiance to his wife? Annie, she was caught in the middle.

"For Christ's Sake! Tom was an adult, a father. This was his second marriage. Why did he have to make a choice?

Annie suspected that somehow, (as crazy as it seemed) — that his mother was *evil*! Threads of these thoughts flew through her brain. You could go to central casting and wouldn't find a more malevolent character than Tom's mother. Ursula was manipulative, at times malicious. Oh hell, Annie was always thinking in terms of bete noire movies. Silly. Maybe the booze was exaggerating her judgment. Sure! Ursula's behavior was merely that of a strong-willed woman — albeit, a dominating mother-in-law. Forget about it! No! It was more than that. Tom's mother was sinister — someone who would destroy anything or anyone who got in her way.

What could she do? Annie felt powerless.

Like a tornado of truth and dare and life gone askew, Annie was suddenly overwhelmed by all that had happened to her and felt punch-drunk with self-pity. She'd grown up in some ways, down in others.

The down was the drinking. Sure, she knew something was wrong. She even went to an AA meeting or two in Queens after Tom told her how she'd behaved one night. She didn't remember any of the crazy things he told her she'd said at the family dinner. But she'd really crossed the line as far as Tom was concerned and embarrassed him in front of his mother and brother. And then when his mother commented about her conduct, Annie insulted her too. This was a no-no. No one hurt the feelings of Ursula, the overseer of the family.

Yes, sometimes she knew she drank too much, but not like the people she saw at AA meetings. They were really old and alcoholic. Not Annie. Besides, she didn't drink every day. Well, maybe sometimes. (She didn't know it then but *denial* was the name of the game.)

— ❧ —

The Whirlwind Courtship

They had met on March 4, 1967, married on May 16, 1967, and she was out of town, working in Cleveland part of that time. Talk about tumultuous. It was passionate, a magical, mysterious time, as close to whatever one thought of as love as she'd know in her lifetime. She adored him, every single atomic bit of him.

Annie never really liked how she looked. When she gazed into the mirror she didn't see a pretty face looking back. Even though others considered her attractive, and although she received her share of compliments, it didn't matter — she felt ordinary. But Tom had chosen *her*. That had to count for something.

He was so handsome…the first time she saw him, she thought he looked like that Italian movie star, Marcello Mastrionni. He had the same strong square jaw, perfect nose, a full head of wavy brown hair. And that he was also attracted to her was incredible. He was sexy, tender and very passionate. What a wonderful feeling to love someone who loves you. Oh when it was good, it was very, very good!

Now it hurt too damned much.

Why did opening yourself up, being in love, taking risks have to ache so much? She desperately wanted to hear his voice, go to sleep every night with his warm, sexy body beside her.

The sex was so good that once Tom joked that *even the neighbors had a cigarette.* The Irish side of him had a sardonic wit. Too bad he was only half Irish. The Ryan aspect was the happier one. It was his Teutonic maternal traits that made him obdurate at times.

While they enjoyed each other physically, she couldn't fight it any longer — in bed they fit, out of it they fought. If only their entire marriage could take place between the sheets. Annie knew how ridiculous that was.

— ɶ —

"It's still a man's world, women's lib or not," Maureen said sympathetically as Annie walked into the living room. "Hey kiddo, I've got to get to work, and you're looking like a mess. Take a shower and go for a walk, for God's sake. You can't keep hiding out in here. Crying and feeling sorry for yourself isn't going to make a dent in this chaos," she added. Maureen was kindhearted, but she also suspected that the marriage between Tom and Annie was so volatile, it would never ever work.

"You've been phoning me every week telling me how awful you feel after he and you argue," she reminded Annie. "You have to get back in shape. Drinking in the morning, honey — now you know I'm not the kind to pass judgment, but this ethyl alcohol isn't going to solve the problem. It's going to make you feel worse. It's a *depressant*. I know. I've been off the sauce for three months now. And I feel much, much better. Just smoke joints if you want to zone out a little. Maybe you ought to see a shrink or something?"

"Oh Maureen, I know you make sense. You're a good friend and I can be a pain, I know. I'll drink less, I promise. Thanks for being here for me."

"Don't worry about it. I learned a long time ago that if you're too busy to be there for a friend, then you're too busy," Maureen answered, lighting a cigarette.

"Remember this: Men still rule. We just don't get the same picks and choices," Maureen continued, pouring herself a quick cup of coffee. "Let's face it, there are too damned many married ones and too many gay ones, and too many who play games. Besides, there are many more of us than them, kid. It's not even. It's not fair. It never will be," Maureen added, putting her empty cup onto the pile of dishes sitting in the sink.

"You have to stop this downward curve you're on," Maureen added. "Christ, Annie, pull yourself out of this, or get some professional help. You've been in a crying jag for the last week. It's senseless, Tom's got a dark side to him, Annie, you just couldn't see it, not the way you met and married so quickly. It was a damned cyclone of a courtship. You've admitted that yourself!"

"Cyclone? Totally! We met through that ad I placed, and we didn't see each other much before I left for the interview for the agency job, but we spoke every night, sometimes as long as 2-3 hours, even when I was in Cleveland, Maureen. There was this immediate warmth, connection. It was definitely love at first sight. The chemistry was there. I loved the way he looked, his hands, his face, his voice. He was so dynamic and he seemed to feel the same magnetic draw towards me. Why wouldn't I think it was real? And why couldn't it last?"

"You are a dyed-in-the-wool romantic! What is real, Annie? What can we believe in?" said Maureen. "Why do so many of our hopes and dreams end up evaporating like we're stuck in some quicksand? We're sinking, going under, and poof! He's gone! That special man is no longer there."

Annie just shook her head; she was exhausted with the trueness.

"Come to think of it, why do they all have to say that they love me as they're having their orgasm and why do even I believe some of the sons of bitches anyway?" Maureen took another drag on her cigarette, then put it out. "They're all scum bags, at least 80 percent of them are, Annie. Look how many marriages end in divorce. Men are led by their penises — like Geiger counters. All they really care about is a good fuck."

Annie ignored her friend's bitter testimonial. "He'll call me, I'm not going to call him. It was his fault. He has a terrible temper, but it's so hard, so daunting without him," Annie reasoned, still totally absorbed in her mental masturbation. "Yes I know he sometimes is immature. But he's been through so much and he can be so loving too." Annie looked at her glass. "Get me some ice, hon?"

"You've had more than enough," Maureen chided her. "You've spent the last week sleeping on my couch and drinking most of the time; not that I don't want you, but aside from the sofa not being very comfortable, you have to get out of this terrible state you're in. You've got to start working again. I can get you some catalog work to do. Altman's will be doing their back-to-school supplement soon. Let me talk to them. And by the way, how can Tom call you when he doesn't know where you are?"

"He knows I'd probably come here. You're about the only single friend I have. Maybe that's why he resented you. He thought I envied your freedom. And in a way I did. I felt like a prisoner out there. Tom was the one with the wheels, the ability to go where he wanted. When we had an argument, he wouldn't talk, he'd just take off in the car. It was awful, being out there in the boondocks all alone. It's not what I thought it was going to be. But I still love him, oh God, how I love him, even when he's getting mean on me."

"Mean? Abusive is what you should be saying. You already told me he's hit you twice. Annie, that's no good, it's wrong, it shows a darker, violent side to Tom."

"But I provoked it," she said imperceptibly, biting her lip. While it was hard to admit, Annie knew Tom had an impenetrable part to him, something in his past that affected his mood, that could bring rage to the surface. All those times she was awakened by soft sobbing noises, he had to be reliving something gloomy from long ago. Was it his first wife's sudden death that was so disturbing? He wouldn't talk about it. Ever.

It had been a rocky year. They fought bitterly, reconciled, separated, and then came back together, desperately craving one another. Always the passion, the lovemaking was good. He kept promising not to get angry, and then she'd say something stupid, and he would go over the edge again.

Twice he took Colleen and headed for his mother's house. That bitch, Annie thought — No! Annie never could feel convivial toward his tall, blonde, very opinionated mother. Ursula always took Tom's side, even when he was wrong. And oh how she loved it when Tom came home. "I told you so," was written all over the smirks upon her face.

— ∞ —

It didn't help that Tom lost his first wife in such a tragic manner. Patty had died suddenly at age 32. It happened soon after they buried their second child, a son — Kevin, who had died of leukemia on his first birthday.

It was a real Irish nightmare. The poor woman had buried her pain in booze. Tom told Annie that it was from cirrhosis of the liver — that he never knew Patty was really drinking that much.

After their baby boy had taken sick Patty began her hidden drinking. Tom was working two jobs. (He later admitted he was also "running around.") How could he know that his little girl Colleen was not being properly fed? Patty was falling apart — running back and forth to the hospital to spend time with the baby, who was growing progressively worse. So she drank. And swallowed her misery.

"Tom, I think Patty is drinking too much," her mother Noreen had warned. She spoke to him more than once about her concern. Nonsense! He said it was only because the baby was so sick. He didn't see it as a real problem; it was easier than asking questions.

Patty was the nervous type. They'd married too young when both were 18. The first baby was stillborn, then two years later Colleen came along and then little frail Kevin. Now Kevin had died. Patty was devastated — she just couldn't get over it.

Three months later, one hot August night, his wife had sat up in bed and let out this awful moaning sound, (which he later realized was a death rattle,) and just fell back and died right there beside him.

Tom's mother never cared for Patty. Ursula was unyielding. They were too young to marry, this was a mammoth mistake. She damned well knew that Patty Sunshine would never make a good wife. Still, Ursula, always concerned with propriety, visited the baby in the hospital, even went over to Tom and Patty's house a couple of times but was irritated with her daughter-in-law's sloppy housekeeping. Dishes were piled up in the sink, dirty laundry on the floor and Patty, she was either crying or sleeping or drinking too much. What a spineless woman she was.

"She never kept a clean house," commented the first-generation German woman who had married Tom's Irish father. "She got Tom to marry her. *Trapped* him. Patty was pregnant, you know," she said with a smirk. "Then the baby boy — he got leukemia. A real curse on the family. He didn't make it. Patty fell apart. She was weak. Too fragile. She smoked like a chimney and probably was drinking then too. When she lost that first baby, that's when my Tom should have walked out. That Patty was very mixed up," Ursula added with little sympathy. "She hurt Tom — and in the end left him a young widower with a child to raise."

Ursula, who doted on her two sons, never thought any girl was good enough for them. Her sons were *special*. They went for dumb women, though somehow she suspected that Annie wasn't so dumb. But she was also a *Jewess*. Her son had married a *Jew*. Maybe that's why she resented Annie even more.

Her older son, Joe, 38, was already divorced and remarried. A handsome chap, Joseph Ryan was 6 feet tall, blond and blue-eyed and more Arian looking like his mother. Tom looked more like his Black Irish dad. Joe wouldn't put up with any nonsense from a woman. His mother was right. His first wife was lazy and a gold-digger, she just couldn't tolerate his mother's imperious nature. The two women clashed. It couldn't last. And it didn't. No, Joe wouldn't put up with that kind of disrespect. Ursula expected a lot from her darling sons. Tall, beautiful, used to getting her own way, she adored them and they adored her right back. Too much.

They wanted someone just like mom. Mom was a tall, 5'6" beautiful blonde who was very disciplined, very dominating, very selfish. On the living room wall hung an oil painting of Ursula. It was unusual to have a portrait painted of oneself in the middle-class community in which they lived. But she wanted it and Tom Sr., did whatever his wife required.

As for Patty's untimely death, Tom had some sense of humiliation — a deep, all pervasive guilt about it all. Annie wasn't sure why, but she thought he blamed himself, though he would never admit it.

She knew it bothered him, that his in-laws reviled him and held him responsible. He felt at fault, that was obvious; but he refused to talk about it. All Annie knew was the little he'd shared when they first met. That first night he poured out his heart. He described how she had died so suddenly, how he had called his brother to help, how much of a shock it was to everyone, how Patty's family blamed him.

It was only when Tom's older brother Joe arrived at the apartment that the police were called. Later they phoned other family members. Then they made a startling discovery. Before awakening Colleen to take her to Ursula's, they opened the three year old's dresser drawers. There they discovered the empty vodka bottles, dozens of them, hidden, displacing most of the attire. There was no clean clothing for the child to wear. Was Patty crying out for help by hiding all those bottles instead of throwing them out? Now they'd never know.

Why didn't he look before? Why didn't he know Patty was drunk most of the time? Why didn't he pay attention to his mother-in-law's warnings. He couldn't deal with it. Tom took Colleen and went back to his parent's home on Breezy Point. It turned out the child was severely malnourished. While Patty drank away the better part of the day, her little girl would nibble on cookies and crackers, whatever she could find. Tom's mother was furious. "See what this woman was like," she spit out. "You never should have married her, my dear son. Now you have a child to worry about." Ursula nursed Colleen back to good health, cursing her dead daughter-in-law over and over again. At least now she had her son back with her.

Then just 10 months after his wife had died so suddenly Tom met Annie. You can imagine what his mother thought about that!

And what about Tom? If he wanted to think about it, but who wanted to think about anything — when he first met Annie she was drunk. She got off the damned plane smashed as can be. He should have run the other way. In fact he had to pull over to the side at La Guardia Airport, because while they had met through that personals ad, and spent quite a few nights talking on the phone, all he knew was that she lived in Greenwich Village, but not exactly where.

He sat there, quietly, in the car, for more than an hour, while Annie slept it off. He told her later that he thought she was pretty, looked a lot like that actress, Natalie Wood...but wow was she zonked. Yet he found himself immediately attracted to this girl he hardly knew. How lucky was she! How naive was he?

The reason Annie was so drunk had to do with her fear of flying. She had always been afraid. That's why she felt so comforted when the nice voice on the phone that turned out to be Tom's told her he'd be happy to pick her up at the airport after her initial weekend interview in Cleveland. He seemed so warm, so understanding.

Annie had flown to Ohio with immense trepidation. It was her first out-of-town job interview and she wasn't sure what lay ahead. Fortunately, she liked Rob Matthews, the president of the agency, and he liked her and her work. He offered her the job. Oh my God, she was being hired to write television advertising in Cleveland. Annie was thrilled to death. Then, just before she was scheduled to leave she heard about it — there had been a major airplane crash.

The kindly hotel bellman told her about the plane crash. "I have a bad feeling, mam, that there'll be another one. It's very stormy out there," said the elderly Black man. "If I were you I'd wait 'til the storm clears up."

That was more than enough for Annie. She rescheduled the flight, went down to the package store and bought herself a bottle of vodka, a container of orange juice and proceeded to spend the next 3 hours getting zonked. Good. She wouldn't feel a thing on the plane. She called Tom and asked if he'd meet the later flight. Of course he would.

And that is how six hours later the two of them had met. An out-of-the-ordinary start to an even more extraordinary relationship. *The love of her life.*

— ଔ —

— ✂ —

Chapter 13

Christmas Eve, 1969

They drove back from Breezy Point late that Christmas night. The exchange of presents, the smiles and kisses were over. Of course, the kids had fun; it was Christmas time at the Ryan's. There was laughter and kissing, but underneath the phony holiday cheer, there was only angst and misgivings.

While the atmosphere seemed hospitable, it didn't include Annie. As usual, she felt left out. After all this time she recognized the harsh reality — that she really wasn't accepted — the family just tolerated her, the Jewish girl who'd married their darling Tom.

Worse, although she'd gone to so much trouble to beautifully wrap Tom's mother's present, and most important, had spent far too much on the gift — a stunning pearl necklace with sapphire clasp — it was received with a cold kiss, like it really didn't matter at all to Ursula.

It did indeed matter. Annie had put the expensive necklace

on their charge account without Tom's knowledge. When the bill arrived she was home, got the mail, was able to tear it up. But she was worried about the next month. Maybe when the next bill arrived he'd be home and get to the mailbox before her. Oh my God! When Tom discovered what she'd spent he'd be very angry. The necklace had cost $300 at Fortunoff's, more, much more, than Tom's weekly paycheck. What was she thinking!

What a waste. Her mother-in-law couldn't care less what she bought her. Annie finally got it: there was no damned way she'd ever impress her, nor win her respect, never mind her affection. Truly, she was tired of trying and sick of the way she was treated by Tom's family. It was almost like a cartoon, this thing about in-laws, but it was real life and it hurt. Annie was the outsider — she'd never belong. Even her sister-in-law Margaret, had a holier than thou attitude.

"You know she did it for spite, Tom," Annie cried, tears floating down her face. "Margaret knows I have good taste, why would she give me *plastic*? A cheap *plastic* wallet for Christmas?" she complained, not really expecting Tom to give her an answer. How could he? On some level she knew he knew she was right.

For the love of Christ! Leave me alone," he yelled back. "So she's not so thoughtful. Why do you always have to put me in the middle? How does Margaret know that you think the wallet is crap? Maybe it's all she could afford. Just forget it, okay? If you're not nagging about my mother, or my brother, then it's about Margaret. I'm sick of it, damn it," Tom answered, gritting his teeth.

He had a habit of setting his jaw when he was angry. You could see the muscles and veins tense up on his temples. It was a warning that she'd better slow up on him. So then why did she never heed the warning?

"You women are all the same, fighting like cats and dogs" he continued, obviously annoyed. "I told you a long time ago, stop nagging me about my family. You don't like 'em, then stay home.

I don't need you to go with me. You only aggravate my mom, anyway. She saw how you didn't like the turkey she made. You didn't even touch your plate. So she's not the best cook, but she's my mother, damn it."

"And how come she opened the velvet box, and saw the beautiful pearl necklace — she held it up, and then didn't even try it on? How come? It was beautiful...and it was *real*, Tom, I made sure we gave her a really nice gift."

"Yeah? Where'd you get the money from?" he asked.

Ignoring him Annie continued, "You never ever take my side, honey, never." She tried to say it softly, afraid of angering him any more than this, hoping to gain his sympathy, some understanding of why she felt so hurt. She saw she wasn't getting to him; that he just wasn't listening. It was so damned frustrating.

Tom said nothing and drove on. She felt his rage, the fury he inevitably displayed if she said anything about his family.

But she was like a time bomb, ticking away. Annie couldn't hold it in any longer. Enough was enough. She felt a rush of adrenaline, a fury that couldn't be held back, that came from some dark place inside her that was a hurt from long ago. She had to speak up. To tell Tom how she really felt — how hurt and upset she was. But it was senseless because he wouldn't really hear her, understand her feelings, but only care if what she was saying affected *him* in any way. It was a spiral of futility – this arguing, this trying to make the man listen. He just couldn't or wouldn't do it.

"Okay. You win. I don't want to go out there any more. I've had it with your family and that *Eva Braun*. She obviously hates me. She's probably having a bund meeting in the morning," Annie added, referring to the Germanic background of her mother-in-law who never let Annie forget that she was Jewish.

Damn it! Annie knew it annoyed Tom when she called his

mother 'Eva Braun', but hell, the woman was so mean, so cold. And really — she only cared about her darling sons. In Annie's desperate and imaginative mind, Ursula was as rotten as Hitler's girlfriend. Besides that, half the time Annie didn't care what she'd say to get Tom's attention. She hated it when he ignored her. That was the worst of all. He had a way to freeze her out, to detach. More than anything, she couldn't stand Tom acting indifferent towards her. No, Annie couldn't shut up, she had to talk and talk and talk, to answer him back. She couldn't hold it in any longer.

"I hate your family, the whole freaking group of them, they're only out for themselves!" she shouted.

"Cut it out already. Can't you shut up and give me a little peace? Why do you always end up complaining about them? Damn it, your people don't even celebrate Christmas anyway, so what's the difference? You know I hate it when you jab and dig and jab and dig into my mom. Leave her alone, for God's sake. So — she's not in love with you. She didn't marry you. I did. What the hell do you want from me? What do you care, what anyone in my family thinks, as long as I love you?"

Love? Annie wondered if Tom really loved her, when he talked about Christmas and Jews the way he did. She was sure his family was a bunch of anti-Semites. She had a feeling that Tom had his own hang-ups. Even though he didn't go to church or anything, she knew it bothered him that she wasn't a Christian. Ironically, it was the first time she felt Jewish and proud of it.

She'd use this difference between them to tell him of all the people — celebrities, sports heroes, writers who were Jewish. She'd go on and on in a litany of tribute to Jewish creativity and talent. "*White Christmas* it was written by a Russian Jew, Irving Berlin. He also wrote *God Bless America*, and he donated all the money from this song to the Boy Scouts. That's kind of great, Tom. And you always love Kirk Douglas in the movies, well he's Jewish. Paul Newman, he's half Jewish. Same with Goldie Hawn. Most of the songs you like so much — Jews wrote them. George Gershwin, Stephen Sondheim. You like *West Side Story*, don't you? Well Jews wrote it. You know, Jewish people only make up 2 percent of the American population – yet look at all they've contributed to American culture — yet you and your family, somehow underhandedly, you put my people down. And what about Jesus Christ, Tom? He was a rabbi, a Jew. What can you say to that?" Annie ranted on and on.

"Help! Somebody! How can I get his attention?" she screamed without a sound.

Tom had no answer. No answer at all. Maybe he wasn't even listening.

Come to think of it, Annie realized, there had always been an undercurrent, a sense that she and Tom were different from one another, that there was something separating their true union. That's why they'd rushed and gotten married at City Hall and did it secretly — before letting his family know they'd wed. Before anyone could put a stop to it.

To tell the truth, Annie hadn't told her family about Tom, about their marriage either, not for months. When she finally had the courage to tell them, the reaction was odd and edgy. Then she brought him to dinner. She knew they were surprised that she'd married such a handsome young man. But while her parents were polite, and her grandmother seemed pleased and had kissed him on the cheek, overall the meeting was strained. They couldn't accept that Annie Rosenberg was now Annie Ryan. "A goy, she's married a goy," is all her mother kept saying after they left.

No one gave them a wedding present. Well, her grandmother did put a 50-dollar bill in her pocket that night and told her not to say anything. But there were no real acknowledgments, gifts. That was like disregarding that they were even married. It hurt.

Twice, Annie invited her parents to their new apartment. Twice they came up with excuses. Then Colleen turned four and she hoped they'd come to the birthday party. This time they sent a gift. She gave up. They'd never understand. She hadn't married a nice Jewish dentist or doctor or accountant. No, a fireman, a non-Jew. Evidently this was unacceptable to her family. As if they were such pious Jews.

Annie laughed inwardly, recalling her long relationship with Roosevelt. God if they'd ever known about him they would sit *Shiva*; she'd indeed be dead to them. Well, at least Joanie had sent them a wedding card and a bottle of champagne. Her sister understood when she'd said she had finally found someone she could really love. But the rest of her family just didn't accept him, them, the marriage — it was heartbreaking.

So what kept them together when so much could keep them apart? It was a burning intensity between Annie and Tom, a passion that unrelentingly held them together despite all the differences, in spite of all the fights. When the enmity was all over — well, they fit like tea spoons, perfectly together, legs entwined, always holding one another when they went to sleep — no matter what was said to one another during the day. Oh lord, it was so good when they were close and loving – why couldn't it last?

— ❧ —

Tom turned the corner. In a few more minutes they'd reach their house. He was obviously angry. That would mean another argument if Annie didn't back off. Colleen was fast asleep in the back seat; happy with the toys she'd received. But Annie was still miserable. No, she wouldn't let it go. Her judgment, affected by the scotch she'd drunk, and the two valiums she popped before they'd left for the Christmas Eve dinner was off. Mixed up, drugged up, she was fueled and furious.

Annie's mind was racing. No, she wouldn't put up with this shabby treatment. She knew she deserved better. Why couldn't he listen? How could she ever get through to him? It was like talking to a man whose head was encased in a giant plastic bubble. "Knock, knock, can't you hear me?" she thought.

She especially resented his smart-ass brother, Joe calling her 'Tom's Jewish Rose'. Damn it, Annie couldn't shut up. "Your family is prejudiced, that's what. And Breezy Point, it's all Irish and German and Catholic and there are no Jews out there, admit it, for God's sake, admit it," she screamed.

He turned and slapped her hard, so hard her head snapped against the side window of the car. She shut up fast. Colleen began to awaken. She hated the child to see his rage, their fighting. God, she felt trapped.

The next morning Annie awakened with a terrible hangover. And with a black eye. When she looked in the mirror, she saw the black and blue marks, the cut above her eye. Evidently the alcohol had kept her from really feeling the pain. Now, it stung and she hated most of all that after he had hit her — he didn't even say he was sorry. She hoped the dark glasses would hide the marks. She was badly bruised. Inside and out.

Annie spent the rest of the afternoon sipping carefully from the last bottle of vodka she'd hidden under the towels in the linen closet. She turned on the television and watched *It's A Wonderful Life*. But it wasn't a wonderful life for her and Tom was no Jimmy Stewart. Where was Clarence, the angel that rang the bell? She needed an angel. Someone to watch over her. Why were there only happy endings in the movies?

She took a swig directly from the bottle – bitter awful tasting liquor swallowed up in desperate despair. She didn't know what to do. Or did she and was she just too damned afraid to do it? It wasn't working out, and now that he'd hit her like that, she was afraid of where it was going.

The nights Tom worked Annie would phone everyone she knew to complain about what was going on. But this time almost everyone she knew wasn't home. Besides most of them were tired of hearing her whine and bitch about her marital problems. She'd ask for help and then never follow their advice.

She'd try to dull the horrible anger and frustration that was building up in her, but she didn't know what would make it stop. Why did he always strike out at her? Because he was bigger, and stronger, one of New York's Bravest.

"There's nothing brave about hitting a defenseless woman," Maureen had reminded her, more than once. But then Maureen didn't know how Annie provoked him, made Tom so angry he had to strike back. It was partly her fault, wasn't it? Yes, she wouldn't stop talking, she couldn't stop talking, and it was her only way to vent her emotions and to try to reach out to this man. Tom couldn't deal with Annie. He'd go out and play hours of handball down at the city park. He worked off some energy that way. If she started nagging him at night and he didn't want to answer — he'd get dressed, get the keys to his car and he'd drive away. It drove her crazy!

"It's the shout and pout syndrome," Maureen told her. "When are you going to get it, hon? He's never, ever going to hear you!"

One day Tom came home to Annie's pent up anger. And boy was she angry. As soon as she began complaining he locked himself in the bathroom. She'd been drinking. It enhanced every annoyance, frustration, lack she felt. Annie crazily spent a frantic fifteen minutes banging and kicking on the bathroom door. The heel marks would remain. Finally she found a screwdriver and was ineptly trying to remove the hinges (she was never good with tools) when Tom pulled the door open, his face red with rage, the veins in his neck erupting.

Why did he have to hide from her, play sick games with her, what was he doing in the bathroom? Her throat was sore from yelling, her eyes red from crying. He didn't say much, just a "hon," and a look at Annie that told her this time he was sorry. She loved when he called her honey or hon. Those were the sweetest times.

After Annie's tirade she retreated to their bedroom, and lay down atop the soft down bed covers. Tom soon followed her in, leaned down to stroke her shoulders, kissed her, and soon they made love. Of course the lovemaking was always good after the frenzy. What a way to relate, this on again, off again craziness.

He was her fix, her addiction. Better to be arguing with him around, then for him to be at work and her feel lonely. That's when she did most of the drinking. Annie knew booze exacerbated everything. But she didn't know how to deal with the marriage — or for that matter life on life's terms. She had to numb herself somehow and ethyl alcohol was her drug of choice.

"I don't want to talk, you're crazy," he'd say when she'd had too much to drink and was nagging him about some imagined or real hurt. But with alcohol to steel her nerves — she felt out of harm's way. Of course it wasn't true, but what did she know.

Some times she'd grow so exasperated at his refusal to discuss what was bothering her she'd throw something. Once, Annie threw an ashtray at Tom and grazed the side of his head, leaving a good size cut. That time, in a rage, having just come home and still wearing his heavy black fireman's boots, he kicked her hard in the left leg, and then took off. The welt was awful, and a permanent scar remained on her leg, one that would remind her of how crazy their fights could become. It was awful, what they were doing to one another.

Another time after a particularly vicious argument, Annie picked up the phone to call someone. He hated this — he knew she'd be whining away about him. In a frenzy, Tom ripped the telephone wire out of the wall. He got into the car and drove off. Damn it. How frustrating it was for her when he ran away like that. And she had nowhere to go.

Why was Annie the one left behind and helpless? Part of the

answer was that she didn't know how to drive. It was a bus ride to the subway, a major trek on her own. What the hell was she doing out in Queens anyway? Tom was right, she missed the Manhattan scene, and felt lost out there in that bedroom community. All the women in their apartment complex — they were pregnant or already had one or two kids and their interests were so different from Annie's. They wanted to talk about soap operas. She wanted to stop living one.

Sometimes she'd get a glimmer of self-honesty. She realized she was drinking to hide the pain and that even the drinking wasn't working any longer; it was making her horribly depressed. She resented feeling like a prisoner, of feeling dominated and worse, mistreated. It wasn't what she wanted out of a marriage. She'd seen enough of her father's rages. Was she repeating a pattern? She couldn't go to her family for help, all they'd say is *"I told you so."*

Annie staggered into the next room, unsteady on her feet. She'd taken a Valium as soon as she'd awakened. Now with the vodka she was good and numb. Colleen was down the hall at Dottie's apartment playing with her little friend, Joseph. Dottie didn't mind babysitting. Besides, the four year-olds played well together.

Suddenly Annie focused on the artificial 5 foot Christmas tree that Tom and she had picked out together. She'd tried to make it into a special event, their very first Christmas in this new apartment. She bought an abundance of beautiful trimmings for the tree. Dazzling red globes, metallic green ornaments, crystal white teardrop lights. Their tree could win an award; she'd made it so pretty, so special. Tom helped Annie put the star on top and for a few days there was peace. They kissed and hugged and loved each other so. It was fun, buying toys for Colleen, gifts for each other, to place the wrapped presents under the tree for Christmas morning. When it was good, it was perfect.

Now after the holiday, and the awful fight Christmas night,

Tom was working an overtime shift while Annie was home, alone, hurting, disgusted, angry, as angry with herself as she was with him. She hated his night shifts, worse when he volunteered for a double shift to make more money. She was alone too often. And too far away, isolated from friends in the city.

The tree, it's lights out, the presents beneath it long gone, stood silently in the corner of the living room. Suddenly it took on a life of its own. Annie saw it as the enemy, as the symbol of Tom and his phony kissy-huggy relatives who went to church and didn't know the true meaning of Christmas anyway. She'd tried so hard. She wanted to be happy, to make him happy, to please. But it hadn't worked. She ran to the tree, pulled the outlet from the wall, and with strings of lights and wires hanging, and some of the fragile glass Christmas bulbs shattering as she dragged it off it's stand, Annie pulled it across the room, knocking a crystal bowl off the coffee table as she headed towards the terrace.

As she dragged the large inanimate object, she felt the sharp artificial pine needles uncomfortably close, as if the tree was fighting back, trying to save itself from the fate she'd decided for it. Annie used one hand to slide open the windowed doors to their terrace. They'd rented the top floor — a 2-bedroom apartment on the 6th floor, just enough height to make a dramatic difference. With as much force as she could muster, she flung the tree with all the lights and bulbs on it over the brick edge of the terrace wall. She was dizzy, she was drunk, and she felt wonderful, absolutely wonderful as she heard it go crashing down, down, down to the back alley. It was perfect and dramatic enough to satisfy her hurt. Annie didn't care what the hell the neighbors thought; she knew they already knew too much, hearing their fights late at night. She'd show Tom how mean he was, how selfish, how their marriage was no damned good. Destroying the tree was telling him he'd destroyed her dreams, damn it! Didn't he get it? That he was breaking her heart?

"Hey what the hell is going on up there," she heard Clancy, the super, yell. "Who the fuck threw a tree off the terrace? You can kill someone you dummy!" he yelled even louder. Annie ducked quickly and went back into their apartment. It was done; she'd made her decision. Now was the time.

Annie called a private cab company. Since Tom was working a double shift, she'd have more than enough time to take Colleen out to his mother's. This was it. She'd saved the $118.00 with which she was supposed to pay the rent. (He didn't know that their December rent wasn't paid.) She'd hidden the cash knowing she might have to use it to get away.

Any money she had now, Tom gave to her. She hadn't earned much free-lancing, and Annie was tired of having to ask him for anything at all. It was almost as bad as asking her mother for money. Maybe she married her mother? He was certainly cheap like she was. "You never shut the lights out when you leave the room, it's just wasting electricity!" he'd remind her. "Don't you have any value for money?" he'd ask, annoyed, when she came home with too many non-essential grocery items. Annie took to hiding the extra cake and cookies she bought as treats for Colleen. "The kid doesn't need so many cookies. And they're expensive too," he'd complain. He was tightfisted, and she was tired of it. He even complained about how much money she'd spent on a party dress for Colleen. Then, sadly, she remembered how generous Roosevelt had always been, and wondered why this man she'd married, whom she loved until it hurt, was so begrudging with both his money and his emotions.

She used most of the rent money for the cab trip to freedom. True, she'd left before, and yes she'd returned. But this time was different. She couldn't do it any longer. Annie was frightened to death of what lay ahead for her, of starting over without Tom, but she was even more terrified of staying there. The fights had escalated to the point where it was unsafe. She knew she'd have to leave, to escape right now.

The reconciliations were mostly on Annie's part – a phone call to the firehouse made from a bar she'd visited on a lonely night, and then they would meet and make love and they'd try again. Leaving while he was at work was a dull, unhappy alternative to staying on — praying the marriage would improve when it was only becoming sicker. She was gasping for independence, mixed up, scared, and knowing her life was at stake. "Please, God, please," she prayed, "Help me to leave. And help me to stay away."

It had begun to snow as she piled her one suitcase full of clothes and little Colleen into the taxicab. Annie was feeling no pain. Sure she was drunk, but she couldn't have done it sober. It was too damned hard to leave this kid who called her mommy, whom she adored, but Annie knew he'd never let her keep Colleen. Besides, how could she support her, when she'd have to get a full time job? Who'd take care of her? Tom had never agreed to her adopting the child, so it had to be this way, she had to let go once and forever no matter the pain.

"I love you my darling little sweet one," Annie said softly to Colleen, hugging the little girl, who looked confused and frightened. "You have to stay with grandma for now; daddy will see you later," she added.

"But I want to stay with you, Mommy, please, please, don't leave me," Colleen said, tears streaming down her cheeks. It was an awful moment; one Annie would remember the rest of her life. God, why did little innocent children have to suffer because of the acts of their parents, and why did this darling child have to get left and hurt so badly not once but twice?

When the cab approached the house in Breezy Point Annie kissed Colleen for the last time. "Driver, I can't go to the front door, please, go ring the bell and bring her in for me, I'll wait here."

It was a terrible moment. The snow was falling with more vengeance now, the Christmas lights were still on all over and there she was giving away this darling little child who really loved and needed her. "Oh God help me do this. Don't be angry with me. I don't know what else to do, God. I'm so afraid and so hurt and I just can't go on this way," she cried in the empty night. She had to let go, Annie knew. For it was survival. She had to get away. It was agonizing but the pain in the end outweighed the pleasure.

"I love you, Colleen, always remember that, I love you," Annie cried, not being able to avoid tears of her own. She could barely swallow; the lump in her throat was so big. Oh it was awful, so horrible to leave this child this way. She was abandoning her, and she knew it. But Annie didn't know what else to do — she had to save herself.

And finally, on that December 26th of 1969, she had left him for good.

— ❦ —

"One never notices what has been done; one can only see what remains to be done."
— *Marie Curie*

— ⚭ —

Chapter 14

T he taxi driver took her all the way into the village, to Bleecker St. where Maureen was now living.

"If you need to, you can stay here until you get on your feet," Maureen suggested. "And by the way, there's a job open in Macy's advertising department. Heard about it through the grapevine." Maureen was still working at Altman's; had even obtained a raise. She felt damn good about it.

Macy's might be a step down, but hell, Annie needed a job. After getting her feet wet writing for an ad agency before the marriage, she'd hoped to continue on that level — except that during one of their many arguments, Tom had taken her portfolio of clippings, the ones she needed to show during an interview. It was his way of trying to control her, she knew it. Tom was always threatened by Annie's work. The portfolio represented independence. Now she'd no idea where it was. But, what the hell, she wasn't feeling that good about herself — right now she'd take anything.

The booze was wearing off. As much as she ached with the horrible hurt she was feeling, Annie knew there really wasn't any other solution than the one she'd chosen. Still she was filled with doubt and self-pity. The liquor was a depressant and didn't help her mood. Oh Lord, it hurt so damned much. How do you give up the love of your life and also let an innocent child go in the snow? Slowly, slowly, she knew.

While it was dreadful, the common sense element within her told her she had to move on — that she really didn't have a choice. Damned if this wasn't exactly like an addiction. Because with everything she knew on an intellectual level, Annie was dazed, stuck in a groove that kept her feeling desolate without Tom. "*Please God, please help me to stay away,*" she prayed, frightened and forlorn, while on the contrary — to the world she'd show a resolute front — (though it was faintly tinged with anger).

"I swear, Maureen — right now I hate every man walking the face of the earth. I had to be hit between the eyes — and without a wooden plank — before I finally left," she sobbed. "This time it's for good."

"Isn't it amazing – the shit men pull? I will never understand how they justify their treatment of women to themselves. Is there a gene that makes them say one thing with all sincerity and then drop off the face of the earth?" Maureen answered. "Men are mostly A-holes, my dear!"

It was a brittle Saturday morning, the hint of new snow in the air. They sat over coffee, talking. Annie promised Maureen that she'd go to a nearby Alcoholics Anonymous meeting. Maureen had the presence of mind to call ahead. There was a meeting on Perry Street in the West Village. "I promise, I'll go, I'll get to the one that begins at 3 p.m." Annie said.

She didn't know it then, but she'd begin learning, a day at a time, how to stay away from this formidable mood-changer that she'd finally admitted had a control over her.

Maureen lit another cigarette. "Think of it this way — at least

Tom revealed his true colors before it was too late. Once he raised his hand to you, you should have left, honey. It would have only gotten worse. You could have been killed. Who knows — maybe his in-laws were right and he murdered his wife. From what you've told me, his running around while their poor baby was dying of leukemia, he certainly wasn't a star husband, hon," she said, taking a puff.

"Oh Maureen, he may be immature and have a temper, but Tom didn't kill his wife."

Maureen shook her head from side to side. "Well have it your way. I'm not so sure. But at least, you finally saw the truth, Annie. Thank God you're out of it."

While Maureen readily dispensed advice Annie knew that what she was telling her to do was not that easy. Hell, Maureen had her own weaknesses. That's why for the last couple of years she'd stayed totally away from men.

Annie nodded. Her head was aching. She was all mixed up, tired, exhausted. Yet deep inside — somewhere within her weakest self she was playing mind games, all those *what-if's*, for she still dreaded being without Tom.

"I wish they would *all* go away," Maureen commented wryly, taking acigarette out and lighting it with the end of the one she'd just drawn her last puff from. "Not that they're standing in line outside my door these days. But half the time I'd just like to go to bed and pull the covers over my head."

Annie got up and poured herself another cup of coffee. "I have an awful headache. Let me get a couple of aspirins."

"Help yourself. They're in the medicine cabinet."

"You know something Annie? Now that I've passed my 30th birthday I've developed a theory — that most men are looking for a 20-year-old trophy – a long-legged blonde bimbo to boss around. No one's going to tell me what to do! I only hope the heart attack rate for men over 40 increases in proportion to their casting we older women away," she remarked.

Annie had to laugh at that. "Maureen, 30 is not old. Besides, you look like you're 19. Of course, smoking isn't great for the skin, and I notice you're doing too much of it. But really, you're so pretty. Lie about your age if you have to. But I don't think men are all that shallow. Hell, age is for wine and cheese. And besides you're beautiful. Just stop smoking, please."

"I know, I'm promising myself to stop again. I did for a while. It's an awful addiction and don't I know it."

The two women giggled. They knew there was still time — that in spite of everything they had their lives ahead of them — it wasn't too late to change course; there was still hope.

"Annie, when you're in a negative relationship, you feel lousy about yourself. It can do dreadful things to your self-esteem. But I hope you know you're very attractive — you look even prettier now, drinking or not. Maybe you've pickled yourself," Maureen said smiling. "But with your looks and good shape, you'll have no problems meeting men, but now — now isn't the time. You've got to get your priorities in order. First stop the drinking and the pill popping and get yourself a job. Please."

"You're right Maureen. The drinking is out of control. And I really don't know why I do it. I promise myself no more and then something sets me off and I drink again. I feel trapped. Sometimes it dulls the pain, other times it just calms me down. But it's a powerful, addicting drug. I know it."

"Hell, it isn't only the *Irish Virus*, girl. Though my dad had it big time," Maureen commented.

"As for Tom — no woman will ever be good enough for him in his mother's eyes. I am sick and tired of competing with her for his attention. It makes no sense. I think they're too close, that they have an unhealthy relationship."

"But *their* relationship is unimportant. *Your* relationship with yourself is," Maureen stressed. "You have to get to like yourself. Look in the mirror. You have gorgeous green eyes, you're really a pretty girl and bright, too. And you know you have a firecracker personality — I mean — you always make me laugh! But your self-esteem is way down there. Please, it isn't easy the way you feel right now, but try to listen to me, and focus on yourself, as painful as it is. I know; I've been there, done that, moved on."

"That you have. I admire your self-control."

"It isn't self-control alone. It's lots more. It was really a decision that I had to make after the hospital. I knew that taking men home was what led to my picking up a venereal disease, Annie. I have to be honest with you about it. And I had to face the hard facts that I almost died from the peritonitis. It's damaged my fallopian tubes. If I weren't so damned drunk, maybe I wouldn't have jumped into bed so casually. Now, sometimes I'll have a drink, but only at a party or special occasion."

Maureen, while she still drank, was now careful about how much and when. If she drank at all it would be at most two drinks; and for her this worked. She'd attended a few AA meetings herself, but felt that she was best off in the *adult children of alcoholics* get-togethers and went to this support group weekly. Her drinking had diminished greatly after her illness, and the job at Altman's gave her not only a decent salary but also solace.

— ❧ —

It wasn't as easy for Annie. She couldn't have just *one* drink. No matter how she tried, and God, she'd been "on the wagon" a dozen times; she couldn't go a day without the booze. For the longest time she needed it to feel whole, to feel okay. A year earlier, out in

Queens, she'd tried AA. There were too many housewives, too many gray-haired fat and boring people there. She was young, no — she wasn't like them. She stopped going to the meetings, still in denial.

Now this December 30, 1969, she'd go to a meeting, and another meeting, and still another, and finally, slowly, Annie would learn about the disease, and ultimately be relieved, that it *was* a disease, that there was medicine to treat it, that the medicine was the meetings, and they were free too. All you had to do was drop some coins in the basket they passed around. AA worked.

Eventually she'd immerse myself in the program that was begun the year she was born, when a country doctor, Dr. Bob, and a stockbroker named Bill Wilson, came together to help each other. It was a covenant of trust that would help them deal with their drinking problems and then share their discoveries with the world.

How fortunate that in 1935 two men formed an alliance that would eventually save millions of misspent lives. It would eventually be the 12 steps of this program that would be the support Annie would need to become honest with herself. Slowly, she'd learn how to grow up emotionally, to build self-esteem, to relate to people and situations without alcohol or the Valium she was also hooked on.

That New Year of 1970 would be a turning point. Annie had always been a people person, never a loner and so she stayed close to the people she met at AA. It turned out to be a superior form of group therapy, this 12-step program. She'd go every day and when she was aching for Tom, and her brain was spinning with old thoughts, she knew just what to do – she'd double up and go to two or even more meetings a day. She did whatever she had to do to keep from drinking, to keep from picking up the phone and calling Tom. She still missed him, but she couldn't go back.

After a while, the meetings became a good habit, and she'd look forward to the get-togethers, where Annie would see familiar faces, many of whom would become friends; friends of all persuasions. All sharing the same despair and need to turn their lives around. No matter if they were young like her or middle-aged, thin or fat or in-between — they were all hypersensitive and passionate, and every single one of them, when they first walked through the AA doors, was hurting like hell. She'd attend meetings with socialites and actresses, with priests and lawyers. There were members of every religion and color. No one was exempt from this universal disease.

— ❦ —

The 70s was a decade swarming with terrorism as American hostages were taken in Iran. It was also the time of national shock and shame and Watergate. Richard Nixon would resign in defeat and others would go to jail. Who to believe, who to believe? In 1973 the U.S. finally withdrew their troops from Vietnam. In all, 57,000 American men had died there. There had been no victory.

She needed to work and luckily landed a job in the ad department of Macy's department store, writing lack luster copy concerning bed linens and custom upholstery and window treatments. Boring. But it paid the bills.

Annie was lethargic spending half the day typing up lists, columns of numbers about how wide and long a window was and what drapery or curtains were available in which size. But it paid her enough to rent the cute studio apartment on Jane Street, so she could get off Maureen's sofa bed and on her own.

She not only made friends in the program, Annie had obtained a sponsor — Ilene Slovinski, a nice girl from Pennsylvania. While Ilene's background was vastly different than Annie's, they had a common cause — they shared the same disease.

Ilene grew up in a small town in Erie, Pennsylvania and had come to the Big Apple a decade before where she worked as a legal secretary. She was now 35. She also had sight in only one eye, which she carefully hid from the world with an artificial one. A childhood accident had resulted in losing her left eye. It never stopped Ilene from anything. She was earning a good living at a top law firm and more important, she'd recently celebrated five years of sobriety at the Mustard Seed, a small AA meeting held in a brownstone on East 37th Street.

Ilene was like a top sergeant, insisting Annie sit through the meetings from the opening through the Lord's Prayer. "You sat drinking more than an hour, sit here now. Listen, stay put, take it all in. You get well just by being here," she reminded her when Annie got edgy and wanted to go home. She was right. The famed doctor, Dr. Menninger once said that those who shared in the group therapy of Alcoholics Anonymous became "weller than well". Here was a place to share your deepest thoughts and fears in a non-judgmental atmosphere. It was honest, it was real, and it was necessary. And it would change Annie's life forever. Some day, she'd look back, and say, thank God I found AA.

— ❧ —

"Life is not lost by dying; life is lost minute by minute, day by dragging day, in all the thousand small uncaring ways."
— Stephen Vincent Benet

— ⊂℞ —

Chapter 15

Sabrina

April 1970 was also a turning point for Sabrina Aldrich. Her favorite pop group, The Beatles, announced they were breaking up their band, which proved to be the end of an era. She'd miss the mop-topped "Fab Four."

Besides enjoying pop music, show tunes and opera; Sabrina was a voracious reader. She rarely needed more than 5 hours sleep and so some nights she'd read an entire book. She savored the great American novelists of the 30s and 40s and was especially fond of Hemingway and Fitzgerald.

Sabrina took her reading seriously. F. Scott Fitzgerald once wrote that American lives had no second acts. "Wrong, Scotty," Sabrina thought. She'd have a second act and a third. With a serious and steely intent Sabrina was certain she'd meet any and all challenges with success.

Having been raised with many advantages, Sabrina was

uniquely secure in making choices and changes. Her belief in her own will was so strong that she literally thought that wishing for something would make it so. Some days she'd sit down, close her eyes and envision where she wanted to be and she knew if she wanted it enough eventually she'd be there. Long before the self-realization prophets came along, she was a case study in the visualization process that became popular in the 80s. Believe in achieving your goal, set your mind to it, visualize it and get it done!

Born during a hurricane in July of 1942, Sabrina was the only daughter born to the Aldrich's and so she was pampered much more than her two older brothers, one of whom followed his father into medicine, while the other became a prominent attorney.

"I had an idyllic childhood," Sabrina recalled. As a pony tailed, bobby-socked teen, her high school class voted her *Miss Greenwich Princess.*

"Actually, I was a goody-two-shoes. I never smoked, skipped school, did anything bad. I didn't want to disappoint my parents, who showed me such love and believed in me even before I did," she told an interviewer for *Life Magazine* years later.

After college, Sabrina decided to create a niche for herself in the business world. She'd embark on having a career.

At the beginning, it didn't go as well as expected. Unfortunately, because of her golden beauty Sabrina was often underestimated. Besides, it was the 60s and women's lib was just beginning. She had presence, style and poise, but she was a *woman*. It wasn't so easy back then.

While Jane Aldrich was glad her daughter was self-assured, she detected an ennui disheartening in such a young woman. "Perhaps we've given you too much," she told Sabrina. "Nothing seems to satisfy you any more."

"Mom, I know you're concerned, but honestly, I do have many

interests and real goals. What I've done is to set my sites *high* – after all, look at how much you and dad have accomplished. So I don't want to settle for second best at anything," she responded. Her mother smiled. "Good enough darling, and you know I'll support you in whatever you have the courage to take on."

Sabrina smiled, then kissed her mother affectionately on the cheek. Yes, she was serious. *Nothing* would stand in her way. Yet for all her talent and tough exterior, when it came to intimate relationships Sabrina could be vulnerable. She just didn't let people get that close to her, didn't bond easily. While she adored her parents and brothers, and trusted them implicitly, she was careful. She had few close friends through schooling and always kept a part of herself and her emotions concealed. Still, she did savor romance.

For a while Sabrina tried the singles scenes at hot new places like Maxwell's Plum. The swinging singles of the 1960s came to life in this theatrical restaurant that was opened in 1966 by the flamboyant restaurateur, Warner LeRoy. It achieved a social significance that rivaled the Stork Club of the 1940s and 50s and everyone from celebrities to girls from Brooklyn felt at ease at Maxwell's Plum. But Sabrina bored easily, didn't find any interesting men, and soon stopped frequenting the place.

She'd been copy chief at Altman's for two years. Lately she'd grown restless. She felt the fire within her, knew there was reason to stretch herself, to achieve higher objectives.

It was time to move on.

Besides being bored with her work, she was also bothered by her own bad behavior. For Sabrina had a little *secret*. Why she did it she didn't know, but she'd been having an affair with a married man. And that married man, Arnold Schoen, was in the higher echelons of the department store staff.

Worse, after the first few passionate times, Schoen turned out to be a lousy lover. He seemed distracted. She noticed that during their lovemaking he wouldn't remove his watch. The damned gold expansion band on the Rolex scratched her soft skin.

She especially found it offensive when one afternoon, he kept everything but his trousers on. "What is this all about, darling? Are you really in that much of a rush?" she asked sarcastically. He had smiled, undressed and later sent her three dozen roses. Big deal.

After the first few assignations it was like slam, bam, thank you mam. Beautiful, pampered, wanting more, she wouldn't put up with that. Sabrina was amazed at her own stupidity for getting involved in this manner. She realized it was no one's fault but her own. She felt empty, craved more. More of what she wasn't certain. What she did know is that she didn't go for superficial any things. She remembered her mother's caveat, her sage advice: "Sabrina, whatever you are willing to put up with, is exactly what you will have." Sabrina wasn't putting up with this shabby affair a moment longer.

Jane recognized her daughter's need to have everything fit just right. Of course, she knew this was impossible. "Sabrina, wisdom is really knowing when to avoid perfection," her mother counseled. But Sabrina, she didn't get it. Flawless, exacting, she still wanted perfection.

"Now, mother, you can't blame me for trying,"

"It's not perfection you're seeking, its control," her mother wisely stated.

"Mother, you may be right. But let me make my own mistakes. If I fall short again, I'll admit it. I'm not an idiot — I realize that I'm not doing well at finding a great guy. But then, you have him!" she added.

It would be hard finding anyone as terrific as her dad.

At first Arnold Schoen displayed the kind of self-assurance she liked. True he wasn't self-made and like her father, a doctor who contributed to saving lives, but he was smooth. She liked smooth.

Arnold had his moments of accomplishment. In crafting his own image, he'd gone to elaborate lengths to generate an aura of panache about him. He was definitely charismatic. Sabrina once had a schoolgirl crush on the actor Tony Curtis. "Yes, that's who Arnie reminds me of," Sabrina realized. Schoen had a similar facade with a broad smile, curly hair and a charming personality. She was attracted to him because he was young, smart and in a position of *power*. Sabrina was always attracted to power.

What Sabrina didn't realize was that Arnold Schoen was a survivor of the Sixties and that he was born into a poor, lower class family. He had suffered a few encounters with prejudice, growing up in a neighborhood where Jews were in the minority. *Matzos, Matzos, two for five, that's what keeps the Jews alive!* was chanted at him more than once as he walked home from school. It hurt. But education, the line of offense for most poor Jews, would gear him for success. And his good looks helped him make it to the top.

"I've got to dump him, and now," Sabrina decided. Now wasn't soon enough.

— ❧ —

Chapter 16

Arnold

Arnold Schoen's hard-working father, Abe, toiled in New York's garment industry — a *piece worker*, prodigiously sizing and cutting precious cloth for women's high-priced dresses, garb his wife could never afford.

A survivor of the depression, Abe Schoen was determined to give his children the things he never had. He and his wife Esther would do right by both of them. She was a very loving, giving mother, a good woman at home, while *Seventh Avenue*, the fashion center of New York gave him a decent enough living as long as he worked very hard. It was the overtime that made the difference.

"Success is getting up one more time," he'd often say and so he labored long hours without grumbling even though he'd arrive home so late his children were already asleep.

In the end, he spoiled his children with his largess.

Arnold got a car of his own at seventeen and successfully

seduced all the neighborhood girls. A vehicle wasn't really necessary, but he wanted it and he got it, even if it was an old 1949 Studebaker his father bought third-hand. His sister Judy was given piano lessons, expensive dresses from Bonwit's and was sent to an exclusive summer camp. Nothing was too good for the children.

Arnold attended the prestigious Bronx School of Science High School, obtaining good enough grades to win a partial scholarship to Oberlin College, eventually transferring to the University of Berkeley. But he was majoring more in coeds than in any serious studies.

— ଔ —

It was a time of profound social and political change punctuated by assassinations, campus dissent and in 1970 the shooting of students at Kent State. Arnold was troubled and dedicated enough to join the protestors at Berkeley. There he affiliated himself with the radicals and participated in the "Free Speech Movement." His sister, Judy, two years behind him, stayed at home, kept out of trouble and received a scholarship to Barnard College. She would work hard to become a biologist.

Like other young men of his time who protested the Vietnam War, Arnold Schoen dodged the draft; dissatisfied with his studies, he began experimenting with drugs. Fed up with what was going on, sufficiently smashed by the uppers he was swallowing by the handful, Arnold soon lost any interest in earning a degree. By 1967 he'd left Berkeley, moved back to New York and much to his father's consternation, became a field coordinator for the anti-war march on the Pentagon.

In 1968 he became acquainted with Jerry Rubin and Abbie Hoffman, the founders of the Yippies, which stood for the Youth International Party. In those days Arnold also experimented with the Timothy Leary brand of tuning in and turning on — LSD.

Fortunately for Schoen, results of laboratory studies linking LSD to genetic damage began to appear in scientific literature. He was no fool. Pot, yes, harder drugs, no. His sanity was at stake and he knew better than to squander it. His father, Abe, had taught him well. It would be madness to struggle for independence and give up one's own personal freedom.

He knew drugs could control and destroy you. Arnold witnessed many of the voices of the 60s that were tragically extinguished, voices like Janice Joplin and Jimmi Hendrix. Hendrix had died of a drug overdose in London on September 18, 1970. Sixteen days later Janis Joplin was dead as well of a drug overdose in a motel in Los Angeles. *"Freedom's just another word for nothing left to lose,"* wasn't working. They *were* losing.

From the end of 1967 through 1968 the Maharishi and his Human Potential Movement, based in California, made all the cover stories of leading magazines like *Time, Newsweek* and *Life*. Transcendental meditation was what he espoused, and while it had little impact on the west, it did influence the lives of those young Americans who wanted to find a way to *turn on* without drugs.

Arnold found himself doing a 180-degree turnaround, practicing Yoga, reading Eastern religions and learning to meditate. Always known for his unpredictable temperament, veering wildly between violent rages and boyish vulnerability, meditation foiled some of the turmoil within — his compulsion to win, his endless quest to succeed. But he would never be serene.

Next, he stopped smoking and joined the small counter culture that was now into treating and respecting one's body like a shrine, a temple.

"Pop, you gave me an enormous amount of love and attention. I guess it worked. I'm now on the straight and narrow," he said hugging a grateful Abe Schoen.

By the time Jerry Rubin was called to appear before the House

Un-American Activities Committee in Washington, D.C. and showed up wearing a Santa Claus outfit, Arnold Schoen had taken the positive energy he newly felt, one that clearly detached him from the protest movement, and moved back home. "You're right pop, you're right."

"I want to go back to school," he announced to his father, who would spend all his meager savings to once again help his son.

The little man, for Abe Schoen was barely 5'3" tall, gave his son some words of advice: "Arnold, trust only those who stand to lose as much as you do when things go wrong. And stay away from the *misha gash*, the *pot and the pans*, the junk out there," he said, somewhat confused about the terminology that described marijuana. Arnold smiled, his father was a good guy, old-fashioned or not, and often came up with amusing malapropisms.

This time Arnold made it into Columbia, where he enrolled in its distinguished journalism program. He liked it, envisioned himself as a possible newscaster. After all he had the looks and a good speaking voice.

— ❦ —

While Arnold had changed his political stance, there were still many ardent protestors on the new campus. After a four-year history of agitation at Columbia University, the spring of 1968 saw a wave of new demonstrations sweep over the campus.

Mark Rudd, the president of the Students for a Democratic Society gave a speech before the students. Eventually radical students barricaded the entrance to the mathematics building. This time Arnold stayed far away. He wasn't getting involved any longer. His private revolution was over.

Schoen was determined to look the other way. He'd smartened up. Just a bit ahead of the "Me" generation that was to follow, Arnold already knew to take good care of Arnold. He sought out social groups that signified status. Like *Zeta Beta Tau*, nicknamed

"Zillions, Billions, Trillions," because it was a Jewish fraternity peopled with wealthy members. The fraternity needed smart, presentable pledges and Arnold, though not moneyed, fit the rest of the bill. He was good-looking and friendly, although some found him pushy.

— ❦ —

It was at the Lion's Den off the Columbia campus, where the juke box was consistently playing the latest hits by the Beach Boys, the Rolling Stones, the Byrds and Sonny and Cher, that Arnold ambled in one evening to meet his future.

She was a sinewy, petite eighteen-year old with teased auburn hair worn in the beehive style of the day. She had big brown eyes and an assured look about her. A member of Iota Alpha Pi, the sister sorority to ZBT, (known for counting the campuses wealthiest and prettiest Jewish girls among its members), the very wealthy Roberta Gottleib, a junior at Barnard, was majoring in finding a husband.

She was a slightly built young woman of 5 foot five, who could fit into a svelte size 4. After a successful rhinoplasty at 15 to correct a rather sizeable nose — followed by the removal of braces that rectified a distinct overbite, Roberta was plastic but pretty, and easily attracted men. Best of all, she was very, very rich.

Going with the *rich* went being *thin*. All through her adulthood no matter what she ate, Roberta remained remarkably slender. Of course, eating sparingly, and only two meals a day insured her figure would stay slim.

Roberta was good at getting what she wanted. She'd have it no other way. After all, she was the daughter of department store magnate, Frederick Gottleib and was always daddy's little girl. It wasn't long before she had her sites set on Arnold Schoen, 6 foot, handsome, maybe no money, but to her a real catch. After all, her sorority sisters all swooned when he walked by — "why he's the spitting image of Tony Curtis," some would say. Yes, he was considered quite a hunk. She liked his good looks and she had enough money for both of them.

A friend, recalling their courtship years later commented "They were perfect for each other, because Arnold's first interest was Arnold and Roberta's first interest was Roberta."

Soon she was enticing him with invitations to play tennis at her family's lavish Great Neck Estate. It wasn't long before Arnold found the Gottlieb's lifestyle intoxicating. He met world-renowned musicians like Isaac Stern and Leonard Bernstein, and even one of his favorite actresses, Barbara Stanwyck, who was a guest one weekend. He was easily convinced that this was what was missing from his life.

The Gottleib's traditional upper class environment quickly transformed Arnold's agenda for his own future. He was in awe of these third-generation Jews who had carved a secure niche in society. It was easy to get used to the good life. When his prospective father-in-law, Fredrick Gottlieb, talked to him about going into the family business, of giving him the opportunity of running the famous B. Altman's department store chain, the final seduction took place. Yes, he liked journalism, but he liked even more what this family represented to him — a quick leap to financial security, a lifestyle that was irresistible.

Roberta was his anchor, and better still, his entrance into a standard of living that he never dreamed would be his. What did he care that as soon as they became engaged she dropped out of college? Roberta would be busy planning their wedding, their home, and their lives.

Roberta's father was only too pleased to bankroll her fantasy blowout. Gottleib put $400,000 where his mouth was, and the September 23 nuptial between his only daughter, Roberta, and this young man, whom he would groom to take over the family business would be newsworthy. He'd see to that. Publicity never hurt.

They pulled the strings, and Arnold subtly but without much struggle, allowed them to dominate his sphere. His likely-to-succeed drive was happening, so who the hell cared what tune he danced to. But in the end, no one would dominate Arnold Schoen.

— ℛ —

The wedding took place at the glitzy Hotel Plaza. Gottlieb saw this as an investment. Not only did he hire Johnny Carson to emcee a special talent show, with the Beach Boys singing and the hit comedienne of the day, Totie Fields, telling the jokes, he flew guests from other points of the country in on private charter planes, put them up at luxury hotels for four days, ferried them around in limos.

"Arnie, such a wedding, I can't believe it," his mother cried out. His father looked pleased, a little awe struck, but happy such a good union was taking place. They posed for the family photos proud that their only son had married into such a good Jewish family, a family with roots and accomplishments that they'd never attained.

"It's something I'll talk about for the rest of my life!" Roberta raved.

"Daddy, I wanted it to be the party of all parties, and you did it my darling," she said kissing the balding millionaire.

Almost $200,000 had gone for the flowers, the decor, and a staff of 100 waiters, bartenders, security guards, chefs and guides to see to the comfort of the 400 guests. Food featured two kinds of caviar and three varieties of crabs and oysters flown in fresh from Nova Scotia. One triumph in excess was the wildly imaginative mold of the department store that had helped build this family's great fortune — a four-tier replica of the B.Altman flagship store on Fifth Avenue made entirely out of chopped liver. While there was a reform rabbi, the only compromise with Jewish tradition, there was also the standard wine glass the groom would stomp on at the end of the ceremony.

"Hey, you can always make more money," Fred Gottleib said, shaking hands, and posing for the press photographers from *Life Magazine* who came to cover this high-flying million dollar wedding. This was news in 1968 and good publicity for the Altman business. Gottleib had recently extended his business interests investing heavily in a new venture he had been introduced to on the west coast. In 1969 Gottleib had attended a reception given by the Sony Corporation at the Beverly Hills Hotel. Sony was demonstrating its new consumer videocassette machine, which utilized a three-quarter-inch tape like that used by television stations.

Eventually Gottleib invested in this company that would make megabucks for him and others. His skill as a note taker and list maker came to the fore. In business affairs, the domain of contracts and legal documents came easy to Gottleib; he had two years of law school before deciding to join the family business. He liked this new challenge, and would bit by bit do more flying to the west coast to make contacts. Soon he was looking for the right home in Brentwood so that he and his wife could entertain there too.

— ❧ —

After the first few months of marriage, Arnold found some of Roberta's dominating ways a turn-off. Damned if she wasn't spoiled rotten. But it was her lack of interest in sex that was a real disappointment. Roberta was small, her vaginal area was always too tight and too dry, and so sex was painful. Sex also held little interest. She just didn't get turned on, and besides, his damned *shwanz* was too wide and big. "Hurry up, will you, hurry up and come," she'd command.

While their lack of a decent love life was a disappointment, the life pattern they soon adapted suited him just fine. Within the first two years of marriage Roberta's interests focused on her friends, their newly born son, her family, and very little regarding him. So what. He'd have his cake and eat it. Roberta's lack of interest allowed Arnie the luxury of flirtations and eventually illicit extramarital affairs.

All his wife was concerned about was that he be available to accompany her to the parties she told him were *the* parties to attend. She was usually right. He even met Henry Kissinger just before the Berrigan brothers were indicted for a wide-ranging plot to kidnap the Secretary of State. It was amazing with whom the Gottliebs were friendly with on a first-name basis.

If Roberta found out about the few times he made it, even once with one of her bridge partners, he doubted she'd mind — just as long as she didn't have to be bothered. They had enough sex, she felt, to give them a son, which absolutely had thrilled her father. No, she didn't hate sex, it was just bothersome, and painful, and finally, her excuses were good enough to allow them the discretion to live together, but in separate bedrooms.

Affording a large home bestowed upon them wonderful conveniences. Roberta wanted the larger of the master bedrooms, the one with the enormous dressing room and a sauna in the bathroom. She told Arnold the other bedroom was good for him; it had its own library and den. What the hell, why complain, he never had it so good.

Roberta enjoyed her bridge playing, tennis and shopping at chic stores like Henri Bendels and the shops on Madison Avenue. She wouldn't buy anything at Altman's, which she considered an 'old ladies' store'. She spent half her days talking on the telephone to her friends, planning parties, gossiping. Most of the other half was spent in visits to the nail salon, the beauty salon, and a private masseuse that came to the home. She believed in total maintenance. But sex had become a mute issue. After all, didn't she suffer through the caesarian section? Didn't she bear him a son?

Only once did Arnold catch her in the act of enjoying herself physically. He hadn't knocked on her bedroom door and didn't realize the music playing so loudly was to drown out the sounds of her moans. There she was using her trusty vibrator feeling horny before her period. So what. He laughed to himself – actually he was a little turned on. He smiled and quickly excused himself, a tiny smirk on his face.

It never entered Arnold's mind-set to leave her, even when he told Sabrina the day she confronted him about being married. What he didn't realize was that Sabrina never considered him marriage-material. But then Arnold was always the most dedicated member of the Arnold Schoen fan club.

Leave his wife? How could he leave Roberta, who came with all the trappings of success, the beautiful home, the Porsche he drove on weekends, the exciting life he led? Arnold had swiftly catapulted himself into the rounds of corporate warfare, in a race with Lord & Taylor and Saks Fifth Avenue to be the biggest chain of upscale department stores.

At the beginning, Arnie loved the competition, and in one characteristically brilliant move, visited each chain store to interview top management. If he found a lack-luster staff, an executive doing a poor job, he fired the person on the spot. Then again, when he discovered a hard-working employee, he promoted the man. In style, Schoen foreshadowed the yuppie corporate warriors of the eighties.

Strange, just two years before he was out there with the rest of the rabble rousers. Now he was a major participant in the mainstream he once criticized. And guess what, ladies. (Just in case this should come as a surprise.) No matter how many times he insisted to Sabrina and all the other women he romanced that he wanted to leave the bitch to whom he was married, it was all talk, all lies. He liked his life the way it was. He'd married well. Arnie had a way with words, explaining his life choices with his own brand of philosophy: "All great discoveries are made by mistakes. Roberta is my greatest mistake."

— ○⃥ —

"Hello, lovely one," he greeted Sabrina when they met for the first time at the annual stockholder's meeting. She just shook her head and smiled politely. While he admired her tall chiseled beauty, he never gave her a second thought as a possible sex partner. She seemed aloof, very self-assured, and then again, he learned she was the daughter of the Aldrich's, waspy enough to be in the 400.

It was months before he and Sabrina really took notice of one another. Schoen had just been named a vice-president of the 5th Avenue Store and executives were invited to meet with him. Since the Gottliebs had no sons, they hoped Schoen would become an integral part of this retailing dynasty.

"Here, here, good fellow, you deserve our congratulations," intoned a rather oily, slick-back haired Justin Schwartz, the treasury officer for the store. Justin knew it was a slam-dunk, that Schoen got the job because of family connections. He raised his glass in a toast. Everyone applauded, including Sabrina, who suddenly caught Schoen's eye. This time, he really liked what he saw. And she was partial to his debonair style. He could be very smooth.

While he was astute enough to do an effective job in the administration of the retail chain, after the first year, Arnie found nothing challenging. It was fool's work; often boring, little that stimulated his interest. Eventually he grew accustomed to the routine, the limousine that picked him up at the door each morning at 9 for the ride downtown, the glittery dinners, the easy life. Boy, was it easy.

Roberta was another story. She'd turned into a goddamned cold bitch. Looking back, he couldn't remember feeling any real affection for her. Sure she was stunning and with all the pampering, always looked ready and perfectly groomed. But she was not what anyone would think of as an admirable person. The flaws were apparent and Arnold saw them right away.

Although Roberta believed she was well-bred — after all she'd attended the best schools and associated with the "best" people — her paramount philosophy could be summed up in her favorite motto: "The secret of success is sincerity. Once you can fake that, you've got it made."

However, Roberta really had no concept of how to feign sincerity. She was spoiled rotten. Arnie was astonished at how she treated people. Though her voice was delicate, her tone was abusive. He detested how she talked to the help. Roberta was good at dictating orders without ever saying thank you — even to her hard-working housekeeper. She was short-tempered with deliverymen, abrupt with anyone she felt was beneath her. A *Princess*, that's what she was, and while he realized it was ridiculous for him to look at her as a "JAP", the disparaging name for a spoiled Jewish girl, Arnie recognized that sometimes the worst anti-Semite was a Jew.

He thought about his sweet Jewish mother. She was always kind and simple and loving. "You know, Roberta, if you had even an ounce of decency in one of your red-painted toe nails you still couldn't measure up to my mother – who is good through and through," he yelled at her one night, when he just couldn't take Roberta's supercilious attitude towards the help. "Can't you just once — say thank you?" he asked. "Oh leave me alone, already. Just leave me alone," his wife answered, and left the room.

Yes, his dear mother, Esther Schoen was a giver, a fixer, and a gem. He would always be devoted to his undemanding and decent mother and his equally wonderful father. As soon as he could arrange it, Arnold bought a beautiful home on Long Island for his hard-working parents. It was payback time and Schoen rose to the occasion. He was so proud that he could do this for them — a feel-good moment when he'd done the honorable, right thing. So maybe he was a heel with women, wasn't always above-board in business, but damned if he wasn't a good son.

— CR —

As far as Arnie and Sabrina's little affair went — it had been a mistake, one that Sabrina would quickly lay to rest and move on. She wasn't the type to look back. Soon after the break-up, when Sabrina had finished telling Arnold it was over —that four and a half months was more than enough, thank you — she quickly implemented a new strategy.

"Yes, it's time to make some adjustments. I'm going to take some time off, and then settle on what I want to do," Sabrina explained to Maureen. A while ago, she'd told her of the affair, had mentioned she was tired of retail advertising work and was thinking of moving on.

Still her announcement seemed to catch Maureen off guard.

"Gee, Sabrina, you're a good friend and a real advocate for me here. You've always liked my sketches and given me more full-page ads than the other illustrators. Do you think they'll keep me on?" Maureen asked, still insecure about her abilities.

"Look you survived the Mary Quant mini dresses, you survived your illness and the hospital stay and for sure — you'll live to tell the tale of my leaving," Sabrina joked. "You're good, you're quite good at what you do, you know."

"Gosh, thanks. But why now — why are you leaving so suddenly? You wouldn't let that schmuck, Arnold you-know-who bother you, now would you?"

"Now you know me better than that Maureen. He's not worth the conversation."

"But you'll be so missed. Especially by me."

"I have many reasons, some I'd rather not share at this moment. But Maureen, don't feel bad about this. We'll remain friends, I promise to keep in touch." And Sabrina meant it. She didn't make connections easily but when she did she'd keep them for a lifetime.

'I despise that expression 'keep in touch'…it's usually so final."

"Nonsense, I give you my word — we'll always be friends. And you, you're in good form, you have a body of work now, a decent portfolio. You could move up. Try for an agency job, honey."

"Hell I like it at Altman's. It's easy for me. I don't know if I want the hassle of an agency. But, tell me just a tiny little bit — please, Sabrina?" Maureen knew Sabrina had a goal in mind. It was so like her.

Sabrina laughed. "I'm going to carve a new career for myself. I've thought about it for a while. I want to be a television news reporter. My father has a few contacts at WPIX, the local TV channel here. I know I can get in as an intern. Maybe even a spot on a show. That's why I'm not jumping into anything — so I can see if I can search out an opening in the editorial department. And of course, I want to try my hand at working in front of a camera."

"Fabulous. You're blonde, beautiful, sure of yourself. You'll be a star!"

The two women smiled, hugged spontaneously and said goodnight.

Sabrina went home to relax. She would draw the water for a bath. She loved adding some essential oils into it, and luxuriating in the tub for as long as an hour.

The doorbell rang. It was a delivery person with a box of flowers. "Sorry, I don't want them," she said, turning them down. "Here, take this," she added, giving the elderly messenger a $5.00 tip. She didn't need to read the gift tag to see the elaborate signature. She was merciless. That Arnold Schoen, what a conniver. As if flowers could make a difference.

— ❦ —

"It is never too late to be what you might have been."
— *George Eliot*

— ∝ℛ —

Chapter 17

Sabrina was now a practiced player in the sacrament of single women — ending a relationship that was going nowhere. Damned if she didn't know better. She should never have gotten involved with the prick in the first place.

Four months was a long time to have been caught up in this negative state of affairs; worse, Arnie was smug and conceited. But what troubled Sabrina most was that he was *married*. Not right, not ethical — she knew better than that. Yet, perversely, she stayed in it far too long. "Holding on to Arnold Schoen is like trying to get a drink of water by cupping my hand. Far too much slips through, little of value remains," she said.

"That's a funny way of putting it," Maureen, (who'd been the one person in whom Sabrina confided,) smiled. Amazingly, Sabrina and Arnie had been so discreet that although Maureen worked in the same department — she hadn't noticed a thing. Remarkable! When she found out about the affair Maureen could barely believe Sabrina's choice, never mind that a romance was happening within the hallowed walls of B. Altman's.

Somehow Arnold Schoen didn't seem like someone Sabrina would find interesting. Sure he was handsome. Strutted about in those $400 Saville-Row suits, the custom-made monogrammed cuffed shirts, the imported Italian shoes — always preening like a damned peacock. But, no way did Maureen see her friend finding Schoen worth more than a possible romp in the sack. "Sexy he was — but intellectually stimulating — and good enough for a woman like Sabrina? — never," Maureen opined.

"Not only was he no *Captain Thoughtful*, he was just about the romantic equivalent of a dim night light," Sabrina admitted. "Frankly, Maureen, Arnie can't really pay too much attention to any woman — he's too fixated on Arnie. As for my work here at the office — there are no challenges left. It's time for me to stretch myself."She knew her friend was still dismayed with her decision to leave. But good-old Maureen quickly demonstrated her love and support.

"Hey! Then it's time. After all — change is inevitable, except maybe from a vending machine!" Maureen laughed. Truly, she was the last person who should sit in judgment. "And God only knows how many mistaken alliances I've made!" Maureen admitted. Wasn't Sabrina lucky? she realized — she had no addictions, no skeletons in her closet, no bottoms in her life to hoist herself up from. With her in-bred confidence, shifting gears had to be easier. Or at least Sabrina made it seem easy. The poise was always there.

"Let's meet later at Dino's," Maureen suggested. It was a favorite watering hole.

"Excellent idea, I'll call and make a reservation for 8," Sabrina retorted, relieved that Maureen was taking the announcement so well. She'd share more of her plans then. "My treat, please. This will be a celebration."

Next on Sabrina's to-do list would be telling her mother. About her leaving Altman's that is. Not a word about the illicit affair.

"Please, mother, you can always find what you're *not* looking for," Sabrina commented in a telephone conversation. It was easier than she realized it would be — telling her mother that she'd given notice. "I'm just tired of having to be perfect at everything I do," she joked.

Her mother laughed. "Perfect, I don't know, but nearly so, yes. I suppose we raised you with enough love that you feel good about yourself, as well you should. But you drive yourself far too hard my darling."

What Sabrina didn't disclose was the sorry state of affairs she'd just ended. Sabrina knew her mother would have been mortified that she'd squandered her time on a married man. She was raised with good solid Christian values. She really didn't know what made her engage in this behavior, being the "*other woman*," and why it didn't bother her conscience more, but it didn't. Still she was sensitive enough to know it would offend her mother.

After a quick shower, Sabrina changed clothes and dashed out the door. Soon she was on Lexington Avenue, hailing a cab going downtown to meet Maureen for dinner.

The headwaiter brought her to the back table where Maureen was already sitting, sipping a Virgin Mary, resolute in staying away from the hard stuff. Maureen, her blonde hair gleaming in the candlelit room, had a big smile on her face. She knew that Sabrina would share with her, but to put her at ease she said, "You have the right to remain silent, my friend. Anything you say will be misquoted and then used against you," she winked.

Sabrina laughed. "Hey, I know you can be trusted. So just let me order a drink, because yes, I have much to tell you."

"Good, good, my friend. I'm all ears. And remember. I always keep my circle of friends small and their secrets confidential. Even the ones that are in prison or drug rehab," she joked.

Over dinner, Sabrina confessed to Maureen: "I don't feel good about admitting it but right now I hope Arnold Schoen is miserable — and as far as his wife is concerned — well, I'd only heard horrible things about the woman — and when I met her at the Christmas Party she lived up to the reviews. Frankly, my dear, I envision her falling into a big man hole somewhere and getting swallowed up in the city sewers."

Maureen laughed. "You actually met her? Tell me about it!"

That past Christmas, Sabrina had finally encountered Roberta Schoen at a charity ball the department store was hosting at the Plaza Hotel. It was the kind of party that made the newspapers and was good publicity.

"Talk about awkward! Martin Gottleib had spotted me at the get-together and insisted on introducing me to his daughter."

"Wow!"

"She was svelte, hair swept up — in an over-busy do, and it was also apparent that Roberta Gottleib Schoen had undergone a very poor nose job — the kind where the tip of the nose is so pinched in you wonder what huge proboscis the surgeon had started with. Overall, the woman is plastically pretty — even though her dedicated husband had suggested more than a few times that she's repulsive. But come to think of it, Arnie never had a kind word to say about her."

"Oh Sabrina, what a happening, I don't know if I could have pulled it off."

"A *fait accomplis* – you should have seen how the woman held herself. There was something so off-putting about her demeanor. A glass of champagne in one hand, pinky finger up, wearing this ultra expensive emerald green Dior gown, and jewelry, far too much jewelry beginning with chandelier earrings, necklace, bracelets and rings, rings, rings. She was decked out like a Christmas tree. But worse — Roberta made the waiter stand an inordinate amount of time while she decided what canapé to select from the tray. Then when she spotted some salmon canapés she lunged for them all."

"Yuck, salmon is so fishy," Maureen commented, all ears.

"She was snide, snippety, the ultimate snob, there was no thank you offered to those who waited upon her. It was like everything was due her. I hate to admit it but her poor behavior made me feel less culpable about my mucking around with the lady's husband."

"Indeed," Maureen nodded.

"Then she insisted I try one of the canapés, telling me they were 'utterly divine'. She snatched five of them off the waiter's platter; luckily she only handed me one, without a napkin, I might add. They were fatty little things and the salmon was salty as hell."

Maureen laughed.

"Best of all, she told me – let's see if I remember this right – she leaned over and whispered to me: "*It's really lox, you know. But uptowners say salmon — salmon, schmamon — it's lox!*""

"Well — I took a quick sip of punch to wash down the extremely salty taste and of course she was insistent on asking me what I thought."

"*Aren't they heavenly?* Roberta pushed.

"It's alright; I don't really like salty foods," I told her, hoping to make a quick get away. Then, this is the quirkiest part — Roberta said: "*Oh well, that's what makes the world go round 'ya know. I mean my mother used to say if we all liked the same man we'd be in trouble — well we all have different tastes in food and —*"

"Oh is that a riot!" Maureen whispered.

"I couldn't believe what Mrs. Arnold Schoen had just remarked. I truly wondered if she had any suspicions or if I was just feeling guilty?"

"Oh Saints Preserve Us!" Maureen proclaimed. She almost didn't trust what she was hearing.

"Anyway, after she called the waiter back (a little too loudly,) she seized a few more of the canapés and finally took her leave of me: *"Nice to meet you, dear, I have to work the room, if you know what I mean!"* she added and walked away."

"Lucky you!"

"That's when I noticed the back of Roberta's designer gown. Guess what? Adhering to the long satin skirt was this really large piece of fatty pink salmon."

"Here's to salmon canapés," Maureen said, lifting her glass. "And you know what, Sabrina, somehow I think Arnie and Roberta deserve each other."

— ✄ —

The two women also conversed about careers. Especially Sabrina, who was steadfast in her plans to move up the executive ladder.

She was ready to try her hand at Television. Sabrina wanted a more serious and *national* career and women were slowly gaining clout as commentators on the television screen. Now was the time to concentrate on getting herself into the intriguing and relatively new industry. The idea of becoming a news reporter was uppermost in her mind. She'd been reading up on the business, knew this was where she might make her mark. What Sabrina wanted, Sabrina got. Even if she had to begin as an intern, she'd make it.

She'd studied the network news shows and noticed a flurry of young attractive women getting small but nevertheless on-camera spots reading the news or doing weather reports.

And then there were the pioneers.

While Betty Furness was getting rich demonstrating refrigerators on the black and white TV screen, other females like Faye Emerson were hosting talk shows. Women were becoming more visible on the small screen. Most visible lately was Sabrina's heroine, Barbara Walters.

Barbara Walters was getting the spotlight on the Today Show on WNBC. Sabrina knew that Walters had begun on the early morning television show as a writer and within a year had become a reporter-at-large, developing, writing and editing her own reports and interviews. By 1974, NBC would officially designate Walters as the morning show's first female co-host.

Sabrina was also keenly aware of the visit to the People's Republic of China made by President Richard Nixon in 1972. Barbara Walters won a coveted spot on the NBC News team that accompanied the president. She wanted to get to where Walters was, to pursue such a course with the same fervor she did anything — with confidence, determination and a winner's attitude.

— ೞ —

After coffee and the check, the women got up and warmly embraced. "I'm so glad we're friends," Maureen said with affection. "And I just know you're going to be a shining success!"

"I have a strong feeling, that for both of us, the best is yet to come," Sabrina predicted.

— ೞ —

Oh Life is a glorious cycle of song,
A medley of extemporanea;
And love is a thing that can never go wrong;
And I am Marie of Roumania
  — Dorothy Parker

— CR —

Chapter 18

Annie

In the mid 60s a fashion revolution had erupted with Puccis and pop art and dazzling colors everywhere. There were high-style boots made for walking and mini skirts made for gawking. Annie studied the latest issues of *Glamour* and *Mademoiselle* to make sure she was in tune with the day's trends. When the outrageous miniskirt that Mary Quant inspired became the uniform, Annie Rosenberg Ryan was stepping out in the shortest of them with her thigh-high boots.

Now it was the beginning of the 1970s and Annie was buying the most outrageous platform shoes she could find—the ones with the skyscraper heels that made her 5'2" look a lot taller. She didn't care that half the time she was too tipsy to stay in them for long. The look was "in"—and that's what mattered.

At the moment, Annie was putting together an outfit. Her purpose – to attract a man. She stood in front of her full-length closet mirror, turning from one side to the other, and decided this hot pink lace top played up her figure just the way she wanted. And she absolutely loved the way the fringed edges moved when she did. Now she reached for her tightest velvet jeans — the ones she'd found on sale at Bloomies. Annie slithered into them, zipped them up, and looked at her reflection unsparingly. "Okay Annie," she thought. "You look good! Maybe this time it'll get you *Mr. Right.*"

Gazing into the mirror once again, Annie appraised the finished look. Damned if she didn't look voluptuous. She checked the eye shadow, rouge, eyeliner, all the tools to embellish her twenty something "M.O." She looked sexy — it went with the territory. After all, who wants to sit still and feel what's going on inside, who wants to hurt? Not Annie. No, it was better to be out there — *searching, looking for someone to take care of her. Poor, dearest Annie, would she ever discover that inside, deep down, it was all right there?*

— ଔ —

In fleeting moments of self-honesty, Annie knew there was something wrong with her drinking. But she still hadn't found sobriety. She did find a job—a decent one—back at Macy's —writing retail copy on linens and home furnishings. It was a bus ride away from the small walk-up apartment she'd rented on Bleecker Street in Greenwich Village. Getting a job, especially one as a copywriter, was a step up. And Macy's was paying a decent wage of 115 dollars a week. It was easy, real easy to write the household ads and the inane two-for-one in-store sales circulars. This wasn't exactly creative writing but hell it paid the bills.

Still, life seemed a struggle. Sometimes she felt ultra wonderful and hopeful, but more of the time, there was the drinking, the doubts, the depression. Well, at least she was working. On her way home from work — dreading yet another evening alone, she'd stop and buy a pint of the cheapest vodka, and maybe a take out sandwich or a serving of hot lasagna from the neighborhood deli. But it was the vodka, mixed into some Fresca or other citrus flavor soda that numbed Annie and got her through the long and lonely night.

Damn it! Something was always missing. Annie was flooded with fears although she displayed a different edge to the outside world, wisecracking her way through the workday, glad to be among people. It was probably her good sense of humor that saved her most of the time.

Of course, AA was in the backdrop, a place Annie visited intermittently— but she was still lying to herself, still not surrendering by stopping the drinking that was causing the chaos in the first place.

When Annie attended the AA meetings and listened, she began to understand what was really exacerbating her problems — the *alcohol* itself. But her other addiction — to men — only complicated her dilemma. Her AA sponsor Irene stressed the unwritten rule: "No dating, no relationships, no major changes in *any* area of your life the first year you're getting sober."

Flirting with men in the program was totally taboo. As for those males who were attracted to newcomers, the ones who were extra friendly, always offering help, and preying on the vulnerable — that was called *pigeon-fucking* and was frowned upon.

However, Annie didn't like rules — especially ones that touched upon her weaknesses. She painfully missed Tom and Colleen and the consolation of belonging. Incessantly, she'd tell whoever would listen about her broken marriage. Just letting someone know she'd been married made her feel better — like the label meant she'd at least attracted a man who truly wanted her.

Irene would have none of it: "Annie, anyone who lives with an active alcoholic has emotional problems as well. Can't you see it? Your husband has his own demons to deal with. You've got to let go and let God. Put one foot in front of the other and just *surrender*. The meetings are the medicine. Please give it a chance."

No, Annie just couldn't see it. There had been nothing wrong with Tom. It was all *her* fault. After all, didn't her mother always say, "you're living in a dream world, wake up to reality!" And didn't she foolishly expect a Hollywood romance with a happy ending? To her way of thinking it was she who'd made most of the mistakes. It was impossible for Annie to comprehend the advice being offered. Irene was a good person, but she didn't understand. And so she'd go on, persistently and morbidly recalling the good times with Tom, conveniently forgetting the rest.

Clichés! Damned if she didn't hate the platitudes and sayings that AA'ers repeated ad infinitum. Were they all brain washed? Didn't they realize that not everyone was molded from the same cookie cutter? While she still went to meetings, when she couldn't take the loneliness, the doubts, she'd secretly drink, if only a glass or two of wine.

"You're into a real pity party," her sister Joanie reminded her, when she phoned to complain, usually slurring her words. Joanie was no fool; she always knew when Annie had been drinking. "Get off the wine, honey, or whatever you're drinking. You should know better by now!" she warned.

But it was the only way, the most comfortable way Annie knew of to get through the emptiness that seared her soul.

Over and over again she'd pour herself a glass of spirits, put on some music, and soon tears would well up in her eyes. She'd play Streisand singing, *"Have I Stayed Too Long at the Fair?"* and felt that she wanted the music to go on forever and that she had stayed far too long.

At other times, she'd play love songs that reminded her of Tom. One of her favorite downers was *"Let It Be Me,"* sung by Roy Clark. She'd obsess over the lines, "Each time we meet love, I find complete love, without your sweet love, what would life be?" and the tears would come quickly. Why did life have to be so unfair?

Why couldn't she have someone to love who loved her? Why?
Why? Why? The ethyl alcohol fueled her self-absorption. And so the
make-me-miserable-music played on and on – fueling her fantasies
and increasing her obsessions. It was becoming Annie's major
occupation.

— ೞ —

Then in the summer of 1972, something inside of Annie began
to change. It had to do with what happened in Munich when one
of the worst terrorist attacks in the history of the modern Olympics
occurred. The nightmare took place at dawn. A group of Palestinian
guerillas scaled the fence surrounding the Olympic village, stormed
a building housing the Israeli team, killed two and took nine
hostages, demanding the release of 200 Palestinians held in Israeli
jails. The nightmare ended with a gun battle at a military airport. A
rescue attempt that went tragically wrong resulted in the murder of
all nine hostages.

Her sense of Jewish identity had begun before this tragedy,
when Annie first perceived the anti-Semitism in Tom's family. Who
the hell were these small-minded people to hate her and her people?
But it was when the terrorist attack occurred in Munich that all of
her sensibilities surfaced. At that heartrending instant Annie became
proud of her Jewish legacy. Her father had once shown his children
tattered old photo postcards of lost relatives — two brothers and
their families — who hadn't left Poland like he did, and eventually
perished in the concentration camps.

Damn it. Why did so many people hate and mistrust Jews?
Didn't they realize that Jesus was a Jew? She loathed prejudice
of any kind but the focus on Jews was incredible. Annie couldn't
understand why a tiny country like Israel, a true democracy in a
region of states of kings and despots, was always being attacked.

In between her own chaos — the familiar yo-yo syndrome
that came with drinks and tranquilizers — Annie was a bright

young woman with flashes of insight and awareness. Interested in nationwide and international issues, she conscientiously read *Time Magazine*, and daily, the *New York Times*.

But what good was her concern with starvation in India, if she was starving for balance within her own life? Annie was ill equipped to do anything for anyone else, never mind herself. Nothing seemed quite right. So she continued self-medication desperately trying to feel okay. Caught up in denial, the obliteration that came with using mood changers, her real world was whittling away. She'd never learned to live life as an adult, to take responsibility for herself, existing instead with haunted remnants of her past. Especially of *Tom*. She would dream of him continuously, reflect back on only the good times.

She remembered Tom's chiseled good looks, his wonderful, muscular body. One night he had come home from the firehouse with a big smile on his face. "The fellows put one over on me, big time!" he announced. "They sent in my mug photo to a modeling agency that's booking men for the new fireman's calendar. And Jesus, Joseph and Mary! – Someone from the agency called the firehouse today and asked if I'd pose for the 1968 New York City Fireman's Calendar," he said, not seeming to believe it was for real. "Bravo, my gorgeous husband!" Annie responded, giving Tom a big round of applause. "Naturally, I didn't want to do it, but I found out it pays $250. That's like stealing the money! It would be a sin to turn down the bucks," he laughed. They hugged one another warmly. What a terrific turn of events!

He became *Mr. October.* She not only kept copies of the calendar and his picture plastered all over the walls, but had Tom's sexy photo folded up in her wallet to show to anyone willing to look. Yes, this fabulous hunk, he was her husband, or at least he had been. Of course she never mentioned the bad parts.

— ☙ —

Again and again Annie played the heartbreaking songs that evinced the only emotions that made sense: rejection, frustration, sadness. Somehow, feeling bad felt good. It was all she really knew.

Much later, when Annie had finally found sobriety and a sensible, sane way of living through the 12-Step Program, and when it was her time to tell her story, (or "qualify" as the members called it,) she'd describe how she used to feel — like *someone who had cellophane enveloping every brain cell*. Everything was muffled, seen through the shrouds of self-absorption and fear.

"But then," Annie pointed out, "look at the history of so many women who were victims of drowning their emotions in alcohol and pills. There was Judy Garland and Marilyn Monroe and Edith Piaf and Billy Holliday." — she could have gone on and on with a list of hundreds of the wounded and the dead who didn't get the chance to get it — that the chemicals and mood changers didn't work, didn't help, didn't give them what they needed.

It didn't come easy. Even in her newfound sobriety, Annie was still absorbed with filling up the *empty hole* she felt inside with something from the outside. "I hate to admit it, but my all-consuming thoughts, are still that I need someone to care about me, someone to be with, someone to make me feel whole," she admitted to her sponsor.

Like many women raised in the 50s, Annie wanted to be rescued by the hero on the white horse, a Prince Charming. Where was that *"Someone To Watch Over Me?"* It was so isolating. Working all day and then going home to nothing but the four walls — that's when the loneliness set in and it ached. Most of all she couldn't stand the silence. That's why music worked.

The music especially brought Tom closer. Sometimes she'd write him long letters, pour her heart out, hoping to reach his soul. She tore them up the next morning. When she couldn't stand it any longer, she'd dial his mother's number, hoping to get Tom on the phone, to tell him how much she missed him, to ask that they get together. But he never answered the phone. And she'd hang up when she heard a woman's voice.

"It's not going to work, Annie, I can't be your listening friend, I'm only here to carry the message," Irene complained one evening, when she'd called her at 2 in the morning. "You've got to come to the meetings. Bring the body and the mind will follow," she quoted one of the many aphorisms in AA.

Most of the time Annie didn't remember the calls she'd made in the middle of the night.

Oh well. Being irresponsible made living easier. It certainly masked any stress. Since she couldn't assume the postures of an adult, of being on her own and feeling okay, then her main goal was to look for someone to do it for her. She tried to find him, this magical, mystical Mr. Right, over and over and over again. Of course, Annie really wanted Tom, with all his faults, but the fury in how she'd left — not paying the rent, throwing the tree over the apartment terrace — had caused a greater rift than she'd imagined. He wasn't making any attempt to contact her. She'd really put nails in the coffin this time.

— ❧ —

And the lord said love is near, and I answered what should I wear?

She had written those lines in high school and twenty years later she was still living it. Annie was still turning the pages of the fashion magazines, still dressing for love.

Oh how Annie ached for attention. For tenderness. For a partner. She needed to feel attractive. Gorgeous is what worked with the opposite sex. At the AA meetings, she couldn't resist looking at the men — looking and hoping and wishing.

And there were many men at the meetings. While alcoholism knew no gender, more men than women attended the meetings in

Manhattan in the 70s. Some were quite good-looking. There were even a few well-known actors among the members of this special club. Fascinating to sit across a table from someone she'd seen on TV or in the movies; Annie was pleased. It helped to bring her back to the meetings, even if for the wrong reasons.

But it was really *any* single, available man that caught her interest. Many of these were the "old-timers," — men who had a few good years of sobriety, but came regularly to meetings. Some of them would stand in the back of the church halls like members of an old boy's club, talking among themselves, looking the room over for pretty new faces.

Yes — Irene had warned Annie to stay away from the men; that a few disingenuous ones sought out naïve, newly sober women.

No! She'd do it her way. Resolutely, stupidly, Annie struggled on.

Then along came Kevin.

She first saw Kevin Grace at a Village AA meeting. Thin, with a wiry build, Kevin had a strong square jaw line and unusual gray eyes, and when he smiled amazing dimples. There was an elegant air about him. Although he was attending meetings in dusty basements of churches, his most casual attire would be a blue shirt and tie. A member of a well-known shipping company family, Kevin had grown up with a silver spoon in his mouth. Unfortunately he replaced it with a silver keg that held scotch or bourbon. He'd made a mess of his life. Separated from his society wife and two children, his family was supporting him, but was not in high spirits about his joining Alcoholics Anonymous. It was the early 1970s and AA hadn't received the respect that would come later with the publicity surrounding stalwart members of society, like Betty Ford, talking about the disease of alcoholism and the value of 12 step programs.

Annie plotted her course of action. She knew Kevin usually joined the others who retreated to one of the many coffee shops after the meeting. It was a social hour, where AA congregated

— over a cup of coffee and maybe some cake. Going for coffee was an opportunity to extend the camaraderie of the meetings. A compendium of society was always well represented.

Seated in one booth might be an out-of-work actor who drove a cab, a priest who was into more than the Mass wine offerings, a nurse who also dabbled in stealing pills, an attorney who kept up his successful practice but spent most nights in a blur of scotch and sodas and a housewife who vowed never to drink. After all— her father was the town drunk, and now there she was asking for help, knowing booze was destroying her and her marriage.

Each person, known usually by their first name, sat over coffees and sodas, clinging to friendly words shared — small talk — a vital connection that kept them away from the seduction of alcohol.

Kevin attended the Workshop Meeting regularly and afterward could be found sitting at one of the group tables around the corner at the Java Café. Most of the time, Annie noticed, he'd be seated with a few of the more attractive people who'd been at the meeting.

Even in AA there was a pecking order of sorts, (though no one would acknowledge it). The "higher order" was usually successful, professional, good looking, more confident than some of the more troubled beginners. Although Annie was merely a writer of sales copy, she felt like she belonged to the professional contingent. The table where Kevin was seated included an actress who had a major role in a television sitcom, a Daily News reporter who'd been in two drying out places before he got serious in AA, a successful lawyer who only drank on weekends, (but oh did he make up for lost time!) and a beautiful model, sans makeup and absolutely beautiful in her repose.

And then there was Kevin.

It didn't take long. Within a few nights of going for coffee Annie cracked a few remarks that evinced laughter from the group. She felt comfortable and accepted. Best of all, she noticed Kevin had noticed her too. That was enough for Annie.

"Hi Annie, come, sit here," Kevin beckoned.

Within two weeks of a mild flirtation Annie invited Kevin home after one coffee shop meet. They'd discussed music. "I have some really rare old Verve albums, of Fred Astaire, the dancer, singing the movie hits he made famous," she announced. "Yes," Kevin said, "I love Astaire, he's a better singer than people give him credit for."

"So come back, come listen with me," she coaxed.

That's all it took, then some low lighting, the music and a kiss. They slept together. No, that wasn't true. They had sex. Kevin looked uncomfortable about staying the night. Keeping his socks and his watch on were a clue. And the sex, it really wasn't very good. She thought he was far too fast, and not enough preliminaries. Maybe if she'd been a little tipsy it would have been better? No, it was that when she came, and she did come, she instantly thought of Tom, of how much she loved him physically. She knew in that truthful moment that this man — maybe *all* other men – could never make her feel like she did with Tom. The realization, the fear, the sense of loss was devastating.

— ❦ —

Don't cry because it's over, smile because it happened.

— ❦ —

Chapter 19

Annie and Jim —
April 1973

It was the spring of 1973. Elton John had a number one single with *"Goodbye Yellow Brick Road,"* and in April the 1,350 tall World Trade Center in New York City was officially opened. And Annie Ryan had finally put together six months in the program, back-to-back, day-by-day, total sobriety. Yes, she was able to stay away, a day at a time, from booze. She began feeling grateful, thanking her "higher power", working the AA program.

Her job was improving. Or was it Annie? She didn't have to show up late or give an excuse about dragging through the day because of a "headache" or a "cold," since she wasn't waking up hung over. Life was getting better.

One night at a meeting she ran into an old friend, Jim Phelan. It was in the basement of a brownstone on East 37th Street. There he was, leaning against the wall. She could hardly believe it. Just another drunk ready to attend the regular 7 p.m. Mustard Seed meeting. She'd lost track of Jim a few years back when he'd moved to Connecticut. She'd heard he was living with his sister and her children. Jim often talked about his sister.

Jim Phelan was a larger-than-life character who consumed 16,000 calories of life a day. He was bright, intellectual, discerning, yet a mass of contradictions. While he had his undergraduate degree from Yale, and dressed like Madison Avenue, and was damned good looking, he lived like a slob. Ever the roaming bachelor, looking for the perfect Miss Right, Jim compared every woman he met to his golden-haired sister, Casey, with whom he was very close. Casey Coughlin, who lived in Westport, an upscale town in Connecticut, was a widow at age 28, left with two young daughters to raise after her air force pilot husband was killed when his plane was shot down during the Viet Nam War.

Jim played surrogate father to Casey's children, first spending weekends at her home, and finally giving up his Manhattan apartment to move in with her and the kids.

It wasn't such a good idea. He was reverse commuting to his Madison Avenue agency on the New York Central, which took an hour each way, resulting in his getting back to the house at 8 o'clock or later most nights and so he rarely had time to spend with his nieces. The commuting also eliminated him from the bar scene — the nightly singles meat market where he'd search for someone special. As if he was going to meet anyone special in a Village saloon. But, ah, he enjoyed the hunt.

"The best way to escape your problem is to solve it, Jim," his sister wisely intoned. "You're a good guy, you know how much I love you. And I appreciate your hanging out with us. The girls like having you around — but really; you need to find your own way and hopefully your soul mate. Life's most precious moments, they don't have value, unless they're shared," Casey reminded him. "I had ten wonderful years with Gary, and I have his daughters. You have no one. Please, you need to be in the city."

Casey spent the better part of two months urging Jim to go back to New York and "get a life," that she would be just fine on her own; and so after much talk and prodding he reluctantly returned to the city.

Jim, now edging towards 30, was no closer to finding his own way, nor his perfect lady, but hell, his sister was usually right so he'd give it another try. Soon enough he returned to the singles bar scene, bounding around, drinking a little too much, looking for the right one night after night after night.

As for Annie and Jim's history — it was back in 1966 when they were both living in the West Village that they first met. Where else but at a bar? There she was, propped up on a stool at the old Cedar Tavern. She flirted; he flirted back. Damned if he didn't have a great smile and a sardonic Irish wit. He was awfully handsome. But somehow there wasn't the right chemistry, no romance. Well at least, not on his part. If the truth were known, when Jim and Annie partnered up to bar hop — if he lucked out and found some beautiful babe — she was a bit jealous. And even when Annie found an interesting man for the evening, she always wondered what it would be like if Jim had been that man. It didn't seem to be in the cards.

Theirs was a comradeship of convenience. Lost souls, drifting through the castles-in-the sky taverns dotting every corner of Greenwich Village, they would lead parallel lives that crossed every so often as they returned to these watering holes, to their old hunting grounds.

Finally, Annie got tired of the bar scene, threw all caution to the wind and brazenly placed an ad in the personals, where she'd meet Tom Ryan, and after a whirlwind affair, marry him. (Of course she was drunk when she placed the ad, drunk when she met him — but that's another tale that's told within these pages.)

Jim Phelan was an account executive at Davis and Company, a small advertising agency, where he handled the Norelco electric razor account, and was doing rather well. Holding a master's degree from the prestigious Wharton School of Finance, and having good looks, Jim rose fast in the corporate world.

Although Jim had a top-notch position and earned triple what Annie made, he was often piss-poor since he'd spend every cent he made — and was never really good at budgeting. While Annie wasn't exactly the world's most logical being she certainly had a better handle on the common sense practices of living one's life than Jim did. When he set himself up in a new apartment, his notion of how to decorate it involved a comfortable club chair and footstool, a small table that invariably held an open can of Spanish peanuts, a bag of chips and a half drunk beer. (This was usually his lunch or supper depending upon the time and day of the week.) There was one floor lamp for some light, a TV that was almost always on, and for sleeping, a large mattress in the corner, and wouldn't you know it — on the floor. "What more do I need?" he laughed.

The worst she encountered of Jim's indolence was the Thanksgiving of the year they met. It was 1966 and Jim was living in a walkup on Cornelia Street in Greenwich Village. Annie had just had an argument with her mother, who hung up the phone, with her usual teary "*do whatever you want, Annie. You don't really give a damn about me!*" Annie decided right then and there, holiday or not, she wasn't going to Brooklyn to hear the rest of the lecture. Feeling forlorn, with nothing to do, Annie walked over to Cornelia Street, took a chance and rang Jim's bell. The buzzer let her right in.

There he was, sitting in his club chair, a mess of newspapers beneath him, a half chewed cigar in a tray, ashes spilling over and blasting loud from the TV was the football game of the day. It was a wonder he'd heard the bell at all.

"Where's all that smoke from?" she asked, choking up a bit at the acrid billowing fumes coming from the direction of his kitchen.

"Don't know. Could be dinner. Am cooking myself a turkey. Maybe I better check it," he responded, taking another sip from his beer can.

"Allow me," she volunteered.

"'Wild! Crazy, Jim!" she shouted, after opening the oven door in the tiny kitchen to see the fat dripping all over his oven, a turkey inside, large, plump, and *without* a pan. "I mean, don't you know enough to put the bird into a roasting pan?"

"Thought something was missing," he said, smiling.

They both laughed.

"Hey you know something, he or she who laughs…lasts," she said finding a way to put a light top note on the moment.

"Tell you what, if you stick around until the game's over, I'll take you out for a meal at Tony's," Jim suggested.

Annie loved the home-baked lasagna at Tony's. Better still the opportunity of being treated to dinner because Jim was always generous, and so she gladly accepted.

Tony's was one of those obscure little restaurants on the west side of the Village. The tables were covered with paper tablecloths in a homey red checkerboard pattern. There were matching paper napkins and tinny flatware, but the food, large, ample portions, traditional Sicilian type of cooking, was superb. She ordered her favorite plate. Jim, who had grabbed and devoured a drumstick from the scorched turkey while watching the balance of the football game, really wasn't hungry and was nursing a Guinness Stout. He'd ordered the shrimp scampi, but picked at his dish.

Annie wanted to help Jim. He was a good-looking young man with a future. He earned a comfortable living, but really, his personal habits left much to be desired. But Annie couldn't believe the sink, piled high with dishes, the discarded cartons of take-outs from the local Chinese restaurant, and the empty cans of beer overflowing the garbage pail. And so she was relieved to be out of there and sitting in this warm neighborhood eatery.

She made an attempt to talk to Jim about his bad habits. "How do you expect to attract any woman long-term, when you have such a mess of an apartment?" Annie scolded. "A woman is going to take one look and run the other way, Jim!"

Jim, his black Irish face breaking out in a large grin, displaying those ever-present dimples, just laughed it off. "Oh hell, Annie, I go to *their* place, not mine for screwing."

"That's your problem, Jim, the screwing. You say you want to fall in love, get married, but you're into one-night stands, and you don't give anyone a real chance that way — even yourself."

"Hey, hon, I don't want to cast aspersions, but where are you in the long scheme of things?" he reminded her.

She knew he was right. Annie didn't have any answers, only questions. And she'd done her share of sleeping around. But at least she had a friend in Jim — they were kindred spirits, and he was a good guy to hang out with. It was far better to go to a watering hole with him than alone. Since he was handsome – well, some men thought he was her boyfriend — what the heck. It couldn't hurt and in fact made her look more appealing in those busy bar settings, where the competition was keen.

— ❦ —

They'd lost touch sometime in 1968, but then a couple of years later; here they were, meeting at an AA meeting. In a way the two mirrored each other — each of them was seeking something in someone else that would make them feel whole, all the while assuaging their defeats and disappointments in drink after drink. It was serendipitous that they'd come across one another at an AA meeting.

Annie learned that Jim was staying at a friend's loft, but was looking for an apartment. It turned out that he was sharing space with a co-worker, Sean, who was the art director at the Davis Ad Agency. It was the odd couple all over again. Sean, who liked neatness, wasn't happy with Jim's ways. So Jim had taken a sublet, this small studio apartment, but he'd never really moved in. In fact, one suitcase was still packed and the other lay open, so he could pick and choose shirt, underwear and socks for the day.

"I have an idea, Jim," she suggested. "My Bleecker St. apartment is really very large, and there's a section with a loft bed. I never use it. Too much trouble to climb up into it anyway. It was left by the previous tenant."

Jim looked at her and smiled. He got it right away. Her idea was appealing. He really didn't dig living alone, nor with Sean, who was compulsively neat.

"Why don't you stay at my place for a while until you find yourself the right apartment? You can chip in for rent and utilities, and we can share any food expenses. I'll even do the cooking, hey, what do you say?" Annie suggested.

"Hell, why not? Life's a journey, not a destination, my friend. Let's enjoy the trip for a while as roommates," he answered with a twinkle in his eye.

And so, even if it were only for a little time, she wouldn't have to be alone.

— ◌ —

"The nature of reality is this: it is hidden, and it is hidden, and it is hidden."
— *Rumi, 13th-century Sufi poet and mystic.*

— ∞ —

Chapter 20

April 1976

It was a time of soul searching, of seeking spirituality through meditation and swamis, an era when both flower children and even those in the establishment were seeking new answers. The trend was set after the well-publicized journey of the Beatles to India, where they studied Transcendental Meditation with the Indian teacher, Maharishi Mahesh Yogi. Surely there had to be something of value, something more to life than making money.

News traveled fast. Mainstream publications like *Time Magazine* and *New York Magazine* were now covering meditation and the expansion towards Eastern religions and philosophy.

Annie read the article in the April issue of *New York Magazine* with rapt interest. The piece of writing told of an Indian spiritual leader, a guru (teacher) named Baba Muktananda who had been attracting followers from the West Coast to the East. A new devotee of the Swami, Sally Kempton, an established journalist and the daughter of a well-known newspaper columnist, Murray Kempton, wrote it with passion.

Kempton had described her meeting the Indian guru, first when he was in California, then getting so caught up she joined his American tour. Now, almost two years later she was fervently telling of the incredible experience that came with spending time with "Baba", as he was affectionately called.

Baba now held meditations in an old Catskill Hotel, once known as the DeVille, in South Fallsburg, New York, a part of the Catskills. The area was once a thriving vacation Mecca called the *Borscht Belt* where old time comedians like Milton Berle, Eddie Cantor and singers like Eddie Fisher once entertained visitors from the city. Now the old hotel had been turned into an ashram, and people were traveling from all over to be with Baba.

The story peaked Annie's interest. A guru, whatever that was, and wow, people from all over the world following him, and now he was in upstate New York, where, she later learned, even some well-known names from Hollywood and Broadway had come to visit. John Denver, Marsha Mason, Dave Brubeck were among the regulars.

The Catskills was a two-hour trip away. Why not go there and see what all the brouhaha was about? Of course, some of the motivation came from Annie's involvement with Alcoholics Anonymous. The 12-step program emphasized spirituality, of the need for a "higher power". The 11th Step stated: "Sought through prayer and meditation to achieve a conscious contact with God as we understood Him, praying only for knowledge of His will for us and the power to carry that out."

"Maureen…what are you doing next weekend?" Annie asked, dialing up her old friend. "There's a guru up in South Fallsburg, supposed to be for real. We can rent a car and go see what it's all about," she suggested, knowing Maureen was always fascinated by new experiences.

"I read the piece in my dentist's office," Maureen responded. "Sally Kempton is a damned good writer, and if she's gotten involved with this swami, then he may be bona fide. It's certainly worth a trip. Count me in. Just as long as we leave Saturday morning; I have theater tickets for Friday night. Sabrina got them for me as a birthday gift…we're seeing the new Sondheim musical, *"Pacific Overtures"*.

"Lucky you! I've heard some of the music…it's beautiful. We could leave in the morning… it's only, like, a two-hour drive. Guess what? I already called Jim at his office. I talked him into it…he'll rent the car and do the driving."

"Beautiful. A trip to the country!Hey, I think I can get Buddy to come along. He's open-minded and would enjoy the adventure. Just tell me how much it will cost, and where we'd stay overnight?"

"I've already called up there," Annie answered. We stay right at the Ashram. Girls with the girls, boys with the boys; dorm style I hear. Nothing fancy, but doesn't it sound like a dynamite trip? And, it's dirt cheap…$15 each per night with three meals. Vegetarian meals –- but — sounds exciting. Besides, what do we have to lose?"

And so plans for the next weekend were set. It was ironic, that in the early stages of her life Annie avoided reality, and after AA, she really wanted to know everything. She'd seek answers wherever she could find them. And eventually she would.

— ෩ —

It was magical. The air was filled with the smell of sweet flowers and intoxicating incense. A mellow, orange and spice milieu drifted through the old hotel, which had been transformed into a beautiful ashram. It was crowded yet the atmosphere was calm, peaceful, quiet. Devotees, some wearing the traditional yellow and saffron colored robes, others in simple American style yoga outfits had come to be with Baba.

The girls were aware they were attending a phenomenon, something unique and special and holy. Some of the attendees were curiosity seekers, but most were there seeking spiritual knowledge, of getting to know the Self, through meditation and lessons taught by the guru.

Buddy and Jim seemed less impressed than the women; Jim made a few jokes about the sign-in lines, how it reminded him of registering for college classes. But mostly he was impatient.

"Well, Jim, we're here to learn something, and since they're all volunteers at the reception desk, we'll just have to wait," Annie explained defensively.

Maureen immediately liked the ambiance, the laid back, very relaxed feeling. There was soft chanting and in some areas of the Ashram, gentle music playing. There was much to explore.

Annie was absolutely exhilarated — took in the entire experience, cognizant that this was a sacred place, a place to learn, to be at one with whatever God you believed in. And then a significant, a magical moment happened.

There was an energy field, something one could sense but not see. A boundless electricity and magic filled the air. First a flurry of activity, then suddenly a small man, wrapped in gossamer orange flowing robes quickly walked through the hallway, passing before Annie and the others. It was *he*. Instinctively she knew this incredible and exhilarating energy that had so suddenly filled the room when he entered it, was coming from this very exceptional individual, the guru known as Baba Muktananda.

"It's him," whispered one of the many who had come to witness this happening. There were sighs and smiles. Like little children, they felt they were in an enchanted land, transported from their daily lives, in a warm, inviting, otherworldly setting.

Annie didn't know why, but she was sure that he was a blessed

man, someone very special. Call it a sixth sense — she experienced a
spine-tingling sensation, a deep recognition that this is *where*, at this
very moment, she had to be. Instantaneously she recognized that this
joyful man could imbue unceasing and effortless love, that if one was
ready and open to it, he could be an uplifting teacher.

Soon they all gravitated towards the main meditation hall,
where they learned the guru would eventually enter and sit on a
small velvet chair at the center of the cavernous room. At times
he'd hold a spray of iridescent colored peacock feathers in his
hand, feathers used to lightly tap the head of a devotee. After the
chanting, Baba would hold a sidda yoga meditation session where
one would become quiet, chant the mantra, *Om Namah Shivaya,* and
possibly experience a sense of self and of God within that made it all
worth while. And then, the payoff, Annie learned, was that after the
meditation was over, one could go up to the guru, and ask for his
blessing.

"When the student is ready the teacher appears," she whispered
to Maureen, who had taken a seat on the floor next to her, her lithe
body already in a comfortable lotus position. Annie's legs hurt, and
while the pillow she was given at the entrance, helped make the hard
floor in this main meditation hall a little less intrusive, she wasn't
very comfortable sitting with legs curled up like a pretzel.

The music began with a few young men, with guitars, singing
songs about the guru. They possessed a gentle folk music quality,
and the hall grew even quieter as everyone listened. They knew that
soon, the guru would enter the hall and take his seat on the orange
velvet throne at the front of the auditorium's stage.

"Be with Baba, Be with Yourself…." the guitar-playing singers
intoned. The music was beautiful and beckoning.

Later on, Annie walked along the Ashram paths. Overwhelmed
by the bucolic atmosphere, the birds singing sweetly all around
her, the sun shimmering over the beautiful landscape, the horizon

seemed endless and life's possibilities limitless. She couldn't tear herself away. Far off in the distance Annie saw black and white swans swimming in a lake. She walked over to the wooden bridge to get a closer view. Later on she learned the swans were symbols of the spiritual nature of our souls. She'd return time and again to this enchanting spot and always be stirred by the experience.

...Maybe God wants us to meet a few wrong people before meeting the right one, so that when we finally meet the person, we will know how to be grateful.

— ❧ —

Chapter 21

South Fallsburg in upstate New York is a small town with old-fashioned wooden homes, narrow, winding streets, inexpensive shops plus the usual Woolworth's 5 and 10 cents store. On the outskirts of the municipality there are small farms earning a modest trade. In the past most of the townspeople had earned their living working in the big resort hotels in the vicinity.

Then, with the financial recession in the 1970s, there was a rapid decline in attendance at the hotels. Widespread unemployment ensued. The old crowd just wasn't coming to the countryside these days. And so, there weren't many hotels still operating in the area. Only the Concord and Grossinger's, the biggest of them, were still going strong with their predominantly Jewish clientele.

These days it was more likely one would find a Buddhist retreat nestled in the hills than a kosher-food hotel.

The SYDA Foundation had purchased the run-down Deville hotel and 30 surrounding acres for a song. Within six months of taking it over, volunteer carpenters, electricians, painters had refurbished it into a simple, clean and exceptional environment.

The main entertainment ballroom had been converted into an inviting meditation hall. Soothing, shimmering colors festooned the room, while attractively framed portraits of past Siddha Yoga Saints hung upon the walls. The sweet perfume of Blue Pearl incense permeated the room. Intoxicating and lush and inviting it appealed to Annie's senses.

Daily assemblages were held. It was then one could go before the Guru, bring him questions, ask favors, perhaps pray for something desperately wanted. A procession would form, people patiently waiting to go up to Baba, to receive his blessing. He sat cross-legged, a friendly smile upon his face, his countenance warm and welcoming. Dressed in a sleeveless orange garment and wearing a knitted cap, he would listen carefully, whisper his answer to his interpreter, and then gently swat the person who came up to see him with his wand of iridescent peacock feathers, bestowing his blessings.

Some would ask philosophical questions. Others brought gifts. A few brought an assortment of personal effects, from packs of cigarettes to chocolates, mostly items that represented the person's addiction. Give it to the Guru, and he will take it away from you, take on your bad karma.

— ᘓᴙ —

Annie and her friends had arrived at the Ashram before 11 a.m. "It's not a bad drive at all," Jim commented. "I take the same general route when I'm going skiing."

"Skiing, huh? The last time you took me up to Sugar Bush I don't think you did much, skiing," Annie reminded him.

"Well, there were some really beautiful Canadian girls up there and...."

There was no need to say any more. Annie laughed. "Well, I can't say I did much of anything myself. I was scared to death of those chairlifts, and by the time I walked up the side of the mountain, I was too tired to do much skiing down it!"

"You're not exactly the athletic type, my dear," Maureen said, laughing.

"Yeah, but I'll try anything at least once!"

"Let's get out and stretch our legs," Buddy suggested. "I'm ready for anything now, but the ride was rockier than I expected."

"That's because he wanted to get here before lunch," Maureen commented. "So we made it without any pit stops. But, bravo, Jim, you can really maneuver through the turnpike traffic."

"Thanks, kiddo. Now let's park and find out where we check in. I don't know about the rest of you but I've got to use the rest room," Jim added.

From the start Annie sensed a difference in the surroundings. There was almost a dreamlike quality, as if time had stood still, or at least didn't matter. A lulling pastoral texture so lush one wanted to touch it welcomed the visitors. There was a hush, and at the same time, expectancy, like one was about to enter a different world.

"Hey, I feel like Dorothy, going to visit the Wizard of Oz," Maureen commented, by now so exhilarated that she began skipping. "Let's follow the Yellow Brick Road...."

"Oh really, then who am I? You took the female lead, so who's the cowardly lion, and who's the scarecrow and which one of us would be the tin man?" Annie asked lightheartedly.

"Well — you can be the good witch, the one who showed Dorothy and her friends the right way to get to the Land of Oz, that's who, Annie!"

They all laughed. "Count me out on identifying with any of the other characters," Jim said. "Ditto man," Buddy chimed in.

"Okay, girls, we'll take the suitcases in and meet you in the lobby."

Of course, Annie was the first one out of the car. She was in a rush — for what she wasn't sure. All she knew was she was very glad they'd come.

An air of anticipation resonated throughout the Ashram. Both Maureen and Annie were aware that they were attending a phenomenon, something unique and special.

Buddy and Jim seemed less impressed. Their body language was kind of laid back, bored, show-me types. Jim made a few jokes about the sign-in lines, how it reminded him of registering for college classes. "I thought I was done with standing on lines like this."

"I dig what you're saying, but it's not exactly a hustle," Buddy said.

"I think this is for real, at least let's check it out."

They dutifully lined up.

"Welcome," said a soft voice as they approached the registration desk. A lovely, tall thin woman, her hair pulled back, wearing a simple Indian-style sari, handed the next in line an index card and pen. The friendly smile was reassuring. Jim approved of her appearance, and suddenly felt better about being there.

Maureen liked the laid back, hassle-free feeling. There was soft chanting and in most areas of the Ashram, mellow music playing. Later on she wandered into the bookshop and purchased some tapes of chants and Siddha Yoga music to listen to when she got home.

Lunch was satisfying enough for Maureen and Annie, but both men disliked the vegetarian fare. "I can see why everyone looks so lean up here. Hell, I can just about swallow another spoon full of this rice," Jim commented.

"Hey for this money, what do you expect?" Maureen joked.

"The damned thing tastes like library paste," was Buddy's critique. He went to the modest Siddah-operated ice cream shop and bought himself a double dip cone. Sweets were big at the Ashram. The ice cream would have to sustain him for the afternoon.

Afterward they explored the grounds, talked to some of the other visitors, and waited for the 5 p.m. meditation service, which was to be the highlight of the visit.

"Get there early for a good view of Muktananda," a slim young man who was visiting from Chicago, said. "And an aisle seat is great, because Baba comes down the aisle and you can get a better view that way."

"How long have you been up here?" Jim asked.

"Came last weekend and decided to stay through this one. It's been some trip! I'm graduating next month. From the University of Chicago. I read about this happening in my local newspaper. Thought I'd come and see what it's all about – and it's really worth it."

Later they attended the meditation service. After, they sat out on the green lawn and talked.

"Muktananda is a realized being, Maureen. That's what Sally Kempton's article explained. That he doesn't know how to judge anyone. It's probably why we're finding all of this…well, so spellbinding," Annie said. "Because being around a divine being raises one's consciousness. There are special, gifted teachers in this world. Individuals like Gandhi, and Jesus, and I think even Muktananda, they're all self-realized beings, saints," she said with reverence.

"You know, you're on the right track, Annie. The Saints of my childhood, what I learned in my catechism – was that they devoted themselves to others. The saints saw Jesus in all of us. In the most distressing of disguises, enlightened people see the good. And I think Muktananda, he holds a mirror…or maybe he is a mirror that reflects the purity in our souls."

"Profound, Maureen!"

What Annie already knew was she liked the meditation because it made here quiet down inside, to feel — well — at peace. Prayer was asking. Meditation was listening. If this process was created through the chanting and prayers, the stillness of meditation, and if it meant that she could be a calmer person by learning how to still her mind, then this was better than any pill, any drink, any elixir known to man.

"We both have had our own hard times, I guess. But you know, people can rise above it, and build good lives for themselves. It's what I think I've gotten from the 12 Steps in AA. I need to get rid of the negativity. And not to be so judgmental, both of myself and of others," Annie continued. "I suppose I had a poor role model in my mother. She was constantly judging everyone including herself."

"Ditto on the mom part. My mother decided what was good for me according to her own limited views... and when I didn't want to live my life her way, well - you know what happened," Maureen said solemnly.

"The thing is...I don't want to blame anyone any longer, even my parents for anything that's happened to me. I've had to pray for those I feel hurt me and forgive them. I learned this in AA. It's a daily process, but I'm going to move on, or I'll never feel okay."

"You're right Annie. Let's both try to move on. And I like the meditation — there sure is a lot to explore and learn up here," Maureen said. "I'm going to sign up for one of the weekend Intensives. Want to do it with me? We can share a room. I found out that there's a van service that leaves from the West Side that we can take up and back. We won't have to rely on anyone to drive us up."

"Yes, count me in."

By the next day Maureen had become drawn in by the music, and soon someone gave her a guitar and she sang along. Funny, the joy of the music, the harmonization seemed vital here. She loved the chanting, the soft, loving songs that were sung. Without realizing it, she was going through a metamorphosis, one that would take her on a journey into the music world.

The next morning, awakening early, the girls rushed to the meditation hall. Again, chanting, then meditation and a beautiful sense of tranquility and comfort surrounded them. It was truly an extraordinary experience.

At the end of the program, they got up from their pillows in the fast emptying meditation hall and looked around for the men.

"There's Jim, he looks bored to tears," Maureen said, seeing Jim leaning against the wall in the large meditation hall.

"Well ladies, have you had your fill? I'm just about ready to leave.

Let's find Buddy and head on back, okay?"

"Buddy is out on the grass dead to the world. I saw him before. I'll go get him," Maureen remarked.

"Didn't you score with any of the ladies, Jim?"

"That's a low blow, Annie."

"Well, it may be, and I apologize. What about breakfast?" Annie asked.

"We can stop on the road. I don't think my stomach can take another vegetarian meal…and those Indian spices…my stomach is erupting," Jim said, rubbing his abdomen.

"Okay, hon. No problem."

It was only 9 a.m., but the women didn't resist. They knew they'd both be back. To be with Baba.

— ❦ —

Know then thyself, presume not God to scan;
The proper study of mankind is man.
— *Alexander Pope*

— ᴄᴙ —

Chapter 22

It was a warm and languid July day 200 years after 1776. And so on this extraordinary Fourth of July weekend there would be grand celebrations throughout America. In New York City, the fleet was in and the Bi-Centennial would be celebrated in splendid fashion.

Annie and Maureen had chosen this holiday weekend to return to the Ashram. For Annie, this was a time to declare her *own* independence. She'd been going through a subtle but significant metamorphosis and so the reverential setting of the Siddah Yoga meditation hall and the soft bell-like chanting helped her focus on the authority inside of her. For most of her life, her thoughts ran wild. Now, as she became more proficient at meditation, the racing thoughts slowed down. She needed this— to rest within a deeper place.

After the early morning meditation, Annie meandered outside into a bucolic setting of plush green lawns that looked like majestic soft carpeting. It was difficult not to be seduced by the sounds of birds singing in the trees and the subtle scent of the incense, so breath-taking that it wafted in waves to the out-of-doors and mingled with the sweet air. No one seemed to mind where anyone walked or sat or lay upon the soft green grass. A fresh, warm breeze drifted by, fanning the good feelings within her. Amazing! She felt safe, secure, really okay.

Beyond a small footbridge, regal looking swans, both black and white, glided along in a lake that gleaned in the sunlight like prisms of a mirror to the soul. She moved closer, peered in and saw an ever expanding circle of peace and calm resonate, halos of water spinning about as the beautiful swans – the guru's symbols of devotion — slowly sashayed along.

— ∞ —

Everyone pitched in at the Ashram. Volunteers cleaned the lobby, or the public bathrooms, while others helped prepare the vegetarian food in the kitchen. Visitors on their first day were amazed at the way this very large former hotel was run so perfectly. There wasn't a drop of litter around, the bathrooms were ultra clean and the crowds of diners lined up silently and patiently to get their food in a cafeteria-like setting. Each one worked with joy, as if it was a privilege to serve. It didn't matter if the individual was a highly paid advertising executive in the city, nor a celebrity visiting from Broadway — participating was a source of pleasure.

The next day, Sunday, Maureen, guitar in hand, having learned and practiced an old Hindu chant, sang at the morning meditation. She sounded bell-like and beautiful and was clearly touched when Muktananda blessed her with his wand of peacock feathers.

"I'm going to try my hand at writing some music," Maureen shared later. "I feel like I should be writing and singing my songs." Maureen's face was glowing, her eyes sparkling with happiness. She too was finding something special here.

"When we get back to the city, I'll look up an old friend, who's in the music business. I got to know him when I worked at a record company. He's an A&R man, and has written a string of hit songs too. I'll bet he can help you, Maureen," Annie suggested, thinking immediately of Roosevelt.

Oblivious to her remarks Maureen went on: "I want to come back — spend my vacation up here," Maureen said. "I get two weeks in August. Muktananda, he's very special, isn't he?"

"I know what you're saying…I feel like there's something magical, very powerful here…that I can learn from the experience too."

"When I went to see Baba before, on line — I asked him how I can get rid of negative thoughts. He answered that I must just view them without judgment and then I will see them for what they are…that's simple, and yet, well kind of profound, isn't it?" Maureen commented.

"I tried that during the meditation," Annie answered. She closed her eyes and waited a moment. "And I noticed that I felt less judgmental after it all. That I could let go of some of the negative thoughts that keep crowding and running through my brain."

What Annie didn't share with Maureen was that she was also hoping that Baba had magical powers that could overcome all the obstacles she'd experienced in her broken marriage, that somehow he'd be able to reconcile Tom and she. It was so long since they'd spoken anything but brief words to one another. They were divorced, and yet she still thought about him, still missed him, still wished they could work out their differences. Incredible, that he still meant so much to her. She yearned for something from him that no matter what, she just didn't get from others, that didn't make her feel good even when she was successful in her writing. After all of this, after all her searching and learning, it was still Tom she wanted.

"I asked a question too," Maureen responded. I wanted to know about unconditional love. Do you know what Baba said?"

"No, What?"

"*The core of compassion is unconditional love.*" That's what Baba said. I figured out that he wants me to be more forgiving. You know I still hold anger towards that creep who transmitted the gonorrhea to me, and also, I get angry at how my mother — well, she seems to favor everyone else in the family but me. I think I have to find a way to forgive them all, to be more compassionate," Maureen said thoughtfully.

"And you know what, Annie? When I play and sing up here, I feel really good. Maybe it sounds crazy — maybe it is crazy — but somehow I feel that the guru is telling me I should be singing and playing my guitar, not painting. I don't know where this is coming from, but I'm going to explore it, I am...."

The women felt a kindred ship that was very unique. They embraced. It was good, this deliberate but momentous change, this reaching out, this spiritual journey they were both on.

— ൕ —

She awoke from the disturbing dream...no, nightmare and couldn't believe the panic she felt. Her tee shirt was soaked with sweat. Rid yourself of the f—-ing demons she thought. She felt such rage. How come 60 years later you still remember the hiding in the closet, the horror of it all? Will you ever grow up? And why, when you practice forgiveness and understanding and intellectually agree that yes, your mother was a sick, fragile woman, why in your dreams do you still hear her saying, "NO, NO, NO" and rejecting you all over again?

— ∝ —

Chapter 23

March 1979

"Fabulous! Maureen," Annie said, viewing the brand new cover of Maureen's first album.

"*Rockin with Love*" was the title.

"Is that one of the songs?"

"Yup. Roosevelt wanted an up tempo tune as a lead-in. I also open my act with it."

"That's right...now I remember. You do a great job with it. I heard you sing it at the *Blue Note*." Annie observed.

"Correct, my darling friend! That was my first big club date. I can't believe it yet. All this stuff happening to little ole me! Wow, and now after the *Blue Note* I've cut my first album."

"So much has come to pass for both of us, so much good!" Annie said, an immense smile upon her face. She was really happy for Maureen.

"Actually *"Rockin with Love"* was the first song I wrote by myself — words as well as music. And with Roosevelt doing his usually great arrangements, well, it certainly took on a life of it's own."

"Boy am I glad I called him for you! He was so helpful to me for so long, he has a really good heart. He's really a wonderful person, never mind so talented." There was a lot Annie didn't say, couldn't tell Maureen about Roosevelt and herself.

"I'll always be grateful to you, Annie. He's a gem — a real genius! And…well, you know how much experience he's had. I can't believe he's worked with top singers like Dinah Washington and Sam Cook, and that he agreed to work with me. He's written the music to four of the other selections — and the rest of the album — Annie, I wrote both words and music on these. I did 'em all myself," she said with great pride.

"Wow, and after all those years you spent on the abstract art, all those paintings and work. Here you are using your beautiful voice – l loved it from the time you used to sing in the school cafeteria, way back when. Remember?"

"This just seemed, well *authentic*, Annie dear. I was always expressing something in my art, but it didn't seem right. This, the music, the singing, now I feel I'm giving of myself, that it's what I should do."

"Well, come to think of it, I never really thought I'd end up writing for a living. I had all sorts of ambitions, but never dreamed I could really be paid to be a writer."

"Take it, Annie," Maureen said, handing her the CD she had been holding. "It's the very first one off the press. I want you to go home and play it and let me know, truthfully, what you think. We're going to go on tour next week. We start in Philadelphia."

"I know. I spoke to Roosevelt last night. I'm going to have dinner with him tomorrow. At Jilly's. Maybe I'll actually see Frank Sinatra there! You know it's his favorite hangout when he's in New York. But more important, I want to see Roosevelt. I haven't seen him in so long…it's going to be special, getting together with him again."

"Yes, I know you were close," Maureen said.

How close she didn't know. Some how, that secret, the long term romance, the time they lived together — Annie had respected Roosevelt's wishes — and never told anyone of their intimacy. He was wise. He knew that an affair between a black man and a white woman was still shocking to most people, even those who claimed to be highly liberal in their views. "No sense talking about it to anyone, Annie. It was wonderful, the time we shared. I'll always care about you, and I know you feel the same about me. But it's better to keep this between us," he'd suggested.

Only when Annie talked with Irene, her AA sponsor, and worked on her 5th step, which had to do with sharing one's past indiscretions and misdeeds, did her very private life become known to anyone. She knew it was safe with Irene, as safe as going to confession with a priest. She'd always remember Roosevelt with love and appreciation. And while she was actually rather proud that this man who was so successful and such a public figure had thought so highly of her so long ago — keeping it *their* secret — she knew it was better for everyone that way.

"Well, Roosevelt encouraged me to try writing when I first got to know him. We became friends when I was at that job at Triumph Records. Seems so long ago now. But he really encouraged me. And he never laughed at any poems or lyrics I wrote. Some were good, I see that now; I read a few of them the other day. But I had no confidence, no belief in myself at all. Roosevelt took the time to listen and to be supportive. No matter how busy he was, he listened. He was always a generous spirit," Annie explained.

"Generous he is, almost to a fault. I think that man helps half the world. There's always someone with a down-on-their-luck story, and he never says no," Maureen noted.

"Yeah, he used to give anyone down on his luck — a musician, a songwriter — anyone who stopped by the record company money. He understood how hard it was, what a parasitic industry it is. Some of those people at the top — the ones who run the business — they take advantage of too many of the writers and artists. Roosevelt — he's never forgotten his own battles. He's really a very decent person. He even helped me pay for college and other expenses, and wouldn't take a penny back," Annie said, hoping this wouldn't be revealing too much.

"Well, now he's sitting on top of the world. A real dynamo! Did you know he's building a home in Los Angeles? He's going to be doing more arranging and recording for the movies. He wrote the music for the last Sidney Poitier movie. In fact I think the title song is going to be nominated for an Oscar."

"Yes, he's almost larger than life. I see his name in the columns from time to time. I'm happy for him. He's a giant of a talent and he deserves all the success."

"And wow, Annie, look how far we — you and me have come! What magic, what a miracle!"

"You know, when I look back at it — I tried to instill magical powers in Muktananda — like he was the Wizard of Oz or something. I've always wanted instant answers, quick solutions. But I think what I learned most of all from being with Baba, is that, well, the guru bestows his blessings, which enables people, through their own self-efforts, to overcome the obstacles in their lives."

"Yup, Annie, you're right. We were inspired by Baba, but I think it was through our own efforts that positive changes were made. Still I feel a wonderful connection to him and the SYDA Foundation. In fact, next break I have, I'm going up to the Ashram for a weekend Intensive. It always centers me, makes me feel better."

"Lucky us. We've both gained from the fruit of having Baba's *darshan*," Annie added, realizing how much there was to be grateful for. "What a wonderful, incredible journey!"

For Maureen, it had been three years from the time she first sang along at the Ashram that her singing career had taken off. Actually it first began with an old guitar and her harebrained singing at Village taverns, and then her entertaining at parties. Afterward there was the life-changing meeting with Muktananda. And now, through her affiliation with Roosevelt, she was on her way. She was actually becoming a successful recording artist. Hard to believe but miracles could happen.

She started training with Roosevelt in 1977. He began by doing the arrangements for the songs she brought to him, then writing a few with her, and finally, coaching her until she was ready to appear at small club dates. She enjoyed the work, even if there were some seedy joints in New Jersey and Pennsylvania where she first appeared. She knew she was appreciated when she heard the applause.

Next came a few demo records, which were produced by Roosevelt. Soon, she'd cut her first record: Maureen McDermott sings *"Lovin You is All I Can Do"* and the "B" side was *"Praise God and Be Free,"* an up-tempo gospel-type song. "You know, Annie, even my first record got noticed," Maureen reminisced. "Both sides got air time, and the love song, it made it to the charts, though not that high up. But heck, I heard from some old friends who'd listened to my song on the local radio station. Better still, one of my brothers called, amazed that his sister was singing for a living!" Maureen added. She was full of pride that someone in her family found out she was doing well.

By the time of the record release in 1977 Maureen, taking a big risk, resigned from her illustrator's job at Altman's. She continued to work at her music, to write, record, and finally, in 1978, she had a real hit on her hands, "*Baby Let's Make Music Together*." It had made it to number 8 on the Billboard charts. Finally, Maureen was earning real money.

"Have you heard anything from your Mom?" Annie cautiously asked. No sense bringing up old wounds.

"We speak. She hasn't been that well. She's developed awful arthritis in her knees and hands. Danny, he came to see me when I was performing on Long Island. Brought his wife along. I felt real good and they came back stage. But the rest of them, well Danny said they're proud of me, but they haven't let me know it. I did call my mother a few times — and I've sent her the records to listen to. Funny, she just couldn't say she was happy for me. I don't understand it. But perhaps someday…," she said in a plaintive tone.

"Maybe her idea of achievement must be marriage and babies — perhaps that's the only thing she can relate to. But I bet she's glad that you're making a success of yourself. Why don't you go out and visit her or ask her to come to see you the next time you perform locally?"

"I suppose I'm as stubborn as she is, that's why. But you're probably right. Anyway, when I find that I'll be out on the Island again — there's a chance I can be the opening act for one of the comics out at the Westbury Music Fair next fall — my manager is trying to book it for me — then I'll ask her. And I'll send a car — a big stretch limo — maybe it will impress her. But at least she won't be able to give any excuses — say she can't come because it's too difficult for her. I'd like it, if she would see me perform," Maureen said wistfully.

"Ta Da! My friend has a real manager! Wow, you've come a long way Baby!" Annie said happily.

They both laughed.

"I have you and Roosevelt to thank for this Annie. You

introduced him to me. He's really helped and encouraged me. It's been a trip, a beautiful experience, thanks to both of you — and oh yes, thanks to Baba."

It was true. What a small world it could be. Annie knowing Roosevelt and then putting Maureen together with him — it had worked to their mutual benefit. Wow, she was overjoyed that she had been a part of this and actually had made a difference in someone else's life.

She also knew that the life-affirming time spent up at the Ashram, learning from Muktananda, had positively affected both their lives. What Annie had derived from it was that her sense of self and entire approach to work had changed. She'd become more positive since practicing daily meditation. Somehow through that quiet time, going inward, being still, she became more at ease with expressing herself.

"You know the very first serious piece of writing I did, was when I wrote about the opening of the Siddha Yoga Ashram on 86th Street," Annie reminded Maureen.

"It was Baba. He asked for the *"writer"* to do it, and he was referring to me. *Me*, the writer! When they told me that, well, I was astounded, that this great man was giving me the title of "writer." You know, Maureen, I was never very sure of myself. Then going up to the ashram all those weekends, that first summer, well it was the very first time anyone actually referred to me as a real honest-to-goodness writer. Maybe it sounds peculiar, but I believe it was Baba who began me on my writing career," she whispered, almost shy about sharing her thankful thoughts.

"The guru is an enlightened being and he can shed light for all of us.

I suppose it's what happens in all great metamorphoses. It's like being reborn, Annie."

"Well rebirth started for me when I finally got the AA Program. There was a lot of denial until I did it *their* way, not mine. All of this, all of these experiences, and I don't think I'd even trade the bad ones, have helped me to learn better ways of dealing with life and being more accepting."

"What a rip-roaring hell-of-a-trip!" Maureen added. "And who would know, when we started out, that we'd have a chance at grabbing...not that we wanted it — the gold ring!"

"Speak for yourself, girl! I like the golden ring, both on my finger, and well, every way!"

"You've got a point there," Maureen said.

They giggled like little girls.

Annie was now a full-fledged writer and doing double-duty at that. She was a reporter and weekly columnist for *Our Town Newspaper* and a full-time editor for Harcourt Brace Jovanovich, in its major trade publishing company. Besides this, after a year of writing beauty and fashion columns she'd obtained a literary agent, a top-notch one at that, Connie Clausen, who handled works by Francisco Scavullo, Quentin Crisp and many other best-selling authors. Annie came up with the ideas, wrote the proposals and Connie successfully sold 'em.

Her first book, "*Look Super for Less*," a paperback published by Dell, was now in its second printing. A whole new career facet, writing how-tos, mostly on beauty and skin care had opened up for her. One thing led to another, and her name was getting well known. Her married name, that is.

Annie Ryan, was her chosen byline, the name she used when writing. Frankly, she associated her birth name, Rosenberg, with the fragmented family life, the unhappiness she'd suffered, and felt more comfortable with Ryan.

Of course Annie's parents resented her not going back to her maiden name, but Ryan was lucky for her. "How can you use a goyisha name, instead of your birth name, Annie?" her mother reproached her.

Hell, if Ryan had been her maiden name and her married one Rosenberg, Annie would have still chosen to write under the latter one. Her mother just didn't get it, the long, sad history. But maybe that was because she was still caught up in it.

Annie Ryan, the writer, was getting to be known and she liked that. When an opportunity came up to write on restaurants for *Our Town*, alternating with the main reviewer, Annie grabbed it. "*The Epicurean Explorer*" was the name of her column, and soon her reviews, and her name, were blown up in windows all over Manhattan. What a fantastic deal. Free food, inviting friends to join her, and a byline.

She was now working on her next book, "*A Year of Beauty and Exercise for the Pregnant Woman*," a hardcover for Lippincott-Crowell, a top-flight publisher. Odd, she had never been pregnant, but this book, it was like her baby. It took a good deal of research, but she liked to investigate, to delve into subject matter, and long before others had written about the hazards of alcohol and pregnancy and the fetal alcohol syndrome, Annie developed a chapter on not smoking, never mind one on not drinking nor taking any questionable medications during pregnancy. Her own experiences in AA played an invaluable role in making her aware of the subtleties in how chemicals and cigarette addiction affected the body.

Still she coveted approval from her mother. And so Annie dedicated the book to, who else, but her Mom. After all, pregnancy was the ideal subject matter. It worked. Sara Rosenberg actually said something nice about her daughter when Annie sent her one of the first copies. Well sort of —. She was never very good at being direct in positive comments. They were all together for one of their rare family dinners. It was to her dad that her mother directed the good comments: "Sam, look, our daughter is now a writer and she thanks _me_ for it."

Then a few months later, when her next how-to was published: "*A Man's Guide to Plastic Surgery*" Annie thanked both her mother and father in the acknowledgements. Evidently her mother didn't like sharing the limelight. When she called home to ask what her parents thought of her latest book, her mother commented: "Well, to tell you the truth, the quality of the paper isn't so good (as your other one)."

In January of 1979, Annie queried *New York Magazine* about writing an article on advertising for love in the personals. After all – she'd done it. That's how she'd met Tom. Met and married him. She'd learned to write good proposals, and sure enough, *New York Magazine* bought the idea.

In April 1979 Annie Ryan's story, along with a half page photo, appeared in *New York Magazine*. Television producers called to talk to her about a spot on their talk shows. The public relations department of *New York Magazine* set up contacts. Soon, she found herself doing a string of television appearances, including appearing in Baltimore on a morning talk show co-hosted by a young, and relatively unknown Ophra Winfrey.

Her major appearance took place on the David Susskind show, a popular hour talk show on a local New York station. Ironically — she didn't plan it that way — but she essentially became the star of the show. Susskind introduced Annie both as a published author, the current entertainment editor for *Our Town Newspaper*, and the writer of the *New York Magazine* story. She was pitted against other guests who'd advertised in the personals, including a really obnoxious professional bachelor, who professed that his main goal in advertising was to get himself '*one-nighters*', ratcheting up his conquests like a warrior. The verbal banter between Annie, who was always good at wisecracking and this slobbering example of a man was beyond belief. When the host, Susskind, asked if Annie would consider dating him, she laughed. "Of course not, I consider him nothing better than a *Chauvinist Pig.*" The audience laughed in approval and gave Annie a thunderous round of applause.

The TV show was taped. When it was time for its airing Annie rushed over to Jim's apartment to view the production. Jim had bought himself a large screen TV and she wanted to see herself on the biggest screen she could. What a terrific experience, watching yourself on TV and being witty and a hit on it! Yes, Annie's life was changing fantastically!

She was good, really good. Wow, what a fantastic feeling it was to be the main subject and to come off so well in a television program. When Annie returned home later, there was a host of congratulatory messages on her answering machine from friends who had seen her on the Susskind show.

There was also a call from her mother. The message was: "*You didn't look so hot, Annie. It's Mom.*" Like anyone else would have left such a cutting remark.

— ❦ —

The difference between life and the movies is that a script has to make sense, and life doesn't."
— *Joseph L. Mankiewicz*

— ❦ —

Chapter 24

I t was April 23, 1979, and there she was — sitting contentedly across the table at Jilly's restaurant, gazing at her once grand amour, Roosevelt Jones. It felt oh so good that the fascination still lingered; Roosevelt possessed a magnetic force that would forever move her spirit. He smiled at her and it was like the world took notice; but then he'd always had this incredible way of illuminating a room.

She'd noticed the warm welcome he received from the maitre 'd when he walked in. Having appeared on a number of television shows, and after touring with major musical stars, Roosevelt was now ministered to like a celebrity. Gosh, she realized — he *was* a celebrity. But he had no entourage, no phony conceit about him.

"You know Annie, I'm really glad for your success. I told you that you had it in you, girl, that you'd become a full-fledged writer. And you've made it. And — I caught most of the Susskind show, and you were terrific on it, terrific," he said, rubbing her shoulder gently.

"Thanks. You know hearing it from you, really means something to me."

He grinned. "Let's order something to eat and then we can talk."

She really wasn't hungry. Somehow she never had an appetite when she was around exceptional people. Like Roosevelt. Annie was so glad she'd met him and that they'd remained friends. For a while he'd been her mentor, had continued to help and encourage her. She was really fortunate to have known him and even though she had to keep their intimacy secret, it really didn't matter; they'd always share a special bond. Besides, times were changing, and maybe in a few years, an interracial relationship would be acceptable. But this was still the late 70s, and she'd never betray his trust by revealing their affair.

This evening, she noticed a few heads did turn when a black and white couple sat down alone to dine. But at least in the world of show business, most people looked the other way; there was far more tolerance shown. Why *'Ol Blue Eyes'*, as Frank was called, had become good friends with Sammy Davis, Jr. Things were changing, but slowly.

Too bad Sinatra wasn't at the restaurant, which she knew was one of his favorite places. Jilly, of course was the owner and Frank's long-time pal. Annie heard he was making a movie on the West Coast. But still the place was packed.

"Annie, I have something for you," Roosevelt said, reaching into his pocket and placing a small blue velvet box on the table.

"For me?" she said flirtingly. It was difficult not to flirt with him.

"We haven't seen each other in a long while, but well, you brought a really good singer to me and this is my modest thank you. Open it, why don't you?"

It was a heart-shaped pendant encrusted with brilliant diamonds. Spectacular diamonds. She knew it was expensive. Roosevelt was always the sport, the big spender, generous to a fault. But the cost really didn't matter half as much as the incredible gesture – that Roosevelt thought of giving her something so beautiful and loving. She'd treasure it always.

Tears welled up in her eyes. "I know it's silly, because it's been so long, but you know how I've always felt about you, Roosevelt, and this gift…well, I will wear it and think of you, and be grateful…."

"Hey, enough little girl," he interrupted. It's from my heart to yours, but I don't want you to cry over anything I give you," he smiled.

They both laughed a bit, as they clicked their water glasses together. (He knew Annie no longer drank and had ordered a bottle of imported water.)

As always, he was a thoughtful, considerate human being.

Annie would remember that dinner always. But not just because Roosevelt had given her such a lovely remembrance. It would turn out to be the last time she'd ever see him alive.

— ○℞ —

May 25, 1979

It was Friday, the end of a long workweek. Annie had just come home from the office. She decided to stay in and just take it easy. She was exhausted after a few early mornings of working on a chapter of her latest book, while still toiling all day as an editor at Harcourt Brace.

She really didn't mind doing the double duty. An editor's salary just wasn't very lavish… good secretaries made just about the same amount, however the "glamour" of being an editor had attracted droves of young women and men into the field. Publishing was not a high-paying field — not unless you were a managing editor of a major magazine, or a best-selling author of a popular book. And that was not Annie's status.

Actually, working as the editor of a small trade publication, *"Hosiery and Underwear Magazine"* wasn't exactly what one would term, glamorous. Her friends laughed at the title of the weekly magazine. But Annie didn't mind the underwear reference…hell, it was a good training ground and she did get to do some first-rate profiles of executives in the hosiery industry; had even made trips down to North Carolina where the major manufacturing took place. She was collecting by-lines, was building up her portfolio, and maybe, just maybe — one of her how-to books would make it. As for the "underwear" title to the weekly, she never could figure out why that wasn't dropped, since there were no articles in the publication on this topic.

That upcoming weekend, Annie was planning to see Maureen perform at the Westbury Music Fair out on Long Island. She knew that Roosevelt, who was rehearsing with another singing group in Chicago, was due back and would be accompanying Maureen at Westbury. What a double treat to see them both.

She took off her work clothes, threw on a robe, put up her feet and turned on the television. A bulletin interrupted the regular programming. It was news of a major disaster. There had been a plane crash. Somewhere in Chicago. She listened carefully. The newscaster was reporting that earlier that afternoon an American Airlines DC-10 lost an engine and crashed on takeoff from Chicago. There had been many fatalities. A foreboding feeling overcame her.

The telephone rang. It was Maureen. "Annie, 274 people died on a plane out of Chicago. I think it was the flight Roosevelt was booked on. I called his office. They sounded frantic," she said, barely containing tears.

"Oh my God, my God," Annie said. "Don't let it be true."

But it was. On Friday, May 25, 1979, Roosevelt Jones was one of 274 passengers who did not survive the fiery crash of the American

Airlines plane that had lost an engine on take-off. A brilliant career, the splendid life of an extraordinary man had been tragically shattered – gone at the age of 46. His death left an abyss, an empty hole in so many lives.

...Life is what happens to us while we're busy making plans.

— CR —

Chapter 25

Sunday, May 27, 1979

The funeral was bleak and black and painful. The loss of a man in the prime of his life, never mind so unexpectedly and violently, intensified the somber mood.

Roosevelt was so loved and admired that the Campbell Funeral Home on Madison Avenue was overflowing. Mourners spilled out from the church steps and then into an extended line that turned into an ever-widening crowd on the street below. Black umbrellas trailing down the sidewalk gave the scene a morose look, as the heavens opened up and poured forth huge hailstone-size raindrops, as the sound of the rainfall thumping on the tops of the umbrellas muted the organ music playing solemn hymns inside.

While Annie knew she had to be there, she felt unbearably awkward. She stood in the back — way back. She considered staying outside, but the warm spring rain was a hard one and she didn't have an umbrella. Somehow the rain was comforting, bearing witness to the natural rhythm of life—and if only for a brief moment, allayed the harsh reality — that a young man had died.

At the front of the room, the gleaming copper casket held the mortal remains. The casket was closed; the air crash had mangled the victims' bodies. The lid was covered with a blanket of red roses, and surrounding the coffer were so many floral tributes that there wasn't much room for the mourners to come up and bid their goodbyes.

One tribute came from Pricilla Presley. A heart-shaped wreath of white roses and orchids was banded about with a wide ribbon inscribed with the words: "It Was A Night. Oh Such A Night". The card read "in memory of you and your song for Elvis." Presley had made a hit recording of Roosevelt's song in 1964. Biting her tongue, as if that would stop the tears, Annie wept inconsolably.

But what moved her the most was getting a glimpse of Roosevelt's mother. Annie knew how very important she had been to Roosevelt; he'd talked about her often. Stooped over with the ravages of osteoporosis, this once robust woman appeared frail and far older than her 68 years on earth. Her hair had turned snow white and she walked with an unsteady gait.

There were tears welling up in Rosella Jones's eyes, yet her inner strength and resolve shone through as she grasped the hands of two teenage boys. Roosevelt was a private person; hadn't shared that part of his life, but evidently these were his youngest children. It saddened Annie to see any family member so tormented. It was obvious that they were traumatized by his death. Only the good die young, that's what they say.

Then she noticed a tall, regal looking woman in a simple black suit. It had to be Roosevelt's wife. Annie could see her face, the exquisite features, as well as the reddened eyes. Though it happened so long ago, she felt shame for her role in taking him away from his family.

But she also knew he'd had many long-term affairs. Besides, Roosevelt traveled so much for his business that his family probably didn't expect a normal amount of attention. *"No, shut up!"* Annie screamed to herself to stop the racing thoughts. *"What do you know of what they expected? Or got?"* Damn it, she felt guilty.

"Would you like a seat?" the usher asked.

"No, no thank you. I'd rather stand here on the side," she answered, her words stuck in her throat.

She felt dreadful. *"This isn't the time to worry about being embarrassed. Just worry about his family — his sweet old mother, his wife and kids and hope they're well-provided for. Stop thinking about your minor part in all of this,"* Annie chided herself.

As if anyone might be listening to the thoughts that were chasing through her mind: *"You've no right to assume anything about his family. Sure he was a good provider, but he wasn't a faithful husband, and that had to be a cruel state of affairs for his wife. But he's gone now, Annie, he's departed from this earth, he's lost to everyone, this wonderful, generous man with so much talent. Feeling to blame, making judgments, is self-centered so let it go, let it go."*

At that very moment Annie glanced up and noticed Maureen seated in a back pew, of the chapel, eyes shut, praying. She was kneeling on the padded knee structure. At the conclusion she made the sign of the cross. A fallen-away Catholic — yet there she was — asking Jesus to help Roosevelt and his family. Maureen was devastated; her childhood religion gave her comfort.

Annie gazed around and saw some of the luminaries of rock and roll in the front pews. Chuck Berry, Little Richard, the group of girl singers — the Shirelles — were some of the artists who came to say farewell. She also recognized members of the Modern Jazz Quartet. Roosevelt had talked of their artistry often, and counted two of the members of the group among his closest friends.

Disc jockeys, presidents of record companies, celebrities of stage and screen were there. Roosevelt would have taken pleasure in the turnout, she thought. He was a people person and seeing his friends, so many of them — would have made him feel good. She only hoped he could see them all there, know he was sorely missed. Was there a heaven? Was there someone who was watching over him? She was confused, but wanted so to believe.

Bayard Rustin, the black social and political activist, who had known Roosevelt since the early beginnings of his career, gave the eulogy. They had become good friends. A Quaker, he spoke of Roosevelt's incredibly generous heart, his support of all nonviolent causes, his wonderful talents and the songs that would live after him.

But his eldest son, Roosevelt Jones, Jr, spoke the saddest words of all.

"My father, he was there for us when he was needed. He always attended our little league games, and he helped me through one bad period, when I have to admit I was drinking too much. Sometimes it's not easy being the eldest and also carrying your famous father's name. I got into some trouble a few years back, smashed up a car pretty badly, but Dad, he was there for me. I went in to one of the 12-Step programs, and I've been straight ever since. *'Dad, I love you for what a great man you were, what a powerful example, and I'll always love you,' just like all your children do,"* he said, tears rolling down his cheek.

Now Annie realized why Roosevelt had been so understanding, why he'd taken care to order the bottle of imported water that last time they met for dinner. He'd seen first hand how alcohol could devastate a life.

They performed some of Roosevelt's compositions on the chapel's organ. It was glorious listening to his body of work. Heartbreaking too. There was an intense silence throughout the room, an awareness that a brilliant and creative artist could no longer contribute in this life. And then, a wonderful new singer,

Aretha Franklin, arose to sing a few Negro Spirituals, and soon the church was filled with hand clapping and warmth. Soul music, it was the best way to send Roosevelt Jones on his way. The passion of the chorus that accompanied Aretha, the glory of the gospel songs that went on for more than half an hour held one and all spellbound. It was an exhilarating experience worthy of the man.

Before the final words were spoken, the last goodbye said, biting her tongue to keep from crying out loud, Annie just had to get out of the memorial service. She couldn't hide her hurt much longer and even though she was in a sea of fellow mourners, she felt oddly conspicuous. She'd go to a nearby church and light a candle for Roosevelt. It was all she could think of doing, Jewish or not. And for the next week, every day she'd go and light another candle in his memory. She was sorry now that she hadn't spent more time with him and kept in closer contact. But then there was that crazy period when she'd gotten married and sort of dropped off the earth and lost contact with most everyone. Besides, Roosevelt was a very, very busy man, immersed in his successful show business life and then of course — his family. But still the loss was beyond measure. She felt a terrible numbness inside her. The first man she'd ever really loved, could he really be gone?

She was relieved that they'd met for dinner not so long ago. She went home, opened her dresser drawer where she'd placed the velvet box for safekeeping. It held the special gift Roosevelt had given her the last time they were together. Annie carefully took it out of the box, kissed it and put the diamond heart around her neck. She'd wear it every day from then on, for the rest of her life.

— ◌ɞ —

Chapter 26

March 1981

More than a year had passed yet a sense of loss lingered.

"Life has to go on. We all know that. But it must be brutal on Roosevelt's family, losing him like that," Maureen said. "I called his wife once and she was very pleasant. But there was so little I could say except to let her know how much he'd helped my career. "

"I'm still numb over it," Annie replied glumly.

"His mother suffered a stroke a few months later. She's in a nursing home now. He was everything to her," Maureen added.

"Oh, wow, I didn't know that. How sad. He loved her very much and took such good care of her. "

"You know Annie, we never know what's going to happen in life. I called my mom and told her that I loved her. I don't know — I hope it got through. I know she's softening a bit, but somehow I've always been the black sheep in the family. Now, well, we'll see.

And losing Roosevelt — it hit me hard too. It was touch and go the first year, but because he was so prolific, he'd prepared many of the arrangements for the new songs. I have more than enough material in the hopper for maybe two more albums. Besides, I lucked out with a good manager and I've been getting plenty of club dates — so I'm more than alright," Maureen continued.

"I'm glad for you. It was pretty traumatic when we all heard about the crash. I try not to think about it because when I do I get down in the dumps about his going that way. So horrible. He was such a good person, so very giving to me. I'll never forget him," Annie whispered sadly. "Never. "

They hugged one another — as if closeness would assuage their loss.

Maureen tried to lighten the conversation: "I was hoping you were coming to my show in New Jersey. "

"Oh, Maureen, I'm sorry. I wanted to see you. Truly. But I had to spend time in Brooklyn. My mom. Sick again. I'm the only one around right now, with my sister in Arizona. No fun, but I had to do it. "

"What about your brother?He's been out of the service and in school for a long while now?"

"Sid — believe it or not, is working on his second master's. I think he's become a professional student. Besides, he's just not the accommodating type. Actually, he acts offended by my mother's illnesses. And she's always favored him, there's the real irony!He's very selfish. Says our mother is doing it for attention, that she's a hypochondriac, that she'll get some quack doctor to remove organ by organ if it helps her stay in the limelight. I won't argue the point – yes, she's neurotic, but she had medical tests that showed some serious problems. This time, it meant surgery. On her pancreas. She's not recovering very fast. "

"Still — Sid's probably right. She's controlling you through her poor health, and from what you've always told me, does little to help herself. "

"You're sharp, Maureen. I think they call that kind of behavior *"passive/aggressive"* — don't think I haven't noticed. But the fact is, she was bedridden and she's still my mother," Annie said, realizing she was caught between a rock and a hard place. "My dad asked me to stay at the house for a few days. It was hard to say no. And, believe me, she's a horrific patient. It wasn't easy, but if I didn't do it, I'd feel so guilty it was better saying yes. I had some vacation coming so I took some days off. She never did eat right. Wanted ice cream one hour, cake the next. And she has diabetes on top of it. "

"Ironic isn't it — she once had gall bladder problems, didn't she? Something is eating her up," Maureen commented.

"You're right. She's always retreated to food, and of course, continually eats the wrong stuff. She's fanatical about Indian nuts, has been devouring them for years. They're so fatty, which is no good for anyone with pancreas problems! It's a wonder she still has a stomach left. We've all told her — but no matter what, she just doesn't connect the dots. "

"She's a tortured soul. I think she should have left your father a long time ago. From everything you've told me they're like night and day. But since they're from another generation they'll probably stay married 'til death does them part. You can't change anyone else, and if they don't want help, then you really can't lend a hand. "

Well, if it's some kind of mental illness, and I think that's what it is with her, nothing is going to make it go away, if the person isn't dealing with it. I think she's too far gone, secreted so long in a shell, that it won't get any better. She'd never admit to needing help. Most of all, she wouldn't want our relatives to know that there was anything wrong," Annie added. "But I'm sure they're aware of something. "

"I understand, but it's rough, watching someone slowly destroy their self. And it can't do you much good, Annie, going back to the wrong well. There's nothing there to drink from — no nourishment for you. "

"But, still, it's better that I went. I feel I've paid my dues. She'll never change — I know that, Maureen. For as long as I can remember, my mother's always had difficulty bridging the chasm between expectation and reality. She's lived in the world of "If Only. "Except "If only" never came. All of her life she's escaped — into food for comfort — books for fantasy, soap operas on the radio and now television — where everything has a happy ending. "

"Happy endings, nice and easy…that's a rule I learned at school…." Maureen began to sing softly. It was a line from "The Three Penny Opera," a show she'd seen in the Village the prior week.

"Well said, Maureen, you ought to hang out a shingle. You're very sharp. It was emotionally draining staying there. And never once, not once did she show any appreciation. Sure, when I was leaving she said thanks, but you know, I don't think she meant it — she felt it was due her — my waiting on her hand and foot. And yet when I was little and helpless she never really mothered me. I guess…I guess she just didn't have it in her. "

"There are so many laws - people must pass tests before they can drive cars; you'd think some legislative genius would come up with a bill for mandatory lessons in mothering. "

"Well, at least I've got my grandmother's unconditional love - she's always been there for me. She's a great lady! No more — I'm not going to my mother's house just to serve her; they can well afford a nurse. Besides, I have my own problems. "

"Like what?"

Annie hesitated. She knew Maureen would be disappointed in what she was going to tell her.

"Like — well, I'm sort of seeing Tom again. I hadn't heard from him for quite a while, he'd gotten married again — you know — and I didn't want to interfere. "

"So what's new? Tom's the marrying kind!" Maureen said sardonically.

"That was a couple of years ago. It didn't surprise me. I don't think he can be without a woman in his life. I know he lived with some waitress he met soon after we broke up — for about a year. But that didn't work out. "

"Nothing ever does with Tom, he can attract them, but can he keep anyone — with his immature ways?" Maureen commented.

"Anyway, he phoned me about a month ago and asked if I knew of any singles dances in Queens. Evidently he picked up the '*Our Town*' newspaper and saw my new singles column — he can get it when he's at work. It's mostly listings of dances and a few private parties for singles. But he knows I don't cover the boroughs — just Manhattan. Yet he called to ask me about Queens. "

"He was letting you know he was available. "

"Well, I'd heard he was having problems with his wife. She's someone from out in Breezy Point. A young woman who lived two or three houses from his mother's, if you can believe that one. And she'd never been married. I suppose she was like the rest of us... couldn't resist Tom's movie star looks, his little boy quality; I mean there's no denying that he's the kind of man women are attracted to — and sexy as hell. "

"So what happened that made the marriage go wrong this time?"

"I'm not sure. But when I first learned he was going to get married, it was about the time that I was doing the television tour for the *New York Magazine* piece. He'd heard about it and naturally, he watched the Susskind show. He called to congratulate me... but he couldn't really talk much — I heard screaming in the background.

He told me later that his fiancée was there – that she was livid that he was watching anything that remotely had to do with me. She was definitely jealous. "

"After all the two of you have gone through — after all the grief – you were still keeping in touch?" Maureen said, looking exasperated.

"Well…you know I've always cared about Colleen…and so after things calmed down a little, well, finally he let me speak to her. Of course, his mother doesn't know, she absolutely hates me. And I'm sure she's tried to turn the kid against me. But Colleen, she's so sweet and good. We were close when I lived with Tom, and I think, that whatever else, Colleen knows I care about her. She's so precious. And I've sent her some gifts, especially for her birthday.

"Was it really Colleen you cared about and missed or was it wanting to reconnect with Tom?" Maureen asked, already knowing the answer.

"At first, I think the connection was really to her. If there were any feelings, I'd buried them deep inside of me. I worked on the 12 steps in the program and I forgave him but I don't think that he ever knew how he played a part in all of it. He was the *enabler*. I don't think he really is aware of the role he played. "

"Well, I remember a dozen or more times when you phoned me, whispering about the pain you were in, crying into the phone — of how you felt so abandoned out there in Queens, how you just didn't know what to do about Tom and his family. How quick we forget!You know it's often a package deal, don't you?It's not just him, honey, it's his family too. "

"Maureen, don't be so tough on him. I don't know what to think or feel. I've looked at it inside out. I've talked it through in therapy, in group and private sessions and worked it through the steps and prayed a lot, and you know what?I don't have a good answer; I don't know what to do. All I sense is I still feel so much for him — that if you take away the anger, the verbal abuse, the mistrust, the jealousy — all the hurts — if you scrape each and every one of the negatives away, underneath it all, there's still love. "

"I don't know what to say, kiddo. I think you're really treading on dangerous ground. And you've come so far on your own — done so well with your career. I just worry for you. And I really don't have the answers," she said, getting up from her seat. "Hey, would you like anything to drink?" Maureen asked, pouring herself a cola.

"No, I'm good. I just wanted you to listen — and — well – maybe — to say it could be different now," Annie said faintly, knowing it'd be difficult to gain Maureen's seal of approval. "I didn't really get in touch with Tom until a few weeks after we'd been up at the Ashram. Somehow I felt it was okay after that to write to him. For a long time, I avoided direct contact with him, and just sent things addressed to Colleen. "

"Contact? Yikes! You knew it was like a child touching a hot stove. You were fearful — because you could still remember the bad parts. I think you're in some sort of denial now, Annie, if you think it will be different. You may have changed and grown, but has Tom?"

"Well, with time, he doesn't seem to have such a short fuse. He was very angry when I first left. It took a long time before he was in any way approachable. Then, after Baba, I prayed a lot and listened to my heart and I finally did it, I wrote Tom a note. He called me. So we sort of got over the worst part…and well we're at least on civil terms with one another. "

"Sorry, hon, but since you're asking my advice, well, I think that's where it should remain — on civil terms. "

"But, Maureen — I've changed, years have gone by…."

"Annie, what makes you think he's changed? You once told me he laughed at the thought of going to 'Al Anon'. The man is close-minded. "

"Well you may be right. At the beginning, I listened to my sponsor and knew it would be bad for my sobriety to see him. Irene told me that a person who lives with an active alcoholic is also sick. I could never see that — thought it was *me*… but after a few years, I realized his role in all of it. "

"Glad to hear you're in touch with reality. "

"But that was then and this is now. I've changed, grown up a lot, and see things differently — and I have 8 years in the program. I still care about him, never, ever, have I found anyone to make me feel so much. "

"Feelings can fool you. You're asking what I think, and you know I love you like a sister — and you've always been a good friend. But I hate to see you hurt again. Sorry, but I think you're flirting with disaster. And boy, would I like to be proven wrong! You know I only want the best for you. "

"Love is not something easy to find. I didn't leave him because I didn't love him, Maureen. I left because I couldn't live with him. But it's a different time now. I've become more independent, have a career — and yet, with all the success, I still have feelings for him. I'm sober, have a lifeline with the program — it's ongoing therapy — it can bolster me. Sure, it's great to be published, to see your name in print. But you can't go to bed with a book. In the last analysis if I had to choose between a career and a successful marriage, I'd opt for the marriage. "

"Marriage. Look at your parent's. Look at mine. Look at half of them. You know it's damned hard to find one person you can live with, grow with, not get tired of — and well, Tom's track record ain't so great either!"

"So call me a romanticist, an optimist — there are happy marriages. I'm not willing to give up yet. You know, in all these years, I've never found anyone else that I really cared for like I cared for Tom. What could a few dates mean? All I've done is ask him if he wants to come in and do a restaurant with me…he doesn't even have to pay since I'll be reviewing the place. "

"I don't know, Annie — somehow I think the two of you are like oil and water. Or should I say oil and fire? You're a combustible combination — you have to be careful or you'll get hurt all over again. "

"I'm praying a lot. And he sounds like he's done some growing up too. "

"Maybe — but he's also just failed at another marriage. That doesn't say much for his mental health!And from what little you told me of the first one, it was a real Irish soap opera with his wife drinking herself to death because he just wasn't around. I don't know if he has the capacity to change. I hope for your sake — if you're going to see him again — you'll go slow, very slow," Maureen advised.

"I'll try. I really will. I don't want to get hurt again either. He's coming over to my apartment tomorrow…just the lobby. He's meeting me there. All we're doing is going out to dinner. I'm writing up a new Italian restaurant on East 72nd Street. I know he likes Italian food. What harm could there be in that?" she said.

Little did she know.

— CR —

"To fear love is to fear life and those who fear life are already three parts dead."

— ႙ —

Chapter 27

It started with the one dinner and later on, at Annie's suggestion, (everything was always at *her* suggestion,) a movie. Sitting in the theater, in the dark, so close to him, Annie had to keep her body intact, not let her leg touch his leg, not allow her arm to make contact. Tom was always laid back, never made a physical move unless he knew it would be welcomed.

The magic of a movie, the muted lighting, and the larger-than-life figures on the silver screen stirred her deepest, most quixotic fantasies. Every sense — touch, smell, taste – were so much more *alive*. It was safe yet stimulating, being this physically close. And she enjoyed the pretense, the temptation of the game. Oh yes, she knew it was a game, this sitting next to one another in the dark. But it was exciting — it tingled and felt so good.

At the beginning, Annie made sure she didn't invite Tom up to her apartment. Everything was tentative. Like they were friends. She knew he was more afraid than she was to get involved. Yet something was drawing them together — part of it was a soft, silent tenderness and the rest — an electrifying force that glimmered just beneath the surface.

Sometimes she thought Tom was too passive, too shy. Maybe he was still the way he was years ago — the little boy lost — a participant who could not— would not take responsibility for anything that happened. Was it the *Peter Pan Principle*? Maybe he hadn't grown at all.

Yet, he was so reassuring, so pleasant, so easy to be around. Annie could relax and feel completely comfortable with Tom. He was always polite and sweet and then, wow, all she had to do was look at his face, the square jaw, the perfect nose — his was really a movie-star handsome face — and all she wanted was to be held in his arms, to be wrapped up in his sexy body.Soon Annie was feeling that old intensity, a rekindled interest, a wonderful exquisite warmth. It didn't take long for her to realize she was still passionately in love with this man. Or was it just a physical fervor and not real love? What the heck was real love anyway? She didn't want to repeat old mistakes, she'd changed and grown and was sober and sensible and yet, and yet — she wanted him so.

Was this right? Should she trust her emotions? Truly, she was bewildered with what was real and what was not.

And then there came a day, May 16th.

Truth can be stranger than fiction. Who would believe that exactly on May 16, the anniversary of the day they were married 14 years before, that they'd end up lying in each other's arms, giving way to the passion for one another.

— ᙭ —

It had begun that Saturday morning when he had called to say he was nearby. They'd met and gone for coffee and then taken a walk around Annie's neighborhood in Murray Hill, which was a quiet residential section of Manhattan. They ambled by the brownstones and tall buildings and past the trash containers lined up on the sidewalks. Then while passing one of the high-rise buildings on

Second Avenue they came upon a discarded Christmas tree, an artificial one, but in rather good condition and amazingly, with most of the ornaments still attached. There it was, in the merry month of May tossed out on the sidewalk waiting for garbage pick up.

She couldn't help but giggle. Annie felt so good being with Tom, and now this prize discovery! It was an *omen*, of this she was sure.

"It is a rather strange time to find a Christmas tree, now isn't it?"

Tom laughed. "And it's in pretty good shape at that."

"Let's take it back to my apartment," she suggested. She'd store it in the basement for the following Christmas. But what she really was thinking, was of long ago, of the larger Christmas tree she'd tossed over the balcony of their apartment out in Howard Beach, just before she'd left Tom for good. She wouldn't mention this to him, why bring up old hurts? The apartment was gone, that bleak winter they'd broken up was long over, but this symbol, discovering a Christmas tree in May, surely it was a message, a positive sign — something that was saying pick up where you left off.

Carrying their find with them, Tom and Annie went back to the building, dragging the tree through the elegant marble lobby, right into the elevator, bringing it with them to the 19th floor. "Leave it outside the door," she suggested, "I'll get the super to store it for me later."

Once inside the apartment, they embraced and kissed like they'd never kissed before. It was sweet and delectable and delicious. An instant touch, a word, a smile, the electricity was still there, the incredible bond, the connection, that feeling of utter ecstasy just beneath the surface, it had been there all the time, waiting to be reawakened. Everything began happening rapidly — like a fast-forward on a videotape.

"Oh Annie, I've missed being close to you," he said, holding her even tighter.

"You know I've never forgotten you, that no matter what...."

Annie couldn't finish her sentence, as Tom kissed her long and passionately. "Oh my God, this seems so good, so right, I love him so,

But is this for real, is it?" the thoughts raced through her mind.

Yet she still wasn't sure what Tom was feeling; he was always passive, not easy to read, while Annie wore her heart on her sleeve. Sure they were kissing, but a man, he was always more physical in his response. And sexy, well that he could always be.

Without a word, Annie began to open up the sofa bed in the living room.

"Here, let me do it," he said. She smiled, walked over to the window and closed the blinds.

Quickly undressing, they lay down and made love, passionately, over and over and over again. Was it possible that they could have done it three times, that he could have had three erections, that she could have achieved such a luscious orgasm so many times, that there was so much love, so much passion, and so much hunger to be satisfied? God, how could she have ever forgotten the exquisite rapport, how sublime the sex was with him. They fit just right, always slept with legs intertwined, were ideal, passionately, purely perfect in bed. If only that harmony existed in other areas of their union.

Annie whispered, "I love you" when she came. Did he hear her? Oh yes. He said, "I love you too." But so what? It was orgasm talk. What did it all mean? Nothing was said after.

Tom was tentative in his words. But then he had never been much of a conversationalist. She always knew he had a shy side, or what she really suspected was an inferiority complex. He just didn't feel at ease in most social situations. Even when Annie was welcomed into the upscale restaurants she was reviewing for her newspaper column — when she'd invited Tom along — he'd feel out of place. He was a fireman, a blue-collar worker; he just didn't feel comfortable in the world she'd made for herself.

She was aware that his mother had taught him not to think he was any better than anyone else. Tom told her how he and his brother were raised, and while it sounded good on the surface — somehow this got translated as thinking he wasn't as good as others.

When she'd comment on how handsome he was, Tom would inevitably answer: "Come on... stop it. You're off the wall... I look like everyone else. My mom told us a long time ago, looks don't matter — that I'm no better than anyone else."

While Tom might deny her flattery, he didn't argue with the way they both were feeling towards one another. He knew, like Annie, that the incredible connection they'd made once again, the fierce physical attraction, was very real, and couldn't be ignored. For better or worse, they'd fallen back in love.

But he wouldn't, he couldn't reveal this to his mother, or his brother, and not even Colleen. "No sense stirring up old memories, Annie. My mom, she feels we're better off apart. She's been good to me and especially to Colleen, took care of her these past years while I was working. There's no point upsetting her."

This wasn't exactly what Annie wanted to hear.

Tom was cautious and not sure if he was ready to become seriously involved again. He knew he'd made mistakes, that something was wrong with how he handled things and while he felt so much for Annie, he was afraid of getting back in there, of any more marriages. Hell, he was no good at it; that was becoming clear to him. But he couldn't contend with Annie's headstrong nature. She was totally, illogically in love. And though he didn't know it yet — she was determined to go all the way.

— ❧ —

"Yes, you're sober a good while and you've gotten your life

together and I agree, you're in better shape, but that doesn't mean that Tom has also grown," Irene reminded her.

Annie had phoned Irene, had confided in her AA sponsor, the woman who had been there at the beginning, who had heard her fifth step, who had seen her evolve from an unsure, shaking, alcohol-addicted young girl into a poised, seemingly happy young woman.

"Just go slow, Annie, _slow_," she urged. "He's been through another divorce, right?"

"But we're so close, and he's so nice and I love him, and…."

"That doesn't mean you have to move back in."

"But I want to be with him *ALL* the time, I miss him so when he's not around."

"Look I'm not a therapist, and you know we're only supposed to share our experiences, not our opinion. I haven't been married, nor divorced…so maybe talk to a rabbi or a priest, or see a shrink, but please, don't jump right back in. And go to more meetings. Meetings are the medicine."

Meetings? All Annie could think about was Tom. What a thrill, what a terrific sensation to savor the delicious, dazzling, dizzying emotions of love. She would obsess about him all day long. She loved everything about him. His voice, his laugh, the smell of his body. She was addicted. No one else ever made her feel so good. Meetings, Schmeetings.

A day at a time, Annie did not drink. And though she asked advice of Maureen and of her sponsor, she really didn't accept any of it. After all, Irene was 45 years old, had never married and wasn't even dating, so what did she know? This just felt right to her, and whatever differences Tom and she had in the past, that was ancient history. She'd summon up the pleasantries and fail to recall the faults. After all, forgive and forget. *And let the music play on.*

In the end, for some inane reason, a marriage certificate, saying he belonged to her and she belonged to him, *legally* that is, mattered most to her. Playing house — shopping for new dishes and pots — redecorating his house — which was dreadful in dark brown colors and a hodge podge of furniture — this appealed to Annie's take-charge character. Finally, she had a chance at a happy marriage. She'd changed. She'd grown up. She'd make it work. Besides, she was tired of their clandestine meetings, of his having to make excuses for coming in to the city. How could he be ashamed of her, be so secretive?

And so, after just a few more months of surreptitious dating (he didn't dare tell his mother, who still had nothing but animosity towards Annie) she convinced him that they should marry again. As smitten as he was, it didn't take much persuasion on her part. It was still early in the relationship, the sex was fantastic, and they were still ultra respectful of one another.

Annie went to Saks Fifth Avenue, chose an elegant off-white silk suit, asked for a day off from her editorial position, (excitingly telling all in earshot that she was getting married!) and two days later, took the subway out to Queens, where she'd meet Tom at a small Unitarian church. The minister of the church had been a long-standing member of AA and Annie had first met him at Manhattan meetings. It seemed like a good way to be married, with good positive people and in a simple church ceremony.

Simple it was. They were married with no guests and the required two witnesses. One of the witnesses was the housekeeper of the church. The loud hum of the vacuum cleaner went on until the minister called the woman to come in, that she was needed for the ceremony. What the hell, this was one step above their first marriage. That time they married at City Hall. Here, at least there was some hopeful blessing from God. And most important, the main object, marrying Tom, it was a done deal. His mother or brother couldn't stand in their way. She was his wife all over again! Another chance at happiness, with someone she truly loved. Happily ever after, could it finally be coming true? Annie wanted it so much, God, she prayed so long for this to come to pass. Please, please, let it be true.

Lovers' oaths are thin as rain;
Love's a harbinger of pain...."
— *Dorothy Parker*

— CR —

Chapter 28

October 28, 1981

"Oh, honey, I love you so very much," Tom said to Annie, as he held her face in his hands and kissed her gently — soft, precious, tender kisses — on the cheeks, forehead — all over.

"You're the only one I've ever really loved," she said softly. She remembered the anniversary cards he'd given her — with the one line he'd always added that ended, *"Love is Eternal"*.

"Hhmmm — you smell so good!" he said, smiling.

"Courtesy of Joy perfume — I saved the last of my bottle for this," she answered.

"You smell delicious too," she remarked, knowing he was wearing the exclusive after-shave she'd bought him.

"Hey, isn't it nice to have a mutual admiration society?" he laughed, hugging her so close to him she thought she'd come out the other side.

"Well if we didn't have it on our honeymoon night, then when," she bantered back. Oh, she was so happy, so very happy.

It was autumn in New York — a sparkling, leaf-changing season with promise in the air. The World Series was being played with Annie's all time favorite team, the Los Angeles Dodgers against the New York Yankees.

It was also Annie and Tom's first night of 'remarried bliss". They were spending it in a first-class hotel, the Doral Park Avenue. Best of all, they were given the penthouse suite, with fabulous views of Manhattan; a courtesy gift from a major public relations firm Annie dealt with in her work for the newspaper. She'd long ago become proficient at currying favors as a "member of the press".

The air was cooler as it was wont to do on a late autumn day. They'd checked in early, eager to make the most of their one-night stay; Tom had to return to firehouse duty the next evening. But this time alone was theirs to savor and share. As night fell, with the brilliant white stars twinkling in the navy blue sky above them, the view from their suite was breathtaking.

They embraced, swathed in each other's nearness. Tom, a half foot taller than his petite bride, bent his head to kiss Annie again. The touch of his lips was soft and sweet and tender. Giddy with desire, she felt nothing would ever go wrong. She touched his hair. It was so nice and familiar to her. When he was working, he'd often come home with the smell of smoke and ash lingering there. Scary, to know he'd been so close to a dangerous fire. But now it smelled fresh and delicious and to Annie, sexy, like the rest of him. He kissed her again. Later, Annie melted away into Tom's strong, protective arms. There was magic in their lovemaking, a gift that never went away, no matter what else their differences might be. He was just the perfect lover — thoughtful, patient and passionate.

After, room service sent up dinner — a romantic candlelight service with Tom's favorite, filet mignon, and for Annie, Dover Sole and for both, a special non-alcoholic cranberry orange cocktail to toast their happiness. All was right with the world.

They were both avid baseball fans and the World Series game, just beginning, was their choice of entertainment. Amusing, watching baseball on their honeymoon night. But they enjoyed every wild moment of it, wagering small bets, applauding each run brought in for their teams. Tom rooted for the Yankees, and Annie, ignoring the fact that her beloved Brooklyn team was now the Los Angeles Dodgers, excitedly cheered them on.

Life was so very good. The glow of romance, that first kick when everything seemed fresh and promising seduced both of them. Annie, her heart overflowing with joy, silently thanked God for her blessings. She'd finally received the answer to her prayers.

It was an irreplaceable moment in time. She'd always remember their extraordinary night of sharing.

But after that, slowly but surely, a day at a time, reality began to seep in. Annie knew she'd have to relinquish living in her Manhattan apartment and move out to Tom's house in Queens. He wanted her there with him. It would involve a daily commute to work by bus and train. She'd always hated commuting. But she was so much in love. She'd do it—move there, be by his side—show him her devotion and commitment.

1981 was a year when many major events took place. The minor but positive one for Annie was that the Dodgers had defeated the Yankees in the World Series. She gloated with joy and lauded the fact to anyone who'd listen that her *'bums'* had done it.

But the year was also an intimidating time when the ravaging disease of AIDS was first identified. Some of Annie's good friends, gay men she'd met and come to know well at AA meetings, were the first victims of this horrific plague. The year was also marked by a dark chapter in history: the Mid-East quest for peace was set back by Egyptian President Anwar el Dadat's assassination by

Islam Extremists. The world situation was growing tenser with terrorism. Hi-jackings, car bombings, the violence and awfulness kept escalating.

Ronald Regan, who was the new president, nominated the first woman who would serve on the U.S. Supreme Court, Sandra Day O'Connor. Women everywhere were doing better. Later on, Regan would survive his own encounter with an attempted assassination.

Meanwhile Maureen, as much as she tried to keep it hush-hush, was becoming romantically entangled with her agent, John Turner. John, who was legally separated from his wife, was eight years younger than Maureen, but he was absolutely taken with her. In one careless moment, Maureen admitted to Annie: "He's really very special. Such a good guy. And smart! I know I said I wouldn't get involved any more — but — this is different."

"I'm happy for you, Mo, go for it!" Annie was so very glad for her friend. It'd been a long time since Maureen had any man in her life. Trusting men after the serious consequences of her one-night stands was difficult. For the last few years she'd concentrated on her singing career. Then one day, she was recommended to a top-flight agent, John Turner.

Maureen had met with John to discuss his representing her. She really needed an agent; especially after Roosevelt's sudden passing — for a while there was no one to look out for her best interests.

She was taken aback at how fine-looking John Turner was — and even more so — that he really seemed to be a nice fellow. Never mind, that he was so successful. His management offices on Madison Avenue occupied half a floor, had a large staff and a stable of well-known singers. How lucky was she when he took special notice of her and they began dating. How really lucky when they both felt the same and fell deeply in love.

Maureen was on *Cloud Number 9*. After a long time of dating doofuses and dopes and going through the crazy free sexual period in her life, she'd given up. For certain, she never thought she'd find real love and a solid relationship, one that might lead to marriage. But John was talking about it and she was listening.

As for Annie, she'd soon learn that life is not a fairy tale and living happily ever after is a gamble at best. What was she thinking when she thought this time it would be different!

"You know Annie, you can put your money on it—that there will always be a certain amount of tedium—the tedious, every-day deadly requirements and restraints of life—rules and regulations that come into play in marriage," Maureen philosophized. "If you're feeling some doubts now, I'm not surprised. You've always seen marriage through rose-colored glasses with happy endings, hon. But it takes work, and it's still a damned f—-ing gamble, that's for sure! But stick to it, give it your all." Annie knew she was right.

And so it played out. The next phase of Annie and Tom's marriage would be a transformation, an up and down, in and out, constantly evolving and changing metamorphosis of feelings and actions.

"When are you going to tell your family?" she asked Tom.

"Let me get through the night tour, and I'll call my brother."

"I'm tired of your telling me not to answer the phone," she screamed. It was *their* house now. She was also annoyed that Tom's mother called him so damned often. The woman was still grasping, controlling.

"Hey, chill out, sweetheart. You know my mother's from the old school. I'm going to tell her. I'm not going to hide it forever. I'm just waiting for the right moment and I'm hoping, Annie, that she'll give us her blessings."

"Blessings? Fat chance of that!" Annie answered irritably.

No! Stop! Annie bit her tongue, halted her negative thought pattern. She didn't want to think this way this time; she'd try to overlook his mother's bad points and look for the good. There was good in everyone. She'd keep an open mind, do all she could to befriend his mother.

"And just when are you going to tell *your* mother? She's the real problem, isn't she?" Annie persisted.

"Please—let me tell Joe first, and then I'll take a drive out to Breezy Point and talk to my mom," Tom said.

They'd been living together for three weeks before her gentle urging had turned into nagging. She hated living a secret, hiding something she was so happy about. Finally, Tom agreed that it was time to talk to his family.

But wait. She wasn't blameless in all of this. He questioned her about her own truth saying and why she still hadn't told her parents.

"While you're complaining every day and nagging me to death, how about your side? When are you going to tell your relatives?" he asked. "Honey, what's fair is fair. You haven't told your family a damned thing about us, have you?"

He was right. Annie wasn't comfortable about telling her family much of anything. It had been a long time since she let them know what was going on in her life. She knew how much they disapproved of her life in the city. She was the odd duck, the black sheep, the one who wouldn't take her parents' advice. It was hard to tell them anything at this stage of her life.

She'd confided in Maureen and her other friends, happily announced wedding plans to the people with whom she worked. But she'd neither written nor called her sister, Joanie, and certainly had avoided telling her parents. She knew they knew what a mess the marriage had turned out to be the first time—and for sure, her mother would be critical, as always.

But it had to be done. She was an adult and while she knew that they could push her buttons—especially her mother—she had to tell them. Besides, who were they to judge anyone else's marriage when theirs was such a mess?

Finally, Annie picked up the phone and called and in her best casual manner — (she didn't want to let on that she was nervous, that she wished somehow that they would show their approval and support) — matter-of-factly announced that she and Tom had "gotten together" and "after dating for a few months, well it worked out all summer, so we've gotten married."

Dead silence. Not a word.

"Are you still there, Mom?"

Finally her mother responded:

"Listen, no one could ever tell you what to do, so what do you want me to say? You'll do what you want anyway. But you married a "Goy." You should know "Goyim" don't make for good husbands. Or don't you remember how miserable you were the first time?"

Annie felt her stomach turn. But she would not let on—not give her mother the satisfaction of knowing she'd struck her where it hurt the most.

"It has absolutely nothing to do with if someone is Jewish or Catholic or Buddhist! I've been out there for a long time, Mom. I've gone out with plenty of men—even had a few serious relationships in the last four years and in all that time I've never found anyone that seemed really right for me. I feel more for Tom, much, much more, so I'm following my heart."

Again, dead silence.

"Anyway, I just wanted you and dad to know."

"Your father is sleeping. I'll let him know. I don't want to aggravate him right now. Leave him alone, " her mother answered, and then hung up.

Later that week Annie was surprised to receive a congratulatory card along with a gift certificate for $500 to Macy's. Annie knew it was her father who was responsible for the money part. He could be so good-natured. That made her feel much better. But when she called to thank them and ask if they'd come out to dinner, they turned down the offer. "Your mother, she's not well, you know that. When she's feeling better, we'll try—okay?"

Well at least there was some acceptance shown. Better than the hostility and coldness that emanated from Tom's side.

"I want Tom to tell his mother and if necessary," she grumbled to Maureen on the phone (and she didn't doubt it would be necessary) "to defend his decision to marry."

"You know I'm not going to sugar coat anything, Annie. I'm your friend. But for God's sake, you're 46 years old now, and how old is Tom?

"He's just one year younger—he's 45."

"Well, hell, at this stage of your lives you shouldn't need your family's approval. I mean if you didn't want in-law trouble, you should have married an orphan."

"Look, Mo. What you're saying makes perfect common sense, and I'm more of a realist now. I didn't expect the *Good Housekeeping Seal of Approval* — especially from my mother. If I married a drop-dead gorgeous, successful Jewish doctor, she'd still find something to complain about. I'm okay with it. But—Tom—he's very close to his mom and his brother, and I think it's important to him."

"Well, you know I wish you only the best, honey, but please, please—keep your expectations low and your antenna high. That way you won't be disappointed. Neither of you came from a *Leave it to Beaver* family."

Annie laughed nervously. It was true. They both had more than enough background garbage they'd brought with them.

"Hey, not to change the subject, but John and I are having a party a week from Saturday night. At his apartment. It's downtown at Battery Plaza. Fantastic place — two bedrooms — fabulous views of the World Trade Center and the harbor. John loves any view with water and this one is spectacular. I'm sending out invites today. It's — well, to announce our engagement. His divorce just came through. We'd love for you and Tom to be there."

"Oh Maureen, I'm so really happy for you, so glad you've found such a wonderful guy! I'll check with Tom, see if he's on duty. But no matter what, I'll come. I wouldn't miss it for anything in the world."

Maybe Maureen was right. Annie knew it wasn't very mature of two 40-year olds to be so concerned with family approval. But who was 40? She certainly didn't feel or look her age; she looked years younger, and Tom — he still seemed like the dashing, virile young man she'd first married so long ago.

Eventually Tom got up his nerve. He told Colleen first. She was the easiest. After all, Annie was now living with them — this was obvious. A legal document didn't mean much to a kid.

But when he told the rest of his family — it was obvious that it didn't go well. They were taken aback. If the truth be known, they didn't like it one bit. Tom's older brother, Joe was still married to his wife Marilyn; they had a seven year old son and a nice home out in Breezy Point, only a few blocks away from his mom's. They just couldn't believe Tom jumped right in all over again. This was now his fourth marriage and he was in his early 40s.

But it was his mother, consumed with rage, who really reacted poorly to the news. She was overprotective, domineering. She adored her son but sometimes couldn't figure him out. She'd have her say.

"I can't believe you did this without talking to me first," Ursula said, her voice filled with fury. "By now — after three failed marriages — don't you think you should have waited? Sleep with them if you have to, but why marry them? And Annie—well you know she doesn't have our *beliefs*..."

Tom interrupted. The dig at Annie being Jewish didn't escape his ears. He knew his mother lived in a narrow Christian-only world. She'd rarely left her home on the Breezy Point beach in the last 30 years—met and mixed with few outsiders. She was prejudiced against all minorities. Blacks, Puerto Ricans and most definitely Jews. For him to marry someone Jewish—never mind someone as strong-willed as Annie—well, she was still raging over his poor choice from the first time. The two women had always clashed.

"The world changed about fifty years ago, Ma, and you're standing still. Annie is a good person and I don't care if she's Jewish or not." Hell he'd given up the Catholic Church years ago, so what did it matter anyway?

Ursula let out a sob. "I can't talk about it any more, not now," and hung up.

Damn it! It wasn't like he was marrying a stranger. He had remarried his ex-wife. It was a done deal, so why couldn't his mother say something nice? He felt like shit. He was between a rock and a hard place. Damned if he did and damned if he didn't. Tom was sorry he told them at all.

A week passed. Then another.

There were no warm congratulations, no cards, no presents. But this time Annie was determined to make a go of it.

"So we already know how they feel. I'm going to try anyway. Let's invite your mom to dinner," was her first suggestion.

He admired her spunk. And he missed his mother. He wanted to be close with his family like always. He'd work on it.

It took a month of negotiations with Tom going out on his own to visit his mother a few times, but finally, he got the two women together.

They took his mother to a local diner out near Breezy Point, where she'd feel comfortable. She was polite enough. So Annie bit the bullet and invited her to join them the following weekend. "I've been asked to write up the Sunday brunch at the Plaza Hotel. They have a wonderful atmosphere, very elegant, and lots of variety in foods. I can bring guests and Tom is off from work, so maybe you could come with us?" she asked.

"Okay, that sounds real nice. And Tommy, you can pick me up out here next Sunday, darling?" she asked him, rubbing his shoulder in a coquettish manner.

"Sure Mom, *we'll* pick you up at 10. The brunch goes on well beyond noon, doesn't it, hon?" he asked Annie.

"Yes, we'll have plenty of time to make it. I'm so glad you'll come — it's a spectacular hotel and the food — I've eaten there before — is wonderful."

She hoped this would impress his mother, earn her some points.

It didn't.

Over the next few months, Annie reached out, called to ask how "Mother Ryan" was feeling. She felt ill at ease using the term "mother," but bit her tongue and did it anyway. She made every effort she could to make friends, always leaning over backwards, inviting her to join Tom and she when they went to Manhattan restaurants she was covering for the newspaper.

At one crucial juncture, she took his mom to a glittery Revlon p opening at the famous *Studio 54*, where elegant gift bags filled with women's toiletries were dispensed. She thought Ursula would lov being amongst the high fashion models and the well-known gues especially getting all those goodies. But on this occasion, Tom wa duty at the firehouse. His mother seemed disappointed, hardly s during the entire afternoon. It dawned on Annie that it wasn't t going out, but going out with her son that was the main appeal

She did whatever she could to placate the woman, going all out to impress her. How else to create harmony in the family? At first she thought she was making some headway, but about five months later she knew it wasn't working. Ursula seemed to dote on her other daughter-in-law, and of course, both her sons. But Annie was only to be tolerated.

She was viewed as "the Jewish girl" he'd married and that was that. His mother really hadn't changed her critical impression of her daughter-in-law. As for Annie, she still insisted that it was the Teutonic influence of Tom's mother — after all, she was German — that this was the reason for her anti-Semitism. Damned if she wasn't *"Eva Braun"* the pet name Annie had given her mother-in-law the first time around. It seemed to fit just as well now.

But the painful truth was that no one would ever be good nough for Ursula Bruckmeyer Ryan's son.

Once again, Annie shared her exasperation with Maureen.

"Hey kid, you're playing out scenes from *"The Way We Were,"* erse the roles and well, you get touches of *"Annie Hall."* You n't going to get the age-old religious and ethnic differences all d out, the acceptance you hoped for," she opined.

t's 1982, the world has changed," Annie said vehemently.

half the world and certainly not for the enclaves out at You know it's still a restricted community. Hey, I'm tell you there's plenty of blaming for the Crucifixion aming it on your people, my friend. They don't get a Jew. And they don't want to change anything, on't think bigotry is only in the South and towards r here, but they're still racist diehards, Annie. There s all over Manhattan that have no-Jews accepted 's not just your mother-in-law, who's old and e your choice — there are thousands of ordinary ots! It's much easier to stay with what they know, to have someone to blame for the ills of the world."

Annie went home that night, deflated, depressed and disgusted at tilting at windmills. It seemed insurmountable, this need to win the approval of Tom's family.

Then there was Colleen, whom Annie truly cared about. Annie bent over backwards to understand this troubled and sensitive teenager. A few times she took her shopping, bought her some high-fashion teen clothes that Colleen really wanted. One evening she took her to Manhattan to a play and then out to dinner. Overall, she showed a real and loving concern. At the beginning it worked. Colleen seemed at ease with Annie and pleased to see her father and Annie together. But she also had her own hidden agenda. Old ghosts and past conflicts emerged. She was older now, asserting her independence, and was used to having the run of the house. The cliché about you can't have two women in one kitchen held true.

Annie liked to "potchka" around, prepare dishes to please Tom. But the kitchen was a mess. From the day she'd moved in, it was obvious that the entire house needed an overhauling. Dust everywhere, a tired look to the boring masculine style furnishings— the house was not attractive and definitely needed revamping. Annie had enjoyed redecorating; she had a real flair for it. But cleaning up—that was a different matter.

The stove was especially difficult to use when Annie first moved in. Colleen was used to heating up pizza in it. She never did clean off the old burnt cheese spills. Then there was the sink. Dishes were piled high; pots never scrubbed. "Doesn't anyone clean up after they eat?" she asked Tom. "Colleen is absolutely no help and by the way—I'm not the housekeeper," she complained. He didn't answer. Resentment was setting in.

But Tom loved her cooking and Annie so wanted to please him. He'd always loved her veal parmigiano and her pasta Bolognese dishes. She made a mean meat sauce and was especially adept at preparing Italian fare. "I must have been Italian in another life time," she commented, "because I damned well can make Italian dishes better than any I've tasted in some top Italian restaurants." And she was right.

Satisfying Colleen was another matter. She had a whole set of new problems. Some of them came with being a teenager. Besides, she'd already subsisted through three different mothers. All the more reason to rationalize why she was smoking pot. Where she got it from, they didn't know, but for a 15-year old to have such easy access was surprising to Annie.

They'd come home and Annie would immediately smell the acrid odor. The pungent stench emanating from the bathroom was easy to recognize. The girl was smoking pot there and Annie loathed it.

"I gave up smoking years ago. I'm allergic to regular smoke — never mind this awful smell," she'd complain. She was livid. How could Colleen be so damned disrespectful? Then she realized that addictions had no room for respect. What to do? What to do?

Annie was beginning to notice what a master Tom was at avoidance. And now he had a new diversion — an autograph collection that had taken on a life of its own.

This hobby soon became obsessive, frenziedly taking up increasing amounts of his time. Tom would collect in-person signatures of whoever was famous and happened to be appearing or visiting in New York.

Past presidents like Ford and Nixon, ballet star Rudolph Nureyev, playwrights Tennessee Williams and Arthur Miller, singer Frank Sinatra (who would stay at the Waldorf Hotel whenever he was in town) would become targets for Tom's autograph practice.

Tom's particular modus operandi was to dress up in his official fireman's dress uniform, take along 8x10 photos or first edition books by or about the celebrity who was in town (Tom read the daily papers, as well as purchased the show business weekly, *"Back Stage"*, since it listed what major stars were in New York) and then would approach the individual, asking for autographs for "the men at the firehouse."

His system worked rather well. Long before 9/11, most people respected New York City firemen. Remarkably, even the Secret Service allowed Tom to get close to anyone they were guarding.

At first Tom only went out once a week to collect. But soon the hobby took another day. He once stood at the garage entrance to the Waldorf Towers for four hours, knowing Sinatra's car would enter that way and that he could get *Ole Blue Eyes* to sign a few photos for him.

"No, I can't come back now. I'm too close to getting the signatures. I have a lobby card from *"On the Town"* that I know he'll sign. Just shut off the stove," he'd tell an exasperated Annie. "I gotta go now. I'll call you when I'm getting on the train."

Tom was slowly but surely amassing a unique and valuable collection of in-person autographs and for him, this became more and more time-consuming. He loved it.

Then there were the auctions and paper memorabilia shows. Most of these took place on weekends or on days when Tom was on an off-cycle at the firehouse. After a while, rather than become "an auction widow" Annie went along with him to auctions at places like Charles Hamilton Galleries, where one afternoon he bid on and won a vintage Oscar Wilde signed portrait and a Pavlova small picture postcard signed by the celebrated dancer. He was spending all his extra money on this pastime and amassing a small fortune in autographed photos and books.

"How did he ever get started on this?" Maureen asked, after Annie related this new aspect of Tom's.

"You know he's always loved art and the theater. Tom's really a very cultured person, fireman or not. He even went to Europe twice in the years after our first divorce. It seems he met some autograph collectors in London. Got involved there and bought some items at shops there—and cheap. He got hooked, I guess. He's always been someone who likes collecting things."

"There was an auction at Sotheby's last week—of Hollywood memorabilia. I read about it in the newspaper," Maureen reported. "I think Judy Garland's ruby shoes went for $20,000 and a signed photo of Carole Lombard and Clark Gable for at least $900. So there's a method to your husband's madness."

"Oh sure, if nothing else, Tom's shrewd. Some of the autographs are worth a lot of money and he goes after the ones who ordinarily don't sign. So he's building up quite a collection."

"Well, kid, I hate to say it, but it doesn't sound like love has found Andy Hardy. I think you better keep your head, keep your apartment and go to more meetings," Maureen responded. She didn't want to say it, but it sure sounded to her like there was disappointment ahead.

"The whole conviction of my life now rests upon the belief that loneliness, far from being a random and rare phenomenon, peculiar to myself and to a few other solitary men, is the central and inevitable fact of human existence."
— Thomas Wolfe

— CR —

Chapter 29

"*Shit, piss and corruption!*" Annie didn't want to admit it, but she knew the marriage was unraveling.

"Hey kiddo, I've heard all sorts of one-liners, but where'd you get that one from?" Maureen asked.

"Heard it years ago — from some one in my illustrious family. I still say it every once in a while…especially when I'm totally frustrated. Like now. I hate to grumble, and I know you're going to say you told me so, but I'm in over my head."

"That you are. But you're doing something about it. You're going to a therapist. You're going to meetings. You're talking about it. Don't be so hard on yourself."

"Thanks. But I've also gone up a dress size. Two months ago I went to Weight Watchers. I took off five pounds and put back eight. Tom actually remarked about my getting a little *zaftik*. But if I'm alone when he's on all-night duty at the firehouse, I make myself a steaming pot of spaghetti, drown it in some rich tomato sauce, and it's comforting."

"It's an international disease, this overeating," Maureen said glumly.

"Oh well, it's a little safer than booze I suppose. I'll call you tomorrow. Maybe we can make a date for dinner soon?" Annie suggested.

"Sure, would love to see you. But call early — I'll only be in until noon. I've got rehearsals after that."

— ℭℛ —

While Tom's fixation about money troubled Annie, she still blamed his family for their main tribulations. She knew when she married him it was a package deal but she didn't think it would just be a repeat of history — that she'd feel the same as she did the first time — isolated, on her own. And when it came to Colleen, she felt even more discouraged.

She could ignore the family, but Colleen was a teenager and living with them. Besides the pot smoking it was evident that she was drinking too much. On at least three occasions since Annie had moved in, Colleen had come home intoxicated as all get out. Just how could Annie say something? Surely not when Colleen came home smashed. Talking to someone who was drunk was like trying to blow out a light bulb.

Suddenly Tom wanted Annie to manage the situation: "You've got experience, so talk to her, please," he pleaded. But this pitted Annie against her only ally. At least before this, Colleen seemed to trust her. Now Annie had invaded her stepdaughter's space; for her to question her would be treading on risky ground.

As usual, Tom looked the other way. Annie finally realized what was going on and that it was a *pattern* — he rarely brought up Annie's drinking the first time they were married. And, now, only after her bringing Tom to the point of exasperation did he talk at all about his daughter's behavior.

"This is ridiculous! When I was 16 I couldn't even come in after midnight, and drinking, that was totally out of the question;

Maureen has to know about boundaries," Annie said.

"Well you may not have drunk then, but you certainly made up for lost time later," he commented sarcastically.

"True, but my father set rules for all of us that we had to respect. At least I had an 85 plus average and got into a decent college. I was much older before I began drinking. If Colleen continues at this pace, with her failing grades, and hanging out with some of the hair-brained kids I've seen her with, she's going to do what they've done — drop out of school. She'll end up ruining her life."

"I don't get it. If Colleen is smoking marijuana, where'd she get the money for it? I only give her $5 a week allowance," Tom said. "I figured out that she was drinking when I noticed the few cans of beer in the refrigerator was gone. But that she got right here. That's it, no more booze in the house."

"We're all better off without anything around," she reminded him.

He looked at her, weariness in his eyes. Tom just didn't know how to deal it. First it was Patty — now Colleen was coming home drunk. Christ, why was this happening to him? How come he got all the boozers?

Annie took a few deep breaths — she'd offer advice even if she suspected it'd fall on deaf ears. "Colleen's taking advantage of the situation. In a way she's been a helpless participant in your life — in dealing with all of your women, including me. She's also had too much freedom. With your revolving work schedule, there hasn't been enough supervision."

"The kid's a good kid. She's been through a damned lot. But, alright, I'll try to talk to her later," he promised.

Later. Everything with Tom was *Later*.

Tom would say anything to get Annie off his back. When she started on a subject, she'd harangue him for days. He'd enough to contend with. If Colleen was like her mother, if she had the

'*Irish Virus*', what in the hell could he do about it? He was totally disgusted.

Why the hell couldn't life be easier? What did he do to deserve all these ditzy broads drinking and drugging around him? In the past he'd tried talking to Colleen. She had a way of making him feel guilty. She did lose her mother. Tom just didn't feel right bullying her. But he also knew the kid was headed for trouble.

Christ, he had to do something about it. This was his daughter. His only child. Maybe Annie was right. Maybe it was a disease. It was a good thing Annie had gone to AA. Now she could help Colleen.

"Annie – please — can you talk to her?" he asked once again. "See if you're able to reason with her," he said, a resigned look upon his face. "Maybe you can tell her how the AA program worked for you."

"At fifteen, she may not be ready for a 12-step program. I didn't get it right away and I was much older. But I'll talk to her — and see if she'll go to a meeting with me. I know one where there are young people. If she refuses, isn't ready, then you take her to a therapist, Tom, she needs some kind of counseling."

"I'm gonna go out for a while, play some handball."

How often had she heard that?

Tom had to get out of the house. Get away for a while. He really loved hitting the ball hard against the wall over and over and over again until he'd forget about problems and work off the anger. He'd play down at the schoolyard for hours on end with whoever showed up. There was usually someone on the handball court.

— ❧ —

Later, Annie approached Colleen. She should have known better.

…."You've gotta be kidding. I don't need AA or anything like it! Sure, I've had a few drinks at a party, but so did all my friends. There's nothing wrong with it. Just because you had a drinking problem you see it in other people. No, I don't need your Holy Roller group. There's a bunch of old people there. I'm 15. Why can't I have a little fun on a Saturday night!"

"You've a right to your opinion. Still – 15 is young, it really is too young for drinking and please won't you try? There are plenty of young kids at meetings, not just older people," Annie answered defensively.

"Mind your own business, why don't you!" Colleen screamed as she ran out of the room slamming the door behind her.

Annie could've kicked herself. How dim-witted of her. She knew she was too close, too familiar with the situation to help.

Colleen was afraid, in denial, not ready to get honest with herself. The program was for people who *wanted* it, not for people who needed it. And some people never did get help. Fortunately Colleen was still young. Maybe later. Maybe.

After that, she kept her opinions to herself. The less she said, the better. But these days the atmosphere was charged with antagonism. Ironic, the little girl she held so close to her a decade ago was now a rebellious teenager who was acting out in perilous ways. What on earth could she do about it?

Maureen offered wise advice: "The dynamics of your relationship have changed. Once you moved back with her dad, and you're all living under the same roof, it's a different game. You can't be her friend, like it or not — you're her step-mother."

"It's true. For almost a year she had her father all to herself and now here I am. Almost like the *other woman*." Annie thought about it and had a split second insight: Most of her life she had to compete with her mother for her father's attention, and now she was competing with both Tom's mother and his daughter for his attention.

"Damn it. You know what, Maureen? As much as I don't want to admit it, in all these years that Tom's life has been affected by alcoholism, he hasn't joined Alanon, sought counseling, hasn't really done anything to change or grow."

· She was beginning to realize that she would have to accept him the way he was, or… she didn't want to think of the alternative.

— ❧ —

Thankfully Annie held on to her Park Avenue apartment. She'd have been crazy not to. After all, it was rent-stabilized and in a great old building. Her apartment was on the 19th floor with a spectacular view of the city. The Empire State building — brightly lit up at night – glistened in all its majesty from her west windows, while the unique vista of the Pan Am building could be viewed from her northern exposure. The rent was affordable: just $400 a month for this great apartment in Murray Hill, with a Park Avenue address, never mind the 24-hour attended elevator service. No way would she give this up.

Besides, Tom was at work two nights a week, and now that Colleen was already 15, she sometimes stayed at friends or visited with her grandmother.

Months went by with no change in the situation. Some days were better than others. But while Colleen no longer smoked in the house, she was now staying out late. Worse, there were nights she surely was drinking because she'd awaken the next morning with an obvious hangover and skip school that day. Annie couldn't bear it. She'd bite her tongue, try not to say anything, but more than once, confronted her. Naturally, it didn't work.

Now, after shouting at each other one time too many, Colleen and Annie were barely on speaking terms. Home life had deteriorated for each of them. What a mess.

Annie plodded on. She reverse commuted to her job for a few months, and then, when the magazine folded, she was almost glad that they'd had to let her go. She hated traveling into the city. She'd take the time off to concentrate on the marriage.

She could collect unemployment benefits for six months, keep up the columns for *Our Town*, and find some 'off-the-books' free-lance work. Maybe this way — with her days free — she could find a means to make things better. She'd remain full time at the house. At least she could spend Tom's off-days with him. Fireman worked a two-day on, two-day off schedule. There was plenty of time for them to spend together.

Annie liked seeing Tom so often. If it involved going to the movies, or a half-priced Broadway matinee, he was really the best of companions. It was nice, having him at home during the day. They'd take drives to Rockaway Beach, where she loved having clams on the half shell, or go to Lundy's in Sheeps Head Bay, Brooklyn, where they both enjoyed the shore dinners.

And after a while, as he became more obsessed with his autograph collecting, she'd go into the city with him to attend the auctions. Her not working for a while — was going to be like a vacation. She'd try her damndest to make the marriage work.

But as her main income dwindled — unemployment paid her only $150 a week — the economics of the situation changed. Soon the subject of money and how to spend it reared its ugly head.

Annie was still paying the rent on the apartment in the city. She also wanted to keep up with her personal luxuries — be it haircuts, manicures, or a new outfit. Suddenly she realized that money was needed. With only a marginal income from unemployment, she'd have to depend upon Tom for some of the big-ticket items, and for all the grocery money, to which she'd formerly contributed. Tom didn't like that at all.

She was stunned at how quick everything changed. Changed

was a nice word for it. Deteriorated was closer to the truth. She knew Tom was tight with a dollar. He used to complain about paying the toll to go to Breezy Point to visit his mother. He resented *all* the bridge tolls. *"Jesus, Joseph and Mary, the public was finished paying for the construction years ago, yet they keep raising the damned tolls."* But his penuriousness had grown worse with time. He'd walk from room to room shutting out lights. "I'm not supporting Con Edison," he'd say irritably.

Now Tom asked that Annie wash the dishes in cold water. She couldn't believe it! "I pay too much for the oil to heat this house and too much for the damned water. The water bills are over the top and the fuel costs are robbing me blind. You can't use so damned much hot water," he'd remind her, over and over.

"What the hell are you doing in the shower for half an hour?" he asked another time, exaggerating the amount of time she'd spent there. This was ridiculous. She laughed. She had to. If she hadn't she would have cried. He walked out angry with her for not taking this seriously. The next time he complained she'd bite her lip so as not to react. But she was stupefied. What could she do if he was acting like a stingy Scrooge?

The friction between Annie and Tom persisted over the most trivial of things. She was annoyed at his petty comments about how much money she spent grocery shopping. My God, he wanted her to buy the cheapest kind of toilet tissue, anything to save money. "I'm not going to wipe myself with that stuff," she complained. And then, knowing it would annoy him, she bought the softest, most expensive brand of tissue in the store.

"Here, here's the $1.00 extra for the tissue," she said, handing him the money. He was furious. What was her ass made of, for God's Sake, that she couldn't wipe it with the same brand as the rest of them?

After the anger subsided they'd kiss and make up and then the love making, it was even better. A truce of a week or longer would develop - he'd be on duty a few nights, she'd be in the City, Colleen was sleeping at a girl friend's. All was quiet and at peace in the world and the time shared was *let's pretend.*

But then there were the inevitable episodes when they'd clash. She thought his attitude about the hot water was ridiculous. He was as relentless with Colleen, who spent what seemed to be an hour every night washing her long hair. "Get out already," he'd knock on the door. Annie couldn't believe it all. She tried to ignore it, unless he noticed. And notice he did when she was washing the dinner dishes.

His face would redden, his jaw tense up. He was annoyed, you could see it. "Are you kidding? I can't wash anything in this icy cold water...you can get arthritis that way," she'd shriek at him. "Move over," Tom said and finished the dishes. In cold water. But he wasn't happy about it.

Annie bit her tongue. Like that would numb her from the knowledge that there were too many fault lines in the marriage.

— ∞ —

That Friday evening she met Maureen and Sabrina for dinner at an upscale French restaurant. It was Sabrina's treat. She'd just landed a plum assignment. Finally, she was going to do hard news on the local channel. "What a relief to get out of that puff stuff and move on and up, ladies!" Sabrina said with a smile. "Let's celebrate!"

"Bravo, Sabrina, and more of it!" cheered Maureen, who was looking truly beautiful. She took far better care of herself now that she was in the public limelight. Her nails were done, her hair glistened with just the right amount of blonde highlights and best of all, she exuded confidence and joy.

"Let's toast to all of our successes," Sabrina suggested. Annie had a Bloodless Mary. And no real success to toast about.

"I don't know," Annie said glumly. "I feel like I've taken two steps forward and one step back. Maybe I'm just on a treadmill going nowhere. I don't feel like I have much to celebrate, but of course, I want to toast both of you."

"Baloney, Annie. Your marriage is getting you down. But you're a fine writer, have done some great magazine pieces and they've published some of your books. Never mind, Connie Clausen, your agent — is top-notch. You'll be finding yourself with a hit on your hands one of these days. Just keep on keeping on," Maureen said caringly.

"I wish I felt better about myself. I sure hope you're right. But I'm big time bewildered about Tom. Sometimes he's so romantic, so endearing, so wonderful to be around, and at other times, so damned petty and insensitive and ready to erupt. It's like living with Dr. Jekyll and Mr. Hyde. And I can't blame it on drinking or drugs, because he doesn't drink much at all and he's never smoked or taken drugs."

"Who said, *Hell's afloat in lovers' tears* — because each and every one of us has gone through an agonizing time when we risk love?" Sabrina asked.

No one seemed to know the quote. "Have you tried marriage counseling," Sabrina suggested.

Annie was embarrassed. "I'm dragging down the conversation — all I do is vent about Tom and my problems." She realized how fortunate she was to be sharing dinner with Maureen, such a good friend, and Sabrina Aldrich, already a television personality, yet all she could contribute were a litany of complaints about her dum dum marriage.

"Hey, slow down. Been there, done that, you're not alone, friend," Maureen interjected. "We've all had men problems. It's the way of the world."

"Well thank you both. And I'll look into counseling — good idea," Annie answered. She quickly changed the subject to

Maureen's upcoming singing engagement. She'd be headlining at the Blue Note, a jazz club in town.

All three toasted Maureen's success.

— ☙ —

Back home it was round and round again with no easy answers. Just angst and arguing and opposition. Lord, how it hurt.

Maybe Tom's choice of drug was money. First it was the damned toilet tissue, now the heat and the electricity. My God! What was next? He was so damned anal-retentive, she decided. No wonder he'd collected postage stamps and coins as a kid, and now he was into collecting books and autographs. This collecting had become a fixation with him. He wanted things and more things and more things.

There was an extra bedroom upstairs that Tom had turned into a private room. He even installed a lock on the door. It was where he secreted first-edition books and signed photographs and playbills. She'd peek in when she walked by and see him sitting at a desk inside, making notes. But it was *his* room, *his* house, *his* collection, and now he was keeping the autographs under lock and key. It just ran through her, this horrible separating he was doing, his keeping his prized possessions to himself, his obvious lack of trust in her.

Annie also realized that he considered the house *his*. After all, he'd bought it while they were apart. While she had an income coming in, everything was fine…but if she wasn't earning, she found it creepy to ask him for money. Yet every day he'd come home, empty his pockets of loose change and put it into a large 20-gallon glass bottle that sat on the floor next to his bedroom chest. It must have contained hundreds of dollars in coins and yet here he was raging over the latest utility bill.

Sometimes, while Tom was sleeping, or in the bathroom, Annie was so disgusted at the entire state of affairs she rifled through his pockets to get an extra $20 bill for herself. She was enormously frustrated at how things were going and rationalized doing this because he was so ungenerous, so stingy, so sick.

One night, when he was on duty, and Colleen was staying at a friend's house, Annie snuck into the autograph room. She'd picked the lock.

She had a plan she'd purchased a couple of throwaway cameras to take pictures of what she saw. Rows of first-edition books, all signed — an extensive collection, albums and more albums of signed photos — and most important of all, lists Tom had made indicating his estimation of the value of each item. Was he planning to go into business as an autograph dealer one day? She wasn't sure what he had in mind, but she couldn't help but notice that his estimates added up to thousands and thousands of dollars.

She recorded all of this. If there was no way to save this mess of a marriage — if there was another divorce — and Tom claimed that he was living on a New York City Fireman's salary, Annie could prove that he was worth much, much more. That in fact he owned an immense and valuable collection. She clicked away, making sure she got close-ups of lists in his handwriting, opened up the rare first-edition books to the pages with signatures, made certain that she'd recorded the most valuable items in the collection and click, click, click, took close-up photos of them all.

The next afternoon, after Tom's night tour, he asked once again:

"Why don't you give up your apartment, or at least sublet it? Are you just playing house out here?"

She just couldn't give up all of her independence. The city apartment represented freedom. Funny how she once thought living alone there was so lonely. Now, living with Tom in Queens, she could be right there with him and still feel deserted. What was that cliché about the grass always being greener?

Fortunately she was still collecting unemployment insurance, but still, Annie didn't like being obligated. She'd have to find a new editorial position before the money ran out.

Annie detested admitting admit it, but it was difficult making a life out there in the boondocks. She was so used to the ease of living in the heart of Manhattan. If Tom didn't harp on the petty things, if he was more generous of spirit, it would have made it easier. When they were in bed and making love, Tom was always loving, tender, and the negativities melted away. But the rest of the time, the other 23 hours of the day, reality reared its malevolent head.

It was a drag getting into the city. Annie needed to take a bus to get to the subway station and then ride the crowded, dirty subway train. There was only one time in all that first year of their marriage that any of her friends from Manhattan came to visit. It was such a schlep. She could tell they were not thrilled with the trip. And her parents, no they'd never come. She gave up asking.

By the second year, she saw that the differences between them, how to spend money, what to spend it on, had became impending battle areas. The difficulties of a decade ago had not gone away. So it wasn't all her drinking that contributed to the heartbreak.

Intuitively, Annie had known that she should hold on to the apartment. In the ensuing months it would become her haven, where she'd retreat if they argued. And after the first few months, boy did they argue. Some were major. He still had a violent temper. He'd yell or worse, run out of the house and stay away all day. Those were the bad arguments. The kind where she didn't want him to touch her when he was ready to kiss and make up.

Annie fumed silently, tried not to provoke him, but some things had gotten worse. Yet even now, when it was good it was very, very good. Tom had a little boy quality about him that was endearing. But the differences were like a cancer, invading every phase of their lives, little by little eating away at their souls.

And so when Cosmopolitan Magazine sent her a confirmation letter, that they would accept her story *"Why I Remarried My Ex-husband"* she made every effort to write a charming upbeat article. They'd pay her a whopping thousand dollars for it, and besides she wanted a byline in Cosmo.

But after a month of false starts on the project, of thinking of the healthy, positive reasons of why she remarried Tom — she could no longer deny the truth — it was really hard to tell their story in encouraging terms — Annie knew she really couldn't think of one good reason for doing what she did.

How could she write the article? It would be foolish of her to influence other Cosmo readers to remarry their ex-husbands, if they were going to base it on her experiences. She'd be leading them down a no-win road. No, she couldn't think of any rationale for the remarriage. She felt smothered, controlled, and sadder than she ever thought she could about long-term happiness with Tom.

Finally she consulted a marriage counselor. Tom came along a few times, just as long as she paid for it. Absurd as it was — (and she sensed the counselor's mockery when she talked of Cottonelle and Kleenex brands,) all they dealt with was toilet tissue and who'd pay for the expensive brand. This is where their future began falling apart.

Annie continued to see the counselor for more than a year before she finally began to get it: She couldn't reach Tom. It was like talking to a man encased in a glass shield. He could see her, but didn't hear her. Not the real things — her feelings — her concerns. She just couldn't figure out a way to penetrate that shield around him. It was like there was nobody home.

She called her agent to tell her of her decision and then wrote a note to the Cosmo articles editor, advising the editor that she wouldn't be submitting the story after all.

Depressed, Annie sought help. First the therapist, then a rabbi, then a priest, and finally a doctor who prescribed anti-depressants.

She was miserable. So she popped a few pills. Even this didn't work.

She began to overeat. Oh how she loved Sara Lee, especially the cream cheese cake; half the time she didn't even wait for one to defrost! Late at night, when she was alone, she made even bigger plates of pasta with sauce. It filled an emptiness inside. In just two months she put on ten pounds. This was awful. She couldn't admit that the marriage was over, and so she'd stay on, then go away, then come back then separate, then reconcile, in waves of hope and despair for the next two years.

Yes, Annie wanted to be rescued and she thought this was her answered prayer — that Tom was the someone to watch over her, to care for her, to love her like she'd never ever been loved before. No, she couldn't, she wouldn't give up this dream. A horrible seesaw of can't live with him, can't live without him went on and on and on.

But in the end she knew that the marriage was debilitating, humiliating, the breaker of hearts, the murderer of promises and the burier of goals. She had to escape or die.

And so in late April of 1985 she left. It was over for good.

"Human existence is always irrational and often painful, but in the last analysis it remains interesting."
— H.L. Mencken

— CR —

Chapter 30

September 1986

"**W**FD Seeks detective-type for romance and more" *began* the cryptic ad in New York Magazine. The W stood for white, the F for female and the D for divorced. Well, not quite. Annie had hired a divorce attorney, served Tom with papers, but the battle was only beginning. He was bitter, hurt, and wouldn't, he swore, give her a damned cent.

Numb as she was from the finality of the breakup, vowing to get a cash settlement, Annie now sought diversion, maybe even romance, but for sure, a man to rescue her. Viewing herself as a 'damsel in distress' she advertised for a *detective-type*, because Annie still lived a part of her life as if it were a movie script: Dashing man comes to the rescue, happy ending after all. Our heroine was on her own once again, needed help, reassurance, and yes, a take-charge man.

She wouldn't go to bars any longer. Bars were for drinking. So where else to look? What better place than the personals?

She rented a Box at the Murray Hill Post Office, and placed the ad in the magazine. (Of course Annie told the ad-taker of her article six years before – the one that helped make the personals popular.) But damned if they would even think of giving her a discount. Yet it was her success story that had made the ads socially acceptable, so much so that where she'd once spent $20 for an ad, she now paid $150. Worse, there were three pages of ads, with her small one lost somewhere in the middle. Would anyone read it?

— ᏯᏭ —

Annie needed a romantic distraction. The ending with Tom had been miserable. It was so damned hard to leave when she still felt such ecstasy in his arms. But that was at night, in bed, asleep. Awake was another story. Eventually, when they argued too much, when there was more negative than positive, she'd go back to her apartment, disappear for a while. Sometimes, they didn't talk for weeks, then he'd call and she'd return to the house.

At other times she made the first move. They spent one entire summer apart, Tom staying out at the beach in Breezy Point. With his mother, of course. They didn't speak at all. Annie grew increasingly depressed and finally, morbidly maudlin. Depleted, she ate too much, slept too much, isolated herself for days on end, crying.

Eventually she missed him so much she thought she'd die from the pain. She called the firehouse. They met, "just to talk" and soon they were back together again. A seesaw of emotions kept her from leaving for good. It was absurd, ridiculous, childish, but inevitable that they would want to see one another. They just couldn't seem to live together, that was the problem.

Over and over and over again, until the pain was far more than the pleasure, months and then years passed. How could anyone in their right mind consider going back for more? And then in one moment, not much different than the rest, she knew it: She was sick and tired of being sick and tired. At long last, when no one thought she would ever give up, Annie admitted defeat. She talked with the right people, got recommendations and then, consulting with the most suitable attorney, filed for divorce. There was no going back now. Not if she valued her sanity.

— ❦ —

Annie opened the latest issue of the magazine and flipped through the pages to the back personals section. Her ad appeared on page 107, buried amongst countless others. Bad spot! She was worried if it would even be seen. A week later unlocking her post office box, she was pleasantly surprised.

The personal ad had been seen and answered. By some wannabe's and some bores and by one highly interesting man. And if he weren't exactly *"Mr. Right,"* he would turn out to be someone who was wonderfully supportive and caring. Annie would later play the Bette Midler hit song in homage to her new male friend, for he would turn out to be the 'wind beneath her wings' for the next critical couple of years.

His name was Salvatore LoBianco and although he wasn't a detective, he was the next best thing to it: a Supervising Fire Marshall with the fire department, whose main expertise was in surveillance. The marshals were the men who investigated suspicious fires. They were the policemen of the fire department, carrying firearms, acting as detectives. Sal had a squad of men who worked under his supervision. Just the right mix of he-man and mystery to capture Annie's imagination. Wow, she was playing a role in an old Sam Spade movie. Wouldn't this be fun!

What was it about firefighters? She definitely liked the heroic image. Now here was another one, one smart enough to progress through the ranks and have a higher echelon position in the division. Not only would Sal, who was madly attracted to Annie, help her, he was clever at getting inside information on Tom, since he had access to fire department personnel records.

What Annie learned was unexpected. Tom had studied and passed the Fire Lieutenant's test the last year they were apart. Ironic. For years she'd urged him to move up higher in the department, but he always made excuses — he really didn't want to do all the preparation involved in taking the exam — he was happy driving the chief — he had other interests — he didn't like to study.

Now suddenly after she'd left, he'd accomplished it. Damned if it didn't bother her! Furthermore, he was no longer working at the same ladder house. Tom had been transferred to a firehouse in downtown Manhattan, which meant, he'd be closer to the theater world, something Annie knew he'd find irresistible. He was also earning much more money. Big deal. For him. Not her. Her attorney informed Annie that whatever Tom's present salary, never mind any accumulation of pension interest would not enhance her settlement. Anything she'd be entitled to would be based solely on the four years they lived together.

It was all about money now. Annie finally faced the barefaced facts: the end of a marriage involved the green stuff. A financial settlement, who got what and why, this is what the great love of her life — the man she married twice amounted to. Who got the dishes and pots (she'd bought all of these items, Tom didn't spend a dime) to the bigger benefits — like what portion of house, pension and savings the partners were required to share — in the end, this was all that was left of her love-will-conquer-all dreams.

She knew Tom's financial worth had escalated considerably during their marriage. He'd accumulated what she now estimated was a half million-dollar collection of signed limited editions and autographs. The few times she'd slipped into that locked room, she was amazed at how much he'd amassed. The collection kept growing. Annie was relieved she'd taken so many photos. Tom would probably ask his brother to help him hide the valuable things. He'd no idea she had proof of what he owned.

The first time it ended, she wanted nothing from the marriage; she wanted out. Annie knew her drinking had contributed to its demise. This time — she had sacrificed three and a half years of working on her career — tried her damndest to make the marriage work — had lost valuable professional connections, friends, time, and — he was far from broke. Yes, she wanted a settlement.

The divorce lawyer told her she was entitled to a percentage of the increased value of the house. With real estate values in the Northeast rising through the 80s, it was worth considerably more than when she moved in and helped refurbish it.

A battle loomed ahead. Tom wouldn't give her a nickel if he could help it. Especially because she'd left him, he'd have gone on in that miserable, non-communicative, repressive manner — just as long as he didn't have to change and didn't have to pay out any money. No, she was the one who wanted out, complained, left him — Annie didn't deserve a dime. He'd wage war to keep what he worked so hard for, damn it!

There was to be *discovery, a* term her lawyer explained meant that each side would get court-sanctioned opportunities to examine all financial holdings, be it stocks, bonds, or personal possessions. She knew Tom would be adamant; that what was his was his. He was fanatical when it came to his belongings, especially his memorabilia collection.

— ❧ —

"He who dies with the most toys wins," Maureen wisecracked, hearing Annie's plan to go out to the house to take inventory. "Besides, you don't really think he'll leave any antiques or those valuable autographs you've been telling me about around, do you?"

"No, he probably has carted it all off in boxes — to his mother or his brother's house. The Ryan's will stick together, I'm sure. But he doesn't know that I took plenty of photos, even some close-ups of his handwriting that show his listing items and marking dollar amounts next to them. There were pages of listings — a fairly complete inventory, Maureen — like Fred Astaire and Ginger Rogers, co-signed photo, $50, Tennessee Williams, first edition, *Streetcar Named Desire*, $200, all of this written down in Tom's handwriting...I have proof," Annie explained. "I showed the pictures to my lawyer, and he said he can build a considerable case — especially if Tom tries to conceal his property and I know he will."

That's why Annie needed a detective, someone to find out if Tom had hidden away his assets.

She explained it as well as she could to Sal. He was a good listener. "Our marriage was a back-and-forth soap opera — of neither of us being able to let go. Four years — and I think more of the time was spent apart than together."

"Hey, more than half the marriages in the U.S. end in divorce. Don't fault yourself. It ain't easy living with the same person day in and day out, year in and year out. I know," he said.

"Well, for a long time, neither one of us was strong enough to admit that it was over. Maybe we were too much alike in some ways? We're both Librans, me Oct. 9th, and he's Oct. 10th. "

"Well, whadda you know! I'm October 4th, the same day as St. Francis. Guess you like us October men. But I don't think it's that easy an answer, Babes."

He began calling her Babes early, and she liked it. Sal was a real take-charge person; just what she needed right now. She was worn out, nervous, worried. Going through this divorce was like fighting a bloody bitter battle and she was in it all alone.

She was thankful Sal had come into her life, even though he had lied by describing himself as divorced in his initial note. Annie soon discovered that he was only separated from his wife — separated for more than 10 years.

"She's unable to work; doesn't hold down a job very well — gets into arguments with people. We got married because she was pregnant. Two of our three kids are grown up now."

"But you all live together?" Annie asked.

"Yeah, we live under one roof, but I have my bedroom downstairs and the wife's upstairs," he explained. "The kids are still at home but only one is around much, and he's a teenager, so I eat upstairs a couple of nights a week, because of Sal, Jr. But the marriage; it's fucking dead. I just don't want to get divorced. If I did I'd have to give her half of my pension, damn it. So let her live in the house — I pay the bills and she just sits around on her big fat ass watching soap operas all day."

It didn't take long for Annie to have qualms about some of Sal's tales. Like the derisive way he talked about his wife. Yet he was always pleasant and kind to her. His marriage, the way he described the separation sounded genuine. He did have his own phone line at home. She could call any time. And she did. Sal would always listen and be sympathetic to her concerns. For now, it's what she needed. A good listener, a friend.

And so she'd accept him on his terms. Annie couldn't admit it, never mind understand it, but while she'd grown up in many ways, she was still morbidly dependent upon men. She just didn't think she could support herself totally, be independent and be happy on her own. And so while she wasn't really mad about the guy, it was helpful that he was so wild about her. It was kind of nice to be wooed that way. Certainly good for her bruised ego. The failure of her second marriage had slashed her self-esteem.

And so it went. Sal would be her substitute. Big Sal with the graying dark brown curly hair, brown eyes, a grin from ear to ear, and in a robust baritone voice, (sometimes a little off key,) he'd serenade her with "*Cara Mia Mine.*" He always had a romantic Italian refrain with which to croon his affections. It was amusing, seeing this bear of a man, gun holster strapped to his shoulder, doing his finest imitation of Dean Martin singing *Volare*. It made her feel good.

He was old-fashioned and kept sending flowers, big beautiful bouquets of red and pink roses. She said, "no more Godiva chocolates," after she devoured the first box. Then Sal presented her with a thoughtful gift: he'd spliced together a dozen of his favorites and presented her with a cassette of splendid Italian love songs. Proud of being Italian, he found it important to share with her the warmth of his heritage. Always motivated by music, Annie was soon seduced by the romantic refrains.

Sometimes Sal went over the line. He was excessive at buying her gifts. To commemorate the first month they'd met, he gave her an expensive diamond tennis bracelet studded with enormous stones. "Sal, please – this I must refuse," Annie said, meaning it. He looked disappointed. She didn't care. It was too much. She didn't want to feel constrained or obligated in any manner. Sal had a possessive quality about him, which was ridiculous, considering his marital state. But still, it was nice, feeling so special in a man's eyes. Parched for approval, she drank up every compliment he bestowed.

At times, during his day shifts, she'd visit at his Brooklyn headquarters. The Fire Marshall's office was situated near the old Brooklyn Navy Yard, in archaic quarters. He loved for her to come by so he could show her off to his staff. Annie was like a trophy for Sal. It was good for her too – she gained enormous gratification from someone appreciating how she looked and acted. When she was among this group of men she was the star. Aside from a file clerk and a secretary, who were female civil service employees, this was a man's world. Women were beginning to make inroads in the fire department, however the fire marshal's office was still a male bastion.

Some evenings, he'd pick her up while he was on duty and they'd have dinner together. A few times, he'd be called on his radio and would have to put the flashing red signal light on his dashboard and rush off, with Annie in the car, to the scene of a fire. This was especially exciting. Sal, whose job ranked not far under the NY City Fire Commissioner, would often have to go to 2 and 3-alarm fires to confer with those on hand. If the fire was determined suspicious he'd assign some of his crew to investigate it immediately.

"Hey, you're out of work. Why not apply to the *Staten Island Advance*?" Sal suggested. He lived out on Staten Island and knew the workings of the borough. "It's a strong newspaper, part of the Newhouse chain — maybe they'd have a reporter's opening for you. If you want I'll go over and talk to the managing editor and see what's up. They've done a few interviews with me since our department handles suspicious fires in Brooklyn and Staten Island.""That would be great, Sal. But not right now. You see, I've talked to my sister about visiting her...."

"Oh yeah, you mentioned her. She's older, right?"

Annie smiled. "Just by a couple of years. I don't know if I told you much about her, but she moved out to Arizona five years ago and she loves it there. Joanie's a schoolteacher. We haven't seen each other in a long while. She wants me to go there while I'm still not working."

"For how long?"

"At least a week since it takes like 6 hours or more to get there... and I want to spend some quality time with her. It's a good time for me to go. Right now, my lawyer tells me nothing will happen for a couple of months. There are always delays in these divorce suits."

— ೞ —

The week before Annie had called Joanie. They had a very long conversation. First Annie told her of the divorce. Joanie thought it was the right move. Annie also learned that her sister was seeing someone.

"But I don't want to get married again, it's good this way. Eric is a principal at another school. We met at a conference. He's divorced. Has a young son and a daughter. He sees them on weekends. It doesn't interfere at all and they're really wonderful children. But it's better this way. He lives in his place and me in mine."

"Gee, I'm glad to hear some good news. That's terrific."

"Why don't you come out and visit? You're still not working anywhere special. Before you get yourself into another job, come on out here. You've never been to Arizona, and it's beautiful. I have a lovely home out here, and plenty of room. Please, please say yes."

"Why not! I've already given the divorce lawyer a $10,000 retainer, and he tells me that it will take months before we get anywhere. I'd really like to see you, spend some time. Yes, I'll come."

"Where did you get so much money from?"

"I'm really lucky. You know all these years I've been writing for *Our Town*? Well, I've made a lot of friends, some of them rich and influential."

"Sometimes that's the best kind!"

"Well, I've covered plays, night clubs, restaurants, the whole nine yards. And a man I've known now for many years — his name is Jacob Meyers — well, he's filthy rich, owns lots of real estate in Manhattan. He also owns a small theater off-Broadway and I've done some reviews of the shows there."

"Sounds like the right man to know."

"I've come to know him pretty well over the years — and even his family. He, his brother and sister — they're all in their 80s, but they keep the family real estate business going. He's always liked me. We met about 3 years ago — at the newspaper — he's really good friends with Ed Kayatt, the publisher — well one day he offered to drop me off downtown, and that's how we got to be friends."

"During the ride we talked. I was upset and crying about the marriage and he was very nice and ended up sending me to see his lawyer, who referred me to a top divorce lawyer…and well, Jacob, that's his name — he said, he wanted to help me out, no strings attached, and he's backing me."

"Oh come on! Nothing expected back? No romance?"

"He's got a beautiful girlfriend. Young too. She's the manager of the real estate office. Meyers has been a widower for 20 years; his wife died of a brain tumor early in their marriage. And he doesn't want to marry again. He figures they're all after his money. Not that he has anyone to leave it to. He has no children. I think he's going to leave it all to foundations the family has set up."

"Lucky for the foundations."

"He and Rosemary Robbins — she's the office manager — they keep company. Believe me, the man is so rich he couldn't spend his millions in a dozen years. He owns two high-rise buildings on Third Avenue and a few Brownstones in the East 60s, and also his own theater. I'm just lucky that he's always liked me, loved the write-ups I did for his theater — and he's offered to help."

"Well I guess you can finally say your luck has turned, sis. If he backs you through this divorce, and you know how expensive lawyers are — you'll probably come away with something worthwhile."

"Yeah, if I can struggle through it. This is only the first six months and it's already so damned ugly. I'm told with lawyers getting delays and more delays and the court system here so inundated with cases, it could take more than a year or even two before this is settled."

Little did Annie know then that it would take more than three years, and two different divorce attorneys, as well as $30,000 of largess supplied by Jacob Meyers, before the ugly battles over money would be over. The wheels of justice moved slowly indeed. Especially in divorce court.

— ❧ —

Sal was disappointed that Annie would be away but he didn't let her know it. "Hey, family is family. You go, and when you get back, let me talk to them at the *Advance*, and see what's up. They're a big newspaper there and pay well, I know. My cousin used to be in the sports department."

"How would I get to work? It's over the Verazzano Bridge?"

"You can lease a car. If the job is right, don't let anything stand in your way, okay? They'll pay enough that it would be worth getting a car."

"Okay, I'll consider it, and thank you as always, for wanting to make things easier for me."

"Hey, Gorgeous, helping you is a delight!".

Annie felt good. Sal was a nice guy, so ready to lend a hand. And this was a good time to finally visit Joanie, to see Arizona. "I'm going to look into the cheapest round trip flight, call my sister and tell her I'm coming."

"And you let me know your schedule, so I can drive you to the airport, Babes. You know I've gotta kiss you goodbye."

— ❧ —

A week later, they said their farewells.

"Babes, I'm going to miss you, you know it. But I'll call you every day."

"Well, let me tell my sister about you. And allow me to call you the first time, okay?" Annie needed some space, knew that Joanie would question why she'd already gotten herself so involved. And Sal, he could be suffocating, calling her all the time.

She liked Sal as a friend, but underneath it all, while she knew it was over with Tom, there didn't seem to be anyone who could measure up to her magnetic attraction to him. Inevitably she would compare any man to Tom's good looks and sensuality. Sal was just a regular looking guy, a few pounds overweight, with some pockmarks on his face, a rather large nose, well, he wasn't exactly anyone's idea of handsome. But for now, he was the wind beneath her wings.

....."By the time you swear you're his, shivering and sighing. And he vows his passion is infinite, undying — One of you is lying."
— *Dorothy Parker*

— ⚭ —

Chapter 31

Welcome to the West —

Opulent red hues and terra cotta tints of the desert landscape, bordered by majestic mountains shimmering in shades of mauve and purple were breathtaking. The sky, which appeared to tilt down to meet the mountainous terrain, was a luminescent turquoise blue sprinkled with gauzy puffs of cotton-candy-like clouds, clouds that dangled in the air, sometimes drifting so close you wanted to reach up and touch it. And the sun, incandescent and immodestly bright, shone sumptuously almost all the time. For this was Tucson, Arizona, where 350 days of the year there was sunlight.

Annie had arrived in Tucson on the 10:35 morning flight from her connection in Dallas. Joanie was there waiting at the arrivals area, with a big smile upon her face. The sisters hugged warmly.

"Here, let me take your bags. Eric's waiting in the parking lot. It's so terrific, really terrific to see you… and you look so pretty!"

"And so do you. I love your turquoise jewelry. And your outfit. So Southwestern! You look great, Joanie!"

The two sisters had changed and both for the better. Joanie had lost some weight, wore her hair simply with a fringe of bangs that highlighted her large hazel eyes. There was a beautiful glow to her skin — a gift from the Arizona sun. She seemed more relaxed and happy, and looked far younger than her 48 years. It was evident the Southwest agreed with her. As for Annie — she looked her best in years — blonde highlights in her hair, and more important — a new poise and confidence. It seemed both sisters had grown from their experiences.

They left the air terminal, arm in arm, and walked out into the brilliant sunshine.

Tall cactus stood imposingly all over the landscape, as well as an overabundance of beautiful desert plants and flowers. Desert lilies, with purplish spikes grew along the roadways. Palm trees, bougainvillea, jasmine, and dozens of variety of cactus, and beautiful eucalyptus trees, tall and emitting sweet pungent fragrances filled the air. It was a paradise, so lush and unexpectedly verdant.

"Yes, here we are in the old West, the Arizona desert where many a cowboy movies been made and yes, real cowboys lived," Joanie announced. "This is the territory of Rio Bravo and John Wayne — a land first inhabited by the Indians — Pima, Apache, Mohave, Hopi Tribes. Now, what's left of them, are living on reservations."

"Incredible — it looks just like it does in all those Westerns," Annie observed.

"And, two hours across the border is Nogales, Mexico and a whole other culture. It's also a great place to shop for bargains!" Joanie reported.

The mountains, spectacular in their asymmetry, were a constant stimulation to the eye. Shimmering shades of colors would change with the time of day. From some vantage points the clouds would create shadows over the mountains, in shades of charcoal and slate. At other times, the silhouettes of the mountains would appear almost navy blue, with powder blue and charcoal shadows in broad strokes painted over them.

"Best of all, Annie, is the humidity is so darn low that even in the hot months of summer when the temperature rises above 100 degrees, the air is still comfortable — feels more like New York when it's in the mid-80s."

"No wonder you love it here. Smells good too," Annie commented.

The air was fresh and smelled sweet, a touch of jasmine and eucalyptus encircled them as they walked outside.

Eric, a good looking man, light brown hair worn a little long, tall, lanky, with great blue eyes was leaning casually against the Ford Bronco. "I've heard only good things about you," he said in his soft-spoken voice, shaking Annie's hand with such vigor, she winced a bit.

On the ride home, they all talked.

"About a third of Tucson is inhabited by retirees, another third by natives, both Mexican and American Indian, and the other third, are professionals. Many are associated with the university here," Eric explained.

What a nice man, Annie thought. She was pleased for her sister. Eric was polite, assured, and besides all that, an intelligent, articulate person, and a principal of a high school. Neat. Joanie used to be involved with an assistant principal — seems she'd moved up in the world. But this appeared to be a more solid relationship. It looked as if Joanie had found a compatible mate, and hopefully a measure of the happiness she deserved.

"It's really a stimulating society, with Southwestern art

and culture dominating the scene. You'll be surprised at the sophistication in some areas — after all this is a college town. There's input from students from all over that come to study here at the University. It's what makes this a broad-based community, Joanie added. "I think you're going to like it."

The house was beautiful. An imposing brick ranch with red tile roof, an imposing red brick wall decorated with turquoise wrought iron and a big wrought iron gate surrounding it. Of all things there was an actual guest cottage in the back. "Well, there's far more room in Arizona than New York for guest houses and many have separate cottages. Great for guests, and some you can rent out as well," Joanie explained.

There was a small waterfall and pond off the rear patio, thriving orange and grapefruit trees and absolutely lovely plants and rose bushes flourishing all around that made it look like the Garden of Eden. Joanie was always into gardening, and now she had a place where she could indulge her interests. She'd done a splendid job.

Out on the patio Eric prepared a chicken barbecue while the women sat down in the "Arizona Room," a beautiful space filled with Southwestern style furniture. The windows in the room overlooked the patio. There they sat for almost an hour and talked and talked and talked. There was so much to catch up on.

As always, Joanie was filled with anecdotes, dotted her conversations with funny lines and possessed a witty observation on whatever was going on. She really had captured the art of enjoying life. Now, it was good. But it hadn't always been that way.

Joanie's droll sense of humor had steeled her through the dark disappointments in her life. She had her share of suffering at the hands of their miserable mother. Actually it was a sense of humor that saved all the siblings in the Rosenberg family. "You'd better learn to laugh at the family foibles or you'll become a basket case," was the sisterly advice she'd given to Annie early on.

At one time, Joanie had so many stories and one-liners that she was encouraged by her friends to do some stand-up comedy. And she was really funny when she got up on a stage on amateur night. She did it twice, but felt awkward, not really wanting to perform publicly. She decided that her comedic talents weren't for unrestricted musing.

The two women were attractive but in very different ways. Annie was a petite blonde, with good features, (and after the minor rhinoplasty to remove a bump in her nose, she did have a perfect nose), Joanie, while her mother insisted she looked more like her — really looked like her father — was big-boned, 5'6, and nice-looking in a dissimilar way.

In fact, they didn't look at all like sisters. Annie, bore a remarkable resemblance to the actress Natalie Wood while Joanie had more chiseled features with elegant planes to her face. If one was comparing them, Joanie looked more like Rosalind Russell, the actress who interestingly enough played Natalie's mother in the movie version of Gypsy. Joanie had a distinctive chin, and a long, straight nose. She did enjoy changing the color of her hair and did it with the change of seasons. A brunette, at times, she would become a red head, at other times a blonde.

Joanie's take on life was to dismiss any of the bad parts as learning experiences. Trying her hand at relationships, failing at a marriage and having her own dismal romantic liaisons, it was in finally picking up roots and moving to the Southwest that she would find a peace and contentment.

Annie liked the glamorous life, living in the Big Apple, writing and being involved in the arts. Joanie preferred the simpler things in life, be it listening to her favorite Gershwin piece, *Rhapsody in Blue*, enjoying a chocolate milkshake or languishing in a bubble bath for an hour or more. She also loved flowers and so having her own small home and garden was a dream come true.

Long drives on the dusty trails and roads surrounded by the mountains, watching the glorious Arizona sunrises, getting out of bed every morning and thanking God for another beautiful day was all that Joanie needed. Eric was the plus factor, and she was thrilled to death to have found a partner as loving and understanding as he.

With Eric and his two children, Joanie felt needed. It also seemed to be a love match. Well, at least, she found him passionate and affectionate and a stimulating partner. "It's one of the reasons I invited you down to visit," she told Annie. "I'm so proud of Eric; things are really good. Besides, it's been far too long since I've seen you!"

Annie smiled. She was truly happy for her sister.

"It's easy living here, Annie, and the people, they're really so nice. No angry horn honking, rude loud people! Why don't you come out West, move here?"

"Because — at least for now — I'm not looking for a geographic cure, Joanie. I love New York, it's the hub of the publishing world, and I have many friends there. Sure, it's easy to like what's here; I can see what you see in it. But not now, no, it's not for me."

"Well, let's at least spend quality time together... it's really good to see you, sis. You can just relax and enjoy. Anyway, we have a few days off from school and Eric is going to take us sight seeing."

"We're going to show you some fantastic places here — the GeoSphere project, Mount Lemmon — we've skied there in the winter — and all the wonderful elements here — there are beautiful homes situated in the foothills of the mountains. And real estate prices in Tucson — they're like half of New York's!"

For the first time in a long time, Joanie felt needed. By both Eric and his children. His ex-wife traveled a lot, and the kids spent a good deal of time with their father. They seemed to like Joanie and there was absolutely no discord there. The kids were really nice kids.

It seemed to be a good, wholesome relationship. "He's so thoughtful and affectionate," she said to her little sister. "We've grown closer. In fact, Eric and I are talking about moving in together. His house is larger, and Annie, I could rent mine out for income."

"Not bad Joanie, not bad at all," Annie laughed quietly.

"Now to you, dear sister! We'll have a great tour of Tucson. And we'll point out some of the wonderful vegetation and history here. You know, we have Saguaro cactus growing all over — it takes two centuries to grow some of these giant plants, and they're awesome. There's really so much to see and do."

"Great! I'm looking forward. And I brought two throwaway cameras so I can have lots to show back home. Joanie…you know I love Mexican food so we can eat out Mexican, right? There's got to be lots of Mexican fare out here!"

"Sure, Annie, but you'd be surprised at the variety of cuisine available here.

"Eric and my favorite place is Japanese…"Sushi Saga" — they make fantastic sashimi."

"Love sushi too. Frankly, from dining out all these years and writing my column, I've tried just about every ethnic cuisine and Japanese and Thai are high on my list, besides Italian, which I've always loved."

"Hell, I remember Luigi's on West 70th Street. Remember our eating there, hon? We both love Italian — remember?"

"Funny, I forget you're my sister sometimes — we're so much like good friends, and you're right, gosh, we always liked Italian food, didn't we?"

"Hey I don't want to interrupt, but the ribs and the chicken are all done, so why don't you two ladies come on out and join me," Eric said, poking his head in.

"Now all we need is a recording of Gene Autry singing "*I'm Back in the Saddle Again*," and I'll know we're in the West!", Annie laughingly said.

The phone rang. "It's for you, Annie. Some man named Sal."

Damn it, couldn't he have given her a day, respected her wishes, she thought, as she picked up the phone.

"Hi, we're about to have a barbecue. Can't talk now. I'll call you in the morning, okay?"

"Just wanted to make sure you got there safely, Babes. You know I love you!"

Funny, she wasn't happy at all to hear from him, nor his declaration of love. Gratefully, Joanie didn't press her for an explanation.

"When we have more talk time, I'll tell you about him…he's more like a good friend."

"No problem. Never complain. Never explain. Besides, he's a *Man!*"

They both giggled and walked out to the patio.

— ଔ —

....."Perhaps they were right in putting love into books...Perhaps it could not live anywhere else."
— *William Faulkner*

— ∞ —

Chapter 32

The week had flown by. A wonderful week. Eric and Joanie had turned Annie's visit into a guided-tour of the Southwest. She became a wide-eyed spectator at a rodeo, went to Tombstone, Arizona for a re-enactment of the shoot-out at the Okay Corral, drove across the border to bargain shop in Nogales, Mexico, and dined out in astonishingly good restaurants in Tucson. It had turned out to be a real holiday. For a while Annie even forgot about the drag-on divorce. She also appreciated the wholesome bond Eric and Joanie shared.

"Eric's terrific. You're really lucky to have found him. He's a really nice guy."

"Yes, I'm lucky. But I sure kissed a lot of frogs until the Prince came along!"

"Well, at least one of us has found more than a frog. We didn't exactly begin with a good gene pool, you know — I mean, our parents are not exactly great role models."

Joanie smiled. "That's for sure! And the kids... what do you think of Eric's children?"

"Oh, they seem really nice — good manners, good kids."

"Yes, and you know what? There's no friction between his ex-wife and me. She's a nice person, just completed her master's degree and she's getting married again. So it's been really easy."

"And all the people I've met — your friends — Joanie, they're really cool. Amazingly, an awful lot of them look a little like Ken and Barbie — they're all so darn good looking. But real, too."

"Well many families have come here from the mid-west, so you get a lot of blonde blue-eyed people, I guess. And an amazingly nice group, not affected, nor materialistic — and even though they're so good looking, they don't seem to be aware of their appearances. Did you notice, the women — they wear little or no makeup?"

"Yes I noticed. No 4 inch long acrylic nails, no crazy hairdos, no high heels either."

"It's much more casual here. And everyone is really considerate."

"A little white bread kind of community, I'd say."

"No. '*Tostadas*' are all around here, too. There are many Mexican families here — I think almost a third of the population is originally Mexican. They're all hard working, and in this community, while there's a significant below-the-poverty-line population, many are living the good life. The second and third generations, they're integrated. Actually, the singer Linda Rondstadt's family lives here and very, very well."

"Yeah, somehow I knew that. She did a fabulous recording of "*Someone to Watch Over Me*," you know. One of my favorite songs."

"There's the really bad side of town, like in any place," Joanie added. "It's on the South side, where there's a drug culture, gangs, drive-by shootings, great poverty amongst the immigrants. That's because there's so much destitution in Mexico that they're constantly sneaking over the border. It's a big problem here."

"America, the land of the free and opportunity. Well, it helped our grandparents."

"Yeah, but most of them settled in the East, learned English and assimilated into the general society. Here, Spanish is the primary language, and still spoken in many places. Many never learn English. And there's less opportunity for work out here. Tucson doesn't have that active a work pool. Most of the immigrants who come here are day laborers. But where it's good, where people have professional jobs, well, yes, it's a bit like a *Leave it to Beaver* society, with happy marriages and happy children… the whole nine yards. But don't let it fool you; don't forget Eric is divorced. Not every story has a happy ending. There are split families and divorced couples here too."

"Not to change the subject, sis, but what are you going to do about this man Sal? He's called so often."

"He's a good guy. I like him a lot, but not like he cares about me. He sometimes is too damned possessive — it's like he's breathing down my back and I feel suffocated. Isn't it always that way, the ones you don't care about?"

"I know what you mean."

"Oh, I almost forgot to tell you. I received some good news. I spoke to my attorney this morning — he told me the judge should sign the papers for discovery next week — finally, they've set a date. If that's the case, then I really need Sal's help. Tom will hate my getting court approval to go out to his house and go through all of it. It's going to be a hairy situation."

"Is it really worth it? This endless fighting?" Joanie asked.

"I left the first time with nothing. Just the clothing on my back. Not this time. Not that I don't dread the thought of going out there. He'll probably have his brother or someone else around and it will be very awkward. I really don't want to face this myself. It's nerve-wracking. Sal, he's so gallant that he actually said he's going to have bodyguards go out there with me. You can't beat that kind of consideration."

"Bodyguards? How solicitous of him! This is beginning to sound like a "B" movie, Annie! I just hope you get through the pain and peril of all of this quickly. Fighting over money is what makes divorces drag on and on and on and usually makes the lawyers rich if no one else."

"Don't I know it? The lawyer is charging $150 an hour. But lucky for me that Jacob Meyers is paying for it and wants me to win. When he's behind something, he doesn't care what it costs. It's his money backing me. I could never do this on my own. I've just started to make some money, but my books, while I did get some good advances — only one book so far has gone into a second printing. The advances are against *royalties*. And you have to sell lots of books to get royalties. I haven't."

"So it's mostly glamorous but not very satisfying for your bank account."

"Yup. That's the problem. Publishing is not a high paying field. Not unless you get a best seller. So far, my how-to's have given me a good reputation, but no real money in the bank. You need the publisher to put money up for a promotion tour — and so far they haven't done that with me — they usually get the banners out for a celebrity-backed book."

"Well, I loved your Dell book. Great tips."

"Thanks. It did go into a second printing. And wasn't it neat getting Vidal Sassoon to write the book blurb? You know, maybe, when all of this is over, when I can get some distance from it, I'll write about my own experiences…they're exciting enough! I've long thought of putting it all down. So keep your fingers crossed."

"You know I will. And, Annie, I hope, maybe by next year, you'll come back for a longer visit?"

"When it's all behind me...I promise. And you can also come back to New York, you know. Maybe you can bring Eric along for some sightseeing."

"That's a good thought. He's never been there. And I really need to visit Mom and Dad. I asked them to come here. They're just not travelers."

"Well, I've had a really great time. It's so good to have you for a sister, Joanie. I rarely hear from Sid... we're really like the only family we have. I'm sorry we haven't seen each other in so long a time. It won't happen again."

The sisters hugged affectionately. It was tough saying goodbye.

— ❧ —

Sal was at the airport, waiting with a big smile on his face. "Hi Baby, boy did I miss you." He grabbed Annie and gave her a big wet kiss. She couldn't help thinking of Tom, comparing him, how much more tender and pleasant his kiss was. No, stop! Back to reality, she reminded herself. It was over, over, over and her comparing two such different men — was brainless.

On the drive back from La Guardia Sal talked of his plans for Annie. "I've gotten a big bear of a guy — Cookie is his name — he's actually the brother of the Borough President on Staten Island. Cookie's going to accompany you. He does a lot of bodyguard work. And he'll bring along an assistant...just in case. You never know. They owe me, so the price is dirt-cheap. Your soon-to-be ex will shit in his pants when he sees you with these muscle men. You won't have to worry about a thing," he said, a big grin on his face.

To tell the truth, she was relieved. And a little thrilled. Hey, why not go out with some great big guys? That should annoy Tom...and make her look good. Why not? Annie was still hurting, her ego was bruised, and although she was the one to end it, she knew it was because he was pig-headed. Like she really had no choice.

Annie had worked on looking terrific — exercised, dieted, lost some weight. She was determined to come across at her very best when they saw each other again. She'd wear a drop-dead outfit, casual, but special — one that showed off her figure. She just had to look beautiful, better than anyone he was dating now. And Annie was sure he was dating, if not more involved. Tom liked his women, didn't like being alone. She'd go over to one of her favorite Madison Avenue boutiques and splurge on something special. After all, dressing up for a court-ordered proceeding demanded high fashion.

It was almost a year since they were in each other's presence. The last time was in Family Court. That's where Annie had to file the separation papers. The Courthouse was a cold, remote building with grimy windows and soiled, heel-scuffed floors. The walls were painted a standardized tedious green, almost the color of puke. At least that's how Annie described it: "puke green." Here's where inquiries were held daily for broken marriages and broken hearts. Single mothers, abused women seeking orders-of-protection, foster children in anguish — the building was brimming with life's troubles.

When Tom wasn't looking, she quickly stole a glance. His shoulders were hunched over, he looked sad, but she also detected an anger. Strange, so near and yet so far. No more declarations of love. Oh if only they could talk. Now they dealt through lawyers in a declaration of war. Annie hadn't seen nor spoken to him in a very long time.

It would be grueling, but she'd have to go through the discovery process, prove that he was financially far better off than she. Annie felt she'd lost so much, all her hopes, all her dreams. This was the final damned dissolution, the downfall of her loving this man, the failure at the end of 19 years. Surely she could assuage her hurt and wounded pride if she was paid off in dollars.

"I'm going to follow you in the van. That way I can sit across the street, conduct surveillance, make sure everything is okay. But you know why I can't go in with you, Babes," Sal explained. "It's better for me to stay out of the picture. I'm still active in the Fire Department, it wouldn't look good for me to be involved with a fellow fireman, that could be a very delicate situation."

"Whatever you say, Sal. I really, really appreciate your having those men go out there with me. My lawyer says it may not happen all in one day. If we can't find things — if he isn't cooperative — we may have to go back to court and then back out there again."

"Well, let's take it one step at a time, beautiful. If you need to go back, you'll go back with protection. Hey, want to have a good Italian meal? Bet you haven't had some real New York Italian food in a while, huh?"

"Actually Joanie took me to a great Italian eatery in Tucson. I was surprised but they have excellent restaurants there."

"Yeah, but we're going to Bay Ridge, babes. Where the *real* Italians are!" Sal said with a giant smile on his face, his eyes twinkling.

He turned on his tape system to a Dean Martin song. And off he drove in the direction of Brooklyn. To his old neighborhood, where the food was served family style, and the romantic music he loved, was playing all the time. God she was gorgeous. He was crazy about Annie. Crazy in love.

— ❦ —

"Never appeal to a man's better nature. He may not have one. Invoking his self interest gives you more leverage."
— *Robert Heinlein*

— CR —

Chapter 33

February 1987

The court order had finally come through. The plan for Annie to go to Tom's house with bodyguards was put into place. Now it was time to drive out to Queens. "Yikes, I feel like I'm in a *Mission Impossible* show, or something, with all these fantastic plans," Annie told Sal. "I'm so grateful to you." She felt secure with Sal, and keyed up having his guidance and protection. Yup, for now she definitely had someone to watch over her.

It snowed the previous day. Cone-shaped piles of the white stuff plowed earlier that morning bordered the streets. The piles were already black and brown and in some places urine yellow — corrupted by the exhausts of the cars speeding by and the dogs being walked by their owners. But then this was February in New York, and a snowy one at that.

Sal had arranged for the men he'd hired to meet them on Queens Boulevard at the local White Castle, (which just happened to be one of Annie's favorite burger emporiums). She always loved the distinctive square-cut mini burgers which she customarily ordered 'with extra pickle slices, no ketchup.'

White Castle hamburgers reminded Annie of some of the better times of growing up. Her father used to buy sacks of them and bring them home, along with those salty, crispy French fries. They were about 10 cents a burger back then. It was the junk food of the 50s, and the whole family would enjoy it once or twice a month. Thirty something years later, they still were a bargain, and could still be bought by the sack. Silly, but she wanted to have a few of them that day. And it was only 10 a.m. Probably some of the craving was to cover up the edginess, her angst over the events that would take place later that day.

Hamburgers in the morning? Why not. Anything that touched her tongue and felt tasteful could distance Annie from the real world; buy her a few moments of soothing security. Impractical, sad, maybe even sick, but it worked. She'd also stowed away a couple of Hershey bars in her handbag. She wanted to come across as ultra-calm, hide the edginess inside. Sometimes chocolate worked.

It was a bitter wintry morning. "Ouch, my toes are cold," she mentioned to Sal. He turned up the heat in the car. "Why the open-toe shoes in this weather, hon?"

"I know, it's dim-witted of me," she laughed it off.

Annie wouldn't admit it, but the ankle-strap shoe was just the thing to show off her shapely legs. Tom loved her legs. And those high heels made a flawless fashion statement coupled with the black leather skirt and white cashmere sweater. The look was casual, but sexy. Just what to wear so your soon-to-be ex-husband can see what he's missing. There was no way she wasn't going to dress up to meet her destiny, even if it was a doomed one.

Sal turned up the heat in the car so she'd be more comfortable, but later, at the house, it was staggeringly cold. Evidently Tom didn't want to spend the money on the heat, or was he purposefully making the house sub-zero inside? Annie noticed a window open in the living room. Now she knew why it was bitter cold in there. A game — part of the divorce war game. But the real cold and bitterness was in the air. You could've cut through it with a knife.

The stage was set. How much discovery she'd make was still a big question mark. Tom's brother was there. In fact he opened the door to let them in. She thought he said hello, but Annie was so frozen with anxiety, she wasn't sure if he did or if she answered. The silence was deadening. Tom sat quietly on a chair in the living room, briefly nodding to the men who explained they were there to help Annie make a record of items.

In the background, sitting at the table in the dining room, Annie noticed a young woman, dark hair, pretty, possibly Tom's latest leisure activity? What was she doing there? What was it Annie's business? *She* was the one who'd left. But still, she wondered. Hey, she was wife #2 and #4; the odds were that he'd probably marry again. Was this one to be #5? Amazing, a fireman, with multiple marriage syndrome. Somehow she found this funny, and laughed to herself. My God, maybe she was really getting over him... or was she just numb from all of this?

1987 was an up and down year. The down of it was the "Stock Market Crash" where the market dropped 30% in mid October. Even worse, the deaths of Liberace and Michael Bennett, two talents, both to the dread disease AIDS were downers. And the disease was spreading worldwide. *"Dirty Dancing"*, *"Moonstruck"*, *"Broadcast News"* and *"Fatal Attraction"* were some of the big movies of the year. Fatal attraction indeed.

Andy Warhol, the pop artist had died. Topping the charts that year were songs like *The Lady in Red, I Wanna Dance with Somebody* recorded by Whitney Houston, and *All I Ask of You* from the new Broadway hit, *"Phantom of the Opera"*. And somewhere in Russia, outside of Moscow, on October 14, 1987, Valentina Nicolai Sobstova was born, only to be left by her mother in the hospital there.

Tom's house still looked the same. The few improvements Annie had made, bright wall papering the kitchen, painting some of the rooms, helped open up the place, but it still had dark, masculine brown furnishings in the living room, and a musty smell throughout. It was more like a storage place than a home one really lived in.

But what was soon evident was what *wasn't* stored at the house. Missing were Tom's treasure trove of autographed memorabilia. Sure, he had at least 12 cartons set up in the living room area, loaded with books, one or two of them signed by minor writers — and a stack of old movie magazines from the 1930s and 40s on hand. But it was obvious, this was all for show. The books were not valuable, not first editions, and most of them unsigned. It was a game, a horrible game, and she didn't want to lose.

Annie spent two dark, dismal hours going through the boxes of magazines. She could feel Tom's eyes burning down on her as she leaned down and went through each carton. Damned if she'd back down now. She made notes. And she took photos. She wasn't really getting much information and she knew he knew it too. It wasn't hard to guess — all he'd displayed for discovery was about a thousand dollars worth of goods. Old *Life* magazines, *Time* magazines from the 1930s and some beautiful *Theater Arts* magazines — all of which had some value. But she knew this was the fodder Tom was willing to throw into any divorce settlement — maybe he'd have to give up $500 in what she was entitled to, but no more.

If in the end she could win anything by proving that he had an extensive and expensive memorabilia collection, she knew that any money the court awarded her would be just that, *money*. Tom wouldn't part with one thing he'd collected. In fact, sometimes Annie thought, he'd rather die than part with anything he believed belonged to him. Anal Retentive. Anal Retentive. Anal Retentive. She repeated it to herself like a mantra. Anything to keep herself calm, not to let him see she was in any way, shape, or, form upset. This was hard, much harder than she'd expected.

Out of the corner of her eye she could see him sitting on a chair. Not saying a word. She detected his anger. She felt his eyes on her. Hell, at least, even from the back, she looked good. Still Annie was nervous, upset, and couldn't help but wonder who the hell the woman was that she'd seen at the dining room table. She was now in the kitchen, evidently preparing a meal.

The time was flying by. She'd only a couple of hours more that would be considered reasonable to search the house. Annie whispered to Cookie, "Tell them we'd like to go upstairs now." She just couldn't bring myself to directly ask for anything. Inside she was seething and getting angrier, more frustrated by the moment. Shit! She knew he'd removed most of the collection from the house. When and where he'd taken it she didn't know. But he wasn't that stupid, to leave the really valuable things around. Still she'd have to go through the motions.

Upstairs, she noticed that the framed pictures that had been on the wall were removed and replaced with cheap prints; the kind you bought in a Wal-Mart to spruce up a home. She knew he had a signed Marc Chagall lithograph and at least a few good drawings in the bedroom. No more.

She entered Colleen's bedroom where once there hung a mélange of Oz memorabilia. Tom owned a dazzling Judy Garland signed photo, a very rare and prized original script from the movie signed by Yip Harburg and Harold Arlen, and a framed song sheet of "*Somewhere Over the Rainbow*" signed by the same duo. Thank heaven Colleen wasn't home. Nor, was any of the unique collection. All of it, Bert Lahr as the Cowardly Lion, Ray Bolger as the Scarecrow and Jack Haley as the Tin Man, every signed photo and fragment of the Wizard of Oz memorabilia that Tom had used to bedeck his daughter's room had been removed. Now, cheap posters of the Rolling Stones and the Monkees covered the teenager's walls.

Yes, she had proof. She'd taken a couple of photos of Colleen's room when her stepdaughter was out. No, he didn't know about it. She smiled to herself. Justice would be slow, but it would come.

Finally, she asked to see the "autograph room." The door was closed, but not locked. His brother opened it for them. Annie expected it: The shelves were almost empty. Nowhere to be found were at least 12 albums filled with hundreds of autographed photos of celebrities, authors and composers. The carefully annotated pages where dozens of priceless pictures had been kept were all missing. At least a hundred or more important books were absent from the shelves. As she expected, there was really no sign of the extensive poster, lobby card and autographed memorabilia collection that Tom had been assembling for the past decade.

Fortunately for Annie she'd taken all those secret snapshots when the goods were there. She knew that the signed first edition of *A Streetcar Named Desire* by Tennessee Williams and the signed first edition of Ernest Hemingway's *A Farewell to Arms* had been taken out of the house with all the rest. Those two books alone were worth a thousand dollars.

Even though the tension in the air was unbearable, even though a young and pretty woman (obviously rehearsing to be her replacement,) was now preparing dinner, even though she only caught one brief glimpse of Tom all the time she was there, (and damned if he didn't look good,) Annie grit her teeth, hid her rage, was determined to put up a good façade.

She'd steeled herself for this for more than a year, knowing how hurtful it would be. She'd been warned long ago about the devastation that went with property settlements in any divorce. Still, when you were in the midst of it, it was agony, sheer agony.

Annie's only resolve was that Tom didn't know that she had proof that he did own many of the missing items. She'd have a good case in court, her attorney had assured her.

But it was maddening. She wanted to shout out, "You think you're getting away with it, but I have financial records. I was with you when you bid on the Hemingway and when you purchased the Anna Pavlova signed photograph. I have copies of receipts — from the Charles Hamilton gallery when you bought the Abraham Lincoln document, from Swann Galleries when you bought the John F. Kennedy letter. You're not going to get away with it, you're not," she screamed silently. Oh how it hurt.

Annie bit her lip, remained quiet, pretended she'd been thwarted in her efforts, that he'd gotten away with removing the very valuable cache. Still nothing was a sure thing, and whether she could prove enough to force him to settle in or out of court, in her opinion — was still a gamble.

She was greatly relieved when they finally left the house.

"You did good, Babes, real good," Sal said as they drove back to the city. "Cookie said your husband looked like he was going to blow up a few times…don't think you didn't get to him, because you did. And now, it's just a wait-and-see game. Your lawyer will do the next part."

"I just want it all over already… I hate this, all of this," she said, tears welling up in her eyes.

"Hey, you said your Jim Dandy of a husband has a cool collection — maybe worth a few hundred thousand for all you know — and he got a lot of it during your time together. Remember what the lawyer said, you get a stake in anything accumulated during the marriage."

"I'm tired," Annie said, tears in her eyes. "Tired of it all."She was also thinking of the woman she saw in the background. And she thought of Tom. And of another time when they were so much in love. She just wanted to go home and lie down and be alone. Please, oh please — just leave me alone.

She begged out of dinner. Sal understood and dropped her off at the entrance to her building. "I'll call you later, hon, make sure you're okay."

Okay. What was that? How could she be okay? She loved the hell out of Tom, still felt a passion for him, and yet knew, it was toxic, it was poison, there was no way they could ever be together again, for sure, he'd moved on. And somehow she had to do it too. Annie went upstairs, took off her clothes, curled up into a fetal position and within minutes had fallen asleep on the unturned bed. She just wanted to blot it all out.

"One must never disturb the joy of one's mind. Holding on to distress will not help fulfill one's wishes. Indeed, it will undermine one's virtues."
— Tibetan saying

— ∞ —

Chapter 34

April 1988

"Do you know what I've learned that's helped me get to where I am today?" Sabrina addressed Maureen and Annie. "Whatever women do they've got to do it *twice* as well as men. Fortunately, this isn't difficult," Sabrina said with a wink, as she finished her mousse. Finishing dessert for her meant leaving half of it on the plate. What better way to keep her svelte figure.

The three women had met for dinner at Lutece, the fashionable 4-star French restaurant in midtown Manhattan. Amazing, now all three could afford to pay the $60 cost of a dinner there, although Maureen insisted on picking up the tab as her celebration – she'd married a few months before.

"Tell us about your honeymoon," Sabrina asked Maureen, who'd recently returned from Paris.

"Where do I begin? It was simply wonderful. We went on the

Concorde! It was my first visit to France, and it's just as romantic as they say it is. Unfortunately it was cold in February, but it was still fantastic!"

"And why all the secrecy?"

"We wanted to be alone. Most of all, we didn't want a big wedding."

Maureen paused while the waiter filled her cup with more espresso.

"The engagement party was so immense and public enough. I think John had every client he ever represented there, never mind our families and friends. And I certainly didn't want to deal with the 'McDermott family wrecking party,' which could have happened at a formal wedding, that is, if they'd even shown up. It's still touch and go with them. My mother, she's pleasant when I call. I know she's told the neighbors that I'm singing and she seems pleased that I'm married. But it wasn't in the Church and that was difficult for her to accept...."

"Hey, sometimes you just can't teach old dogs new tricks. My parents are really rigid in their ways," Annie said.

"What the heck is wrong with all of them? Sometimes my mom actually asks questions that sound like she's interested in what I'm doing with my life. Still — in all these years she still hasn't come to see me perform. And only two of my brothers have shown up. I've sent all of them complimentary tickets to every one of my local concerts. It's so sad."

"At least we can pick our friends," Annie commented.

"Anyway, we were married by a judge-friend of John's and left the next morning for Paris. It was really all John's idea. With his being a divorced man, the marriage couldn't have been performed by a priest and frankly, I'm glad we did it this way. I couldn't have gone through a formal big-deal wedding. I'm just not into gowns and bridesmaids and the rest of it. I hope you both don't mind. Believe me, I would have asked the two of you to be my matron's of honor, if that's the right term."

"Well, to tell you the truth, after my dismal experience with weddings, I don't think, as happy as I am for you, that I would have enjoyed dressing up and playing the "she's getting married game," Annie said.

"A bit cynical of you, my dear. But well, you're still battling legally with him, aren't you?" Sabrina inquired.

"Yes, it's been ugly, but it's only three years later," she said sarcastically. "In dog years it would be 21, so maybe we're dogs. It certainly has dragged on and on and on. Now, my new attorney — I needed one who specialized in appeals — has filed papers in the Appeals Court. What I'm contesting is Tom not wanting his pension to be part of any settlement. The lawyer tells me there's nothing a fireman hates more than having his pension attacked. You can even say he's got a small dick and he won't be half as upset as if you go after any part of his pension! I'm told that Tom will buckle in if the court rules that I'm entitled to any part of it."

"I have a good feeling he'll end up settling…just hang in there, girl," Maureen said encouragingly. "Dog years, hhhmm? Funny! Friend."

"Wow, here we are talking about my dumb situation all over again. I'm even bored with it. I'm sorry I got on the divorce track. I really don't want to talk about it any longer, please. I'm happy for you, Mrs. John Turner, that you've found such a great guy. You certainly deserve it. Oh, and, by the way — I absolutely love my job at the *Advance* — so I do have some real positives in my life."

Maureen beamed. "Thanks for sending me a copy of your interview with Marlo Thomas, it was really good. I was proud of you, seeing your byline. And yes, you're right about the Mrs. John Turner. John didn't want me to do it, but on my next record — it's going to be released in about two months — I'll be Maureen Turner, folks. I'm going to become known by my married name. In fact, John is having someone in his office do the promotion on it right now."

"And if anyone can do it, he can."

"Yes, John is superb at publicity!"

"Oh, and I did receive a nice card from my mother. It arrived the other day. And she seemed very pleased that I'd finally married. I wonder if the magic "M" has turned the tide. She wrote that she was very happy for me and hoped I would bring John to meet her. Will wonders never cease! I'm going to call her and set up a date. It will be interesting to bring John out there to Long Island. He's been in the Hamptons, of course, but never in the basic Levittown type of community."

"Parents can have their own expectations, and that's their right. But we also have the right to live up to our own," Sabrina said. "Sure, my mother would have loved for me to marry young and give her grandchildren, but I had to follow my own ambitions…I think we all have to. It's part of the maturing process."

"Yes, we all have life lessons to learn. I for one have found that as I acquire more knowledge, things don't always become easier to understand, but far more mystifying," Maureen opined.

"That's probably the real concept of life — to learn and as we do to know eventually how little we know," Annie added.

"Now about your new job as a reporter? What exactly are you doing at the newspaper? And how long have you been working out there on Staten Island?" Sabrina inquired.

"Well, it's not quite NBC," Annie said, with deference to Sabrina. "But it is a Newhouse paper, and a good one for the borough. In fact, it's the only daily they have there so it's powerful and well circulated."

"Salvatore, was a doll, and definitely helpful. He knows just about everyone there. I think he put in a few good words for me. I met with the editor-in-chief and was hired immediately. I've been in the life style section for 8 months now, mostly writing features, and besides that, they've given me my own beauty column, so I'm doing double duty and love it. And besides that, I'm still writing on restaurants for *'Our Town.'* "

"Fabulous!"

"I really couldn't ask for more, especially since I'm going to do a book on cosmetic surgery for men. I wrote the proposal that was accepted so I get to choose the expert. Connie, my agent, is drawing up the contract with the publisher while I interview doctors, and so I'm really busy and enjoying every moment of it. It keeps me focused, and not dwelling on the damned divorce."

"Good for you. Annie — I know that you're headed for even bigger and better things. That is, if you want it. Just being at peace, centered, we've both learned how much that matters," Maureen added, alluding to their association with meditation.

"How do you get to Staten Island from Manhattan?" Sabrina asked.

"Painfully!"

"Is it really that ghastly a commute?" Maureen added.

"No, I just couldn't resist that opening. It's really not bad at all. A half hour door-to-door if I leave before rush hour. And believe me, you want to avoid rush hour!"

"As for a car, I didn't even have to buy one. Lucky for me that a man with whom I've been friendly, I met him through the *'Our Town' Newspaper* years ago — he offered me the use of one of his company cars, a neat Ford Taurus. And I can park it for free at one of his garages. He's filthy rich, owns buildings and garages all over midtown. He's a really sweet old man, so I took him up on it. I reverse commute and park on the street most days, but when I want to, I just bring the car up to the garage on 60th Street; it's great."

"Annie, it's amazing how you get all these men to be so helpful," Maureen said laughing. "Do you have a secret formula or do they just come to you like pre-programmed robots, ready to do your bidding?"

"Lord knows. But I've been really fortunate. In between the hard knocks, the ups and downs with Tom, I've found some really decent men, and right now the last thing I'd do is look a gift-horse in the mouth. Besides Jacob Meyer — that's his name — he has no offspring, and tons of money, so if he helps some people, well, it's not hurting him one bit."

"It's providential. Like you have a guardian angel or two looking out for you."

"And oh, how I believe in angels." Annie had been collecting portraits of angels, angel figurines and statues for years and kept quite a few in her apartment.

"Not to change the subject or anything, but Sabrina, tell us about your experiences in Calgary," Annie asked. "I saw you doing some of those interviews with the ice skating competitors and they were absolutely terrific."

Sabrina's assignments at the network had broadened. She was pleased when the vice-president of sports selected her to cover the winter Olympic Games in Calgary. It was a plum project.

"Thanks. It was a beyond belief experience. Aside from it being so damned cold it could freeze the tits off a hot witch, it was one of the best assignments I've had so far. And, well, ladies, I have something to tell you," she said with a big smile upon her face.

Both Maureen and Annie leaned in, listening earnestly.

"I've met a wonderful man. He's an orthopedic surgeon specializing in sports medicine. He was in Canada with our ski team."

"…and, and, come tell us more!" Maureen said excitedly.

"It's getting serious. I really care about him. We'll see. With my schedule and his — he travels between his offices here in New York and to visit the teams in Denver — it's a lot. But he's really wonderful."

"Bravo! Cupid has finally landed his quiver in Sabrina's heart," Maureen said. "Let's all have a toast to your new amour. May he have the courage to win you completely! And by the way, Sabrina, freezing the tits on a hot witch? Never heard that one before. And out of your mouth! What a wild way-out expression!"

"What's the lucky man's name, Sabrina? You've never mentioned it," Annie asked.

"Oh sorry. Dr. Mark Le Maux. I think his family was originally from Quebec — some French heritage. He's handsome, a great skier, sportsman, and a heck of a nice guy. I'm *'ga ga'* over him," she laughed.

The women chuckled. And clicked their crystal water goblets together in a toast to one another. It was 1988 and they'd come a long way since they'd first met.

The year 1988 was like any other, one that encompassed defeats and wins, new beginnings, unforeseen deaths.

It was the year that Pan Am 747 exploded from a terrorist bomb and crashed in Lockerbie, Scotland, killing all 259 aboard and 11 on the ground. It was also the year that Annie's team, the Los Angeles Dodgers had won the World Series, defeating the Oakland Athletics. The statistics on AIDS cases kept rising, with 106,994 AIDS cases diagnosed in the U.S. and 62,101 people dead of the devastating disease. Then again, in 1987 Maureen was nominated for a Grammy award, her first nomination for best pop vocal performance, and although she lost out to Tracy Chapman, just to be selected, was blessing enough.

Annie was making plans for change as well. While she loved her apartment in Manhattan, it might be time to move on. She'd spent 20 years there, in and out, in between marriages. It was great, but it was still small, and she didn't want to end up her life surrounded by cement.

Driving back and forth, and throughout the better parts of Staten Island, she'd seen beautiful town homes and houses. Staten Island, was just a stone's throw from downtown Manhattan, and well, she was hoping, since she hadn't any design or plan to marry again, that she might adopt a child. Not a little baby, she'd have to work to support herself and the child. Better someone of school age. And also, as much as she didn't want to admit it she was now in her 50s. Still — maybe adopting a little girl, ready for kindergarten – she really hoped she could do this someday. It would really mean a new start, someone who needed her, someone important in her life.

She'd been reading about foreign adoptions, and thinking seriously of applying. She knew that single women were now being considered, and, well, she'd always wanted her own child, maybe this was a way to make it possible. But Annie knew living in a studio apartment wasn't the right place to raise a child, besides there wouldn't be much extra space. She'd have to bide her time, be patient, wait.

She was giving serious thought to buying a home for herself, that is, if the divorce settlement she was counting on allowed her a decent down payment. She wouldn't be able to afford a spacious enough apartment in the city — rentals were upward of a thousand or more for a one bedroom and $1,500 for a two bedroom. It was well beyond her means. But she could afford the upkeep on a house in the suburbs.

Annie's biological clock had run out. At one point she looked into foster care, then researched adoptions, in fact, researched and wrote a two-part Sunday feature on the thousands of lost children who needed a home, and made up her mind that someday she'd adopt.

Meanwhile, she knew the real estate laws in New York meant she could sublet her apartment, but since it was rent-stabilized, only for a period of two years. Sal kept urging her to move out to Staten Island, but that was Sal's agenda, not hers. She found him more and more suffocating with time. She had two cats now, beautiful Abyssinian cats whom she loved. Sal kept urging her to buy fish. Fish!

"I'll get you a nice big fish tank and you can get tropicals... gorgeous colored fish... I have two tanks in my house, downstairs... they're terrific...let me set you up with this, Babes," he kept urging. "Come on, they take a little feeding each day and that's it...and you never have to walk them, or bother with kitty litter," he said laughing.

She wanted fish like she wanted another pound of fat on her body.

Yet he kept it up, week after week. He would take her into pet stores where fish tanks were set up. He wouldn't take no for an answer. One night he showed up with a gigantic box. In it was an expensive glass fish tank. "No, no, please, return it," she begged. "There's no room here Sal, and really I do NOT want fish."

What a pest. Still, he'd been so kind and helpful to her and was patient and understanding, and well, if he could just be a good friend, that would be just fine. But he was crazy about her, still, and wanted more from Annie, much more than she wanted from him. Like sex.

Frankly, she found him a turn-off. He was over-weight, overbearing, never was a great lover; she just wasn't attracted to him that way. At the beginning it seemed oh-so-romantic, the Italian songs, his investigative job, the shoulder holster and gun, the flashing red lights, his take-care-of-her stance. But it had worn thin, real thin. If they slept together once in a while, she didn't mind, but he was clingy and demanding that way too.

Merd! If Annie had to sleep with Sal one more time she was going to blow up. The truth was she'd lost whatever initial interest she had in him — an interest probably more borne of need than passion. But now, three years later, she wanted out. How could she tell him, what should she do?

In the end, Sal made it easy for Annie to detach. He was so damned jealous and possessive, she couldn't put up with it any longer. She'd met her old friend Jim for dinner one night. Sal had a fit! "I don't have to explain my whereabouts to you, for God's sake — you're a married man!" she shouted, as he ranted and raved on. He didn't have an answer for that one.

Although he'd hidden it fairly well at the beginning, Sal was a control freak. He really didn't like anyone talking back to him, was used to his squad of men taking orders, and his wife obviously had little to say about what went down. Sal had a temper and if he lost it, he had a fast and big mouth. Eventually Annie and he engaged in some pretty vociferous arguments. Still he never held a grudge, would call the next day and apologize. "Hey, let's go to dinner and a movie, I'm really sorry, Babes, you're right, you have your own life to lead."

Still, as she became less dependent upon Sal — Annie was doing very well at work — and was getting ready to begin the new book — he knew that his hold on her was lessening. He didn't like it. She didn't care. She was really pissed off when he complained that she'd stayed out one evening after a meeting with Jim. How was that his business?

As for Jim, poor, poor Jim, they'd lost touch for a while and then Annie met up with him at, of all places, an AA gathering in Murray Hill.

Manhattan was teeming with AA meetings, morning, afternoon, evening, midnight, all over town. As the 80s brought enlightenment — the Betty Ford treatment center was just one rehab center that shed light on celebrities who'd admitted their problems with alcohol and pills — somehow the publicity made it more acceptable for some to admit they had a drinking problem.

News discussions informed the public about the disease of alcoholism, that alcoholism and other addictions, was treatable with a 12-step program. AA became more socially acceptable. Meetings were now crowded and offshoots like Narcotics Anonymous, Overeaters Anonymous burgeoned with new members. Not everyone got it; it could be a revolving door. And there was Jim. She wasn't surprised to see Jim there; he'd drunk along with her many years ago. She knew he'd been sober for a while and then she hadn't seen him any longer.

She soon learned that he was having a rough time and had been in and out of the program. Jim, like many partakers in the 60s and 70s, had dabbled in drugs. It was the LSD that had ruined him; seared perforations in his brain. He'd left his agency job in 1980, declaring that he wanted to pursue an acting career. Actually they were ready to let him go. The quality of his work had diminished severely.

Annie went to the local coffee shop with Jim. "I'm on the acting track," he explained. "I've had it with Madison Avenue."

"How are you supporting yourself then?" Annie asked. "I don't need much. I'm working part time as a waiter, still have some savings left." Annie didn't believe it all. She sensed Jim was in trouble. His eyes had a vacant look. It was obvious he'd been devastated by the drugs he'd done. He just wasn't the same bright light, the good-looking man she once knew. Jim was drained and damaged, looked older than his years. It was also obvious that he was hungry and hadn't eaten well that day. She ordered him a plate of soup and a hamburger. She picked up the tab, and gave him a small "loan." "Here's $20, and my phone number. Call me," she said, "and please, go to more meetings."

It stung, seeing him like that. But Annie knew Jim had to find his own way, that he knew where the help was and if he wanted it bad enough, he could get back on his feet. Still, remembering the good times they'd shared, his wit and good nature, it was heartbreaking to see him in such despair. He was spaced out in a way that only mind-bending drugs could do.

Why couldn't life be easier, less hurtful? Why did so many people go to the wrong well, seek in alcohol and cocaine, in painkillers, in overeating, in any way they could numb themselves a way out? When the truth was, oh if they only knew it, that they could find salvation within themselves. Why couldn't they all get the help she'd finally found? It was painful to admit, but she didn't have the answers, only enormous appreciation that she was one of the lucky ones.

Months went by. She'd pray for Jim nightly — but even when she looked for him at the various Manhattan meetings, she never ran into him again. She had no idea where he was living. She didn't have a phone number, nor could she locate him anywhere in the Manhattan telephone directory.

What could she have done to help? She wondered if she'd done enough.

Poor Jim, was he lost for good?

He never called her again. She would never know.

— ⚭ —

A cathedral, a wave of a storm, a dancer's leap, never turn out to be as high as we had hoped."
— *Marcel Proust*

— CR —

Chapter 35

July 1990

The start of a new decade brought with it an increase in terrorism. In 1990 Iranian-backed Shia groups were believed to be in control of the Western hostages held in Lebanon. Then, after Iraq invaded Kuwait, President Bush set in motion what would become the Gulf War.

On the domestic front, AIDS, was still escalating and now numbered more than 307,000 cases. After a valiant battle, young Ryan White, another innocent victim of the disease, died at age 18. The senseless fatalities would continue, and soon everyone knew someone who knew someone who had AIDS or was HIV positive.

It was also the beginning of a decade of self-indulgence, born out of over inflated stocks and dazzling tech companies on the rise. The age of excess was gearing up. By 1994, young *turks*, gambling on Wall Street would be made into millionaires. Housewives, secretaries, anyone with a few hundred dollars to spare would invest in the market. Some of the small players even made a few dollars, though they were by no means big winners.

Everyone was so certain that it would keep going up, that the economy would remain a healthy one, that prosperity was here to stay — and for an entire decade it did.

This vision persisted over the next few years. George Bush Senior was in office from 1989 through 2001 and then Bill Clinton served a two-term presidency. During the Clinton years, NASDAQ stocks — the Dow — everything seemed to be going up. Money was quickly made and just as quickly spent on bigger houses, more expensive cars, boats and whatever luxuries the conquerors required to satisfy their greed. Though the stage was set, the bubble would not burst until later.

— ℭℛ —

Annie, too, on a much more material level, would find her own freedom. In 1989, when she had just about given up hope of anything emerging from the long drawn out divorce negotiations, her attorney called to say that an agreement had been reached. There would be a cash settlement of $125,000. Did she hear right? $125,000?

It took her months to get over the shock that they were able to pry so much money from the close-fisted control of Tom Ryan, but they'd proved in court that he'd hidden so many of his assets; that she was entitled to the equity accrued on the house *and* his *pension*. Obviously someone had convinced him that legally he wouldn't be able to walk away and not share a portion of what he'd amassed during the years they were together.

At the very bitter end Tom Ryan had given in. And it was bitter. "But hell, Tom," his brother Joe reassured him. "At least you can take some pleasure in how shrewd you were in hiding all the good stuff. They'd never have found it."

"Yeah, it was a good idea to bring it to mom's. It's all safely stored in the attic."

Unbeknownst to Annie and her lawyers, Tom had surreptitiously obtained appraisals on every valuable piece in his collection. It was worth more than $500,000. And she wouldn't get a cent of that.

What made Tom capitulate was that damned pension. In the last analysis, he couldn't accept the notion that Annie was entitled to a vested interest in it. Worse, that she'd have a say in how he chose to distribute it. It offended him to grant her anything, damn it!And it took years of convincing at that. Finally he got smart; he was paying the lawyer $125 an hour. This hurt just as much. The hell with them all! He'd throw the towel in. Relieved to get out without giving her much of the real monies he'd accumulated, Tom refinanced the house to come up with a one-time cash settlement.

At least he owned the entire collection, which he'd continue to build upon, and now, as a lieutenant in the department, he was making a first-rate salary, one that would lead to a damned good pension when he did retire.

— ❧ —

Annie met with Sabrina and Maureen for coffee. She wanted to share the good news.

"I've known him for more than 22 years, married him twice, loved him too much, but finally, it's over. I walked away with nothing the first time. I think after giving it my all, wanting the marriage to work this time, that I deserved something. I know he hates me now, thinks I'm a bitch, but then, Tom's always been miserly about his money. And miserly about his love too. But it's all over; it's got to be over," Annie stated with a fierce determination. Words, they were easier than the feelings beneath.

"Hey, don't I know it? Do you remember way back when, kiddo? I was around then ...listening to you cry, worry, rant and rave, get yourself depressed as hell — I couldn't figure out why the two of you argued so much. Maybe no one can. He certainly had what they call a *passive aggressive* personality. I suppose he just couldn't take responsibility for anything. Many men are like that. But they'll marry over and over again, always blaming the problems on the women."

"Tom always felt it wasn't his fault. Women drank around him, smoked pot around him, got depressed and sick over him, argued with his mother over him and all the time, well, he was like *"Typhoid Mary,"* sauntering around like he'd nothing to do with what was happening. I remember one night — I came downstairs and there he was lying on the couch reading a book. Do you know which one? *"Why Bad Things Happened to Good People."* He was the good person, of course."

"I think he met his match in you. The two of you were volatile together. You were two people who were amazingly attracted to one another, but just couldn't make it work. Now, finally, you can move on. I wouldn't waste another thought on what might have been. Because it ain't gonna be, never is it gonna be, sweetheart. Tom Ryan is NOT for you."

"I know it. I do. I'm numb. I'm dumb. But I'm done with that scum! — hey, bad rhyme, but still it does rhyme! Anyway, Mo, he's already replaced me with yet another victim. Tom is a serial marrier. He'll never grow up. It's enough, believe me. I don't want to run out of time. I'll be 55 come October. I've lots of good things to look forward to and you know something, — living well is the best revenge. I'm going to and I'm never going to look back."

At that very instant, Annie felt a release, the beginning of her liberation from that very long obsessive/compulsive relationship and a sense and wisdom to know she could move on. Well, at least for a while she'd do it. But always, somewhere in the crevices of her psyche, or in dreams she had no control over, thoughts of him returned.

She'd meet with her attorney, sign the agreement, get the

settlement check and deposit it. "By winning the lawsuit I've got more than enough money for a decent down payment — enough to purchase a beautiful home in a better section of Staten Island, a house that's for sale on Todt Hill Road," she explained. "I've looked at it twice, brought a realtor friend out to see what he thought of it, and it's the right one, I'm certain."

It was time to move on, not dwell on the past nor concern herself with what Tom did or didn't have. "I just can't afford to let him rent space in my brain," she announced with conviction.

— ᘓ —

Her decision to move to the suburbs was surprising to Maureen. "You're so involved in theater, dining out, writing for the newspaper, you're a city girl."

"Sure, if I was rich, I could buy a brownstone in the Village and have the ideal life. But I'm not. I want my own home so that I can adopt a child," she explained.

"You know that's a very good idea," Sabrina said. "My mother has long been involved in the field of foster care and adoption and these days many single women are adopting."

Annie was in her mid-50s and alone. She'd always loved children. She wanted a child in her life, someone to love and look after, someone who she could *watch over*.

Sal was still in the picture, but now more a friend, than a lover. They talked on the phone, had dinner every once in a while. But the affair, it was over. She'd said no so many times, he finally got it — decided to answer some other personal ads — he'd always liked the ladies, and from the little she knew, old Sal was out there, busy meeting new prospects. He thrived on the adventures.

Since he knew the leading real estate areas of Staten Island Sal drove Annie around the borough for weeks, looking, and eventually helped her find the house that she chose.

It was a beautiful high ranch, with a rental apartment below, ideal to help pay off the mortgage. Not that there was much of a mortgage. Jacob Meyers, who'd been cheering her on, insisted on giving her one that was absurdly low. The interest would be 3%, and the mortgage was to be forgiven upon his death. Since he was now in his mid-80s, it might mean that Annie would own the house mortgage-free in a few years.

And so Annie was able to purchase the upscale home in a high-end area of Staten Island for $250,000. Best of all, the monthly payments on the house amounted to no more than the rent she was used to shelling out for the Park Avenue apartment.

She'd decided to sublet her Park Avenue studio to a young couple who were graduate students at NYU. She also made an extra $150 a month on the deal and had two years in which she could fulfill this before having to give up the apartment. Seven Park Avenue, like so many other Manhattan buildings, had gone co-op in the early 80s; it was too small to buy, and too expensive to own as a *pied a terre* so Annie was resigned to letting it go. A new way of life, hopefully one she'd adjust to awaited her on Staten Island.

She'd now reverse commute into the city two or three times a week, to call on whatever restaurants she was covering, as well as to stop by the newspaper offices and keep in touch. Annie was still using one of Meyer's company cars. "Don't worry, we'll pay the insurance, you just keep it, young lady," he'd generously told her. What a really nice man.

Ed Kayatt, the newspaper's publisher, was shocked that she'd move to Staten Island. "You're going to be a square peg in a round hole, or should I say a round peg in a *square* hole Annie. They're too square, too conservative out there for your free spirit."

It was true. This was a family-oriented community. Not a place where singles dwelled. More than half the residents had moved from crowded apartments in Brooklyn for a patch of green grass and a town house. Many were blue-collar workers with conservative political views and not exactly great intellects. Annie had gone to the local library branch to take out a few books on George Gershwin. The librarian didn't even know who George Gershwin was.

A few months after moving in Annie described the downside to Maureen: "The damned place is culturally bereft. This borough seems riddled with fat-necked men wearing gold necklaces who like to beep the horns on their cars and who consider reading the New York Post intellectual activity."

"I get it — a bunch of mental midgets, hhmm. That rag is more a scandal sheet than a newspaper," Maureen responded.

"And the wives with their way-out hair do's and sculptured nails — some look more like claws — many women get these acrylic horrors — really freaky nails — and for reading — they prefer the real thing: *The Enquirer* — sells out every week at the supermarkets here," Annie continued.

"Hell, I've seen the nail salons in Manhattan too. They're doing a landmine business in the add-on acrylics. Awful for the nails!"

"Still, not everyone is like this. While some may be uneducated they've got street smarts, that's for sure. And many have really good-paying jobs. Besides, it's safe here, a really secure community," Annie reported. After all — the house was beautiful, not everyone was like the individuals she described, so she'd give it a try. She had two years to make up her mind.

— ❦ —

Todt Hill Road was one of the highest points in the Northeast. Situated on Staten Island it boasted an area of multi million dollar homes at the top of the hill, mansions that were occupied by doctors, successful stockbrokers, and quite a few members of what is known as the Mafia.

In fact, Big Paul Castellano, a Gambino family boss had lived there on a 3.5 acre estate at the top of the Hill, valued at $4.5 million and built as a copy of the White House. Now he was buried at the Moravian cemetery, also located on Todt Hill. He'd been gunned down in 1985 in front of Sparks Steak House in Manhattan. Watching the killing was John Gotti, the man who'd arranged the hit, and who sat nearby in a car with the former Gambino lieutenant Salvatore "Sammy the Bull" Gravano. Sammy also lived on Staten Island, though not on Todt Hill.

The damned "guineas" they make it bad for all us honest Italians," Sal complained. "My father, may he rest in peace, was a hard working civil servant for 35 years. I've served like many other Italian boys in the fire department and in the police department. And then we got these scum of the earth who give all Italians a bad name."

Driving around on the top of Todt Hill, one could see vast estates, and if you got to know who was who, it was evident that a quarter or more of the population had mob connections. Don't ask too many questions and you were just fine. But every once in a while you'd read the newspapers and learn that so and so who lived at such and such address (always on the top of the hill) had been indicted — maybe for running an illegal gambling operation, or for muscling in on the private garbage hauling business, or in some way being connected to the enormous underworld crime families that were involved in bid rigging, the construction business, union infiltration, the rackets, and yes, murder-for-hire.

One advantage of living in this area, Annie soon realized, was it was very clean and very safe. House break-ins were at a minimum. No one wanted to stumble into the wrong house, which could be occupied by a relative of the mob. The only time Annie heard of someone breaking and entering into a house up on the hill, the intruder was shot and killed immediately by the occupant. There was no messing with the *family*.

Then there was the middle class section at the bottom of the hill, which was where Annie's new home was located. Still it was beautiful there, a wonderful home, and she hoped, one that would mean a new beginning. She needed a new start.

— ❧ —

Annie's family had gone through adjustments. Sid had finally married. Her name was Holly, a psychologist whom he'd met when they were in graduate school. Seems they'd been living together for two years and then quietly married, avoiding a big wedding, which made everything uncomplicated for the family.

The couple moved to New Rochelle, an upscale suburb of Westchester, in New York. Sid was working as an electrical engineer, while continuing his doctoral studies at NYU. There'd be a housewarming, their first party. Everyone was invited, even Joanie. She was glad to get the invitation, to finally hear some good news about Sid.

"Come to the housewarming. I have a house now. You can stay with me and visit Mom and Dad and we can drive to New Rochelle to visit Sid and his wife. Come, please," Annie urged.

"Annie, I already have tickets. Dad called me last night. Mom was just diagnosed with lung cancer. It doesn't look good. Didn't he get in touch with you, yet?"

"Oh my God. I haven't set up the answering machine yet and I've been so damned busy, I haven't called the house in more than a week. They don't have my work number. I guess he didn't know where to reach me. Did it sound bad…terminal?"

"I don't know. He was crying so hard it was hard to understand him. I'm taking two weeks off from school. I plan to arrive on Sunday. I thought I'd stay at the house. They'll need me."

Annie was shocked. And worried. More for her dad than her mother. Ironically he'd retired a few years back, and being at home every day with Sara, the two had grown closer. He now catered to her every need and even took over the cooking and baking. Her father had mellowed a lot. And he did adore his wife, no matter what their problems and complexities over the years. He'd be absolutely lost without her. Somehow women fared better as widows than men as widowers. And Sam was very dedicated to Sara. Annie would call and see if she could learn what was really going on.

"Let me find out more. I'll call dad right now. And don't worry, I'll go there and visit and let you know how mom is," she assured Joanie.

Within a few moments, Annie learned the truth. The cancer was inoperable. Her mother had refused to see a doctor for months, even with her coughing and continuing to smoke. It had spread. They didn't give her much time. Her father was devastated. "Come home, Annie, come see your mother," he begged.

"I'll be over in an hour, Dad. Do you need anything?"

"No, nothing. We have a nurse here. Your mother doesn't want to go to a hospital. We've been married 56 years. 56 years, 4 months and 12 days, my daughter. I don't want her to die; I don't know what to do. But she's sick, very sick," he said, and then broke down and cried so hard that it hurt Annie to hear it.

"I'll be there as soon as I can, Dad."

She was trembling, her heart racing so much she could hear it beating, like it was going to burst out of her body. Oh my God. It was really happening. Her mother was dying. She really was sick, terribly sick.

Annie was filled with black thoughts and dread, and worse, guilt. She really didn't like the woman. But it was her mother. And it wasn't just another complaint, minor operation or false alarm. It was the real thing. *The big* "C". Every emotion one could experience raced through her being. Fear. Nervousness. Anger. Anxiety. Sadness. Annie was scared of seeing her mother in this awful condition. But she had to. She'd no choice. She dressed hurriedly, got into the car and drove straight to Brooklyn. No one said life was supposed to be easy.

"You Are Free and That is Why You Are Lost."
— *Franz Kafka*

— ∝ —

Chapter 36

October 1992

A year had passed and it was time for the unveiling of the head stone. The family came together for the funeral, for sitting *Shiva*, and now this. But it was an empty and forced togetherness, for it was soon apparent that Sid and Holly had created their own little social milieu and slowly but surely had detached themselves from the family.

Since the cemetery plot was in New Jersey, it made sense to go to Sid and Holly's home after the unveiling. Meanwhile, their father, Sam, was still numb, very depressed and took no notice of the subtle skirmish that was developing between his daughters — Joanie and Annie — and Sid and his wife.

"It's rather obvious that they consider themselves *better* than the rest of the family," Joanie commented as the two sisters chatted quietly on their brother's veranda. "So Holly has a doctorate in psychology and Sid is working on his thesis. How does this make them superior beings? I've completed my masters, been a teacher for years, and you beat us all out — Annie — you've had four of your books published. Yet they look down on us. Ridiculous."

"Labels whether it's about achieving advanced degrees or having the right designer bag — it's all superficial," Annie opined.

"You're right, but then education is also the way out of the ghetto for the Jew and that's our heritage, isn't it?" Joanie smiled.

Annie laughed. "Well, then — look at this house. In the *right* section of Westchester. It has to be worth a half a million or more. Her father bought it for them. From what I understand, Holly's parents are well off. But guess why? He's a used car salesman. Yes, you heard right, a used car salesman!Yet she acts like she's from some privileged class. I mean, really. She's definitely full of herself, an absolute snob," Annie whispered.

Sid and Holly's home was overflowing with friends and business associates and with *all* of Holly's relatives. Sam, frail and grieving, seemed lost in their midst. Holly, in her late 30s, was in her fifth month of her first pregnancy. Sid was catering to her every whim — waiting on her hand and foot and obviously paying no attention to his father.

As a matter of fact, Annie had just learned that her dad was given the spare room downstairs in the basement, while Holly provided her parents and her sister and brother-in-law the upstairs guest bedrooms. How could they let an old man sleep downstairs? Annie was livid.

"Joanie — dad's still so depressed. And when I suggested his seeing a doctor to get some medication he got annoyed. I've visited him every Sunday since mom died. I usually take him out to brunch or lunch. He likes that, it does help, but I can't be there for him every day. It's just too difficult; I have to work and besides, he's not that near — it's a real schlep."

"I've asked him to come stay with me for a while. He won't,"

Annie continued. He just sits in that big old house in Brooklyn with all the memories. He won't even let me get rid of mom's clothing. It's heart-breaking," Annie said. "Though interestingly enough, I noticed none of her good jewelry was around."

Sure it isn't; most of it was given to Sid for Holly.

Annie wasn't really surprised at the news. "Joanie, did you notice the sterling silver coffee set on the dining table? Looks an awful lot like mom's," Annie whispered.

"Of course it looks like her's — because it is! So is the sterling silver flatware service for 12, which, in case you didn't notice, Holly used to serve brunch. I asked dad about it. He said they gave Sid and Holly the family silver for their engagement."

"So everything of value goes to their son and daughter-in-law?"

"Why not? Do we have any choice? I suppose we were the outcasts, in her mind — the *divorced* daughters. Hell — she never used any of her good, expensive stuff. When did our family entertain? Do you remember the clear plastic covers on all the living room furniture, Annie? Everything was for show, and nothing got used. Mom never enjoyed her jewelry or anything, really. We have to let it go. All of it. It's probably got a curse on it anyway."

Annie laughed, temporarily dispelling her sense of outrage. "The curse of Sara. Well, I hope Holly enjoys all of it. And frankly, I never liked mom's choices anyway. They were kind of "early Jewish" or should I say, "Brooklyn Baroque"?"

"Funny! But you're right. The house was filled with hideous Jewish Renaissance furniture that we rarely sat on or enjoyed anyway. Even mom's jewelry, it was too ornate. Let Holly have it. But really, Annie, it's awfully annoying that everything was given to an *outsider*, and nothing to us. Well, for all I care she can shove it up her rectum!" Joanie said, suddenly revealing her anger. "It's miserable, but typical, that she didn't think of giving anything to us."

"And know what? Mom always favored Sid, even though he was never an attentive son," Joanie added bitterly.

"My God, what an unhappy legacy she's left us. Resentment, rejection, pain. In the end she still ran over us and our feelings — her own daughters — as if we'd anything to do with her unhappiness," Annie said, her eyes teary.

"Pray for her Annie. Keep praying until you forgive her. I've been doing this for the past year. It isn't easy. I'm still angry, I know it. Somehow, even though I know she was a wounded soul and unhappy, it doesn't make it less painful to know she had no love for me. But I keep on praying. I have to forgive or it will destroy me. You should do it too."

"I will, really, I will. But look at all the harm she's caused. We had a rotten role model. You and I both had failed marriages and no children. Sid, at least he had dad, who while he had a horrible temper, was affectionate and caring, and well, let's hope Sid and Holly make it, whatever a self-important high and mighty, vapid, dumb imbecile she is."

"My you're really hot and bothered when it comes to Holly!"

"Yes I am. I just can't tolerate people who think they're superior to others. It's such a phony thing, and really, look at both of them. She's kind of mousy, and, Sid, underneath it all he's still such a nerd, and so petty about things. I don't know why the hell he's acting so superior — he went to a city college just like we did — and he's the son of a plumber. — Really, it just super bothers me. Especially the way she treats dad, like he's a poor relative — when it was *his* hard work that paid for all the sterling and the precious jewelry, which she now owns. He never, ever should have slept in the basement. If anything, they should have given up their own bed if they didn't want to put her family out. And incidentally, have you noticed, how confused he's been lately? He seems in a fog and asks the same questions over and over."

Joanie was silent for a moment — it was clear she'd not really given her dad's mental state much thought until Annie mentioned it. "I've noticed it when I call him. I've been calling two, three times a week ever since mom died. I asked dad a few times to come stay with me in Tucson — even if just for a little a while. Eric got on the phone and told him he could use some sun and a rest with us. We both tried to persuade him. I know he doesn't like flying, but I told him I'd come and get him and go back on the plane with him."

"Yet, now that I think about it, just the next week he didn't even remember the conversation, Annie. I don't know, if he's just depressed, or getting senile, or worse, if it's signs of Alzheimer's. I don't think it runs in our family. I don't know anyone else, do you, who had it?"

"No, not on dad or mom's side. But you know, dad has never had any interests besides his going to work for, what was it, 48 years or something? He has absolutely no hobbies. Doesn't golf, play cards, isn't even interested in any sports. And he doesn't read, never did bother except to come home every day with the Daily News. They say if you don't use it you'll lose it. He has no interests at all now that mom died. At least he had her around and the two grew so close the last few years, and he was busy taking care of her."

"I wish I knew more about Alzheimer's. What I do know is that they really don't know what causes it. But we sure are hearing more and more about it lately. But I suppose that's because people are living longer. They say when someone is over 70 or so, they're more likely to start showing signs of loss of memory…and then by 80 — more likely to come down with something like this. I just don't know, don't have the answers. But I'm going to go home and research the hell out of this," Joanie added.

Concern was fixed on Annie's face as she recalled an incident that happened recently. "Last month he asked me to go with him to the lawyers, to make out a new will. Mom's will, naturally, left everything to him. Now he said, he wanted to leave the estate to the three of us, equally. And you know, he made you executor — I told you that a couple of weeks ago — anyway, I called to remind him that I'd come to pick him up at 3 p.m. that Tuesday and he totally forgot about the entire issue."

"Do you think it could be Alzheimer's? Oh God, I hope not. It's an awful sickness. And I'm so far away," Joanie whispered.

Annie swiftly made up her mind. She knew what the next step would have to be. "I'm going to talk to Sid. He can help me to convince dad to move in with me. I have a three-bedroom home, Joanie. More than enough space for dad and if necessary, I can get someone to spend the days with him when I'm at work, although there are plenty of senior citizen clubs around. I've already checked into that. Maybe I can convince him to join. But I really think he ought to sell the house and come live with me."

Joanie was surprised. Such a thing would never have occurred to her — yet it was so — Annie. She should have known. "You're still young. You could still find someone special and want to marry again. Are you sure you want to do this, Annie?"

"I don't want to marry again. And if I met anyone, it would not interfere with taking care of dad. I don't intend to be a slave, just a good caretaker. The only thing I'll temporarily put on hold is my idea of adoption. I'd see how dad adjusts first, and then go on with the application process.

Annie leaned forward. "There's an adoption agency in Texas that a friend of mine recommended to me. I'm thinking of a foreign adoption. It costs much more, but they accept single moms, *older* single moms."

"You know when you first told me about the idea, I was surprised. But now I think your raising a child would be a fantastic thing, Annie. I'm all for it, and when you're ready, please let me write a letter of recommendation. After all, I know you all your life. I know what a loving person you are, and what a good, kind mother you'd make."

"As to getting dad to move in with you — I think you'll have a better chance at that if you forget about his selling the house. That would be too traumatic for him. It's all paid for. Just close it up for six months or so and see if he adjusts to living with you. Then if he does, we can all convince him to sell it. But right now, he's lived in it almost half a century. It's all he has left."

"You're right. Why didn't I think of that? Okay, but before we leave here today, let's get a hold of Sid, get him aside and talk to him. If all three of us can agree on this — and I don't see why Sid would object if I took dad to live with me — then that's what I want to do."

"It's a big responsibility. Are you sure you can handle it? And what if, what if," Joanie stuttered at the reality of it — he's getting senile and needs nursing care?"

"We have to take it one day at a time. That's the only way I can live my life now, one day at a time. I learned that long ago in AA. "

At that instant in the conversation, Holly opened the door and peeked out on the terrace.

"We're going to have lunch in a few moments, ladies. I ordered from Dean and De Luca, you know, the posh gourmet shop in Manhattan. They have just the right tea sandwiches and wonderful platters of cold cuts and such. And I'm using some of our Tiffany sterling platters. Nothing too good for family, you know."

"We also have some wonderful fruits from Balducci's. You probably have heard of Balducci's. Everyone who is *anyone* shops there. It's not far from Sid's school, so I asked him to pick some up, and to get the best, of course. And I ordered some nova for Dad Rosenberg. Special imported nova that was delivered to us by Zabars, such a landmark store on the West Side. I'm sure he'll love some of it with the Russian rye bread that I picked up at

Bloomingdale's bakery yesterday. So come in, you'll absolutely love the light lunch I've prepared."

The sisters looked at each other, smiling.

"Holly is the all-time champion namedropper, a department store namedropper, a designer label dropper, a grocery shop dropper. She would drop a name at the drop of a hat. She shops at Neiman Marcus, (even if it's only from their catalog), she covers her bed with sheets by Pratesi, but she doesn't even have the class to keep it to herself and let us notice on our own. And I know she's recently learned to play bridge and tennis…that's because…she told me the other day how important it was that Sid and she join the *right* country club, which is really kind of preposterous, since the right country club up this way won't accept Jews," Annie commented.

Joanie chimed right in. "Well I know Sid is taking golf lessons. I suppose they're entitled to their leisure pursuits, but there's just something offensive in the way they approach them. Oh well, to each his own."

— ᦱ —

During lunch, Annie spent more time observing her dad. He was not himself at all. He sat quietly on the dining chair. Not talking; barely eating anything.

It had been a year since their mother had died, and Sam hadn't really come out of the depression. Where he had always been fiercely independent, and would do for others, now he waited for someone to pick out his lunch, make him a sandwich. His behavior was slow and repetitive, like he was in a haze half of the time. Sam was 77 years old now. Something serious was happening. She would get Sid's attention and she, Joanie and he could speak privately in another area of the house while the rest sat around and ate and talked.

"Wait, you can't leave until you've tried some of the Williams Sonoma Chardonnay wine Sid picked out. Sid is taking a course in wine tasting, you know. Here, Annie, have a glass," Holly offered.

"No thanks. I've been in AA for quite some time now. Wine of any vintage or brand just doesn't agree with me. I break out in a drunk."

Joanie couldn't keep the laugh inside. Good for Annie! It was apparent that Holly was taken aback, like someone had announced they had a contagious disease.

"Let's go," Sid said, "we have some family matters to talk over, sweetheart, we'll be back soon."

"Well...well... whatever." Holly turned her attention to her parents, who seemed to be whispering about the public announcement that Sid's sister had made.

Shock, pure shock emanated from their corner of the room. They were not happy to hear there was an alcoholic anywhere in the family; even the in-laws. Like they had never heard about addictions before — and as if they had the right to judge anyone else. Annie didn't know it but Holly's mother had long possessed a diet pill addiction. If she didn't keep her bantamweight of 110 pounds, even at age 64, (when a few extra pounds keeps wrinkles at bay) and although she was 5'6" tall, well, she'd have a hissy fit. The woman was downing amphetamines most of the time, in between her interminable exercise routine of two hours a day. It's a wonder she hadn't had a stroke yet.

"Here, Mother, I ordered the imported Beluga caviar just for you. I know how much you love it," Holly said, giving her scarecrow thin mother the small plate of caviar with some paper-thin wafers.

Sid and his sisters had gone to the back of the house, to the library room where most of the shelves were lined with leather-bound classics that looked like they had neither been opened nor read, but were there for show.

"Yes, you're both right. Dad's not well," Sid said. "Holly tried a cognitive test on him the other day. The kind where you count backwards, and then ask simple questions like who is the president of the United States — things like that — there's a part where you just add up simple numbers. Dad was always a whiz in math. He could total anything without a pencil and paper. He failed miserably in all of it, got little right."

"Oh my God," was all Joanie could say.

"We picked him up on Wednesday so he could stay out here until the unveiling. He forgot there *was* an unveiling. I think he should see a neurologist. Maybe it's Alzheimer's."

"I'll ask around and make the appointment. But whatever happens, Sid, I don't want dad shoveled into a nursing home. He's okay half — maybe more of the time now. He's been a good father, and I don't think he should be warehoused away. It would destroy him completely. I can take him to live with me. I have a nice home now, spacious, three large bedrooms."

"Look if you think you can do it, more power to you, Annie. What about your working? He'll need looking after. But it's your life."

"And it's his life too. Maybe he's still grieving for mom. Maybe some of his problems are the deep depression he's been in. I'll take him to a doctor and see if they can put him on an anti-depressant. He does need to see a good doctor. I'll take him."

"Annie, you're terrific. And you know, anyway I can help, I will," Joanie said, meaning every word.

Sid, true to form, looked visibly relieved. "The will is drawn up, we can always sell the house later, and meanwhile you can take his social security check — he gets about a thousand a month, and he also has a hefty pension from his union — he's always bragged about that, proud of being a union man. You'll have enough to hire someone if necessary as a live-in, and more than enough to use towards food and such. I'll agree to that," Sid said magnanimously.

"Whatever you want, Annie, and if it's not enough, if we need to chip in for a housekeeper, we could," Joanie chimed in.

For the first time, their brother looked worried — this wasn't where he wanted the conversation to go. Holly would have a fit if she knew.

"Well, before we have to shell out money, I'd have to check with Holly.

We've been trying to have a child for a few years. Finally, and she's almost 40, we're having one. We just bought this house, we have big expenses. We can always get power of attorney and spend some of his investments."

"Let's not go into that now. We have enough for today; more than enough to take care of dad without discussing how to get extra money," Annie responded, visibly upset. Anger welled up inside her and she couldn't make herself stop there.

"Besides, I don't think it's fair to talk of power of attorney and things like that right now... in fact, I don't even care what your wife thinks. She's so busy spending on country clubs and Porthault sheets, it's no wonder you're worried about money. Why don't you pawn all the sterling silver and diamonds and the rest you both took from mom without thinking that any of it should go to Joanie and me?" Annie said angrily.

Dead silence. Sid shifted nervously in his chair. Finally he spoke, not looking at either sister, but fidgeting with an imaginary speck on his sleeve.

"You know, Annie, we've never really gotten along. You had a long drinking period. You pranced around the village, lived a crazy life. Don't think we didn't know all about it. Well you made your bed, you lie in it. Meanwhile I've worked hard all these years to get a decent education. You may not like my wife, that's your business.

But when you're in my home, keep your opinions to yourself."

The underlying lifelong antagonism between brother and sister had finally surfaced.

"Look, both of you," Joanie interrupted, struggling with her own overwhelming distaste for Sid. "This is the day of our mother's unveiling. Our father is obviously in need of medical help. And we've all had a very long day. Let's not argue. You two don't have to agree on much. Just how to agree on getting help for dad. And, if necessary, Sid, you call me, or I'll check in with you at least once a week. And if you want, I'll relay any messages to Annie."

"Come on, Annie, let's drive dad back to Brooklyn. The atmosphere is not very warm or welcoming. And Sid, whether you know it or not, being the eldest, I was made the executor of the estate. So I think you ought to cooperate and work with us to keep dad as comfortable and healthy as we can."

— ❧ —

1992 was a leap year. But there was absolutely no one Annie wanted to ask out on a date. It was the year Bill Clinton was elected president and when pop singers Madonna and Mariah Carey had hit records on the Billboard charts. The record of the year was *Unforgettable* as Natalie Cole sang along to her late great father, Nat King Cole's rendition of the romantic ballad. Her silky tones blended with her father's rich voice in a way that would have once been impossible. A new era of electronics was beginning its ascent and amazing things were possible.

It was also the year when Johnny Carson hosted the Tonight Show for the last time. He had ruled the night for 20 years. Now it was time to say goodbye.

And it was also the year that Sam Rosenberg, began his own long goodbye. As best as the neurologist could determine, he was suffering from the mid stages of Alzheimer's.

Annie's dad had agreed to stay with her for a week. She really wanted him to move in. Especially since the doctor had told her that if he continued to live alone, he'd have to have full time help.

"The only way to tell if this is the disease is through an autopsy. That's the best science can do today," explained Dr. Johnson, the neurologist. "But from what you've described to me, your father shows the signs. You told me he's getting up in the middle of the night, sometimes for hours. That's a stage called "sun downing." Very common in Alzheimer's patients. They're restless at night, get up, and walk around. You'll have to be vigilant. He could just walk out of your house and not know where he is during this type of episode. We'll try to slow the progression down with some medications, and see how he reacts."

"Come, Dad, come live with me," Annie urged him.

"Are you sure I won't be thrown out some day? Be in the way?" he said, meaning it. "I don't want to be a burden on you, my daughter."

"Why would I throw out my own father? Of course not, Daddy, I love you and I want you to live with me. Try it, let's go back to your house and pack a few week's worth of clothing. We'll come back later for more, okay?"

"What about my mail? The bills I have to pay," he said in a lucid moment. That was the horror of the disease. Many times he was rational, cogent, his old self. And then suddenly he'd have a far away look in his eyes and fade off.

"We'll do a change of address today. Everything will be all right. I promise you. Come, let's go to Ratner's for lunch. You love the pirogie there and it's on the way to Brooklyn," she urged him. Annie knew her father would appreciate the old-fashioned Jewish style food served at the lower east side restaurant. She would do her utmost to always put him at ease.

How ironic. She finally had her father's attention. For many years, her mother shielded him from both daughters, complained vociferously when she felt he was paying more attention to them than to her. Which was *all* the time. How horrible. But now Sara was gone. And he was still here and needed Annie to take care of him, though he'd never admit it. Annie would do it unselfishly; even if it meant putting off the anticipated adoption for a year or so. She knew she'd have to make sure it would be all right; that her home would be a safe place to bring a child. Hopefully, later on she'd still be able to make this long held dream come true.

Meanwhile, if only for a little while, she'd have her father to herself.

— ᛘ —

"From birth to age 18, a girl needs good parents, from 18 to 35 she needs good looks, from 35 to 55 she needs a good personality and from 55 on she needs cash."
— *Sophie Tucker*

— ❧ —

Chapter 37

January 1993

Almost a year had gone by since Sam Rosenberg had made the move. Remarkably, it was easier than anyone thought it would be. Annie's dad had little difficulty adjusting to living with her on Staten Island. In fact, his mental health seemed to have improved and while he did spend an inordinate amount of hours watching television — all day and evening — he was less forgetful, enjoyed long walks around the neighborhood. It was obvious to Annie that what he needed was *to be needed* and to feel like part of a family again.

"His physical health is very good — strong heart and lungs," Dr. Nelson, the internist, informed Annie. "He's really in good shape for a man of his age."

"It's probably because he never smoked and rarely drank. My father always watched himself that way and was careful with his diet once he passed fifty years of age," she reported. "Good, good," the physician responded. Annie kept in touch with her dad's doctors, brought him often for check-ups. Her father was strong and sturdy, if one didn't count the degeneration of his mind. Sam repeated the same stories over and over again but Annie made sure to listen with the same interest she showed when he told it to her the first time. It wasn't easy.

One unexpected gift— when her dad watched reruns on television — he didn't seem to remember them. So everything he chose to watch was new and interesting to him. Well, sort of. His enthusiasm for life had diminished considerably. He dwelled too much on the past, of his years of successful working and of his Sara.

"It's amazing how he only remembers the good parts now," Annie commented to her sister during one of her regular updates. "He's put mom on a pedestal, doesn't remember any friction, any time it was less than perfect."

"He never had the slightest concept on how bad she felt after his temper tantrums."

"It's amazing how the human mind can filter out the bad stuff. I've done it myself," Annie admitted.

"I know what you mean. Everything looks good or better when you're not living it!" Joanie mused.

Annie laughed. She'd blotted out any bad days with Tom; that was for sure.

"Well then, good for dad. He always loved mom. We both know that. I think he cared more for her – though his temper got in the way of showing it. She recoiled early – and seemed to want to possess him. I think part of their problem was fighting for control. I don't know — it's just amazing that two such dissimilar people lived together for more than 54 years and now he's so lost without her," observed Joanie.

"Men are not the social animals women are. I was reading an article — did you know that at those golden-age dance clubs, the ratio is at most 70 percent women to 30 percent men? The men, if they're alone, stay alone, brood, isolate — whatever. Women want to be out there more. So it's tougher on the men."

"Well meanwhile, we have our own set of problems, caring for dad — and the real burden is on you, dear Annie. I just hope it doesn't ruin your life – take too much out of you."

It was the nights that were hard on Annie. Her dad's condition created nocturnal restlessness. As the disease progressed, he had more and more trouble sleeping through the night. It was a major problem for those with Alzheimer's (or more specifically, a major problem for their caretakers) and was called *sun downing*. Too often her father would get up in the middle of the night, edgy, nervous, unable to sleep. He'd begin roaming around. Twice he'd come to Annie's room, thinking it was his. One night he'd gotten up to go to the bathroom and instead walked into a kitchen door banging his forehead and suffered a sharp gash. A few times he'd gotten dressed and headed out. But he couldn't get too far. As soon as he opened the front door the alarm went off. Thank heaven Annie had installed the system. "You don't have to go to work, dad, it's the middle of the night," she pleaded with him, "please go back to bed."

So far, those were the only warning signs that indicated Alzheimer's. The doctor had agreed with Annie that whatever condition her father had was exacerbated by Sara's death. Now that he was no longer alone, had a caring daughter, he was feeling much better. Most of the depression had lifted, and once he became familiar with his new surroundings, Sam clearly felt at home. So much so that every too often, he'd call Annie "*Sara,*" a bittersweet experience for his daughter that left her feeling sad, yet satisfied that he was at least comfortable.

Annie made a real effort to get Sam involved in outside activities. She urged him to join one of the many senior citizens clubs around. First she took him to a neighborhood non-sectarian club, where he was immediately offended when they offered him lunch for 50 cents. "I didn't work hard all my life to get charity," he yelled and told her he wouldn't go back.

She then attempted to get her reluctant father "plugged in" to a senior club at the local Jewish Center. He was annoyed at how few men there were. "The women, they're like vultures, all over me," he commented sourly.

"Well now, Dad, they appreciate a good looking man," Annie responded, smiling. Her good-natured flattery was lost on Sam.

"And I don't want their meals. One woman, she looked at my meal, and I think she was hungry, even though she had her own tray. She must be very poor. So I told them to wrap it up for me to take home, and then I gave it to her. She probably made it into her supper," he explained. "Tchh, Tchh, such a shame."

"So at least you're making some friends?"

"Friends? No. I have little in common with those people, my daughter. I really don't enjoy sitting there all afternoon. I don't play cards — it's a real mish mash there — mostly women, very, very few men. And why would I want to watch television there? Besides, these old women, they're all over me."

Annie was resigned to the truth. Her father didn't want to join any clubs. She'd have to be satisfied with his staying at home and getting pleasure from his daily dosage of television programs.

Sam was used to watching the soap operas with his Sara. Those last few years after he'd retired the couple had grown amazingly close. He tended to her needs, she sat and smiled and seemed to appreciate having him all to herself. He still had an abiding interest in the overly dramatic fairy-tales. The old standbys — *"Days of Our Lives"*, *"General Hospital,"* *"One Life to Live"* and *"All My Children"* were his favorites. He didn't want to miss any of these daytime soaps. It gave him something to look forward to, something that made the long days tolerable.

Annie hired a woman of Polish extraction to come in 4 hours daily. Maria Politzkiya would make and serve him lunch and spend time with her father. Sam remembered enough of his childhood language to converse with the lady and appeared to enjoy her company.

Annie continued to keep Joanie regularly informed about their father's progress. "Dad's doing real well. I think I already told you that he did have some prostrate trouble in March. I took him to the urologist for a few visits and it's under control now. No cancer, no real obstruction, so we're lucky, or I should say he is," Annie reported.

Joanie, grateful for her sister's caring of their father, strove to support Annie in any way she could. "You're doing such a great job, Annie. I think because he has you around, he's not as lonely, and that's why he's doing better. I'm so glad."

Joanie, who'd finally moved into Eric's home, also had some good news to share. "I was going to retire — after all, I'm 58, but they offered me the job of assistant principal at the school. I'm going to take it. It should be challenging and it will bring me more money."

"Good for you!" Annie was thrilled for her sister. She believed that retirement could spell boredom and early decline for anyone. Annie possessed an inner vitality that was ageless — resistant to time. She had no desire to "grow old gracefully" and intended to fight it every inch of the way. Watching her father's slow descent into senility only increased her resolve to maintain her appearance and mental acuity. It pleased her that her sister seemed similarly inclined.

"You know Jacob Meyers, the old man I've told you about — well he's in his 80s and he still goes to his office every day. Maybe he pushes papers around, but the point is he loves working, meeting people, staying active. And I think it keeps him young. Today, women like us, in our 50s are like women a generation or two ago when they were in their 40s. I think working, remaining active, keeps all of us young!"

Joanie caught her drift immediately. "How right you are. Look at Sophia Loren, Elizabeth Taylor, all the women who are approaching the big 60. They're beautiful and vital. Age, is for wine and cheese!" she quipped, laughing.

Annie's work was part of what kept her feeling ageless. She was enjoying a flourishing time in her career — co-writing a book with a plastic surgeon working as a reporter covering local stories on Staten Island and her restaurant column still appeared weekly in *Our Town*, resulting in her name being blown up in windows all over Manhattan. It was great to walk by a restaurant and see one of her reviews displayed. She felt energized, enjoyed all the work, and aside from interviewing a few "executives" on Staten Island, that she suspected were really mob-connected — she felt good about her efforts.

"The Bilottis, they own bakeries here on the Island. The business editor asked me to do him a favor and interview one of the owners. Tommy Bilotti, he was the driver killed along with Paul Castellano in front of Spark's Steak House," she whispered to a fellow reporter on the Advance. "Isn't that, aren't they part of the same family?"

"Sshh, of course, it's a family-owned business, and you know what kind of *family* I mean, but they're big supporters of our awards dinner, and have been very generous to the college here. They're big donors to charities. The publisher likes them. So you do a few puff pieces, here and there, so what."

So what indeed.

But Annie was tiring of the job at the *Advance*.

"You know, Sal, I've been given a $15,000 advance on my new book. The doctor waived any part of it; he certainly doesn't need the money. I can afford to give up the job at the newspaper now. Frankly, I'm tired of the dim-witted stories I'm assigned there. And I've also noticed that the other reporters in life style, it's more than obvious that they're not happy that I've been given my own beauty column with the byline and photo. There's a lot of back biting, talking behind my back, I can tell."

"Hey babes, so they're petty. It's human nature to be jealous. You write on restaurants in New York, you got a column with your picture in it running out here every week and you've obtained some plum feature assignments for the Sunday edition. You're always going to find someone who is envious. Just look the other way. I've had a taste of this in my own job. When I was made supervisor here, there were a lot of men who thought the job should have gone to them. Just grit your teeth and bear it," was Sal's advice. "And besides, getting talked about is one of the penalties for being pretty."

"Does that mean you consider yourself pretty?" she asked jokingly.

"Sure don't you just love this Italian mug?"

She laughed. "Well, we'll see. But the work isn't challenging. It's still a small-town newspaper. I'm going to apply to the bigger newspapers — I have plenty of experience now on a daily. I just think I've run out of steam here. The women in my department are just so damned small-minded. I'm really only friendly with the fashion editor, who incidentally, has been with the newspaper for about 20 years."

"Yeah, you're talking about Mary Anne Merino. Do you happen to know that she and Rich Strauss, the editor-in-chief have been an item for years and years?" Sal said. "I think Rich's wife even knows about it and looks the other way. But Mary Anne didn't get that position without sleeping with the boss, I'll tell you that much."

"Well if she can sleep with that crocodile, she deserves to be head of the department. He's really a drag most of the time, makes such pompous speeches. Wow, I'm glad I never told Mary Anne what I think of him…that would have been embarrassing. But Strauss is a Class A Schmuck!"

"You're right about that. Rich has a reputation all over town. He can be a devious son-of-a-bitch. But he's the chief at the newspaper. So as long as he's in power, you have to work with him. As a matter of fact, I met up with him at a Republican fundraiser last week. He had only nice words to say about you, so for whatever it's worth, your job is secure there."

"Thanks, but if I can get something better, it's time to move on."

"I'll drink to that. In fact, I'll buy you dinner if you want tonight," he suggested.

"Thanks but I'm taking my dad for a ride later on. To visit his cousin. She lives in Queens. They talk often on the phone. But if I don't take him out there, every once in a while, I feel a little guilty. She's old and can't get to see him and she's all he has left from his immediate family. Some other time, okay?"

"You got it."

— ೞ —

"How many hopes and fears, how many ardent wishes and anxious apprehensions are twisted together in the threads that connect the parent with the child."
— Samuel Goodrich

— ⚭ —

Chapter 38

January 1994

It had been two years since her father came to live with Annie. Overall the adjustment was easy. He was settling in, glad to be wanted and not having to live alone.

Sam, who'd always been a restless type, still had a good deal of vim and vigor. Always a hard worker, he made himself helpful around the house. "Let me do the dishes, please Annie," he'd say, grabbing them out of her hands. "But dad, we have a dishwasher."

"Dishwasher, swish washer!" he'd insist. "I'll make 'em just as clean by hand!" And so he'd wash the breakfast dishes, and the dinner dishes, and clean up after himself, even enjoyed doing his own laundry. It made him feel useful. It was very important for him to be contributing in some manner.

Her father had always been a clean freak, taking at least two showers a day— one when he arose and another at day's end. Now, retired, older, slower — he was down to one shower a day. Annie was relieved but still had a wall rail installed for him to hold on to in case he slipped. So far he'd handled himself well.

When her father was feeling up to it, in warmer weather he watered the garden. He loved the rose bushes, the hydrangeas, and all the tulips and peony bushes that Annie had planted. Both father and daughter had a green thumb. He also enjoyed doing some light cooking; had gotten used to it the last years he took care of his wife. Some times, while she was out working, he'd prepare a big pot of soup.

Sam's specialty was an old-fashioned cabbage soup, a recipe his mother used to make. Annie hated the smell of the cabbage cooking throughout the house, an overpowering pungent aroma that persevered into the night. The soup, which was supposed to have a sweet and sour taste, was vinegary and tart to the tongue, really awful tasting, but she knew how much it meant to him.

"Thanks Dad, this is delicious," Annie smiled, feigning pleasure as she spooned the bowl's contents. She didn't exactly scarf it down. She really detested the damned soup. The cabbage made her feel bloated and gassy.

"Good, very good, my daughter — a *real homemade* soup, what can be bad here?" he smiled, pleased to see her eating his prize recipe. Thank heaven he'd only prepared that soup twice, or she'd have to get her hands on a stomach pump.

— CR —

It had been more than a year since the tragic car bombing at the World Trade Center.

Annie knew Tom's firehouse was nearby. She soon learned Tom *had been* on duty, that he'd gone to the site with his engine company and was one of the many fire personnel who had helped in the rescue effort.

It was good old reliable Sal, who'd found out that he was okay.

"I made the calls for you. Your 'ex' is just fine. The fire marshal's division in Manhattan is looking into this one, Babes. We already know that there were militant terrorists behind the attack. The f — - ing cowards. We think the bombs were planted inside the garage of the building."

Sal had gone down to the bombing scene. He had the right I.D. to gain access. He also possessed a high-octane personality that could shift into overdrive when needed. He figured he'd lend a hand.

"People walked down 50 or more flights of stairs. The stairways were crowded and the lights were out. Many of the workers were old. They slowly marched out of the lower floors. Covered in soot that you could just about make out a human face. Some were badly injured. There was carnage all over; people were lying on the lobby floor. It was bad, but we're going to find them, gonna get those bastards."

And get them they did. It took years for justice to prevail, but eventually all those presumed involved in the 1993 bombing, four militant terrorists, were sentenced to life in prison.

The World Trade Center became a different place after the violence. Everyone needed an ID card, sufficient identifications and someone to vouch for him or her if they forgot their ID. A small price to pay for added security. Little did anyone know back then that this security would do little good in preventing the dreadfulness and terror that would ensue eight years later.

— ❧ —

1994 was a year of ups and downs, of even an earthquake, with a magnitude of 6.7 that had struck the densely populated San Fernando Valley in California. The death toll was 57 and more than 1,500 were seriously injured. The traffic system following the earthquake affected several major freeways serving Los Angeles and temporarily choked the traffic system.

Sabrina Aldrich happened to be in L.A. on news business just about the time the earthquake hit. She'd been pursuing interviews with some of the major participants in the O.J. Simpson murder investigation, talking with friends and neighbors, taping some of the segments for coverage on the nightly news.

Simpson had been arrested for the killings of wife Nicole Brown Simpson and her friend, Ronald Goldman. Sabrina also interviewed some of the lawyers that would make up the "dream team." They were happy to supply her with their "spin" on things.

With most of the nation watching the nine-month trial, the million-dollar defense team would successfully sell their version of events to the predominantly Black jury. The riveting, long-drawn out televised murder trial that had captured the country ended on October 3, 1995.

Few missed an opportunity to comment on the verdict. Most people expressed sympathy for the families of the victims. A majority of whites did not support the jury's decision, which seemed to have been decided on racial lines. There had been 10 Blacks, one white, one Hispanic on the jury.

The three old friends, Sabrina, Maureen and Annie met for lunch at the end of the trial. All three were disappointed in the verdict.

"What a let-down! He's guilty as hell," Maureen commented.

"I know, I know," Sabrina said. "There's an aphorism about crime that I think fits perfectly here: *'I never wonder to see men wicked, but I often wonder to see them unashamed.'* Jonathan Swift, the author of "Gulliver's Travels", wrote it. I think it aptly describes not only the killer, who seems to have no guilt for the crimes he committed — he slit open his wife's throat, almost severing her head — but also it depicts his self-serving, manipulative attorneys. They used the race card to gain sympathy for him and damned if it didn't help get him off. "Sabrina was livid.

"He's a socio-path. I knew he'd done it when I heard about the slashing of Nicole's throat," Annie said. "Let me tell you my theory."

The other two women bent forward to listen, as Annie said in hushed tones: "When Tom didn't want to hear what I had to say, and I'm talking about years ago — the *first* time we were married — well, one night I had too much to drink and I called him at the firehouse. I told him I wanted out — to leave — that I'd wait until he came home in the morning, since Colleen was asleep in the next room — but that the marriage was over. He was furious. He got emergency permission — left the firehouse — came home in the middle of the night — and he almost choked me to death. He didn't want to hear what I had said, that I wanted out. He didn't want to hear anything from me. Well, Simpson didn't want to hear Nicole say she didn't want a reconciliation that it was over. He could have shot her, banged her over the head — chosen many ways to kill her — but he went for the throat. He cut her throat."

"Wow. You're on to something. And Simpson — he's a control freak — has an ego bigger than Times Square. He knocked her around enough. Sure, he didn't want her saying it was over. Your hypothesis sounds first rate to me," Maureen agreed.

"Well I hear that Ron Goldman's family will sue Simpson in Civil Court. There will be a different venue — not in downtown Los Angeles, which is predominantly black. Simpson never cared about his heritage — until now when it's convenient to be a Black man. Let's hope they get a more objective jury — if so they'll snare him there," Sabrina commented.

"Amen," all three said, clicking their coffee cups together.

Suddenly a cake was brought to the table. A birthday cake for Annie. "We know your birthday is almost a week from now, but we wanted to surprise you," Maureen said. The waiters sang "Happy Birthday" and Annie, making a wish, blew out the candles.

"So tell us, what did you wish for?"

"I wished that the immigration department would hurry along with my papers. It's been dragging on, this adoption process," she said.

"Oh Annie, I'm so happy for you. Finally, you're almost at the end of this long drawn out route to adopt a child," Maureen said.

After frustrating, futile attempts to acquire a child from local agencies in New York, Annie had learned of an organization in Texas who had a link to a division for foreign adoptions. She found out that it was fairly easy for an older single woman to adopt through their agency. All it took was money.

She'd begun the course of action in March, had been put in touch with the facilitator, Orson Moses, who ran "The Russian Club" out in California. It was Moses who was responsible for getting Romanian and Russian orphans for adoption by Americans.

He quickly sent Annie videos of Russian orphans, along with a plethora of forms, information on how to go about adopting, and an effective video showing a few of the trips Americans had made to Russia for the adoption process.

The down payment was $5,000 to begin the procedure. Overall, Annie was told, it would cost about $25,000 to adopt an older child. She'd asked for a girl, between the ages of 5 and 8, requesting someone who'd be of school age, so she could continue to work and support the child. Besides, Annie would be turning 58 — an older child seemed the most appropriate.

She had $15,000 in savings from her book advances. Her father insisted on giving her $10,000 from his own savings account — which wasn't even part of the substantial stocks and bonds he had invested with Prudential Securities. She'd easily be able to handle the financial part. But Annie didn't want to travel to Russia, which would involve a two-week trip. It would be too long to leave her father on his own.

And so, for an additional fee of $1,500, which was the cost of the airfare from Russia, via Frankfurt, Germany to Los Angeles International Airport, Orson Moses had agreed to escort a child back to the U.S.

Annie would only have to fly to California to meet her new daughter. Of course, she'd already paid the round-trip airfare in the adoption package, but like everything else concerned with the adoption, Annie soon learned that prospective parents were a "captive audience" and would shell out whatever was asked of them; pay and then pay some more.

Everyone knew how desperate most couples were for a baby while many and others would undertake the care of any child, even some with physical problems. And so costs were always handed on to the prospective adoptive parents. Anytime Orson called — and he'd phoned three times from Moscow — the call was collect. Any gifts to the orphanages, "contributions" to the various officials there, were all mailed, via federal express, and always in cash. At one juncture Annie had to get $10,000 in new 100-dollar bills and mail them via Federal Express to California. "I'm not a drug dealer," she said smiling to the bank manager, "but believe it or not, the man handling the adoption says the Russians only accept new 100 dollar bills, and, well, I've no choice in this, but to hope it gets to the right parties."

It did. It was all legal, but very expensive. But hell, it was 1994 — a good car cost $30,000 or more. A child was priceless. And more than anything else in the world, Annie wanted so much to be a mother.

It would take five long months for Annie's wishes to come true. Standing on long lines to get papers approved, getting a home study prepared, sending in her birth certificate, records of marriage and divorce, letters of reference, fingerprint clearance, financial statements — the paper trail was about two boxes full — and the forms to fill out went on and on and on. But oh, in the end, it would all be worth it.

"I've decided to keep Valentina's given name. It's so beautiful," she told Maureen. "Oh yes – I remember hearing the name — ice skaters, ballet dancers from Russia – it's popular there. I've always thought it was pretty."

The decision was a wise one. Her name fit her perfectly. "What a beautiful name and what a beautiful child," people would say. And she was. Annie was determined to do a good job at helping Valentina grow from the shy, hesitant little girl who first came to her into a self-confident child. Eventually she'd develop into a remarkably lovely young lady.

Having lived in an orphanage from birth, Valentina had missed out on what many American children take for granted. She had a lot of catching up to do and Annie wasted no time in guiding and motivating her daughter. She introduced Valentina to swimming and dance classes, tennis and acting lessons, and gymnastics. Not all at once, mind you. Annie had a lot to learn too. She'd never been a real parent before. But whatever Valentina needed — tutoring in math, help in spelling, dental retainers — Annie made certain she got it. And the giving was just filled with joy.

— ⚭ —

1994 was also the year that Nelson Mandella was elected President in South Africa, and Bill Clinton, the American President, was accused of sexual harassment while he was governor of Arkansas. The charges began with a suit filed by a former Arkansas government employee, Paula Jones. These issues contributed to the Democratic Party's defeat in the 1994 midterm elections and helped the Republicans gain control of Congress for the first time in 40 years.

By 1997 a full-blown sexual scandal involving the President and

White House Intern Monica Lewinski gained national attention, after Linda Tripp, a government employee secretly taped hours of telephone conversations with the White House aide. The tapes later formed the basis of Independent Counsel Kenneth Starr's investigation of Clinton.

But the birth to Annie of a little girl, "she was born from my heart, not my stomach" would be the happiest event of the year, in fact, of any year she could think of. Valentina Nikolayevna Sobtsova, born October 14, 1987, a citizen of Russia, would be admitted to the United States of America as the adopted child of Annie Rosenberg Ryan. Her new name would be Valentina Ryan.

She would arrive at L.A. Airport on August 10, 1994. And while Annie didn't know it yet — when they'd meet it would be instant love between mother and daughter.

*"In this unbelievable universe in which we live there are no absolutes.
Even parallel lines, reaching into infinity, meet somewhere yonder."*
— *Pearl Buck*

— C**ß** —

Chapter 39

October 14, 1994

It was Valentina's 7th birthday, her very first birthday in the
United States, in New York, on the borough of Staten Island,
with her new mother, her grandfather, and a host of little friends
she'd already made in her first grade class.

Annie had hosted the party at the local *Fun Bubble,* a place where
children could play and also celebrate birthdays and, of course, have
a terrific time. A dozen little friends of Valentina's, a few mothers,
Annie and her dad were there. Pizza and ice cream and a big
birthday cake would be served after the children played.

There was a giant trampoline, an intricate jungle gym, video
games and for the six and seven year olds various games to amuse
themselves, like the "Frog Jumper."

"You have to hit frog on the head...see how high it gets,"
Mommy, and I did it up...the very biggest...highest," Valentina
said in her still unsure English. She was always competitive, forever

wanting to do well.

She was also the prettiest child there. Valentina had a radiance about her and a very unique means of taking everything in with a positive, boundless spirit that was absolutely enchanting.

There was no doubt about it, she was a charmer. Valentina made friends easily too. Annie supposed this came from her having lived the formative years of her life in a peer group amongst many children, all of whom had to get along in the orphanage.

Then there was the special birthday gift from Sal. He'd seen Annie's pride and joy the second day she was in America. And he was crazy about Valentina. "Tell you what I'm going to do. Uncle Salvatore is going to make you a doll house, a real-to-scale doll house with all the furniture in it," he promised her.

Sal was always handy. He'd built his own model airplanes for years, and also was very active in a local club that flew radio-operated airplanes at Floyd Bennett airfield. The men had built all the model airplanes that were flown. It was an expensive hobby, and one Sal had been involved in for years.

He started to work immediately on building Valentina the dollhouse. A month later he showed up at the door with a magnificent, very large, 8 room model resplendent with charming miniature furnishings in each room, wallpapered and hand-painted walls, and wouldn't you know it, on the living room wall, a large portrait of Salvatore Lo Bianco, smiling down on all who peered inside the child's house.

"Thank you, Uncle Sal," Valentina said, planting a big kiss on his cheek.

"Mommy look, look how beautiful!" she shouted, delighted at this mystical, magical dollhouse made just for her. The darn thing was so big; it really needed its own room. But Annie thanked Sal profusely, and after he left, took the dollhouse downstairs, into an extra room off the garage. "Here, darling, any time you want to play with this nice house, or have your friends come and see it, you can use this nice big room."

Annie chuckled to herself. Really, what an ego Sal had — to put his own picture on the living room wall. Wait a minute! As Annie peered into the various rooms of the dollhouse she noticed another view of his mug on one of the walls upstairs. His photo was also on the bedroom wall, framed in an ornate tiny gold braid, with a sign beneath it that read, "Our Founder." She laughed herself silly. Well at least he hadn't tried to put a miniature fish tank in it.

Valentina was flourishing. Amazingly, in less than two months, she was already speaking whole phrases of English. Watching *Barnie* and *Sesame Street* every day before she'd begun school, was a big help. *I Love You, You Love Me, We're A Happy Family*, she sang along, over and over again. She absolutely adored the jumbo purple dinosaur called Barnie and all of his friends. On Saturday mornings she would sit mesmerized watching cartoons. There was so much for her to catch up on. She didn't know about cowboys and Indians, Superman or Batman. But yes, she had heard of "Meekey Mouse." Walt Disney was well known in Russia.

Annie registered Valentina in the local public school where English as a second language was taught. She would have preferred to put her into private school, but until her daughter could speak English fluently, she was best off at P.S. 29.

Over and over again, Annie looked at this delightful little girl who had lived all of her young life in an orphanage. She was a beautiful child. Dazzling blue eyes, long dark blonde hair, a warm, loving personality, and amazingly, she adapted immediately to her new surroundings.

"I'm really blessed, Maureen. She's captivating, affectionate, and frankly, she seems less neurotic than me. I've really lucked out with a wonderful child."

"You deserve it, Annie. I always knew you could be a great mother. And by the way, thanks for the photos. Valentina looks amazingly like you. It's remarkable."

"I wish I could agree with you. But I was never that pretty as a child.

She's a natural beauty. I had to have some work done to slim down my nose, and you know I had my eyes done in 1985...didn't have to pay a cent, either. The cosmetic surgeon I was doing the book with — he told me it would take 10 years off my face."

"Well, you never mentioned the eye job. But you do look surprisingly young...closer to 40 than your real age. So I wouldn't worry. And you are pretty, very pretty — even if you had to refine a bit of what Mother Nature gave you. And best of all, you're beautiful inside, my friend."

"Well, thank you very much. And when are we going to see you? I want Valentina to know my best friend."

"Thanks for thinking of me that way. The feelings are mutual, my dear! Well I'm making my absolute last tour beginning on Monday. I'm tired of this nomadic life — the hotel stays, all of it. I've made enough money, can still record, and well, I need to slow down. John wants us to buy a place down in Palm Beach. He loves golfing. He's going to turn 60 in a month. We both want a quieter life. And you know something, after seeing how remarkable your adoption is turning out, I was actually thinking of going to China and getting our own little girl."

"Fabulous!"

"Yes, I read an article about the Chinese regime. They don't want the population to have more than one child and they favor boys, who can do more work. So they've cast off tiny innocent baby girls. Killed some of them, starved them to death. It's a nightmare. I talked to John about it. He said if I want a baby that much, he'd agree. I have the money to hire a nanny if I have to appear somewhere."

"Do it, Maureen, do it! You'll never regret it. A child is a blessing, unconditional love that never stops," Annie urged.

"Well, I'm talking to a lawyer right now, who represents an agency that helps with Chinese adoptions, so I may be going there at the end of my tour. Oh Annie, you're a great role model — you've inspired me!"

"Hey thanks but you know something, Maureen? I'm getting much more than I'm giving. I have a truly loving child."

"I can see it in the pictures. John also said the two of you, you look so much alike."

"Oh I can't wait until you meet her."

"Neither can I. I promise it will be before Christmas," Maureen added.

"Adoption — It will change your life. There's absolutely nothing better in the whole entire world than having a child to care for. It will give you and John an even better sharing — I just know it. An orphaned child is lost, alone, needs guidance and love — and you get it back a thousand fold! It's unconditional love, the feeling of being needed, it's well, like being madly in love every single moment, and you don't have anything to argue about — it's just so super, wonderful. "

They both laughed.

"Oh Annie, I'm so happy for you! And tell me, how's your father doing?

"Dad's okay. He seems to adore Valentina. And it's good that she gets a grandfather, a family figure like my dad right away. They spend time every day together. Even with his failings he's good for her. But lately he's started walking around most of every night – the *sun-downing* has started all over again. He's restless, and after we go to sleep, he gets up. I have to make sure he doesn't go outside, or anything. He was doing so well for so long, but well, he's going to be 84 soon, and he's aging."

"No one ever got out of this world alive, you know. He's up there in years and, well, at least his physical health is alright," Maureen opined.

"Hey I bought a video camera. Took videos of Valentina at her birthday. I'll make a copy and send it to you. But please, as soon as you can take time out, come to visit. And also — let's have one of those long lunches again. And tell Sabrina too. It would be great to get together."

"Sabrina is bi-coastal now. With the Simpson trial dragging on, she does location pieces out there. She wanted a TV career, and boy has she got it. There's talk of her getting the co-host spot on one of the morning shows soon. It's still hush-hush, but I'll let you in on it if she lands it."

"And what about her marriage?"

"Well, Mark still has to work in two cities, and it's difficult, with their both traveling so much. You know, the president had offered him a job in Washington, but Mark turned it down. He's dedicated to his sports medicine, and is completing supervision of the construction on a gigantic sports medicine and fitness center in Denver."

"Wow, I wonder how they ever get time together."

"Sabrina commented about it too. She says after this year she's going to ask that they not give her any traveling assignments. At least Mark is in New York half of the time. They have an apartment down in Battery Park Plaza now. He loves the downtown scene, so they bought a duplex in one of the new skyscrapers there. It's not far from the Twin Towers and really not far from our apartment. I think eventually they'll both settle in one place. For now, their grueling schedule means that they only see each other on weekends — and sometimes not even that."

"Knowing how Sabrina is, I'm sure she'll make it work. When you speak to her, send her my regards. Well, maybe by next spring, we'll finally see one another! Here I am stuck in one place, and the two of you are on the road or in the air so much."

"Don't envy it. I hate the hotel stays, the small towns. This is my last tour. I think it ends in March. And if I'm to go to China, it won't be until June. So if I can't come in by the holidays then I promise to come visit you right after the tour is over. I'm dying to meet the baby."

"Well she isn't quite a baby, but then tell you what, I'm going to wait until you get here, because I'm drawing up a will — now that I have a daughter to be concerned with. And I'd like you to not only be her godmother, but also her guardian. If anything happens to me, I could trust you, Maureen."

"Nothing is going to happen to you. You'll probably live to be 110! But of course I'll gladly be her godmother and guardian. You can have your attorney draw up any papers now. And just send me a copy. But I'm so really eager to meet my little charge. She sounds so adorable on the phone. And I'm coming laden with gifts."

Annie laughed. "She has so many stuffed animals and Barbie dolls and games in her bedroom that I think we need a separate room for all the toys."

"Listen, I have to leave for the airport in a half hour. I'll stay in touch, but have to get off this phone. I hear John coming in and he thinks I'm all ready. I'm not!"

"Take care and be safe," Annie signed off.

— ❧ —

February 1995

On February 4, Sam Rosenberg turned 84. Annie had taken him

to his favorite Chinese restaurant. He loved the shrimp with lobster sauce dish, and ate with a hearty appetite. Valentina giggled when he ate the fortune cookie with the little fortune paper in it. Always in a rush — he just didn't wait to open it. But it was after dinner that he showed more signs of his dementia. He got up from his seat, leaned over the table and picked up the flatware from each place setting and attempted to put all of it into his pockets.

"Grandpa, that's not ours," Valentina blurted out. The little child knew the behavior was odd. The visibly shaky old man did not recognize that there was anything wrong with what he had done.

He looked confused. "Dad we have our own forks and spoons at home,"

Annie reminded him. "You can leave this here, okay?"

He put the flatware back on the table but looked angry that the two of them were telling him what to do. Sam Rosenberg was his own man and he didn't like to be told what to do by anyone.

It was a sign. One of many. At home for the past few months, when Annie served dinner, her dad would sometimes complain that she was giving Valentina "more food than me."

He was getting jealous of the attention Annie showed towards her daughter. "I want more cereal. You gave her more than me," he'd complain.

She surmised he was retreating a bit, like he was the child in the situation.

It didn't happen all the time. He could be wonderfully attentive and affectionate towards Valentina, who loved her grandfather dearly and hugged him daily. She was thrilled to have any relative, and accepted him on his terms, noticing wisely enough that sometimes Grandpa acted a little strange.

It wasn't easy explaining to a child that an adult in the family had a disease called "Alzheimer's," that he was "a little sick in the head;" that if he wandered around at night, he didn't know he was doing it. Annie called the doctor; he said it was to be expected. What did that mean? Expected? Then what next? What next to expect? It was scary. What should she do?

Annie called both Sid and Joanie. Sid had become a father a few months back. A baby girl. No photo was sent, no invitation to visit. Annie sent a present anyway.

Joanie showed more concern about their father. "He sounds like he's beginning to deteriorate. I'll come in on my Easter break. Then I can finally meet Valentina. I'm so looking forward. The photos you've sent me are terrific. And hang in with dad — if you can. I know it's gotta be hard, Annie. But call me if you need any help or just support. I know it's demanding on you and your time. We can talk more about it then."

Annie kept her fingers crossed. The nocturnal episodes were increasing. She took her father to the neurologist. He prescribed new medication and a mild sleeping pill. Still he got up at all hours. One night she found him peering over her face. It was frightening.

"What's the matter dad?"

"Did you take my wallet? I can't find my wallet and my money. It's missing," he said with a strange, vacant look on his face.

Annie knew he had taken to sleeping with his wallet under his pillow, as if someone in the house was going to steal it. She went with her dad and helped him look for it. It was not under the pillow. He seemed frantic. Then for some reason, she put on the light and looked under the bed, then lifted up the mattress — and there it was — sort of pushed there...like he did it himself but didn't remember.

"Here it is Daddy. And all your money is in it. See it's safe. It must have fallen there."

He just stared blankly at her.

The next morning he didn't recall the incident at all.

Annie knew this was getting serious. She wondered if she would have to hire a live-in. Or what she should do. Now her dad was beginning to display signs of forgetfulness during the daytime too.

Annie was concerned about leaving him alone at all. Although she left work early to pick Valentina up from school, she knew her father needed almost continuous attention. Four hours a day would no longer suffice. Not when he went outside that morning at 6 a.m. presumably to get the newspaper that would be on the lawn and swiftly disappeared. He couldn't find his way back. At 6:30 in the morning the police had rung the bell. Annie had been in the shower — even ten minutes for herself turned about to be too long. The police officer had noticed her father aimlessly walking around. It was lucky the patrol car was in the neighborhood and watched him wandering around. Lost. His eyes glazed over. In a robe. They knew something was wrong by his slippers and his demeanor. It took them almost 10 minutes to help him recognize the house. Sam Rosenberg was fading slowly away. And there was nothing anyone could do about it.

"Where is the life we have lost in living?
Where is the wisdom we have lost in knowledge?
Where is the knowledge we have lost in information?"
— *T.S. Eliot*

— ℭℜ —

Chapter 40

April 16, 1995

"Oh, Joanie – I'm so glad to see you. It's been rough lately, with dad not doing so well. But wait until you meet Valentina — you're going to love her!" Annie said as they drove from the airport in Newark to the house. It was the Thursday before Easter vacation and Valentina was at school. While Annie had sent her sister many pictures, this would be the first time Valentina and her aunt would actually meet. Annie was overjoyed that Joanie had come to visit.

"I wanted to come sooner but I had to get through the SAT tests that our school was giving before I left," Joanie explained.

Their father's condition had deteriorated. When they arrived at Annie's home, Joanie ran to her father, threw her arms around him and kissed him warmly on his cheek. He shrank back; it was clear that Sam had no idea who Joanie was. Neither sister was remotely prepared for this possibility. Annie was lost for words. And Joanie began to babble. "Daddy, it's me, Joanie, your oldest daughter,

Joanie, she repeated."

Later in the day he seemed to realize who she was, but kept confusing his daughters' names — much more than the typical elderly person might. They knew then that Sam Rosenberg's mental state was worsening.

The meeting with Valentina was much more joyful. Warm, spontaneous in her affection, she hugged the aunt she'd heard about, happy to see her. "This doll was made by native Americans — Hopi Indians — they don't live far from where we do in Arizona," Joanie explained, giving her new niece the beautifully decorated wood doll called a *Hopi Kahila*. The *katchina* doll was intricately carved, beautifully costumed and painted in rich colors. It was unique — more a collector's item than a plaything. "You can keep it in your room and display it on a shelf if you like. It's not like a Barbie doll but it has much value," she continued. "Someone worked hours and hours to make this so special."

"Can I take it in to school for 'show and tell'?" Valentina asked.

"Sure you can my little darling," Joanie smiled. "Just carry it carefully."

"It's wonderful Joanie. I know those dolls sell for hundreds of dollars — but we'll keep it safe, won't we honey?" Annie said, turning to Valentina.

"Yes Mommy – I promise!" And with that Valentina flew off into the living room to show her grandfather this special gift.

"My return flight is for Thursday morning," Joanie reported. "I really can't stay any longer because school starts on Monday and I have a bunch of things to do to get ready. But let's see how dad does with both of us here."

"You can see how happy he already is for double the attention," Annie responded, because it was obvious, their father enjoyed the gentleness and concern his daughters showed to him.

"Did you make a doctor's appointment?" Joanie asked.

"Yes, but the doctor really doesn't do much. Maybe because there really isn't very much that can be done. The *aricept* he prescribed isn't helping either."

"Getting old ain't any fun — not when you get hardening of the arteries, memory problems, all of it. It's ugly," Joanie groaned.

"I don't mind when dad is just forgetful and wanders around. But it's no fun when his old stubbornness kicks in. You know how obstinate he used to be? Well he'd calmed down, mellowed out with the years. Or so I thought. Not so. This disease brings it back at times and worse — for no reason whatsoever, except what's going on somewhere in the dark crevices of his mind — he gets angry and immovable." Annie commented.

"Well I've noticed that half the time he's just staring at the TV, or falling asleep in front of it," Joanie said. "He's not showing much interest in his favorite programs."

"Yeah…he's losing interest in most everything," Annie said glumly.

"Well, let's get someone in full time. Dad needs to be watched every moment," Joanie suggested. "She can sleep downstairs if necessary. You have no tenant now, do you?"

"No, but frankly, I think the person has to be right up here to watch him. I have to get some sleep. And if the companion sleeps downstairs, that's really no help. Dad's much worse at nighttime. I think whomever I hire can sleep on the sofa bed in the living room. It opens up to a very comfortable bed. Paying $600 a week and feeding the companion – there's nothing wrong with sleeping on a sofa bed."

"Whatever you think is best. I spoke with Sid. He wasn't happy about it, but we have to continue to sell off dad's investments. You did dissolve that trust; it was for about $75,000, didn't you?

"Yes, I did it right away when the lawyer told me that if dad has to go into a nursing home at any point, any monies transferred after two years, will be counted as assets and will go to pay for the home. I did it almost a year and a half ago. It should be safe. It's in a treasury-direct account with all three of our names on it. The attorney did the work for me, so we've salvaged that at the least."

"Good. And whatever we think about Sid, he's been agreeable on this. Though we both know, Sid will always agree to anything if it means he's getting any money. Anyway, we have to disburse more of dad's money, and *now*, — at the least get it into our names, and out of his. If not, if dad ever does have to go into a home, then the government will take all of the monies before Medicaid kicks in with anything. I think Sid is right there, Annie. We need to dole out — to each of us $10,000 gifts, which are allowable amounts from any estate each year."

"You're right. I checked with my accountant, he says we can still get it done for 1994. The amount is actually $9,999. Technically, we don't want to make it for $10,000. So that takes care of almost $60,000 plus even Sid agrees, we should give bequests to both Valentina and his daughter, Rachel. Dad has more than $400,000 in investments. If something happens and I pray it doesn't — well let's try to get a good chunk transferred now."

"Yup, why give it all to the government? Half of them are crooks anyway! Every time I read about another senator retiring on a hundred thousand dollar pension, I wince! Dad worked hard all of his life, it's his money, and well, I'm in favor of keeping as much as we can," Joanie responded.

"Good, we're all in agreement on this — even pain-in-the ass Sid!" Annie said, feeling no warmth towards her brother. Damned families — you couldn't pick your relatives. Arguments about older parents, wills, estates, was not that unusual. Annie was grateful to have one loving member, her sister.

"It's okay by me that Valentina and Rachel get more. Maybe I should run out and get me a child, so I can get the $10,000 bequests for…oh forget it, I'm just kidding!" Joanie said smiling.

"How sad, he worked hard all of his life, got up at 4 a.m. every morning, was out of the house by 5:30, and he never complained, loved working, being a good provider," Annie said, remembering the many years their father toiled and made a good living. "He put in many hours of overtime too. If someone had a plumbing emergency, dad always went out on the job. Even if he was tired, he went," she added.

"Remember, Annie, how he always liked to tell us the story of how he came over from Poland a poor teenager, how he apprenticed himself and studied hard to become a master plumber? Dad made a success of himself, accumulated all these savings and stocks and bonds, and now we have to take it from him. It's kind of discouraging," Joanie added.

"Well, he made the money, but it was mom who did the smart investing. She dealt with Prudential Bache. I remember her on the phone talking to the broker countless times. She was the shrewd one when it came to the money. She deserves the credit for that. Still dad loved to see the statements, get those dividends in. He still runs to the mailbox here to get his pension checks. Boy does he love seeing the checks come in the mail — the money he worked so damned hard for."

"So that's all the money is worth. Dad counting it and us now trying to hide it from the government. How ironic. Almost as paradoxical as mom loving her jewelry, which she almost never wore, and buying all that ornate sterling silver for the house, which she never used, and the expensive furniture covered with plastic that no one really enjoyed…all the material possessions are worth nothing to either of them now, " Joanie reflected.

"You're right. It's tragic. Muktananda, the guru I told you about — he used to say "let go of earthly things. Meditate. Meditate.""

"All the great thinkers and philosophers of the world eschew material possessions. I still remember, *Man is as rich as the amount of possessions he can afford to let alone.* I learned that in high school; think that was written by Thoreau in his book on Walden Pond," Joanie recalled.

"The only redeeming aspect of this disease is that dad doesn't realize what's happening. Thank heaven he isn't aware that we're liquidating so many of his assets. At least he's lucky he has his children to care and look after him. We *can* take good care of him," Annie added.

"It's ironic isn't it, Joanie, how the children have to take care of the parents, and in cases like dad, the parent becomes child-like," she continued. "God, I hope this never happens to me. I'm back to doing crossword puzzles in the Times every day and Sunday too. They say it's a good mental exercise. It's scary, getting Alzheimer's. It's a nightmare of a disease."

"I bought ginkgo biloba, it's a vitamin that's supposed to help your memory. And boy I need it. Ever since menopause I've become forgetful. I just hope it's nothing but just mild aging. My God! Can you imagine, we're getting older, Annie. All of us are getting older. I don't feel old. But we're both in what they call middle age. Wow, it's frightening."

"It's better than the alternative."

They laughed. But it really wasn't very funny.

— ❧ —

Joanie had been planning to leave on Thursday. Then it happened.

On Wednesday, April 19th early news bulletins came on the air. There was a report of a horrible attack. The Federal Building in Oklahoma City had been bombed. Scores were killed as a terrorist's car bomb blew up the block-long structure. Right-wing paramilitary groups were suspected of being linked to the bombing. Television coverage of the event soon showed the ravages of an entire block of debris from the immense damage the bomb had done. It looked like something out of a war movie.

Joanie decided to change her travel plans. "Eric, he's foolish, but he says I shouldn't fly out until the weekend. He says you never know if there are other terrorist attacks planned, until they round up the bombers. Anyway, it just might be better for me to stay on longer. This way I can spell you and spend more time with dad — at least for a couple of days. And we can interview women for the job. I'll change my reservations now."

Actually Annie was relieved. She was glad Joanie was there. Even if their father called her Sara half of the time, and Joanie Annie and Valentina Joanie, that wasn't the worst of it. He was starting to lose his balance, to fall. At least in the house there was thick carpeting. But his bones were brittle. She was concerned he'd break a hip and end up bed-bound, something that would certainly devastate this fiercely independent man.

They'd taken him to the movie that Sunday, a nice treat, though he seemed to drift off to sleep intermittently. Still he enjoyed going out, getting the attention from his daughters. When they left the movie complex and were walking towards the car, even though Joanie was holding his hand, Sam tripped, missed the small step on the sidewalk and fell forward into the gutter.

"Don't move Dad. Just sit down here. Dad's hurt his ankle and he has a big cut on his knee. And look, his head is bleeding. Let's take him over to the emergency room. "

After x-rays were taken, and no break was found, the doctor bandaged up his ankle and gave Annie some painkillers for later. He also advised Sam staying off his leg for a day or two, and suggested that their father use a cane. The cane turned out to be a bigger problem than the fall.

By Tuesday, Sam was feeling better and walking around with the cane they'd purchased for him. He was also using it like an instrument of war. He had swung at the new Polish woman they'd hired. He had a weapon. He was in charge once again. "I'm not going to eat that mush," he yelled at her, rejecting the bowl of oatmeal. And then he raised his cane like an exclamation point. The woman was terrified.

"He's going to need to calm down or no one will stay with him," Joanie commented. He can't run around with the cane like this...or can he? Oh wow, what a mess this is." She phoned the doctor. As if he could do anything. No one could control their father when his ire was up. Sam Rosenberg had always had a temper. While he'd mellowed for a while the awareness that his independence was being threatened, had brought his old anger back. And with a cane, he could be like the Count of Monte Cristo, like one of the Three Musketeers, he would defend his territory, guard the house, keep imagined enemies away.

— C&R —

"Teach me to live that I may dread,
The grave as little as my bed."
— *Thomas Ken*

— ☯ —

Chapter 41

September 1996

S am's mental state was rapidly deteriorating. There were many troubling times when the police had to be called. There were three episodes when he'd wandered away — not too far — but for someone who'd lost his sense of direction and was never totally familiar with the neighborhood, it could have been a continent. Once he was found on the next block sitting on a neighbor's porch. The neighbor called for help when she saw an elderly man seated there wearing only a robe and slippers. Those were minor incidents; no one was hurt, nothing damaged. Still it was daunting.

Then, his behavior became more erratic.

On one calamitous night, her father had embarked on a *work project* — which unfortunately for Annie resulted in his smashing many of the mirrors in the house. And there were lots of mirrors. She'd studied feng shui and employed the use of mirrors to brighten and expand her décor. In fact, many of the rooms featured entire mirrored walls.

Her father began with the bathroom mirrors — taking a
hammer to them — and now was hard at work in his bedroom
on what he described as *renovations*. She'd never be certain why
he chose to demolish mirrors; perhaps he didn't want to see the
reflection of an aging man.

— ○✲ —

Most of the time Sam would speak of the "good old days."
Reminiscing, he would repeat the same stories over and over
again about his work projects and talk incessantly of the crew
he supervised when he'd been head of the plumbing division on
construction sites.

He'd overseen the pipeline installations at the large Blue Cross
Building on Third Avenue, his last major job before retiring. Before
that he'd worked on other large structures in New York, including
some of the key public bathroom installations in the World Trade
Center in 1972 and 1973. Having been the foreman on those projects
for almost two years, Sam Rosenberg would proudly tell anyone
who'd listen that "I'm responsible for the plumbing at the Blue Cross
and World Trade Buildings."

Looking back was soothing. It seemed to be an ideal time — an
era when he'd earned a very good income, lived with his beloved
Sara, was useful and really *needed* and so he often returned to the
reverie. Yes, those were the days.

— ○✲ —

But now he was living in his daughter's home and sometimes he
wasn't sure where he was or what he was doing.

The breaking of mirrors started while Annie was sound asleep,
Valentina curled up beside her in the generous Queen-sized bed.
(Valentina loved to sleep close to mommy, often climbed into bed,
bringing along her favorite teddy bear, the pink one Annie had sent
over to the orphanage.) Annie cherished her affectionate little girl,

but sleeping with her was another matter. Valentina would end up reclining on an angle and took up more than half the space. On those nights Annie didn't have the most relaxing sleep.

It was 1 in the morning when she was startled by the sounds. What on earth was that loud, clashing racket? She soon recognized it as the resonance of breaking glass. And she knew it had something to do with her father. Where was Christa, the woman who was supposed to be watching him? Probably dead to the world. But of course, Annie heard every noise in the house.

"What's that big noise, Mommy?" Valentina asked, awakening from her sleep.

"It's nothing, some glass broke. I'm going to check on Grandpa. You stay in bed, okay?" She quickly got up and went to her father's room.

That's when she saw him — hammer in hand, attempting to finish smashing to smithereens the mirrored-paneled wall. He'd done an expert job so far! All he was wearing was his underwear and surprisingly, socks and shoes. Odd, he must have known there'd be glass splinters or why wear shoes? Annie couldn't get close enough without treading on shards of shattered mirror. It was a miracle he hadn't cut himself. This was dangerous. "Dad, please, wake up. Dad," she called.

"What are you talking about? I *am* awake. I'm beginning the renovation work. You'll have new pipes in soon. My men are on the way. Don't worry, I have everything under control."

She hated calling 911 but had no choice. When the police arrived they observed a white haired old man, small, kind of thin, holding a hammer and smiling like he'd done a good deed. They talked him out of the room, where the floor was littered with sharp slices of mirror; helped Annie to dress him. The EMT workers would take him to the hospital for observation. The police officers were very understanding, exceptionally polite. One even told Annie that he had an uncle who was like "that."

After checking on Valentina and Christa, and locking all the doors, Annie would follow in her car.

Christa, who'd slept through most of the pandemonium could clean up and keep an eye on Valentina. She had to serve some useful purpose — it certainly wasn't taking proper care of her father. The woman had slept through all the thumping and hammering and even through the police arrival.

"Don't open the door Christa — and leave the alarm on. I'll call you if I can't get back before dawn," Annie said, hurrying out the door. "And, please sweep up all the broken glass, then you can go back to sleep. And of course, watch Valentina. I'm going to the hospital to see how my father is doing."

Annie ended up spending most of the night in the emergency room. Her sweet, lost father, who now looked so vulnerable, so confused, would be released the next day. They wanted to do a few more tests and calm him down. There really wasn't anything else they could do for him.

It was, she knew the beginning of the end.

The next time it happened, it was much worse, far more dangerous. He had found a box of matches. He was yelling at Christa and keeping her away with his cane. "Get away from me you son of a bitch! If I want to burn the house down I can burn it down."

The police arrived quickly. Annie's father refused to get out of the chair he was sitting in. Nor to give up the box of matches. So they carried him, in the chair, to the waiting ambulance. He was laughing, seemed happy, and didn't think anything he was saying or doing was wrong.

Perhaps it wasn't. But it was dangerous behavior and Annie knew she could no longer keep her dad living at home. Her first allegiance now was to her daughter — she had to protect Valentina and herself.

The next day Annie called the doctor, called family members and began looking into nearby nursing homes. She called on God to please help her help her father — to do the right thing. She was scared, really scared.

It was time for her dad to live elsewhere. It hurt like hell. Annie felt so guilty. "I promised him I'd never throw him out, Joanie. But it's no good now, it's too terrifying."

"Please Annie you're doing the right thing. Dad's sick and the situation is growing perilous. A fire is the last thing you need to deal with, honey, you've got to find a good quality nursing home now."

Yes, Annie realized it – there were few choices left. Her father didn't know what he was doing. And she believed that if he could comprehend what was going on, he'd agree, that she had to do this for the safety of all concerned. Yes, he'd understand.

Annie was determined to locate the nearest, best nursing home, and find a tactful, comfortable manner to have him transferred into it. The hospital said he was still a little delusional, was keeping him as a patient, so she had time to look. Money would be no object. She wanted the best for their father. After all, it was *his* money. Sid was opposed to the most expensive one on the list. Annie didn't give a damn. She went over, examined the premises, inspected the small but private room he'd occupy, signed the papers and sent a copy to Joanie.

Sam deserved the best care they could get him, and even with the "best", the care was still institutional. All they could expect was hygienic surroundings, pills given on time, three meals a day, and laundry done. There was some recreation, movies shown once or twice a week in the main dining hall, and card games. Again, he didn't play cards, and even if he had, she doubted his mind was up to it any longer. She didn't even know if the movies and camaraderie would matter.

Annie was advised that she could hire an outside companion to come to the home each day to spend time and take her father for walks. The staff was too busy for this. There were many patients in worse condition, confined to wheelchairs or beds because of strokes. They provided a list of outside agencies. "The starting pay was $20 an hour; seems a lot for someone to just sit with him or walk with him," she explained to Joanie. "Yet, I can't be there every day and I don't want him ignored."

"Do it! This way dad will get some exercise, and individual attention" Joanie opined. Annie requested an aide for two hours a day. At this rate, the money would go fast.

She'd visit him as often as she could. She also made a promise to herself, that she'd take him out to dinner at least three times a week. As long as he could interact with Valentina and herself on any level, Annie wanted her father to share time with them. Nevertheless, in the end she was more devastated by the changes that were made than he; Sam Rosenberg was mercifully oblivious to his surroundings.

When she told him he was going to stay at this "hotel" for a few weeks, he accepted it. The room, at the end of a long hallway was private, with it's own bathroom. It did have a television, and the rates, at more than $1,500 a week, meant he was in the best nursing home available. Still Annie felt responsible for leaving her father all alone, this man who had worked hard all his life, who had been so proud. She brought over all his best clothing, and hung up pictures of the family on the wall. Valentina helped make the room more cheerful with a vase of flowers, and some drawings she had made. "Here, grandpa," she'd said, "do you like these?" He smiled and hugged her closely. Valentina proceeded to tape her colorful drawings on the wall. Sam would have a phone in his room, and Annie promised to call every day. Besides, it was only 3 miles from the house, so they'd visit regularly. Valentina loved her grandfather and wanted to see him often.

For the first few months Annie took her father to dinner at least three times a week. They ate in all his favorite places, the local Chinese restaurant, an Italian emporium where he loved the spaghetti dishes, and the coffee shop in the neighborhood where he'd order the same menu item every week, a corn beef sandwich.

But his appetite just wasn't that good. Every time Annie visited she'd bring him fresh fruit. He'd always loved peaches and plums and grapes. Not any more. Some of the fruit rotted. He just didn't eat that much any longer.

And when she had to drive him back to the home after dinner, Annie hated myself for the lies. "I'll be back later," she'd tell him. "If not, I promise to see you tomorrow." She felt awful, simply awful.

As time passed and his surroundings remained the same, Sam grew increasingly morose. Even in his confused state, he knew this wasn't home. He loathed being told what to do. At the beginning, he continued to dress daily in his ultra neat clothing, always wearing a jacket and a jaunty cap. He hated that he could not shower on his own, that a nurse would have to be present. And Annie was equally annoyed, that at that exorbitant rate for nursing care, the residents were only taken to shower three times a week.

By December, Sam Rosenberg had become incontinent. They had him wearing a diaper. It was demoralizing. He would swing his cane at whatever aide came to the room to help him dress. Or to wash him. He was now aware enough that he couldn't leave the "hotel" to know it wasn't a real hotel.

— ❧ —

January 1997

"Goodbye Grandpa," Valentina said, giving him a big kiss. She was only 10 years old but she understood that her grandfather was sick. Annie did her best in trying to explain this strange disease. But no one really understood Alzheimer's so how could she expect this child to know what was happening to her grandfather? Yet Valentina was wise beyond her years. Still she was worried. "You're not going to get sick like Grandpa, are you Mommy?" she'd ask. She was frightened; concerned about losing the only mother she'd ever known.

"No, sweetheart. Don't worry. You see me taking vitamins every day.

I don't smoke or drink. And I watch what I eat. Don't worry, I'm going to do my very best to stay healthy for you."

The next time they went to visit her father, Annie handed him a bag of fresh, beautiful plums. They were ripe and sweet and she hoped he'd enjoy them. He'd always loved plums.

"Thank you Sara, but I don't need all of these. We already have plums in the refrigerator," he'd say, as if he were talking to his wife, as if he were going home to her.

It was awful, simply dreadful, to see her father wasting away. Yet she had to be there. She was the closest, the only one near enough to watch over him. "At least the visits aren't in vain. He's always happy to see both of us," she reported to Joanie. Yes, he did remember Annie and Valentina; recognized them immediately. He might be sitting in the lounge, cat napping in a chair. The minute they walked in, his eyes would open and a big smile would appear on his face. He'd announce: "This is my daughter, my favorite daughter," to the other residents who were assembled in the lounge. "She's such a good daughter," he'd say. It broke Annie's heart.

— ❦ —

The weeks came and went in what felt like slow motion and much of day-to-day existence seemed somber with her father in such duress. But like nearly all aspects of life, there was always an alternative that was full of promise. This was Valentina. Annie's main source of pleasure was seeing her innocent little daughter develop into such a loving and secure young girl.

She now spoke perfect English with no accent at all. Valentina was enrolled at a private school, St. John's Lutheran, situated close to their home. It was a Christian school. That was more than acceptable to Annie. What was most important was that it was a highly rated educational institute and was right in the neighborhood.

Annie didn't practice Judaism, nor did her family. It was more a cultural thing. There were children from every denomination at St. John's. Actually, Valentina had been baptized Russian Orthodox before she was taken out of Russia. Annie didn't care what faith her daughter was brought up in, as long as she had a faith. And it was worth the tuition to keep her out of the public school system, which was over-crowded and second-rate.

Valentina was doing well in school. And to make sure she kept up, Annie had her tutored each term, to supplement the learning process. She needed to catch up on her American history, become more proficient in vocabulary, and grasp the rudimentary rules of reading and writing and arithmetic other children had learned before school. For Valentina, there was only a blank, a dark hole before coming to her new home and country. There were no links for her. She didn't understand the basics that most American children would take for granted.

She hadn't been exposed to Roy Rogers or John Wayne movies, knew nothing of how the west was won, and little about the start of our country. There was no schooling at the orphanage, and what little she'd learned was Russian culture within the asylum's four walls.

Besides that, there was no fluoride in the water, no calcium in the diet, and, Annie had been forewarned before her little girl arrived; most Russian children had bad teeth. It was true, Valentina's baby teeth were all rotting in her mouth.

She'd arranged for a Russian-speaking female dentist to work with Valentina— to remove the teeth that were causing her bad breath and gum problems. It didn't matter what it cost, Annie was committed to helping her little girl be the healthiest and the best she could be — so she could achieve her full potential. And oh, it was so gratifying to watch the changes in this little waif of a child. Yes, as a result of wholesome food, and loving care, Valentina had overcome the inadequate nutrition of her formative years. She was now a healthy young girl, full of energy, and a youngster who loved sports and was good at whatever she attempted.

By 1997 Valentina Ryan had developed into an all-American little girl. As a matter of fact, she didn't like telling anyone she was from Russia…she didn't have good memories. There really wasn't anything very good about living in an orphanage. And when on the few occasions Annie introduced her to a Russian adult, she'd shy away. She didn't want anyone to know she was adopted either. "You're like my real mommy, why do you have to tell anyone I came from Russia, that I'm adopted?" she'd ask.

"I love you more than you know, my angel," Annie said, smiling at this radiant creature who was brought into her life. "You are the *best* thing that has ever happened to me. Now—just because you came from my heart instead of my stomach doesn't make you any less my daughter," Annie continued. "I really believe God put us together. Don't worry, please, darling. And if you don't want people to know you're from Russia, that's okay. But Mommy's grandparents — my mom's parents — they were from Russia, you know. And they were very, very nice people."

Valentina squeezed Annie so tight, she could barely breathe. What a blessing, what a real blessing Valentina was. "I must have done something good in my life to deserve her," Annie decided. They kissed and held each other close.

In the rare moments now that there was time to relax, Annie treated herself to a movie. However, more than half of the time she'd have to sit through children's films — after all, Valentina loved Disney productions. But that's what being a mother was all about.

Sometimes Annie could steal away on her own and see what she wanted. Like *As Good As It Gets*, with one of her favorite actors, Jack Nicholson. Amusing, but it wasn't easy admitting that she possessed some of the character's obsessive-compulsive behavior, like an anxiety about germs. Annie would never touch a doorknob in a public bathroom without first washing her hands, wiping them carefully with a paper towel which she then used to turn the knob.

Because she was so busy traveling back and forth to work and the nursing home, Annie didn't get to see much theater. But she did want Valentina to get a taste of Broadway and took her to see *Cats*, a perfect show for children. Valentina absolutely loved it.

After that, she decided to take her daughter to every musical that played on Broadway, providing her with a stimulating cultural experience. Soon Valentina cherished the music and performances as much as her mother did.

— ❧ —

In 1997 one of Annie's all time favorite movie stars died.

Gene Kelly, dancer, singer, director, had passed away. Annie kept signed photos from *Singing in the Rain* displayed on her bedroom wall, and played some of his recordings over and over. He sang in a warm breathless hush, like he was singing only to Annie. She owned all his recordings including wonderful versions of Gershwin songs, one of her favorite composers.

Annie also admired Fred Astaire and Ginger Rogers. The few framed autographed photos of the dancing legends she'd collected when she was with Tom were hung proudly in the house. The great old MGM movie musicals with Judy Garland, Gene Kelly, Fred and Ginger, were her favorites. She purchased videos of *Take Me Out to the Ball Game*, of *Summer Stock*, of *Meet Me in St. Louis* and of *An*

American in Paris, and when she wanted to relax, she'd play them over and over again.

Silly – but every once in a while a mantra sped through her mind: *If only life could be more like a musical.* She could dream couldn't she?

— ❧ —

The nursing home called. Her father's cold had worsened. They were afraid he'd developed pneumonia and were transporting him to Staten Island Hospital.

"I'll be right over," she said. Annie prayed he'd be all right. She called the family to tell them of the turn in events, drove Valentina to a classmate's home, where she could safely spend the night, and then rushed over to the hospital.

By the time she arrived, her father had an oxygen tent over his head and was in the Intensive Care Unit. "Dad, Dad, it's me, Annie," she whispered, leaning over the bed. His eyes opened, he saw her and smiled.

"Don't talk dad. Rest. Get better. I'll be right here."

She slept in a chair by her father's side all day and night.

"Please, God, let him get better, please," she prayed.

— ❧ —

"All meetings end in partings."
— Buddha

— ‍CR —

Chapter 42

January 1997

On February 4th Sam Rosenberg would turn 90. Would it even matter? He was no longer aware of age, nor years, nor time. His mind was somewhere else—back to when he was young and virile and he was in charge. Who could blame him?

Annie sat by his hospital bed. He looked so helpless and frail. He no longer resembled the robust and resilient man, the proud plumber who worked long hours on major construction sites. "My God," she thought, "is this the father who once terrorized the house with his temper? No, this was the man who was a hugger — warm and giving — a *good* father. Who wanted to remember the bad aspects now?"

"The attending physician, he'd like to speak with you," a nurse came in to say.

"Sure, where is he?"

"He'll be right in."

Annie was afraid of what he might say. Oh don't let it be bad news.

"There's a new drug they're testing. Don't want to promise anything, but if we get your written permission we can try it on your father. Sometimes it clears up the lungs. It's strong. Don't want to mislead you.

But it is my duty to offer you this participation in the study. "

"A study? What study? My dad isn't a guinea pig. He's old and frail."

"It's from Pfizer drug company. They're still test marketing. Our hospital is the only one on the Island using it. It could work...."

"No, no, absolutely not. If it can harm him, I don't want it. I don't want him to have another moment's discomfort. My dad, he doesn't really want to be here anyway. I think he's tired and when he has moments of clarity, he seems so sad being in the nursing home. The diapers, the routine, all of it...he hates it and so do I," Annie cried.

She didn't let the doctor answer.

"Besides, what are the side effects of the drug? What else can you tell me? "

"I won't lie to you. It can cause liver damage. In some it is very irritating to the digestive system...."

"Sorry, Doctor. I don't need to hear any more. I won't sign any forms, give my permission." She had to turn down the testing. She knew her dad wouldn't want it.

Annie fell asleep in the chair next to his bed. His breathing sounded labored. But she'd stay by his side.

The next morning at the break of dawn Annie went home to change and to shower. The mood was somber and too quiet within the house. Valentina was staying at the Phillips home down the street. She and Michelle Phillips both attended the same class. She went by to see Valentina. "I want to see Grandpa, please, Mommy."

"Alright, you don't have to go to class today. We'll go see Grandpa just as soon as I can call my office. Come with me and you can change clothes." She thanked Mrs. Phillips for all her kindness and took Valentina home.

Later that morning they drove over to the hospital. Annie had hired a private duty nurse for round the clock care, so at least she knew her dad was comfortable. But she was worried, was this the end? Was he going to come out of this? And go where? Back to his 10x10 jail cell of a room? Oh my God, why must old age be so dreadful, so punishing? Nobody ever got out of this world alive, she knew that. But a peaceful end, that's what she wished for her father. He had worked hard all his life, did the best he could.

Annie and Valentina both stayed by Sam's bedside. Valentina was magnificent. Most of the time Annie stood near him, holding his hand. And when the nurse said he didn't need the oxygen tent, that he could breathe with the less cumbersome oxygen mask, Sam Rosenberg, small, frail, his life ebbing slowly to a conclusion, looked fondly at Valentina. It was obvious that he was glad she was there. He smiled, winked with one eye to indicate that he recognized her. Annie was glad for that. Valentina leaned down and kissed him sweetly on the forehead.

"We're here Grandpa. Don't worry. Mommy and I are here," she said.

All Valentina really had as her family was her grandpa and her aunt Joanie. Valentina valued family; she had none until she came to Annie. But they were a small family — "well you can pick your friends but not your family," Annie would say, mindful that she'd never be close with Sid or his wife.

Annie called Joanie and Sid to tell them that their father was beginning to slip in and out of consciousness. They needed to know it might be the end.

"Sara, Sara where are you?" he cried.

"Dad, it's me, Annie." She stroked his forehead. He smiled.

And then he closed his eyes. "Is grandpa alright, is he?" Valentina frantically asked.

The nurse took his pulse. "He's as good as can be expected. He needs his rest," she announced.

"Look you two can take a break now — get some lunch in the cafeteria. I'm here."

"Okay, we'll be back in a half hour," Annie said. She knew it was better for Valentina not to be in the room much longer. The child was trying to be brave, but truly, she was devastated.

A half hour later the pair came back and Annie's dad was asleep. Good. At least he wasn't in any discomfort.

The doctor returned: "There's little we can do. His fever has gone down, but he needs bed rest and his lungs aren't clear yet. Go home. I'll call you if there's any change."

Annie leaned down, took her father's hand and held it tightly. "I love you Daddy. See you later,"she whispered.

"Grandpa, I love you very much too," Valentina said, kissing him on the cheek. He opened his eyes, and smiled at her. "I love you too my little darling," he said.

It was the last time they saw him alive.

That night at 1 in the morning the hospital called. "We're sorry to tell you that your father Sam Rosenberg expired at 12:30 this morning. We did everything we could do. You did say do not resuscitate."

"That's right. "Annie knew her father didn't want them to try to bring him back. She knew he wanted to go, to be with his Sara.

"I'll make arrangements first thing in the morning for the funeral home to get my father," she said. She knew where to call and what to do. She'd investigated this a while back. It was awful but necessary.

"Can we ask you if we can have any organ donation? Or a less invasive procedure would be a skin donation?" the nurse asked, softly, respectfully.

"He was old. His lungs were no good. He'd had prostrate problems once. His heart was worn out. No... I don't know about organs. But I'll agree to skin. If you can do this and it doesn't affect anything with his body — I, I," she stammered, " yes, it's alright if you take some skin."

"Thank you. Someone will call with confirmation of your consent."

About fifteen minutes later, another call came in. This from someone asking for basic information, name of deceased, religion, age, and then a few minutes later another call followed. This one confirming that "skin tissue has been removed from your father, Sam Rosenberg. This will be used for skin grafts and we thank you for this valuable donation."

About a month later an actual thank you letter and a donation certificate arrived in the mail, thanking them for the skin donation. Annie never told the others about it. But while it was small, she was glad she'd said yes, that something of her father stayed here to help someone else.

— ∞ —

Annie couldn't wait to get off the phone. To lie down and to cry. But first she had to call Joanie and Sid and let them know their dad had passed. She wasn't quite sure why she hadn't called them before this. Maybe if she didn't tell them it wasn't really true?

In the Jewish religion the body is buried within 24 hours. The mourning or shiva period takes place after. Annie called the funeral parlor. They would transport her father's body in the morning. Oh my God, they're all starting to die off, Annie thought. Lately she'd been hearing about a few people she'd known who had died. Young too. She was into reading the obituaries lately. Amazing. So many gone and some only in their 50s and 60s. She'd also heard about two second cousins, on her mother's side. He was 84, she 83. They passed on just the prior month. She went first; he couldn't go on without her and died the following week. She sent a card and made a donation to the heart foundation. But she didn't go to the funeral. Annie hated funerals. Roosevelt's was the last one she attended. No more. No more.

Though she knew she had to be there for her father. Well at least he passed quietly, without too much pain. And he'd had a good run…more years than many were given on this earth. Was he up there, somewhere, was he with those he cared about and lost? Was there really an after life? She didn't know. She could only hope so. All Annie knew for certain was that she had to go over to the funeral parlor the next day and pick out the coffin. And then go with Valentina to the funeral the following day.

This one she'd have to attend.

— ❦ —

The following week Annie had to clear out her dad's room at the nursing home. No sense paying another month's rent in this overpriced hellhole. She couldn't bear to do it. Even the new TV she'd bought for him, the pictures on the wall — she didn't want them, to have to go there at all. She sent over the cleaning lady with a permission note. They'd allow her into the room.

"You can keep what you want, including the television and the radio. My dad had nice clothes. Take what you want and please give the rest to charity, I don't want anything."

It was so sad. Her father dressed impeccably. Had $80 shirts. Cared about his appearance, and what he wore. He had about 15 pairs of shoes. Most of them new. Beautiful soft leather jackets. And his gold wristwatch and the rings. These Annie had at home. She'd save them and let the family decide who got what. But everything he held dear, whatever he worked all his life for — it meant nothing now. It's true, she thought, we're only the custodians of our riches, our possessions. Her mother, who was so possessive about her jewelry and silver and investments, she left it all behind. And now dad, he was gone, and she had to give his life's possessions away.

— ℃ℛ —

They got through the end of the year. It snowed a lot and somehow Annie took that to be a cleansing process. It felt good to have the sidewalks covered with pristine white snow, even if it only lasted a few hours before the cars turned the snow sooty and black. Then came his birthday. She lit a candle for her dad on February 4th. Valentina and she hugged. And they both prayed. "I know you miss him, honey, but he wasn't well. You know how grandpa changed. He's happier now," Annie assured her. She hoped she was right. Valentina still seemed visibly upset, but was coming around. Time would take care of the rest.

That spring they took a trip to London. Annie needed to get away and while she'd been to Italy and loved it, she chose a shorter visit to England, wanted Valentina to see it too. They spent five days there, visiting museums, attending theater on the West End. Then they traveled to Newcastle. To visit a new friend she'd made on the Internet. Colin was a delight. Loved cars. Had two Bentleys and one old Rolls Royce. Valentina loved the car rides on the opposite side of the road. What a good vacation. And one sorely needed. It was wonderful. And throughout Annie had a delighted traveling companion. Thank the lord for my Valentina, she'd say more than once.

The summer was spent in free-lance writing projects. And her decision to move. Annie wanted to find a decent and affordable apartment in the city. She didn't think she could bear living on Staten Island much longer. The house reminded her of her father, those last years he lived there, the anguish at the end. She'd talk to Jacob Meyers about it. She'd find a way.

And then it was autumn and soon another birthday, on October 9th came round.

Could she really be 64? Impossible, Annie thought. It says it on my birth certificate and on my driver's license, but that's wrong. I am 24, no 34, okay 44, but that's all I'll admit to! I have the energy of a young woman. I look damned good, like I did when I was in my 40s and I feel absolutely terrific. So why does it say that I'm 64? Get real, Annie! The voice of truth told her. Oh my God, I'm almost at that age when I can collect Social Security and get Medicare!

"Age is for wine and cheese." What other sayings could she remember to help her get this age thing out of her head? Then a card arrived from Maureen. *How Old Would You Be If You Didn't Know How Old You Are?* were the clever words on the cover. And inside Maureen had added, *"Dear Friend, we're both growing young together. Love and blessings, Mo."* Annie smiled.

As for her darling daughter — Valentina had made her a beautiful card, all lace and little sequins on bright cuts of construction paper. She had always been very crafty. Besides the card, the equally beautiful picture frame her darling daughter had also made was really striking. It must have taken her weeks of work.

"This is wonderful, absolutely gorgeous, darling. Thank you so very much. "They kissed and hugged and she felt terrific. "After all," Annie thought – "if my daughter is only 12, how old can I be?"

— CR —

"He who created us without our help will not save us without our consent."
— *Saint Augustine*

— CR —

Chapter 43

December 2000

Annie gazed into the magnifying side of the mirror. What punishment — to enlarge every pore so that they looked like crevices on the moon. But that was her plight in mid-life — looking warily for wrinkles and telltale signs. *Vanity, vanity, all is vanity.* Yes, she knew she was vain. Damn it, so what if she was superficial and concerned with looking older? After all, she was the mother of a 13-year old. Except — she was 65. And yet there she was — on the periphery of a much younger group of women— mixing with 35-year old mothers, who waited in the schoolyard like she did for their kids to be dismissed. She didn't want to look like someone's grandmother. Amazingly, she knew she didn't. She could more than hold her own.

"You look like you're in your 40s; how do you do it?" Brenda O'Brien, one of the mothers, asked.

"It isn't from a good gene pool. My mom had creases and folds where she shouldn't for the longest time. But then she also smoked a good deal. Smoking is a horror on the skin," Annie emphasized.

"Don't I know it! I had a yellow tinge on my skin until I stopped smoking six months ago. It wasn't easy but even though I put on a few pounds it was worth it," Brenda said.

"Good for you! You know, I took a course in aromatherapy some years ago— it's about extracting the essential oils of plants and flowers. These precious oils can facilitate the healing of the body and the skin. I've mixed my own essential oil moisturizer for years. It really works."

"Well, I have thin Irish skin. And I've been noticing fine lines around my eyes. Is there any way you could mix some of this magic potion for me? I'd be happy to pay you whatever it costs."

"Not a problem. But only if you'll accept it as a gift."

In due course Annie purchased some brown bottles from an herbal shop, ordered more of the essential oils she used, and made up a few bottles. She sent one to each of her closest friends, Maureen and Sabrina, two bottles of the "REBORN" oils to Joanie, who lived in bone-dry Arizona, and presented the first bottle of the new batch she'd made to Brenda.

Maureen called Annie to rave. She loved the feel, the aroma! "This stuff is terrific. Goes right into my skin," Maureen commented.

"You ought to advertise it. It's terrific!"

"I've thought of it, but right now, my energy is on finishing the beauty book and keeping up with my free lance work. If I had the time I'd market it, but I'm just too caught up in my writing."

"I loved your last *New York Magazine* piece on the real estate market. Boy, it tells it like it is. If you're not living in a rent controlled or stabilized apartment in Manhattan you have to be wealthy to afford to live here at all."

"Don't I know it"! Annie responded.

"John and I bought our condo not a minute too soon. We purchased it for $375,000 and our two-bedroom is worth almost a million now. But then the views of the harbor are spectacular. We love living here — so close to the Twin Towers and everything," Maureen said. "Anyway — you did a great job on the article, Annie. You're a damned good writer!" Maureen added.

"Thanks. Hearing it from you means a lot to me kiddo!

"Hey, you and I go back a long way," Maureen answered.

"You know, for a while I've been thinking of doing a different kind of writing — a book, but <u>not</u> a how-to, more about real things, my life, other peoples, sort of a fictionalized memoir. I'd like to set aside a few hours each day, find the time to do this."

"I read somewhere that all great art comes from a sense of outrage. We've both lived long enough to have experienced a certain amount of indignation over the — how would you put it — the *odious* and *irreconcilable* differences in our lives."

"You're so right, Maureen!"

"My Lord, between my loop-dee-loop family and all the unforgettable characters I've met, if I sat down to write about them, I'd be doing *War and Peace*, Maureen continued. "But you, Annie, you have a way with words, where I prefer to sing my feelings away. Go for it, why don't you!"

"I'm going to give it a try, but, well, not quite yet. There's still so much to do in our moving into the city. But someday…."

— ❧ —

Incredible. Time was flying by far too fast. She'd been divorced and without a man for a very long time. Annie didn't want to admit it, but she was getting that gnawing feeling, the sense of being alone. While Valentina filled a great void in her life, her daughter was growing up and independent, had her own friends and interests, as it should be. And while Annie's daily meditations and prayers, her newfound belief in God, imbued within her a sense that a power greater than herself was watching over her — in spite of everything, she craved affection from a man.

There was still a longing — a lonesome sensation inside. Every once in a while she'd gaze through the personal ads — a long-time habit. After all, wasn't she the one who had expanded the public's interest in such encounters more than 20 years ago? And didn't she luck out in finding Sal? Only now the venue had changed —there were even more personals posted on the Internet.

Sadly, she discovered, there just weren't many ads from men over 55 seeking women of that age or older. In fact, those ads and opportunities were extremely rare. Men in Annie's age group were seeking women a generation younger. Why should she be surprised? Look at all the men who divorce their first wives at 50 and begin a new life, with a woman half their age?

She looked and she looked and she looked some more and still she couldn't find. Annie tacitly accepted the cruel truth — that romance wasn't a likely option for a woman over 60. But it was a bitter pill to swallow. She was healthy. She looked good. But her driver's license told the facts and she wasn't good at deceit. Still, the movie star imagery, the romantic moments imbedded in her psyche, were scattered in the cob-webby crevices of her brain. Annie still wanted to be held, to be loved, to share time with a "significant other." She was still searching for that *Someone To Watch Over Me.*

The significant other in her life was her daughter. She'd have to be satisfied with that. It was more, Annie realized, than many older women had. And truly, Valentina was her biggest and best blessing. For this she'd always be grateful.

— ❧ —

Alcohol-related traffic fatalities often occur on holidays. The year 2000 was no exception. While many people celebrated the coming of the Millennium safely, there were 149 total traffic fatalities, 75 of them caused by alcohol. Surprisingly on New Year's Day there were *more* fatalities — 163; of those 114 were caused by a drunken driver.

In Phoenix where Joanie and Eric had been at a friend's New Year's party, a near tragedy took place. Neither Joanie nor Eric had more than a glass or two of champagne, and Eric was a good driver.

But as they began their two-hour drive back to Tucson, another car, an SUV driven by a drunk driver swerved from lane to lane. In one instant, the driver lost control of his car and crashed into Eric's jeep. The SUV was going so fast that after it side swiped their car it continued on, only stopping when it hit head-on another car coming from the other direction. On impact, the driver of the second car was thrown from his seat, and catapulted to his death on the road.

"It was horrible. Horrible to see that poor man's lifeless body on the road. And the other one, twisted in the wreckage of his car", Joanie reported.

"How are both of you?" Annie asked.

"We were badly shaken up. Eric's arm is broken in two parts, the cast they put on him goes all the way down to his fingers. He won't be able to drive without difficulty."

"Drunk drivers. I've heard my fill of stories in AA," Annie commented; glad to hear Joanie and Eric were essentially okay. "And did you come out of it in one piece?"

"I'm much more fortunate, all I have is a twisted ankle and a few bruises. But we're alive. The occupants of the other two cars weren't so lucky. The drunk driver, he was speeding at maybe 80 miles an hour. He drove right into the BMW sports car and killed the driver. The person in the seat next to the driver is in serious condition; she has multiple fractures. And this insane drunk, he broke his back in two places and had to be airlifted to a hospital. Worse, we've learned he's been arrested before for DWI citations. This time he killed someone. It was awful, Annie, so awful. What a way to begin a new year."

"Well, it's 2001, maybe this year will be better. I have to admit that 2000 wasn't my favorite year. So many disappointments, too many changes. I know I'm supposed to adapt to change — I used to be better at it — but well, I was shocked when my job ended at the *Advance*."

"Yeah, that was terrible. But it was pure envy, pure jealousy, Annie," Joanie responded. "From what you told me, the other women in the lifestyle department couldn't handle your having so many juicy assignments besides all your outside work."

Annie had completed the writing of her sixth how-to book, the one she co-authored with the plastic surgeon. It was a guide to cosmetic surgery for men. Well-reviewed, the book had gone into a second printing and the doctor was now making the rounds of the talk shows. Since he was the expert, there was no call for Annie to do publicity, which suited her just fine. She was busy enough writing her restaurant column and doing the reporting for the *Advance*, where she had been working now for more than a decade.

But while she'd long perceived friction in her department, it had escalated the past year. The women were annoyed when Annie was assigned more Sunday feature stories than any of them could garner. Two women in particular, Judy Bondi, who handled stories on the environment, and her buddy, Rosie Johnson, who covered the social pages, never did like Annie. "She belongs in Manhattan, not here. And her pieces are too damned long," Judy whispered. As if Annie couldn't hear. She did. And it hurt.

The backbiting continued for more than a year. Bondi had an "in" with the editor-in-chief. It seems her father, a local assemblyman, and well-thought of at the newspaper, was instrumental in getting her the reporter's job. She was there for more than three years and still wrote the same boring articles. She never did get to do enough feature stories and was sick of writing on the same issues. Bondi liked the subject matter Annie was covering, wanted more assignments like the ones she got. She'd do anything to get rid of Annie and had her father drop in to express displeasure at some of the articles – especially one Annie wrote about a state senator, John Marchi.

Over the course of time, Bondi slowly, but cunningly, dropped disapproving remarks about Annie to the editor – finding fault with what she wrote, pointing out any minor typo – exaggerating how much time she'd take out of the office on interviews — little jabs here and there.

Eventually, it succeeded. That August, Annie was called in for a review of her work. And subsequently let go.

"You know, we think you're a fine writer. But you're a *book* writer, Annie and a damned good *magazine* writer. Your newspaper articles here, don't hit the mark. They're too long, and don't read like the rest of our reportage," the editor-in-chief said. "We've been over-staffed for some time. We have to make some budget cuts. And well, we hope you understand, *it's nothing personal*, but you're been here a long while."

What did he mean by it wasn't personal? It certainly was personal. Annie's being fired took the wind out of her sails. It wasn't fair. She didn't for a minute believe that it was economics that led to her losing her job, but rather the pettiness and jealousy of a few.

— ❦ —

Annie began querying magazines to write more free-lance stories. Someone suggested she try *New York Magazine* since she'd already written for them. She came up with an idea — to deal with the expansion of the New York real estate market, which had risen significantly in the past few years. She'd begin with Jacob Meyers, interview other hot-shots, come up with a good jazzy type of article. She submitted a proposal. Fine, she was told, go for it. The kill fee would only be $400, but Annie was certain they'd buy it.

That's how she met Dan Little. He was one of the new real estate attorneys who also advised clients on investing in the hot Manhattan market. He was a go-getter, owned a few buildings of his own, and was responsible for implementing a good deal of the new residences and co-operatives on the west side. His offices near Lincoln Center were sleek, gorgeous, had views of the entire midtown area.

Dan was 60, divorced, charming as hell, and quite handsome. He was also attracted to Annie and insisted that they talk about the article over dinner. How could she refuse? Besides, he made for a great interview.

By mid-October, they were dating. Just dinner, a lot of phone calls and smooth talk. They hadn't slept together yet. This time Annie was taking it slowly. But it was hard to ignore the roses he sent her weekly. And the flattering words. Even Valentina liked Dan. He bought her a few gifts, took them both to see *Les Mis* and captivated Valentina as much as he had charmed Annie. She didn't think she would feel anything for anyone ever again. That she'd find someone as wonderful. But she did.

He was so understanding, so really nice, Annie couldn't believe that they were both on the same wavelength. She was starry-eyed over this man. Why not? She'd take the chance. Life was for taking risks; if she didn't believe in gambling she might never have made it this far.

— ✺ —

In the year 2000 *Barbie* turned 40 and Annie Rosenberg Ryan began collecting Social Security. It was also the year that one of her favorite comic personalities died. Steve Allen, who Annie religiously watched way back in the 1950s on the late night show, was gone.

The Presidential election was a cliffhanger; not until December 13, 36 days after the election, was George W. Bush declared President-elect.

Dan had been very attentive and amiable. Until Annie's story appeared in the November issue of *New York Magazine*. She'd been exceptionally generous in her coverage of his real estate holdings, his plans to develop the waterfront area into a high rise complex. A very flattering photo of him in front of one of his projects was the main illustration of the story. Dan Little fared much better with Annie than if he had hired a public relations campaign in getting such a vast amount of positive exposure.

Almost immediately — there was nothing subtle about it — Dan Little had disappeared. Annie no longer heard from him. She called his office when the story came out. She knew he'd be pleased, expected him to thank her. The doorbell rang. She smiled. So, he'd sent flowers. But no, it was just the neighborhood kids trying to sell some school chances. Dan was nowhere to be found.

He was like a lost plane that had gone off the radar map.

She called his home. Left messages on his answering machine. Could he have had a stroke, a heart attack, been hit by a bus?

She bit her tongue, crossed her fingers, and called his office one more time. He was out of town, she was told.

He was. He was on Paradise Island entertaining a longhaired long-legged 35-year-old nymphet. After all, Annie was in *that* age group — *over 60*. What could she have been thinking? Boy, she wished that he'd been hit by a bus.

Annie finally got it. Dan Little wanted his proposal for the new housing he was trying to get passed by the City Zoning Commission favorably looked upon. She'd fallen hook line and sinker for his con game. Bull shit. That's what it turned out to be. She was furious. And hurt.

"It's a man's world, Maureen! Women are discarded for younger women all the time. Look at all the 60-year-old men marrying women half their ages and beginning second families. How many women get that opportunity?" she vented. But damned if she didn't know the truth.

Maureen listened with great empathy. But she had no quick answer, no witty response.

"You're right honey. And you got burned. The guy's a bastard. But not all men are like that. There are some decent older men, widowers, nice men, out there."

"Sure, if you don't mind that they either have had bypass surgery, or are about to have a hip replacement. Most of the others are retired and so boring — they play golf all day and have nothing new to discuss — or worse, have one testicle," Annie said, sarcastically. "Then if you don't mind the disabilities, there's plenty of older men out there."

Maureen laughed. "Well, there's always Viagra, girl."

Annie lightened up. "I don't think so. I think I'll hang up my boxing gloves. I no longer believe that there's a man out there with my initials carved on his forehead. No more *Mr. Right* for me."

"Let go and let God, honey. I never dreamed I'd find John."

"That was 12 years ago. We were both younger and more "marketable" then. Believe me, there's nothing out there but '*drek.* '

"Well, you do have Valentina. And she's truly a blessing."

"Yes, and what really bothers me is how I allowed Valentina to be exposed to this. Dan certainly gave me a good run for his money. He was so very attentive, such a gentleman. So nice to her. She's been asking what happened to him. What can I tell her? That he fell off the face of the earth? I damn well wish he had. I hate that man."

"Hating is like burning down your house to kill a rat. Don't do it, Annie. You've been through much worse than this."

"You're right. Yet somehow it doesn't get any easier. And I just don't bounce back as easy as I once did. But I'll go to some meetings, and pray for the bastard, I will. I have to think positive, be all right for my daughter. She's my anchor, and I *will* survive. I am a survivor, dear friend."

"Is this the time I should break into a few lines of *I'm Still Here*?

… *Good times and bum times, I've seen them all and, my dear, I'm still here*…." Maureen began singing the Sondheim lyric.

Annie laughed. It was really one of Stephen Sondheim's favorite lyrics of hers. *Plush velvet sometimes…sometimes just pretzels and beer. But I'm here…I got through all of last year and I'm here… I'm still here*, she shouted a little off key. "Hey, if I could sing, my mother wouldn't have paid for whistling lessons!"

They both laughed nervously.

Still it was sad, this deception and rejection. Sure Annie was older, but why did that have to mean that it was all over, that there could be no more romance in her life? She had no glib answer for the way the world worked. But damn, damn, damn. It just wasn't fair, life wasn't always fair, but she really didn't have a choice in the matter; she'd have to continue on her own, survive – no — prize life, without a partner.

— ❧ —

Guns aren't lawful; Nooses give;
Gas smells awful; You might as well live.
— Dorothy Parker

— ∞ —

Chapter 44

August 23, 2001

Annie studied her desk calendar. She needed to settle on a school holiday that coordinated with the birthday trip she planned for Valentina – to her favorite vacation place — *Disney World.* Her daughter was still enchanted by Cinderella, Snow White, Mickey Mouse and Donald Duck, every magical character of her missed childhood. Each year since Valentina arrived, celebrating part of her birthday in Orlando was always one of Annie's gifts.

Recalling the shy little 6-year-old with the enormous taffeta bow plopped on top of her head in the adoption video — and considering the confident, beautiful teenager now verging on 14, was mind-boggling. Where had the time gone? It's said that as one grows older time travels faster. It was. Much too quickly Annie decided. "Slow down, slow down," she reflected, talking to whomever was in charge of these things. "I've still so much more living to do."

Staten Island was the only home Valentina had known since she arrived from Moscow, but soon they were going to be moving.

Annie had long grown tired of life in the suburbs. Her friends had been right. Her neighbors were nice, but the *dese, dem and dose* and *hey youse guys* subculture that prevailed was getting her down. Besides, she hated the drive back and forth into the city. And she knew that Valentina was mature enough to adjust to living in Manhattan.

While the move was much smaller in scale — merely from one borough to another — Annie wanted her daughter to feel secure. Valentina had made friends on the Island, loved her school and was well liked. "Hey, Mom, look, the Baskin Robbins lady gave me another free cone," Valentina announced. "She wouldn't take my money!" It was extraordinary, but Valentina was such a loving child — outgoing and friendly, that even the Korean woman who owned the local ice cream outlet often gave her a complimentary cone. Everyone liked her, teachers, classmates, even shopkeepers.

Nowadays Annie was helping Valentina to develop Manhattan connections. Her acting classes in Greenwich Village every Saturday morning, for one, provided a familiarity with that part of the city, and it was also a source of making new friends. They also attended Broadway shows and dined out regularly together.

Annie had made some promises to her daughter: "We'll get a nice apartment, with a view. I'll be able to give up the car and driving. My work now, it's all in Manhattan. You'll be starting high school, and we'll find you a wonderful school, honey bun," she promised. Valentina smiled, her blue eyes twinkling. "Awesome, Mommy! And can we go to the theater more?" Valentina was keen on Broadway.

Annie spent weeks researching and visiting various high schools in Manhattan. Finally she settled on a Jesuit-run high school located on the Upper East Side – St. Ignatius Loyola. She'd heard such great things about it. Sure, she knew it would cost much more for Valentina to attend private school in Manhattan, but with the sale of the house — and a little help from her "friends" – she'd manage it. Annie's major ally was the kindly Jacob Meyers, who Valentina had long called "Uncle Jacob." Meyers adored this vivacious little girl ever since Valentina was first brought to meet him seven years ago. Like so many others, she won his heart immediately.

Annie called realtors and after hearing their advice decided that the market was really good. It would be wise to put her house up for sale — but wiser first to pay a visit to Jacob Meyers and tell him of her plans. After all, he still held a $100,000 mortgage on her home.

The next morning Annie drove into the city. The rush hour traffic was simply awful. Too damned many cars, not enough room on the highways, and because of a car accident that still hadn't been cleared, the East River Drive was totally congested. It took her almost an hour to get there. Oh to be rid of the journey into Manhattan and to live there again! She went straight to Meyer's office. Still very active, and although he was approaching 90, the realty mogul went to work every day. He loved what he did and he did it well. "I brought you this box of Godivas – from me and Valentina — we know how much you love chocolate," Annie said, giving Meyers a gentle kiss on his cheek. "Such extravagance! Thank you darling, but in the future know — a Hershey bar is good enough for me," Meyers said, a sparkle in his smile. And he meant it. Annie remembered a couple of times she found the multi-millionaire reheating up a container of soup on the radiator in his office. He wasn't about to waste anything and while he lived well, he was also mindful of his own humble beginnings.

"Annie, I have some very pleasant news for you. I've decided to forgive *all* the private mortgages I'm holding for my 90th birthday. This, of course, includes yours," he announced knowing how happy this would make her. "Oh my Lord, this couldn't come at a better time. You know I came here to tell you that I've decided to move into the city – to put the house up for sale. Thank you from the bottom of my heart," she said, giving him a huge hug.

Annie was ecstatic. This meant she was free to sell the house, and keep all the proceeds, which had appreciated greatly. Many stockbrokers and lower Manhattan downtown workers liked living on Staten Island, which was a ferry ride away. And Todt Hill Road was a very desirable area. The house was now worth $500,000, double what she'd paid for it more than a decade earlier.

It would provide enough funds to purchase a two-bedroom apartment and to send Valentina to St. Ignatius, her first choice for schooling. She told Jacob of her plans. "I'm not so crazy about a Catholic school," Meyers said, "but let me pay the first year's tuition," he volunteered, not even asking how much it was.

Annie knew that Jacob valued his Judaism, and was proud of his background. His father had been a cantor. She also knew he wasn't small-minded enough to care what religious persuasion her daughter was raised in. "Valentina's been attending a Lutheran school on the Island – because it was the best one around. And St. Ignatius is excellent; I researched it carefully. It's $18,000 a year but when I sell the house, I'll have enough to pay the tuition." Meyers smiled "Well allow me the pleasure of the first year." It was obvious how much he adored Valentina. What a generous man!

Later that afternoon Annie was loading the dishwasher when the phone rang. It was Connie Clausen, her agent. "Annie – I just got a call from Putnam Publishing. One of their authors has developed serious health problems — breast cancer — in the midst of working on a book. It's a natural subject for you — beauty secrets for the over 50 market. They wanted to know if I can help them out, and I told them I have the perfect writer! Don't let me down – tell me you're free and can do this book!" Annie couldn't believe what she was hearing. As if she'd turn down any project right now. But she'd behave with a show of confidence. "What are the financial arrangements?" The answer was almost too good to be true. "Annie, sit down for this one: They'll give you a $20,000 advance. They're that eager to get the book out by spring and I know how good you are on working to deadline. I'd grab it. The publisher is really going to hype this book. They're basing it on tips from celebrities. Once it hits the shelves, it's going to sell like hot cakes!"

"Of course I'll do it," she said, barely believing her good luck. Within the hour she was on the telephone telling everyone about this amazing development. Things were certainly looking up.

Annie immediately began making notes – scribbling an outline for the project. "*Beauty Secrets of Famous Women Over 50*," was a subject she knew a good deal about and would learn even more as she interviewed a lengthy list of well-known women. Of course she'd include Sabrina and Maureen in the book. She'd set something up with Mo right away.

"I'm thrilled, Maureen, I never thought I'd get this far, really. I feel successful for the first time in my life," Annie reported. "Hell! You deserve it; you're a very good writer. By now I hope you know it," her friend reminded her. "You're such a pal. I don't know why but sometimes it's hard to shake old negativities — to believe in myself, but with friends like you, who always give me positive support – it sure helps, Mo."

Annie looked at the clock. School was letting out. "Oh boy, Valentina will be home any minute," she realized. Annie called the local Chinese restaurant to order in. She knew Valentina would love Chinese tonight. They'd have a celebration dinner.

"Oh Mommy I'm so glad," Valentina said upon hearing the news. "And oh boy is this delicious — thanks, you know shrimp with lobster sauce is my favorite." What could be better, more satisfying than this? Annie realized. It was the little things in life like making her daughter happy that mattered most of all.

That night she thanked God for all her blessings beginning with her marvelous daughter. She had so much to be grateful for, and yes, after all these years she was beginning to get it, that the best relationship of all was the one you developed with your self.

Soon enough she found a beautiful two-bedroom apartment on East 86th Street, just off Second Avenue that would be an easy walk to St. Ignatius in good weather and a simple bus ride in bad. The apartment needed work and wouldn't be ready until mid-summer, time enough to move in before school started. Things were looking up.

There, but for a typographical error is the story of my life.
— Dorothy Parker

— CR —

Chapter 45

September 2001

Annie was overjoyed. At last she was back in Manhattan, where being an unmarried woman was not uncommon and single mothers were also in abundance. Staten Island was a bedroom community. She never felt she belonged. From time to time, she still thought about Tom, worse had disturbing dreams about him that always ended with his walking away. Odd— in reality — she was the one to leave. Yet the dreams always ended with his rejecting her.

Life was full — she had Valentina, good writing projects — Annie was gradually feeling good about herself *without* a romantic partner. Yet – old dreams die hard. All those happy endings in the movies faded out on a Prince Charming. Growing up in the 50s, before the pill, before Women's Lib, things were very different. A woman was expected to marry — to have a man take care of her. Now, finally, Annie Rosenberg Ryan was self-supporting. She'd even accomplished the adoption on her own. Role models had changed. Many women now held down major positions in the business world, in politics, in professional practices and were more than content on their own. And although Annie still felt an empty place inside of her – a secret repository of unrequited love — she was tired of playing the litany of the lost.

Besides, at this juncture in her life, she really didn't have much of a choice. Witness the sadness of that Dan Little affair. She'd been hurt by that, really hurt. Annie didn't know if she had another recovery in her. Hard facts, but true. More women than men. More choices for men,

Hell, she knew the drill by heart.

And then the world changed forever.

2001 would become a year of enormous and shattering events.

In January, George W. Bush was sworn in as the 43rd President of the United States. In the entertainment field *The Producers*, Mel Brook's Broadway musical based on his movie, cleaned up at the Tony Awards, taking a record 12 trophies. And the not-very-good movie, *3,000 Miles from Graceland* which featured the song, *Such A Night"* was released. It was the movie Annie had seen that first reminded her of Roosevelt, that triggered within her the desire to write about him and many other now-silent voices that couldn't be heard.

It was also the year when four were declared guilty of the 1998 terrorist bombing of U. S. Embassies in Africa, and when Oklahoma bomber Timothy McVeigh was executed.

And it was the point in time that at 8:46 in the morning on Tuesday, September 11, the first of two high-jacked planes would crash into the World Trade Center. Within minutes, emergency workers across New York City were on their way to the stricken landmark in an attempt to help save thousands of lives during the unthinkable destruction and chaos that followed.

On that day, Sabrina Aldrich was in the television studio

reporting the news when the first plane crashed into the North Tower. And Maureen McDermott had just gotten out of bed in her Battery Park Plaza apartment to shower. By then, Fire Lieutenant Thomas Ryan along with his ladder company was on the way to the scene of the disaster. Concurrent reports soon were told of a plane hitting the Pentagon and another crashing in a field in Pennsylvania.

TV brought images of horror into people's living rooms. The vast enveloping clouds of dense smoke, desperate doomed people leaping from the top floors, the stupefied wounded, then the tons of pulverized building and people that came roaring violently through the streets. Instant death on a scale beyond any comprehension.

"Annie, it's me, Sabrina. I can't stay on but a moment. I tried to reach Maureen. Left a message on her answering machine. I'm at the studio. This is a terrorist attack Annie. Stay where you are. Inside. I've got to go."

Before Annie could mutter more than thank you, she heard the click of the telephone. Oh my God, Sabrina had the presence of mind to call and she was at the television station — she knew what was going on.

Thank the lord, Annie realized, that both she and Valentina were home. Ironically Valentina would have been in her earliest class of the day when the first plane hit and Annie on her way to the main public library to do some research. But by some stroke of luck Valentina had an appointment with their dentist at 10 that morning. So she wasn't in school.

"It felt like a guardian angel had been watching over us," Annie later recalled. "So when Manhattan was completely closed off from the rest of the world, when no one was quite sure what was happening – my precious Valentina was at home with me!"

All over New York panic set in. Rumors abounded, including that terrorists were going to blow up buildings and bridges. Police shut off traffic and entrances and exits to the bridges. "Stay inside for now, darling — until we know everything is safe," Annie cautioned Valentina. They watched the TV coverage, stunned, disbelieving. They hugged each other. They cried. Like so many others Annie desperately wanted to wake up and discover it was only a nightmare. But it was for real.

"Please, get out of the downtown area now. The Second Tower is falling." Annie was in the kitchen, making some coffee. She ran into the living room to look at the TV screen. She had recognized the voice. It was Sabrina broadcasting now from the street — somewhere in the downtown Wall Street district. Heavy white dust and smoke was billowing towards them. "Everyone, evacuate the area."

Annie watched the images over and over and over again, riveted, mesmerized, and horrified. It was impossible to believe. Impossible to describe. Most everyone, including kids — were used to watching bombs and violence on the screen. Movies like *48 Hours* and *Independence Day* were pretty commonplace. She didn't think Valentina realized the actual horror of this real happening. She was glad for that. Let her think this was a movie.

But this was *genuine*. Real destruction. Real death. On an unimagined, unthinkable scale. People trapped in the towers, in an agonizing flight to avoid temperatures of 2,000 degrees leapt to their death. Police, firefighters, more than 2,000 Trade Center workers lost their lives. The terrorists had succeeded, murdering Americans, producing billions of dollars in property damage.

From first reports, at least 200 firefighters were lost or known dead. Was Tom Ryan among them? Oh please God, no, no let it be no. Annie wouldn't learn of his fate for days.

If Tom was dead — and so many firemen had died — it would be a crushing blow. She still had feelings for him, always had. They'd shared a history together. Whatever harm they caused one another – it was fueled by her alcoholism, her insecurities and his own inability to get away from his dominating mother and become an adult. But she wished him no harm, always wanted him to be happy, even with someone else. He'd been so much a part of her, still was, Annie felt it. Now at this crucial time when so many lives were destroyed, she sensed it more than ever. Tom hadn't had an easy life – he'd lost his first wife, buried a baby. Maybe she was too harsh on him. He had many loving ways and struggled to be a good father. Annie's thoughts were racing. She sat down, attempted to meditate. She just couldn't sit still. She was terrified — the ongoing television news reports weren't very good.

She tried Maureen's phone. There was only a busy signal. "Keep ringing the number," she asked Valentina. "Though more than likely all the phone lines are jammed downtown."She only hoped that Maureen and John were okay.

Soon enough Annie learned that Sal had gone down to Ground Zero. He'd called her from his cell phone on a rare break. "Those son-of-a-bitch cock-suckers! I hate every mother-fucking one of them. They come here for their educations, and then criticize our way of living," he ranted for a fast minute — then Annie heard voices calling him. He said he'd be in touch when he could. He'd been with the department for 25 years. He had to lend a hand. He'd be there for days.

There were many fallen heroes. At Ground Zero, metal girders intensely hot, dripping like candle wax could be seen in the days that followed. At night bright floodlights illuminated the scene of piles of rubble. In the coming weeks twenty-seven bodies and enough body parts to fill up several bags were found. There were only stories of death and destruction, harrowing loss and grief.

The public wouldn't know it for days, but in all 343 firefighters and 23 police officers would lose their lives. And then they learned of more than 2,000 civilians, all dead, all murdered, all lost for all time.

Sal volunteered for one of the two makeshift morgues. His job was to help collect the toothbrushes and combs husbands, wives, girlfriends and parents brought in so that the DNA could be taken of them to see if they would match anyone they might find.

Annie didn't realize it but Sal's big, squishy, sentimental streak and his knowing she was tormented — worrying if Tom had survived — had given him another mission. Sal didn't want to be the bearer of bad news, but not knowing if her ex, was alive or dead, that would be even worse for Annie. So everywhere he went, everyone he met — he asked. It didn't seem good, no word, and Ryan never reported back to his battalion chief. It looked like he'd perished with so many others. Sal was disheartened, didn't know what to do, and didn't want to be the bearer of bad news.

He got busy helping to take out the body parts, any scattered remains, a burned credit card, and a bent wristwatch. Those crazy Muslim bastards. No regard for human life. He hated the fact that this terrorist attack on domestic soil would change America forever. If he were younger he'd sign up right now to get back into the army and take care of the dirt bags.

In the end Sal lost at least a dozen personal friends, fireman and police officers who had lived nearby him on Staten Island. He would attend at least 50 funerals in the coming months.

— ❧ —

Early Thursday morning, Annie awakened, beads of sweat on her forehead. She'd been having another nightmare about Tom. Like always, it started out great — back in their house, in bed, making sweet love. Then a bloodcurdling stranger was standing over them, ominous, like she was about to murder the two of them. Yes, it was the figure of a woman. Could it have been Ursula? Or worse, was Tom among the dead at Ground Zero? Was it some kind of awful omen? She awakened feeling on edge, very uneasy.

Worse, by now she'd learned on news reports that his firehouse, Engine Company 231, had lost 6 of their 8 men. They'd never come back from the call that morning. Nor had Tom. With all the commotion, the searching for bodies, no one had heard from him. Annie was sick; sick to her core at the thought that he was dead, gone, departed from this planet they shared together.

The doorbell rang. "I'll get it Mom," Valentina called out.

It was Colleen. Annie was startled to see her. She'd sent out announcements about their move, but Colleen had gone her own way for quite some time, and hadn't called. In fact, they'd barely spoken in the past few years. She'd heard that Colleen had moved in with her grandmother.

"I had to come. It took me a day to find where you were living. I'm so worried about my dad," Colleen said, falling into Annie's open arms. Colleen's eyes were red and swollen. The poor girl was shaking. The two women embraced tightly, united in their concern for Tom Ryan. Yes, Colleen knew it right away — her father was part of the brave firemen who'd been on duty on September 11th. And two days after the swirling fire that extinguished so many lives, there was still no word.

"I just got out of the subway in time. They stopped the trains at Grand Central Station. I walked all the way up here. Everyone still looks shocked, scared," Colleen related.

"Here, let me make you some tea. I have some good herbal ones, that calm the nerves," Annie suggested. If only the damned tea had helped her!

"Oh thanks, anything would be fine," Maureen replied.

"…I suppose it's good that my grandmother died last spring. She couldn't handle this, she'd freak out she was so attached to my dad. Too attached, Annie, I realize that now."

"I had no idea she died. I'm sorry," Annie answered. But really, she wasn't.

Colleen was trembling, shaking, truly upset. Annie briefly introduced Valentina to Colleen, who had heard about the adoption years before.

"It's really nice to meet you, Valentina. I wish we were meeting under better circumstances...." Colleen said. Valentina put her arms around Colleen and said sweetly, "I understand, please, please don't worry. I've been praying for everyone and I just have a feeling it's going to be okay for your dad."

Colleen was surprised at Valentina's maturity and thoughtfulness.

She smiled and said softly, "Oh thank you, thank you with all my heart."

"Come sit down," Annie beckoned to her. Tears welled up in Colleen's eyes. "Here, use this," Valentina offered her a tissue.

"Oh what can I do, I know there's little I can do to make her feel better until we get some news and even then what if the news is bad?" Annie was thinking. Her head was spinning with sorrow for learning of all the violence – the plane crashes, the loss of so many innocent lives — the blood that had been spilled in the last few days. This terrorism was pure evil and now, on this malevolent scale, had changed America ever more.

After a cup of hot tea, Colleen seemed to relax a bit. "Annie, I've had lots of time to think about things — and really, my grandmother was so controlling. She tried to run my life. I stayed with her at Breezy Point for more than a year — but she was suffocating, Annie, just too demanding. Telling me what to wear, whom to date, what to do. And, worse, she still bad-mouthed my mother. It was just hideous," Maureen reported.

"Wow, that's so insensitive," Valentina commented, having listened to the conversation, her eyes wide with curiosity.

"My mom — they said she died of cirrhosis of the liver, yet, my grandmother — 18 years after her death — still talked about her with such hatred, and you know something, — my cousins on my mom's side, they say she didn't drink that long, that she couldn't have had liver damage from alcohol —. I don't think we'll ever know the real answer. And, well I've been sober in the program for two years now," Colleen announced. Annie was overjoyed with the news. "Actually my dad had gone to Alanon - it took about a year but eventually he helped me see the path I was on. Now I'm working on myself with the steps and I'm taking courses at Queens College."

"Oh Colleen, I'm so happy for you, so proud of you," Annie said.

"As for my mom. I've read enough on the subject of alcoholism to know that some people just can't absorb that much, so maybe, she could have destroyed herself with all her drinking and worrying about the baby who died."Colleen stopped, her eyes filling up with tears. "But to die at 32, it's so tragic."

"Your mom and dad married young, and it wasn't easy for her, especially when the baby was diagnosed with leukemia," Annie whispered, rubbing Maureen's shoulder gently. "Just pray for her because she's in a better place. As for your grandmother, she was a rigid woman, unforgiving too."

"Yes, grandma had her faults though I don't think my dad ever saw them. She really loved both her sons. Would do anything for them. *Too much* I believe."

I don't know what to say or think… your grandmother was a difficult lady…and she sure didn't like me or any woman who came between her and her sons!"

"Oh you're so right. She was always very possessive and jealous if she wasn't getting her son's attention."

"And worse, after you and dad split for the second time — when my dad married Maryanne, at first grandma seemed pleased with his choice. After all, she was the one who introduced them. Maryanne lived a few houses away from grandma — she was Catholic and she was even half Irish, half German like dad — and she'd never been married."

"Well that should have thrilled your grandmother — finding someone of her own background had to be a big plus," Annie interjected.

"You think so? Well — after Maryanne had just one minor argument with grandma, everything started to change. I don't know what they argued about — I think it was something petty like where Thanksgiving dinner would be held. But after the squabble — I remember my grandmother stopped speaking to her totally. It didn't take long after that for the marriage to go downhill."

"Here have some apple juice," Valentina offered Colleen, from a tray she'd brought in from the kitchen. Wow, Valentina couldn't believe her ears. This was like a soap opera — evil mother-in-law — and Tom — a multiple-marrier — gosh — was that even a word? She was amazed to hear all of this — she'd never had even a hint of it from her mother.

Colleen took a sip of juice and continued: "I think if Maryanne didn't decide she'd had enough and didn't just break up the marriage on her own...I think it would have been a bigger mess. My grandmother was intent in getting what she wanted. At any cost."

Annie hugged Colleen again. "Here, just relax. It's in the past. Nothing can be done about it any more. Your grandmother is gone now. And your dad, he did a gutsy thing when he went to Alanon. For a long time he couldn't see his role in all of this. I'm so glad to hear it, Colleen, so glad."

"Yes, dad understands more now. We have a better relationship too," Colleen added.

"Let's turn on the television and see what's happening. I've been so worried about your dad. All we can do, is wait and pray. Colleen, I'm very glad you came here, that you're with us now."

Colleen smiled through her veil of tears. "I'm glad I'm here too. I hope we can be friends now, Annie. Somehow I had to respect my grandmother's wishes — she didn't want me to have any contact with you. Annie — she hated you so much. But now, she's gone. Oh God, I hope my dad isn't...oh please...more than anything, I pray my dad is okay," she sobbed. "Oh dear Jesus, please let him be okay."

They waited. They watched television. They grieved. And they prayed.

— ❧ —

Later that afternoon the phone rang, shattering the quiet. Annie grabbed it. "Hello."

It was Sal. "Hey Babes. Listen, I have someone who wants to say hello. Hold on."

And then she heard the familiar voice. The voice of the man for whom she would always feel a passion.

"Hi Annie. It's Hell down here. Absolute Hell. I'm very lucky — I'm alive, and okay. You know...times like this — you think about your life, your past, the good and the bad. I've been thinking about you. Us. A lot. We sure shared some good times. And...I want you to know - that — that I'll always love you," Tom's voice quivered with emotion.

She cried. "I'll always love you too. Thank God you're safe. And...Tom — wait, Colleen, she came here this morning — here, speak to her — she'll be so glad to hear your voice."

Colleen smiled, grabbed the phone and had some quick words with her dad. Joy was written all over her face. "Oh yes, Daddy, yes. I'll be all right now. Just take care," she added.

"Here, a man wants to talk to you…." she said, handing the receiver back to Annie.

"Hey babes." It was Sal — back on the line. "We gotta get back. But didn't want this good news to wait."

"Sal, you're an angel, you know that. I'll always be grateful to you. Listen, when you have time, when things are better, come over for dinner. Please. And thank you, thank you so much."

Miraculously Tom had survived. And still had enough feelings to want to speak to her. She'd always be grateful for those tender words they'd shared. It was all she needed to say goodbye. Or was it? She went to sleep that night thanking God for saving Tom. And praying that maybe, just maybe they might have another chance. She wasn't sure for what, she didn't think she'd ever want to live together again, but she wanted to see him, that she knew.

Later that day Annie heard from Maureen. She and John were fine.

Their apartment wasn't. They'd moved into a hotel uptown. "I don't think we'll be going back there. John has wanted to move to Palm Beach for the longest time. Well, I think this is the time to do it. It was awful, Annie, awful. We saw the tower falling, we saw too much and our apartment, it's filled with soot and dust all over."

"But you're okay, thank God," Annie said. "Oh Mo, I'm so glad you're both alright."

— ❧ —

Within a few days Valentina went back to school. Annie continued unpacking, fixing up the apartment, and of course, writing. The news about the terror attacks was awful. Life would never be the same. She thought of Tom often.

Colleen called. They talked warmly — made a date for dinner. She also mentioned to Annie that her dad was "on his own". He wasn't seeing anyone. He'd told Colleen to say hello for him. What did that mean? In the background she heard the song playing on the radio. Ironic: it was Gershwin's *Our Love Is Here to Stay*, one of her favorites. Who knew what the future held…if there was still time for love.

Annie's life seemed to swing on the hinges of history. The last 50 years had brought change. She could look back at it with reverence. She was glad to be alive. To have survived it all. She prayed she'd have 20 – maybe even 30 more years to live, to see her daughter happily on her own, to enjoy the beauty of life, with all it's unexpected moments. And maybe, just maybe to have some time with Tom again.

Then she heard it on the radio…it was Linda Rondstadt singing the song. It was Gershwin's *Someone To Watch Over Me*. Tears formed in her eyes. As always, the music moved her, made her emotions both soar and plunge with every phrase.

She turned the radio off. Annie was fearful of feeling too much, of playing games with her heart — yet somehow she believed there was hope. Yes, there was always hope.

Tom was right. This kind of tragedy makes you take a different look at yourself and your life. You look back on *all* of it.

Annie decided right then and there to sit down and write about it. So maybe Roosevelt and Maureen and Salvatore, Jim and Sabrina and Muktananda, and of course, Tom, all the wonderful souls who'd touched her life might have their stories told. It was time to put it all down, if only as a legacy to her daughter, another miracle in her life.

— ❧ —

There I am wearing that hideous dress, my hair cut short
— posed against a schoolyard fence. *Send this poor orphan a Care
package* — that's what I look like. Now I'm at my grandmother's
— it's after a Passover meal and I'm sneaking some of the wine.
Now I see my parents fighting, hear them – oh Hell — what awful
yelling. And there, there's Jackie Robinson stealing home again! I see
fleeting images of the 1940s, the 50s, the wild 60s, and the promise of
a better tomorrow. I walk the winding streets of Greenwich Village,
looking for love in all the wrong places. I remember the parties and
bar scenes, love affairs and disillusion, the craziness of my past.
And I hear the music, oh what music, that accompanied my dreams.
Images of long ago keep soaring through my thoughts.

   *"Dear Valentina, there is so much to tell you of my life, of the
past fifty years —. So let me begin."*

— ❧ —